Praise for bestselling author
Rhonda Nelson

"Well plotted and wickedly sexy,
this one's got it all—including a
completely scrumptious hero. A keeper."
—*RT Book Reviews* on *The Ranger*

"Mrs. Nelson surely knows how to
turn up the heat..."
—*Writers Unlimited* on *Unforgettable*

Praise for bestselling author
Joanne Rock

"*Silk Confessions* by Joanne Rock is wonderful.
Tempest and Wesley are strong, attractive characters
with serious heat between them,
and the mystery works."
—*RT Book Reviews*

"Joanne Rock never fails to impress!"
—*Writers Unlimited* on *She Thinks Her Ex Is Sexy...*

A Waldenbooks bestselling author, two-time RITA® Award nominee and *RT Book Reviews* Reviewers' Choice nominee, **RHONDA NELSON** writes hot romantic comedy for the Harlequin Blaze line and other Harlequin imprints. With more than twenty-five published books to her credit and many more coming down the pike, she's thrilled with her career and enjoys dreaming up her characters and manipulating the worlds they live in. In addition to a writing career she has a husband, two adorable kids, a black Lab and a beautiful bichon frise. She and her family make their chaotic but happy home in a small town in northern Alabama. She loves to hear from her readers, so be sure and check her out at www.readRhondaNelson.com.

Three-time RITA® Award nominee and Golden Heart winner **JOANNE ROCK** is the author of more than forty books for Harlequin. When she's not writing or spending too much time on Facebook, Joanne teaches English at the local university to share her love of the written word in all its forms. For more information, visit Joanne at www.joannerock.com.

RHONDA NELSON
1-900-Lover

———————

JOANNE ROCK
Silk Confessions

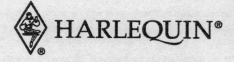

HARLEQUIN®

TORONTO • NEW YORK • LONDON
AMSTERDAM • PARIS • SYDNEY • HAMBURG
STOCKHOLM • ATHENS • TOKYO • MILAN • MADRID
PRAGUE • WARSAW • BUDAPEST • AUCKLAND

Recycling programs
for this product may
not exist in your area.

ISBN-13: 978-0-373-68812-8

1-900-LOVER & SILK CONFESSIONS

Copyright © 2010 by Harlequin Books S.A.

The publisher acknowledges the copyright holders of the individual works as follows:

1-900-LOVER
Copyright © 2004 by Rhonda Nelson

SILK CONFESSIONS
Copyright © 2005 by Joanne Rock

This edition published by arrangement with Harlequin Books S.A.

For questions and comments about the quality of this book please contact us at Customer_eCare@Harlequin.ca.

® and TM are trademarks of the publisher. Trademarks indicated with ® are registered in the United States Patent and Trademark Office, the Canadian Trade Marks Office and in other countries.

www.eHarlequin.com

Printed in U.S.A.

CONTENTS

This one's for you, Granny.
For panty-hose wigs and Martian hats,
paper dolls and peanut butter sandwiches.
For countless hours of undivided attention,
tight hugs, fishing trips and sewing lessons. For
invaluable advice, unwavering support
and unconditional love. You're the best,
and I love you dearly.

1-900-LOVER

Rhonda Nelson

CHAPTER ONE

"WHAT AM I WEARING?" Rowan Crosswhite echoed into the phone, her voice artfully pitched to a breathy sultry purr. Grimacing, she used the hem of her T-shirt and her frayed denim cutoffs to clean the majority of the potting soil from her hands, then took up her watering can. "I'm wearing a black leather bustier, fishnet hose and stiletto heels."

The fabricated description lacked originality, yes, but thus far in her experience in the phone sex business, she'd learned that any imaginative effort she put into her descriptions *wasn't* appreciated. So why bother?

When Rowan had first considered selling phone sex, she'd worried about being appropriately creative, about fabricating a believable performance for the men who dialed her number. She'd even called a couple of 1-900 numbers for research purposes because being prepared was the keystone to any successful venture, and her near-manic obsession with doing everything to the absolute best of her ability—even something as seedy as being a phone sex operator—had prevented her from doing otherwise.

The research had been a wasted effort and she'd worried needlessly about conjuring a suitable performance.

In fact, ironically, she'd learned the less said the better. Rowan rolled her eyes. Hell, all she really had to do was gasp, wince and moan—easy to do, particularly when one was, say, cleaning the toilet or weeding a flower bed—and the guys, thank God, took care of the rest. One of the many advantages of phone sex.

And, surprisingly, there were many.

First of all—most importantly—it was safe. There was no risk of abuse or disease, and if a guy freaked her out, all she had to do was sever the connection and block the number. She mentally shrugged. Simple enough. Furthermore, and equally important given her recent unfortunate circumstances, it was *lucrative*. At $3.99 a minute, where the average call hovered around the twelve-minute mark, that was roughly $240 an hour. Her lips twitched. Considerably more than her previous job as a high-school science teacher.

Just a year shy of tenure, Rowan had been one of the unlucky souls left unemployed by deep state budget cuts. Her boss at Middleton High had promised that as soon as the funds were available, she'd be under contract again.

Regrettably, until then, more panting, moaning and wincing would be in order—and the more dramatic the better—otherwise she'd ultimately starve and, much to the detriment of her heavily padded thighs, she liked food entirely too much to go hungry.

Since she'd been paying off student loans and attending night school to get her master's degree, Rowan had been caught with a grand total of $633 in savings, even less in checking and nothing—aside from a 1962 Chevrolet Corvette that had belonged to her father, and for which she would prostitute herself in the literal sense to keep if need be—of any value to sell.

She did substitute teaching when she could, but that income hadn't been enough, or even dependable, for that matter. Then she'd read an article about a woman who, in similar circumstances, had morphed herself into a phone sex entrepreneur, and the rest had been history. She'd weighed the advantages and disadvantages, deemed it a good temporary choice, then installed her line and invested in a good mobile headset.

This freed up her hands and allowed her to do the things that she really loved—gardening, stained glass and metal-working. *Tinkering,* according to her father. Her shoulders sagged with disappointment. Initially, she'd tried to make ends meet by selling her garden art, but unfortunately—and this thoroughly baffled her—no one seemed to get her style. Rowan cast a glance around her eclectic garden—whimsical metalwork, stained-glass whirligigs, antique roses, bulbs and vines—and swallowed a despondent sigh. Screw 'em, she thought, the tasteless traditional cads. *She* was an *artiste.* Her garden thrived and made her happy, which when one really thought about it, was all that mattered anyway.

A stuttered breath hissed across the line, cut through her musings. "Wh—what about your panties? What do they look like?"

Rowan glanced at her watch. She'd had this guy on the phone for eight minutes. Time to finish up. She had some impatiens to transplant, and her roses were looking a little droopy.

"I don't wear panties," she lied breathlessly. "They… constrict."

Predictably, the line worked. A garbled groan and the telltale whine of a zipper echoed into her ear.

She lowered her voice. "Can I tell you a secret, Jeff?" she asked, purposely using his name. It played into the whole *say-my-name, who's-your-daddy* mentality. Sheesh. Men were pathetically predictable.

"S-sure."

"Sometimes…when I'm alone…I like to touch myself." She barely suppressed a snigger. Rowan Crosswhite, former high-school science teacher turned kinky phone sex queen.

Another broken hiss sounded. "Are you— Are you touching yourself now?"

"Oh, I want to, Jeff. Do you want me to?"

"Oh, God, yes."

"Then I should probably lie down." Rowan affected a dramatic wince. "My sheets are cool...especially since I'm so *hot*." That wasn't a complete lie. It *was* hot. And humid, she thought pulling her tank top away from her chest, a vain effort to circulate a little air beneath her shirt.

A harsh breath stuttered across the line. "How hot are you?"

"I'm on fire, Jeff. I'm imagining that you're touching me. Can I touch you?"

"Yes."

Thirty seconds later it was over. She was thirty-six dollars richer and her sheets were still clean. Honestly, if a woman was going to use her body for profit, phone sex was definitely the way to go. In all seriousness, Rowan knew there were some people who would criticize her choice of temporary employment, but she'd used her own morality meter when making the decision. As far as she was concerned, she was providing a harmless form of entertainment. She simply played a part, catered to men's fantasies from a comfortable distance. No harm, no foul. It was a practical business arrangement, one that benefited her, kept food in the fridge and the power on.

She waited until his breathing slowed before she spoke again. "I've enjoyed talking with you, Jeff. Call me again, anytime."

Jeff exhaled a long, satisfied breath. "You can count on it." He paused. "Hey, as long as you're still there, do you mind if I ask you a quick question?"

"Sure. Go ahead." This was common. Men frequently asked her for all kinds of advice. Everything from how to remove stains, to what brand of fabric softener did she prefer. She didn't mind. It was their dime, after all. *Cha-ching.*

She'd even had a teenage boy call—she'd taught enough of them to recognize the pubescent squeaking croak—and, after she'd neatly avoided the sex issue, she'd ended up tutoring him in science. He'd contacted her several times during one week, then the calls had abruptly ceased. She'd been tempted to give him her home number, but Caller ID and cross-referencing had prevented the impulse. What she did on her own time wasn't anyone's business, but she didn't think Middleton's Mississippi Bible Belt board of education would agree. She'd fully expected a call from an outraged parent, but so far nothing had come of it, and she sincerely hoped nothing did.

"I've got a date tonight," the caller said, "and I really want to impress this girl. What do you think? Burger King or McDonald's?"

Rowan rolled her eyes. Her clients, the poor fools. No wonder they could never get laid in the traditional sense. "Wow her," she told him flatly. "Head for the border."

"Taco Bell?" A thoughtful hum, then, "An even better choice. Thanks."

"No problem." She chuckled under her breath and disconnected. Just in the nick of time, too, Rowan thought, as she watched her elderly neighbor, Ida Holcomb, amble unsteadily across her backyard toward Rowan's fence.

Rowan rented the small guest house, which was located at the rear of Ida's property, from the older lady. The white frame house was small, but two-storied with full, sweeping porches on both levels. It was the mini-version of Ida's grand antebellum home and, for what it lacked in modern convenience, it more than made up for in character.

There was only one plug-in in the bathroom, and the pipes invariably froze in the winter, but the ten-foot ceilings lent an airy mood to the house, and the crown molding, fireplace, and hardwood floors had been hand-crafted with a quality of workmanship which couldn't be duplicated much less found in today's power-tool, particle-board world. The small greenhouse, workshop and attached garden had made it the perfect choice for Rowan.

When Rowan lost her job, Ida had sacrificed part of the rent in exchange for errands and personal services. Rowan did Ida's grocery shopping, took her to and from the hairdresser's, paid her bills and whatnot. She plucked her eyebrows—not that there were that many left because Ida had been part of a generation where having *no* eyebrows was fashionable—and stoically—*miserably*—rendered the occasional pedicure. Her gaze involuntarily moved to Ida's slowly-approaching slippered feet and she quelled a shudder. In Rowan's opinion, there was nothing remotely attractive about feet, and there was something downright *yuck* about knobby, gnarled old-people feet.

Ick.

For all of that, however, she'd nonetheless grown very fond of her neighbor. Her grandparents had passed away when she was small, and her parents had decided to make the most of their retirement by seeing how many stamps they could add to their passports before they grew too old and feeble to globetrot. They were part of the new generation of fashionable retirees. They'd visited the Pyramids of Giza, the Great Wall of China and were currently on an extended tour of Europe.

Rowan had one brother, who naturally begrudged their

parents the fruit of their hard-earned labor and, rather than admiring them for packing as much *living* into their lives as she did, only bemoaned the loss of his dwindling inheritance. Though they both lived in Middleton, she rarely saw him, which, sadly, was fine with her.

Were her parents aware of her circumstances, Rowan knew they wouldn't hesitate to help her out, but pride, the insistent desire to fend for herself and the idea that they might miss another stamp because of her kept her from asking. She scowled. Besides, her brother had his hand out often enough for both of them.

She could make it on her own.

Would make it on her own. All she had to do was get through another month, then hopefully she'd get called back to school. Until then, she'd just answer her 1-900 line every time it rang and take care of her neighbor. It was a small price to pay for her independence.

Rowan summoned a weak smile as Ida drew near and silently—fervently—prayed that the woman hadn't developed another ingrown toenail.

"I swear, you're the dirtiest female I think I've ever seen," Ida chided. "Gardening is dirty work, I'll grant you. But—" her lips twisted with displeasure as she inventoried every smudge and smear on Rowan's body "—I think that you get down and roll in it." Her lined face folded into a frown. "How do you ever expect to find a man when you look more fit to be the bride of a pig?"

Rowan barely smothered a sigh. In addition to being part of the *no-eyebrow* generation, Ida was also of the outdated opinion that a woman wasn't complete until she had a man to make her whole. It was penis envy to the *nth* degree and the mentality never ceased to make her grind her teeth in frustration.

Furthermore, Rowan had been burned once and, call her

crazy, but she simply wasn't up to a repeat performance of that disaster at the moment. She'd been in love, imagining the happily ever after that Ida relentlessly preached—she'd even reluctantly let that bastard drive her car, her biggest regret because he hadn't been *vintage-Vette worthy* and she'd known it—but hadn't heeded her own intuition because she'd been too busy picking out china patterns and bridesmaids' dresses. She'd tricked herself into thinking that she was in love, and he'd tricked her into believing he reciprocated the sentiment.

He'd been reciprocating something all right, but it hadn't been with her.

Two weeks before the wedding, she'd shown up at her fiancé's apartment for some surprise sex. It turned out to be surprise sex, too, only she was the one surprised and he was the one having sex.

Bitter pill, hard lesson.

Since then, she'd developed an unspoken code of sorts, one that her father had unwittingly inspired. She didn't date anyone who didn't fully appreciate her car, and she didn't sleep with anyone who had the gall to ask to drive it. Bizarre? Yes. But it worked.

Rowan glanced at the sleek little convertible parked in her driveway and felt her lips curl at the corners. Dubbed the first American sports car, the Vette was an unparalleled testament to fine engineering at its best. Honduras Maroon with fawn interior and a white ragtop, it had a 327 V-eight with four on the floor, and it purred with megahorsepower perfection. It had been her dad's first brand-new car and he'd cared for it with the kind of reverent regard the vehicle deserved. She'd shared his passion and, as a result, he'd handed her the keys when she'd graduated from high school.

Rowan had decided that while she might not be a '62

Vette, she nonetheless deserved the same care and attention, and the same reverence. Until she found a guy willing to ante up all of the above, she planned to play her cards close to her vest. Did she occasionally long for more? Of course she did. She enjoyed her independence, yes, but not to the point of being a perpetual loner. There were nights when the silence closed in around her and she literally ached for the presence of another body. A big, warm masculine body. Nights when she craved conversation and companionship, a lover and friend. A safe harbor amid the ordered chaos of her life. But she refused to settle for anything less than the total package, and therein lay the rub.

Ignoring Ida's bride-of-a-pig remark, Rowan summoned a smile. "Was there something I could do for you, Ida?"

Ida started. Her preoccupied gaze darted away from Rowan's grimy shirt and settled on her face. Then she frowned, huffed an exaggerated breath and fished a napkin from the front pocket of her housecoat. "Honestly," Ida complained as she wiped Rowan's cheek. "It's all over your face, too." She tsked under her breath. "I hope you're hosing yourself down before you climb into that old tub. Those drains are slow enough as it is."

"I always do," Rowan lied easily. Ida was forever offering little tips on how to care for the aging guest house. *Don't overload the circuits. Use oil soap to clean the floors.* Ida Holcomb was a woman of many opinions and she could be counted on to share them—liberally— whether one wanted to hear them or not. A droll smiled curled Rowan's lips.

Seemingly satisfied, the older woman stuffed the napkin back into her pocket. "There. That's better, though I really wish you had time to change. You're my representative, you know," she said, drawing herself up primly. "How you look reflects directly upon me."

So an errand was in order, Rowan thought, resisting the urge to smile. "I can change in a flash, Ida. Where do you need me to go?"

"To the drug store." She winced uncomfortably and rubbed her belly. "The fiber and prunes didn't do the trick. I need an enema."

And she should definitely be turned out for that mission, Rowan thought dimly, equally horrified and revolted. After all, buying an enema was important business. But just par for the course in her train wreck of a life. She was so used to being humiliated she often wondered what it would feel like to be normal. To not blush or squirm or writhe with embarrassment.

Rowan swallowed, nodded jerkily, not trusting herself to speak.

"In fact, you'd better get two. Better safe than sorry," Ida prophesied grimly.

Rowan managed a sick smile. *Right*. And better this than hungry, she tried to tell herself.

The argument might have worked, too…if she hadn't just lost her appetite.

CHAPTER TWO

AT THIRTY-TWO and in perfect health, Will Foster found himself skating the edge of an anger-induced aneurysm, or at the very least, a massive stroke.

Doris Whitaker had screwed him again.

Not in the literal sense, of course—Will shuddered as her heavily made-up, wrinkled face flashed through his mind's eye—but figuratively, he might as well have painted a big bull's-eye on his ass.

The ass she was undoubtedly watching, the old perv, Will thought with an unhappy start as he strode across her yard to his truck. He cast a glance over his shoulder, and sure enough, she'd been watching him leave. Her painted lips slid into a wider smile and she twinkled her arthritic, bejeweled fingers at him.

Will forced a tight smile and waved back. "Goodbye," he muttered through gritted teeth.

His company, Foster's Landscape Design, had spent the better part of three summers, not to mention thousands of dollars, trying to fulfill their "satisfaction guaranteed" promise.

To no avail.

Though he knew he should simply let it go—should simply concede defeat—perversely, Will couldn't do it. He'd get that satisfied-customer stamp of approval from her, dammit, or die trying. It was the point of it. All bragging aside, he was good at what he did. He *loved* his job.

Loved developing a landscape, then pulling it together and seeing it to fruition. Loved getting his hands dirty, nursing blooms and watching things grow. He had a tremendous amount of respect for the codependent design of the world. The whole oxygen and carbon dioxide cycle that made plants and animals dependent on one another. It was...awe-inspiring.

Furthermore, Foster's Landscape Design was swiftly approaching their ten-year anniversary and in those ten years, he'd *never* had an unsatisfied customer.

He absolutely refused to let Doris ruin that record.

His team had finished up today and, though she'd been pleased throughout the process—had approved the design herself *once again*—she'd decided that it wasn't what she'd wanted after all.

Tear it out and start over.

Will had wanted to tear something out all right, but it hadn't been the cacti she'd decided she hated. This was the *third* freakin' time she'd pulled this shit. He was at his wit's end, and quite honestly, if he wasn't afraid she'd howl blue murder down at that country club she virtually funded, he'd be tempted to tell her to take that cactus and shove it up her—

Two loud beeps, followed by his mother screaming "Will?" into the two-way radio interrupted the uncharitable thought. Despite the fact that he'd told her repeatedly that yelling wasn't necessary, Millie Foster, perversely, continued to do it. On purpose, he suspected, because it never failed to startle the hell out of him.

Will swore, unsnapped the combination radio/phone from his belt and dredged the bottom of his soul for an ounce of unspent patience. He squeezed his eyes tightly shut. "Mother, for the last time, you *don't* have to yell."

"Sorry," Millie replied unrepentantly. "I just wanted to make sure that you heard me."

"I heard you. What's up?" Will detected a bit of laughter and catcalling in the background. He frowned. "What's going on?"

"I just wanted to let you know that you have a dinner date tonight, so be sure and finish up in time to take a proper bath."

Dinner date? Will thought, utterly confused. A proper bath? He hadn't made a date with anyone. In fact, he hadn't had a date in months. Even if he'd met someone who'd sparked any interest—which he hadn't—he wouldn't have had the time. Spring was the busiest season of his year, the time of year when his laughable social life was shoved to the back burner. Besides, his last serious relationship had left a bad taste in his mouth—a combination of bitter regret, bad judgment and plain stupidity—and it wasn't a flavor he wished to sample again anytime soon.

Will frowned as the implication of this conversation finally surfaced in his muddled brain and he mentally swore—she was matchmaking.

Again.

His grim mood blackened further. Though he loved her to distraction, and he knew she simply had his best interests at heart, Will nonetheless was exceedingly weary of her meddling. "Mother, I didn't make a date for tonight, and if you have made one for me, then you'll be the one to cancel it. We've been down this road, and I'm not in the mood to backtrack. Not today."

An exasperated huff sounded. "Don't you want to know who it's with before I cancel it?"

He wasn't remotely curious. "No," he said flatly.

"Fine," his mother replied. "Ordinarily I wouldn't have seen the need to meddle—"

Ha! Will thought.

"But," she sighed, and a curious, almost ominous quiver had entered her voice. "I just thought that, given this ph—phone bill, that desperate m-measures should be t-taken."

More guffaws, more laughter from her end, and he could have sworn he heard his brother, Ben, say, "Hell, yeah! An inflatable woman would have been cheaper." But that couldn't possibly be right, Will thought, thoroughly confused, because it didn't make any sense. And his phone bill? What was wrong with his phone bill, and what did that have to do with her finding him a date?

Will developed an eye twitch. He shoved the key in the ignition and started the truck. "Make sense, Mom. What are you talking about? What's wrong with my phone bill?"

"Nothing…if you don't mind that it's five times more than last month."

"What?" But that would make it—Will did the mental calculation and blinked, astounded—right at a thousand dollars. His jaw all but dropped.

"You sound surprised, dear," she continued blithely. "I guess you didn't realize how long you spent t-talking to y-your 1-900-Lover." She dissolved into a fit of whooping, wheezing laughter that made his face burn. "At any rate, a real date would have been cheaper, which is why I can't in good conscience call Rebecca Hillendale and cancel on your behalf. There are times when a mother simply must intervene."

For the first time in his life, Will Foster knew what it felt like to be literally struck dumb. Not dumb as in he couldn't speak, but dumb as in *stupid,* as in he had a brain, but couldn't for the life of him make it function. Several thoughts swirled simultaneously through his head, but they were disjointed and dim, and he lacked the cognitive ability to put them in any sort of order, much less get them out of his mouth.

The best he could figure out, somehow—and God only knew how—1-900-charges, presumably for *phone sex*—had ended up on his phone bill. Apparently—and much to his immediate, unwarranted humiliation—his mother had broadcast this at the office—where she'd seemingly forgotten that she worked *for him*—and then had taken it upon herself to find him a date.

Meanwhile, Rebecca Hillendale was a humpbacked harpy with the disposition of a constipated porcupine and he'd rather die a slow painful death or have his testicles removed with red-hot pincers than to sit through a meal with her. These were the thoughts roiling through his tortured mind, but when he finally managed to speak, it was in short staccato sentences devoid of any emotion except outrage.

"Mother, I'll be there in a minute." Will slipped the transmission into reverse, backed into the street, then dropped the gear shift into drive. The truck shot forward. "Nobody leaves."

"But—"

"Nobody leaves."

AN HOUR LATER Will's mind was in order, but his temper was not.

According to the phone company, the calls Will insisted that he hadn't made, had, in fact, been dialed from his number. Curiously, during hours that he was at work. Another look at the bill—at the dates the calls were placed, specifically—had shed a new light on the situation.

The calls had coincided with his nephew's visit.

Scott, his sister's eldest son, typically spent every spring break with Will. Usually Will put him to work, but a

four-wheeler accident the week before Scott's visit had
foiled that plan. Scott had been forced to spend the holiday
playing catch-up on his studies, and Will had decided it
would be shitty to cancel the kid's visit simply because
he'd lose the labor.

Given the make-up work situation, he'd had to plead
with his sister for the ungrateful brat to even come, and
now as thanks, Scott had put him in a horrible position—
he'd left him with a whopping *thousand dollar* phone bill
and the unhappy task of telling his sister that her child
had been having phone sex on Will's watch.

Which led him to his present errand.

Before he called his sister and shared that little tidbit—
before he paid the bill, even—he intended to directly contact the author of his misery—the phone sex operator.
Over the top? Probably. But what the hell—his normally
sedate life had been knocked off-kilter today and he had
to do something proactive to put it back on the right path.
He couldn't help it. It was all part and parcel of being a
professed control freak. Will took exception to the unflattering term, but couldn't deny his nature. He liked to do
things *his way,* liked having *his way,* and ninety-nine-
point-nine percent of the time he could say with confidence that *his way* was the *right way.*

Will's first impulse had been to call the 1-900 line, but
he'd quickly changed his mind. The unscrupulous witch
wasn't bleeding another friggin' nickel out of him. Instead,
he'd called a P.I. buddy to do a little snooping for him. The
best Will had hoped for was a toll-free line, but what his
friend had found had been considerably better. A name
and address, and, wonder of wonders, a local one at that.
What were the odds?

He'd been destined to blast her.

Given the morning from hell he'd had, to be honest,

Will didn't think he'd ever looked forward to doing anything more.

When he'd learned that the woman lived here it was as though Christmas had come early. Rather than taking out his miserable mood on Doris—who he resignedly admitted he would be forced to continue to work with—or his well-meaning but meddlesome mother—whom he'd live to regret pissing off—Will had found out that he could verbally assault a perfect stranger who really deserved it, and finally blow off the steam which had been steadily building since early this morning.

What better person to verbally eviscerate than a woman so lacking in morals that she'd have phone sex with a teenager? A minor? A mere child?

Granted, Scott was seventeen and, given the way the girls followed him around, the kid was most likely getting laid more frequently and with more furor than his uncle. Will nevertheless thought the woman should have used better judgment. But she hadn't. She'd crossed the line in order to pad her own pockets—with *his* money, dammit—and for that, she would pay.

A Jackson native, Will had been at once familiar and surprised by the supposed address of the woman. According to his buddy, she lived in an old but affluent neighborhood on a street one wouldn't normally expect to find an unsavory phone sex operator in residence.

Wisteria Court was located in the historical district. Huge antebellum homes reminiscent of a bygone era, with aged boxwoods, magnolias, weeping willows and tulip trees standing sentinel on the manicured lawns. The neighborhood was rife with the scent of mint juleps and old money, and he found the idea of a phone sex operator in residence among Jackson's so-called hoity-toity set perversely funny. Ordinarily, the idea would have drawn a smile.

But not today. Today, he was too pissed.

He slowed the truck to a crawl as he checked house numbers, then finally hitting pay dirt, he wheeled the vehicle into the appropriate drive. Anticipation spiked. *Finally,* Will thought. He purposely stoked his ire on the way to the door by alternately imagining writing the check to the phone company, and telling his sister about Scott's foray into the seedy world of phone sex—*Reach out and touch someone,* indeed, Will thought darkly. So, by the time he plied the knocker every last particle of irritation he'd had that morning sat ready on his tongue. He'd pulled back the hammer, so to speak, and was ready to unload.

It was to his vast disappointment then, when an elderly woman with pink foam curlers in her hair answered the door and he was forced to put on the safety.

Again.

He stifled the burgeoning urge to scream.

"Can I help you?" she asked.

Baffled, Will frowned. He knew he had the right address. But this… He inwardly shuddered. This couldn't possibly be the right woman. "Er…Ms. Crosswhite?"

"Nope. Ida Holcomb. You're looking for Rowan," she said matter-of-factly. She jerked a thumb over her shoulder. "She lives in the guest house in the back." The woman gasped, laid a hand over her belly, and shot him a pained look. "Gotta go," she said abruptly, then slammed the door in his face.

Startled, Will drew back, then, shaking his head, made his way off the porch and toward the rear of the property where the older woman had indicated. He had a bead on her now, Will thought, purposefully striding alongside the house. As he rounded the corner, however, the sight that greeted him caused him to slow and every bit of the anger he'd nursed faded into insignificance.

A vintage Vette—a '62 if he wasn't mistaken—in pristine condition sat in the drive next to the house. He whistled low and, had his attention not been instantly drawn elsewhere, he would have been tempted to inspect the car from bumper to bumper. As it was, his gaze had landed on the house and surrounding property, and any notion of the car, while it was admittedly a fine piece of machinery, drifted right out of his head.

The house, a miniature version of the primary residence sat at the very back of the property. White frame, double verandah, utterly charming. But it hadn't been what made him pause, either—it was the garden around the house that had made such an impact. He blinked, pulling it all into focus, and for some wholly unknown reason, an excited tingle started in the heels of his feet and swiftly moved upward.

Will had been in landscape design for years, had been to countless shows in practically every part of the country, and yet nothing in his experience could compare to *this*.

Though he recognized every flower, vine, shrub and bush—all of them typical to the average bee-and-butterfly garden—the whimsical layout, the use of color and texture combined with what he could only deduce was the owner's original metalwork and stained glass made it the most *unique* garden he'd ever seen. There was no discernable plan, no clear-cut layout, and yet everything grew together in a seamless form of ordered pandemonium.

It was *gorgeous*.

Butterfly bushes, creeping flox, flowering peach and crabapple trees, clematis vines, various lilies, and bedding plants, a variety of ground covers, and perhaps the most interesting of all—antique roses. The swamp rose, in particular, was one that he coveted.

Feeling like he'd been clubbed over the head again, Will slowly resumed his pace. Inexplicably drawn to the roses, the grand dames of antique bushes, he reverently fingered one delicate petal while quietly inspecting the plant. No spots or aphids, and what minimal pruning had been done had been accomplished with a precisely loving hand. Whoever tended this garden had a passion for the process and clearly designed it for their own personal enjoyment.

Not a single detail had been left untended and, despite the fact that he knew this was the work of the skanky phone sex operator, of all people, Will found himself grudgingly impressed. More than impressed. Floored, really. After all, it took a helluva lot of imagination, not to mention a great deal of time and effort to—

The tinkle of feminine laughter drifted to him, snagging his attention back to the task at hand. He scanned the yard and, after a moment, his gaze landed upon a generously rounded, denim-clad rump peeking out from a small raised bed in the far corner of the garden. A pair of tanned, equally shapely legs were attached to the rump. He could see little else save the back of her head, and while he got the impression of long sable-colored hair, in all truthfulness as far as he was concerned she could have been bald and he'd never have noticed—he was too busy admiring her ass.

And oh, what an ass it was.

Full, curvy and heart-shaped, it gently tested the strength of the seams of her roomy cutoffs and accentuated what he could tell even from this distance was a small waist.

She flicked a weed off to her side where a growing

pile accumulated on the lawn. "Oh, you naughty boy," she said, her voice the perfect mixture of flirtatious and intimate. She laughed again, a long wanton giggle that too effectively conjured images of twisted sheets and bare limbs, made the fine hairs on his arms stand on end and a hum of attraction vibrate his spine.

Who the hell was she talking to? Will wondered, trying to peer around her. He frowned, intrigued. Who was a naughty boy? He didn't see any boy. She leaned back on her haunches, seemingly admiring her handiwork and he saw it then—the headset. In a moment of blind, dawning comprehension he realized what she was doing.

Or *having,* rather—phone sex.

Right here in her yard. While weeding her garden.

It literally blew what was left of his mind.

"Oh, Roy," she sighed convincingly. "I'm hot, too. Maybe I should get undressed, slip out of this teddy. There's not much to it, but I like being naked. It makes me feel…wicked. Would you like that, Roy?"

Apparently *Roy* did like the idea, Will thought with a wry twist of his lips, because she chuckled softly again. To his astonishment, he felt that sound hiss through his own blood. Felt a curious sense of excitement—one that was almost foreign to him since it had been so long—fizz through his abdomen.

"Okay, I'm ready," she murmured. "What do you want to do to me first?" Another wanton chuckle, then, "You're right. Foreplay *is* highly overrated. And there's no need, because I'm ready for you right now."

What happened next, Will would have never believed if he hadn't seen—and heard—it with his own eyes and ears.

The woman cooed, winced, groaned and moaned into the phone as though Roy weren't God-knows-where, but

instead rooted right there between her delectable thighs.
Her breath came in short little puffs—while she enthusiastically attacked the weeds, no less—and she threw in
the occasional *"Oh, God! Oh, please! Oh, yes, Roy, God
yes!"* and then rounded out her performance with the most
convincing sounding orgasm he'd ever heard.

When her breathing finally slowed, Will felt like he'd
been through the wringer. Impossibly, his heart rate had
jumped into overdrive, every milligram of moisture had
evaporated from his mouth and he'd come within a hairs-
breadth of an immaculate orgasm himself, a phenomenon
that hadn't happened to him since he'd first hit puberty.
At some point, he'd reached down and held on to her
fence, undoubtedly to remain upright because his knees
had grown decidedly weak.

"Oh, I enjoyed it, too, Roy," she murmured, her voice
laced with feigned pleasant exhaustion. "You're the best,"
she told him, blatantly catering to the man's ego. "Call
me again sometime, okay?"

To his continued astonishment, she blithely ended the
call and went back to weeding, as though nothing remarkable had happened.

Slack-jawed, Will could only stare at her. He blinked.
Then blinked again. Though he'd come here with the intention of blasting her into oblivion, curiously his anger had
been replaced with a combination of brooding fascination,
compelling intrigue and an unwanted smidge of reluctant
admiration.

He'd also found the whole thing hilariously funny.

He smothered a chuckle, lifted his hands and began to
clap.

His prey gasped, then turned and bright green—*true
green*—eyes tangled with his.

Will almost staggered from the impact. The bottom

dropped out of his stomach and, though he knew it was impossible, he felt the ground quake beneath his feet. An electric current zinged up his spine, then back-tracked and settled hotly behind his zipper.

With effort, Will managed to recover. "Very good, Ms. Crosswhite." He summoned a weak chuckle. "I don't think I've ever seen anyone enjoy…w-weeding quite as m-much as you."

CHAPTER THREE

ROWAN WAS ACCUSTOMED to being humiliated. Frankly, she'd long ago resigned herself to the fact that she would stay in a chronic state of humiliation. The level would simply vary, but being humiliated, she knew, was a foregone conclusion.

For instance, buying the enemas today had been humiliating—almost as humiliating as the time she'd had to buy Ida's wart remover.

Or the time she'd inadvertently pulled a tampon out of her purse and tried to write a check with it.

Or the time she'd accidentally crammed a straw up her nose and caused it to bleed.

Or the time she'd shut her *own ear* in the car door.

She was constantly getting herself into situations that made her want to shrink out of existence, or at the very least out of someone's immediate memory. She routinely fell, got choked…*something* all the time. Humiliating? Yes, every last event.

But nothing—*nothing*—in her past or present memory could compare to the absolute mortification of this moment.

She wanted to die.

Truly, desperately wanted to die.

Because the hunk leaning against her fence had apparently heard every last syllable of her most recent conversation, from the first *Oh, God* to the final *Oooohhhh,* and every dramatic pant, wince and groan in between.

Heat scalded her cheeks, and if she hadn't already turned around to face him, she would have pretended to be deaf, maybe even blind. Anything to avoid this panic-stricken *oh-shit-not-again* scenario. Rowan tried consoling herself with the old whatever-doesn't-kill-you-will-make-you-stronger adage—her normal pep-me-up cheer—but for whatever reason, the message fell flat this time.

Though it took every iota of willpower she possessed and because she was the mistress of her world, Rowan stood, dusted her hands off and reluctantly began to make her way across the yard. And the closer she got, the more humiliated she became. Her heart sank and she swallowed a whimper.

Naturally, he had to be gorgeous.

The guy had been a hunk from a distance—casually messy blond hair, a great smile, broad shoulders and nice legs. But up close, he was downright devastating. His hair was sun-bleached, a dark tawny color around his ears and nape, but several shades lighter on top. His face was lean and tanned, with a mouth slightly fuller than average and a pair of light brown eyes that offset the alpha bone structure with just a hint of boy-next-door. It was a face that said, "Best friend or worst enemy? You choose," and the compelling combination made a shiver dance up her spine.

"Can I help you?" Rowan finally managed.

"I'm Will Foster," the guy told her. His smile faded and, unfortunately, a less pleasant look claimed his intriguing features.

So, worst enemy, was it? Rowan thought. Interesting.

"I'm here because your number showed up on my phone

bill this month," he continued, his otherwise nice voice throbbing with barely suppressed outrage. He crossed his arms over his well-muscled chest and an irritating smirk ruined the look of that gorgeous mouth. "But *I* didn't call you."

"If that's the case, then you'll need to contact the phone company," Rowan replied, automatically offering the most expedient solution to his problem. Her nature, she couldn't help it. She could plant a whimsical garden, draw, paint and create different types of funky art, but put a problem in front of her and she'd find the most efficient answer. She was an anomaly, a right-brained thinker with left-brained tendencies.

The left brain kicked in when she belatedly realized that he shouldn't even be here. How had he gotten her address? Her name? A finger of unease prodded her spine. "How did you get my address, Mr.——"

"Foster," he reminded her tightly. "And I did contact the phone company. They told me your number had been dialed from my house, which meant the *thousand-dollar* charges were correct."

Rowan scowled, baffled. "If the charges were correct, then what are you doing here?"

This was over the line, she thought, instinctively backing away from him. If there'd been a problem that the phone company couldn't resolve, then why hadn't he simply called? Why had he gone to the trouble to track her down? Common sense told her she should be alarmed, but the intense irritation stiffening every muscle in her body negated the logical emotion. Her eyes narrowed. *Of all the damned nerve...*

"I'm here because you had phone sex with my nephew," he retorted angrily. "My *underage* nephew."

Rowan's first impulse was to deny the charge—she

knew perfectly well that she hadn't had phone sex with a minor...but she had talked to one.

The flash of insight jimmied an exasperated grunt from her throat and she managed a slight smile. "You're Scott's uncle, aren't you?" She'd been expecting this. Not *this* as in a visit, but at least that explained why he'd gone to the trouble to find her. She relaxed marginally. Things were beginning to make sense.

His lips twisted into another annoying smirk. "I'm impressed, Ms. Crosswhite. For a thousand dollars you should remember his name."

The smart-ass was making it damned hard to forget her self-righteous anger, Rowan thought, heartily annoyed. Pity she couldn't forget how gorgeous he was. "I remember his name because he called me several times."

"I know." He fished what she recognized as his phone bill from the back pocket of his shorts and ran an eye over it. She watched in a sort of drunken fascination as his lips moved, counting off the calls. "Six times, to be precise."

Rowan pushed her hair over her shoulder and assumed a negligent pose, struggled to detach her gaze from those distracting lips. "That sounds about right."

"Did you realize that he was underage? Or did you just not care?"

Rowan knew that he had every reason to be upset, particularly since he was laboring under the mistaken assumption that she'd had phone sex with his nephew. Nevertheless, she didn't appreciate the sarcasm or the censure, and she sure as hell didn't appreciate being tracked down at her house, having her privacy violated.

"Yes, I knew he was underage—"

His lips curled without humor and he rocked back on

his heels. "Then you just didn't care. But you will care, Ms. Crosswhite, when his parents prosecute you."

Rowan felt her eyes widen. "You're probably right. However, being as I've done nothing to be prosecuted for, then I don't have anything to worry about, do I?"

"Phone sex with a minor—"

Her patience snapped and she barely stifled the urge to scream. "I didn't have phone sex with your nephew, Mr. Foster," Rowan all but growled. "I helped him with his science homework."

For a split second his face went comically blank, then a smug disbelieving smile drifted over his too-gorgeous lips. "And what were you doing with *Roy,* I wonder?" he drawled lazily. "Teaching him the difference between a consonant and a vowel?"

Renewed embarrassment flooded her cheeks and while she had appreciated the fact that he owned a sense of humor, she didn't appreciate it being at her expense. Rowan pulled in a deep calming breath and called upon her past experience with irate parents to see her through this provoking scene. She'd dealt with enough of them over the years to handle this, she told herself. One of them had to remain professional, and clearly it wasn't *him*.

"Have you spoken to Scott?" she asked, striving for a calm she didn't feel. "Have you asked him what happened?"

"No, I haven't." A muscle jumped in his tense jaw. "Since I'll have to tell his mother first, it's not a conversation that I'm looking forward to."

"Well, you can handle that however you want to," she retorted, "but as for my part, I have proof that I didn't have phone sex with Scott, Mr. Foster." And she did, thank God, Rowan thought, immensely relieved.

A perplexed line emerged between his brows. "Proof?"

"I have a record feature on my phone. For safety reasons," she clarified at his astounded look. Honestly. "Kooks, weirdoes, harassment—"

Comprehension dawned and he nodded abruptly.

"Anyway, when I realized that Scott was underage— which was almost immediately—I hit record." She pulled a shrug. "In fact, I've recorded every conversation with Scott and will have to insist that you listen to them, just so there's no misunderstanding. I thought I might hear from an outraged parent—or an uncle, as it's turned out— though, frankly, I thought that I'd receive a phone call." She pinned him with a weighty stare. "Which brings me back to my first question—how did you get my name and address?" she persisted. "How did you find me? Because to be quite honest with you, Mr. Foster, it, uh… It kind of freaks me out."

And it did. Anonymity had been her first line of defense. Only one other person knew about her side-job— her best friend, Alexa, and Rowan knew beyond a shadow of a doubt that Alexa hadn't betrayed her confidence. Her friend was one of those rare souls who could actually keep a secret.

But if this guy found her this easily, who was to say that another guy couldn't? One without an understandable cause? It completely unnerved her. In this case, Rowan could easily see what had happened. His nephew had made the calls and, in addition to paying for them, he'd have to tell the kid's parents. She grimaced. Not fun, she'd agree. Nevertheless…

For the first time he seemed to consider that he'd made a mistake, a tactical error of sorts and he knew it. He shifted uneasily, rubbed a hand over the back of his neck,

and shot her an uncomfortable look. "I, uh… I have a
friend in the P.I. business," he reluctantly admitted. "He
made a few calls."

She cocked her head and shrewdly considered him. "I
see. I'm assuming since this friend was able to give you
my name and address, he also had my regular telephone
number." She paused, and was rewarded when he started
to squirm. "And yet you still decided that a visit was in
order."

He winced, looked out over her garden, then shot her a
sheepish smile. That half grin had to be one of the sexiest
things she'd ever seen and it had the singular ability to
drain every bit of the irritation still inhabiting her spine.
"I was pissed."

Oh, she'd just bet he was, Rowan thought, resisting the
urge to smile herself. "Well, since you're here, you should
probably listen to those tapes."

He started. "Right."

Without waiting to see if he followed her, Rowan turned
and headed toward the house. For some unknown reason,
her stomach did a little anticipation-overload flop, and the
back of her nape prickled with awareness. An indication
of just how pathetic she was, she decided with an inward
harrumph of disgust.

Jesus.

This guy hadn't tracked her down to follow through with
an initial attraction—he'd come over here with the express
purpose of chewing her up and spitting her out. He'd bared
his big-bad-wolf teeth and had planned to make a meal out
of her. One, by the looks of things, he'd fully intended to
enjoy.

Rowan darted a look over her shoulder and felt a perverse flame of heat lick her belly. She smiled and bit her lip.

Pity she wasn't ready to be served up on a platter... yet.

CHAPTER FOUR

WILL'S GAZE inexplicably dropped to Rowan's retreating ass. Then the retreating part triggered in his sluggish brain, and it belatedly occurred to him that he was supposed to be following her. Annoyed, he cursed under his breath and hurried after her.

She paused on the front porch, giving him time to catch up. She wore a faint smile, as though she knew precisely why the minimal wait had been necessary.

To his absolute astonishment, he felt a blush creep into his cheeks.

The phone sex operator was making *him* blush.

How screwed up was that?

Hell, he didn't know why he expected anything to be normal today, of all days, when this had been the most bizarre few hours of his life, most specifically the past few minutes.

Only seconds ago, he'd listened to this woman fake an orgasm over the phone, then rather than having the decency to be the stereotypical bored, homely housewife, she had the nerve to be gorgeous. Not passably pretty, or merely nice to look at.

She was gorgeous.

She was hometown-beauty-queen-meets-wet-dream-porn-star and, despite all reason, he found himself absolutely intrigued by her. Hell, who was he trying to kid?

He'd been intrigued by her from the first sultry syllable he'd heard her utter to dear old Roy.

Then, before he'd thought better of it, he'd applauded her performance, and she'd turned around…and he'd gone from being slightly curious to downright captivated.

His impression of her hair had been right. It was long and dark brown, and it slithered over her shoulders, cascaded down her back and landed in a gentle wave a couple of inches below her waist. It was sexy as hell and, while it was politically incorrect, it evoked the caveman in him— not to mention several other primal urges he'd had to forcibly tamp down.

She had a kind, open face with high cheekbones, a pair of bright green eyes that glinted with equal amounts of humor and intelligence, and a ripe mouth the color of a dusky pink rose. And the voice that came out of that mouth…

Mercy.

Sweet and slightly husky, almost sleepy, for a lack of better description. She could undoubtedly read the possible side effects on a medical-warning label and make it sound sexy.

In addition—as though those things weren't enough— she drove a vintage Vette, was obviously a master gardener as well as an artisan and, though she possessed a healthy modest streak—she'd blushed to the roots of her hair when he'd caught her verbally servicing Roy, he thought wryly— she'd chosen phone sex, of all things, as her career path.

The combined incongruity was astounding.

She was the proverbial riddle wrapped in an enigma… and there was nothing more interesting to Will than the challenge of a good mystery.

He let his gaze drift slowly over her as he followed her inside the house and mentally rocked back on his

heels. Figuring her out would undoubtedly be a treat—
one he'd most likely forfeited the minute he'd flown off
the handle and violated her privacy, he reminded himself
grimly. Sheesh. What the hell had he been thinking? Will
wondered. Had he lost his freakin' mind? What on earth
had possessed him to track her down—

She threw him a look over her shoulder, and he caught
a glimpse of continued humor in those leaf-green eyes.
"Let me wash my hands, then I'll get those tapes."

Oh, yeah. The tapes. Will frowned. Considering he'd
made a grand show of running her to ground, he figured
he'd better look interested in listening to them. He arranged
his face into what he hoped look like a serious, slightly
perturbed expression and, rather than continuing to study
her—a perpetual impulse—he let his gaze roam around
her house.

Like its owner, it created an instant impression.

It boasted beautiful hardwood floors, tall floor-to-
ceiling windows and lots of heavily carved molding and
trim work which was a prevalent theme in the traditional
antebellum style.

But the similarities to traditional ended there.

Fresh-cut flowers in old light-blue Mason jars lined the
mantel. Stained glass dressed every window, and hand-
painted furniture and art—obviously hers—rounded out
the eclectic decor. Lots of color, energy and light. The
whimsical design reminded him of her garden—it was
distinctly unique.

Like her.

"Okay," the object of his instant fascination said as she
breezed back into the room. "I've got them."

Once again, Will feigned appropriate concern, but from
the sidelong glance she slid him combined with the slight

quiver of her full lips, he didn't think he'd successfully maintained the ruse.

Hell, he didn't doubt for a moment that the whole damned scenario was precisely as she'd claimed. She wouldn't have offered proof otherwise, and though he'd been initially horrified that she recorded her conversations—his distrustful mind had immediately leaped to some form of blackmail—he had to grudgingly admit that it was quite a crafty move. Smart, really.

An antique display case which housed mismatched china pieces and other bric-a-brac served as a counter of sorts. Butted against the lower kitchen cabinets, the old piece formed a bar between the kitchen and living room.

Rowan shifted a few items aside and hefted a boom box, along with a couple other tapes onto the glass surface. While she wrestled with the plug, the things she'd moved out of the way snagged his attention. His eyes widened and, before he could check the impulse, a startled laugh, which he barely morphed into a cough, broke up in his throat.

A bottle of strawberry wine, three enemas and two treatments of wart remover stood on the makeshift counter.

Rowan started, then shot him a look and ultimately followed his gaze. She inhaled sharply, then closed her eyes tightly shut and groaned miserably. Color bloomed on her cheeks and she sank her teeth into that ripe bottom lip. "The wine is mine," she said haltingly, obviously—adorably—mortified. "The other things…are not."

"That's a relief." Will felt his lips twitch. He crossed his arms over his chest and lifted one shoulder in a negligent shrug. "For a moment there I was afraid you were a warty, constipated alcoholic."

The comment drew a droll smile and, while he couldn't be sure, he thought he saw a flash of reciprocated interest in those too-perceptive green eyes.

"I'm the alcoholic," she deadpanned. "My landlord is warty and constipated."

He grimaced, shifted and rubbed a hand over the back of his neck. "That's…unfortunate," Will finally managed, unable to come up with anything that remotely resembled an appropriate response.

"Ah," she sighed knowingly. A ghost of a smile played on her lips and she crossed her arms over her chest, then leaned a curvy hip against the counter. "So you *can* be tactful." She paused, allowing the dart to penetrate, then continued before he could respond. "I run errands for her," she explained. "As you can imagine, buying those particular items—" she glanced meaningfully at the ignoble remedies "—results in considerable embarrassment. So," she sighed wistfully, "in the vain hope that I could preserve a little dignity, I decided to stockpile them." Eyes twinkling, her gaze darted to him and she blew out a resigned breath. "Clearly, it didn't work."

For whatever reason, Will got the distinct impression that her efforts to thwart humiliation rarely worked. He smiled, unreasonably enchanted. "Ah, well. Better luck next time," he offered, once again unable to conjure an artful remark.

She chuckled grimly, pulled a slight shrug, then turned her attention back to the tapes. "One can hope." She slipped a tape into the player, and hit the rewind button. "So Scott's your nephew? How old is he? Sixteen? Seventeen?"

"Seventeen."

"He seems like a good kid. Bright."

"He is. Though obviously his judgment isn't always on the mark," he added pointedly.

Rather than being insulted, she merely smiled. "He's a teenager," she said, as though that explained everything. "They're a breed apart until those hormones level out. Particularly boys."

Interestingly, her matter-of-fact tone resonated with the voice of experience. Still… Will grimaced. "I don't think that excuse is going to fly with his mother."

She depressed the play button and shot him an enigmatic look. "Then perhaps you should talk to his father."

Impressed with the insight, Will inclined his head. Actually, he'd considered bypassing his sister and talking to Jim. Jim, he knew, would at least understand the motivation behind his son's ignorant, thoughtless episode. He winced.

Lori…wouldn't.

She'd be angry and appalled, and the combination of the two wouldn't leave any room for understanding. Will had initially rejected the idea of bypassing Lori—it was the easy way out for him, ergo it had to be wrong. Now he wasn't so sure. Now he—

His thoughts ground to a halt as Rowan's voice, then his nephew's sounded from the machine—her sultry "Hello," then Scott's nervous squeak.

"Hi. I, uh…" He cleared his throat and his voice lowered to a comical level. "Hey. What's happening, baby?"

Will felt a smile tug at his lips and his gaze instinctively found hers. She, too, wore an amused expression.

"Look, Slick, you're not old enough to have this conversation," Rowan told him, instantly seeing through the ploy. "Call back in a few years."

"Wait!"

From there, things happened exactly the way she'd told

him. They'd chatted, she'd tried to disconnect, citing the enormous phone bill someone would not approve of, and his nephew, to Will's astonishment, had glibly announced that his uncle wouldn't notice another 1-900 number because he frequently called them himself. In fact, Scott had continued, his uncle had probably called her in the past. Rowan had laughed at Will's outraged expression as he fervently denied the charge.

"I don't *need* to have phone sex," Will felt obliged to repeat after she'd turned off the tape. The unspoken *because-I-can-get-laid-without-it* hung between them, eliciting another mysterious smile from her. Her eyes twinkled.

"I'm sure you don't."

He nodded succinctly. "Damn straight."

She chewed the corner of her lip, presumably to keep from chuckling at his expense, and busied herself by putting the cassette away. She was laughing at him, Will knew, and he couldn't blame her because he was making a macho ass of himself. But he couldn't help it. It was a matter of honor, dammit. Men who could get laid in the traditional sense didn't call total strangers and whack off to the tune of a few well-rehearsed pants and sighs.

Phone sex? Will thought dubiously. Come on? He preferred his sexual encounters of the physical kind, thank you very much. He liked slow and tender, hot and frantic, and wasn't averse to a little kinky now and then. Sex was sex and, regardless of the method employed, hell, he thought with a slow smile, it was always good.

He'd never once thought about having a woman talk him through it…but he wasn't averse to a helping hand every now and then.

His gaze instantly drifted to her hands, and it took very little effort to imagine one of hers wrapped around him, touching him the way she'd implied she'd touched good ole Roy. A flash of heat detonated in his loins and a serious sense of excitement, one he hadn't felt in eons, pulsed through him.

She tucked her hair behind her ear. "Do you— Do you want to listen to the other tapes, or will that one suffice?"

Will grunted, unnerved. "That one will suffice."

She nodded, apparently still not trusting herself to look at him. "Good. Could I see that phone bill?"

He frowned, baffled. He couldn't imagine why, but he handed it to her nonetheless. "Sure."

Her lips moved as she silently scanned the bill, and it belatedly occurred to Will that she was tallying the multiple charges. In her head, without the aid of a calculator. Impressed, he readied his mouth to comment, but was interrupted as she handed the statement back to him. "Okay. Let me get my purse and I'll write you a check."

He blinked. "A check?"

"For the charges," she called over her shoulder. She disappeared into the back of the house, then emerged seconds later with a wallet. By the time she'd made the return trip, he'd managed to organize his chaotic thoughts into some semblance of order.

"Look, this isn't necessary. I didn't come here to get you to refund the charges." And he hadn't. Quite frankly, he hadn't thought beyond blasting her into oblivion, but he hardly needed to share that with her, did he?

She finished writing the check, scrawled her name across the bottom, then tore it out of the book and handed it to him. A smile caught the corner of her ripe mouth. "No, you came here to rip me a new one."

He'd opened his mouth to argue, but a guilty laugh

emerged, beating him to the punch. He pulled a shrug. "Like I said, I was pissed."

"You don't say?" She batted her lashes with feigned innocence. "I hadn't noticed."

He owed her an apology, Will knew, and though saying he was sorry wasn't a phrase that came naturally to him— quite frankly, he wasn't used to being wrong—tendering the expected nicety now didn't seem quite so onerous.

He exhaled mightily. "Look, I'm sorry," he said, albeit awkwardly. He glanced at the floor and was momentarily distracted by her bare feet. Lots of toe rings and a small tattoo of a butterfly decorated the skin right above her pinkie toe. Another bolt of heat landed in his groin and he struggled to find the rest of the apology. "I— I shouldn't have come here. I, uh— I should have called."

"Yes, you should have," she replied levelly. "However, when Scott needed further tutoring, I should have given him my home number instead of continuing to let him call the 900-number." Her lips formed another droll smile, and her eyes twinkled with humor. "In my defense, I was trying to guard my privacy." She sighed softly. "At any rate, I intend to refund the charges, so just take the check, we'll be square and we can forget about this mess."

He doubted it, but he reluctantly pocketed the check anyway. "At least let me pay you for the tutoring sessions," he offered. He laughed grimly. "Believe me, if the kid had asked me for help with science he would have been sadly disappointed."

If memory served, he'd barely passed science. Not because he'd lacked the intelligence or ability, he'd merely lacked the drive. Will had been one of those kids who survived high school by way of sports.

And—thanks to the kind hand of his father and grand-father—he'd known from the time he was old enough to plant a seed what he'd be doing with his life, so the only classes he'd been interested in throughout high school had been the ones that had pertained to agriculture.

Both his father and his grandfather had been farmers, had earned their living from the land. Corn, cotton, soy beans. Feast or famine, depending on the weather. They'd expected him to take the same route, but while Will had shared the same enthusiasm for the land, the same fascination with the soil and all she grew—the sheer interdependency of everything—he'd ultimately decided to carve his own path. He'd liked the combination of design, the challenge of outdoor architecture found in landscaping. He'd ridden through college on a football scholarship, had majored in landscape architecture with a minor in business administration, and the rest had been history. Unable to completely abandon his farming heritage, Will had added an heirloom seed catalog to his repertoire.

"No, those tutoring session are on me," Rowan told him, dragging him back into the conversation. She rolled her eyes. "Hell, I needed them as much as he did."

An important insight lurked behind that statement, Will decided. Intrigued, he arched a brow. "Oh?"

From her oh-hell expression, it was obvious that she thought she'd said too much. She swore under her breath, then released a pent-up sigh. "Oh, well," she finally relented. "It's not like you don't know everything else about me." She shot him a wry look. "I'm a teacher. I teach—" She winced grimly. "Correction, I *taught* science at Middleton High. Budget cuts ate my job, so until the system finds the money to put me back to work—hopefully in the fall—then I'm out of a contract." She shrugged, then bit her lip and, though she met his gaze directly, he detected a hint of vulnerability he instinctively knew that she'd resent. Which, curiously, made her all the more attractive.

"For obvious reasons, I would appreciate your discretion. I, uh... I don't think the board of education would approve of my interim job."

Will mentally whistled. She'd certainly mastered the understatement. They wouldn't merely disapprove—they'd freak. A phone sex operator teaching their impressionable youth? Not here, not in this century.

The gravity of the situation he'd put her in finally dawned and he inwardly winced with regret. He'd royally screwed up by coming here. He'd literally jeopardized her livelihood. "Don't worry," he assured her. "Your secret's safe with me."

Her slim shoulders sank in obvious relief. "Thanks. I appreciate it."

"Can I ask you a question?"

She nodded. "Sure. Go ahead."

Will hesitated. "Why phone sex?" he finally blurted out. The question had been burning a hole in his brain. She was obviously smart, educated. Geez, God. Why phone sex, of all things? Granted it was sexy and listening to her had made him unbelievably hot, but still...

Eyes twinkling, she shrugged. "Why not phone sex? It beats checking groceries at the Bag-a-Bargain. It's lucrative, and leaves me time to do the things I enjoy." She gestured around her living room. "Like stained glass, art and gardening." An ironic chuckle bubbled up her throat. "Believe me, I tried other things first. No one wanted to buy my art, and the whole starving-artist gig didn't appeal to me." Her lips curled. "I've grown accustomed to the little things, you know? Food, shelter, electricity." She sighed. "What about you? Aside from tracking down unsuspecting...entrepreneurs, what do you do?"

Will grinned, properly chastised. "I'm a landscape architect," he told her. "Foster's Landscape Design. Almost

ten years in business without a single unsatisfied client."
Will grimaced as Doris sprang to mind. "At least for the
moment, anyway. I'm working with a woman now who
might ruin that particular endorsement."

"Oh?"

He rubbed a hand over the back of his neck. "Yeah.
Doris Anderson." He gave her the abbreviated version of
the past three years, then shared the episode he'd endured
this morning. "It's insane. I can't make her happy, can't
satisfy her."

Rowan's eyes twinkled with sexy humor. "Sounds like
a personal problem to me."

Will blushed, shot her a look from beneath lowered
lashes. "That didn't come out precisely right, did it?"

She laughed. "I sincerely hope not." Her gaze drifted
slowly over him and she rocked slightly back on the balls
of her feet. "*That* would be a tragedy."

Again that little zing of missing excitement buzzed
through him and he barely resisted the urge to preen like
a puffed-up peacock at the implied compliment. His gaze
tangled with hers and he felt a smile flirt with his lips.

"So what are you going to do about her?" Rowan
asked, moving the conversation back onto slightly firmer
ground.

Will grimaced, passed a hand over his face. "That's
the million-dollar question. I honestly don't know." He
glanced out her window, then stilled as an inkling of an
idea began to emerge. He peered out her window, specifically at the garden framed in the multipaned glass.
Another finger of excitement nudged his belly.

What would Doris think of him pulling Rowan in as
a consultant? Will wondered hesitantly. For whatever
reason, he instinctively knew she'd like Rowan's work.
The whimsical layout would undoubtedly appeal to Doris's

own fantastical proclivities. In addition, the idea that he'd pulled in another designer to collaborate on the job would appeal to her "special treatment" needs.

Furthermore, he'd gladly forfeit the entire commission to Rowan—who admittedly needed the money more than he did at the moment—simply to make sure that Doris didn't ruin his satisfied customer record.

That he'd be willing to let go with a sizable chunk of change simply to make that woman happy and to keep his flawless record spoke volumes about his control issues, Will knew, but he was powerless to stop it. He'd worked hard for that reputation and the idea that she could ruin it with a few whiny complaints around town—at the country club, specifically—stuck in his craw and absolutely refused to budge.

Not no, but hell, no.

This could work, Will decided, as his idea gained momentum. Doris would get her dream garden, Will would be rid of Doris and Rowan would be able to earn some extra cash doing something she obviously loved instead of keeping up the phone sex gig.

For some unknown reason, the latter perk appealed to him entirely more than it should have, a fact that would need further consideration at a later time.

"Rowan, an idea just occurred to me," Will began, darting her a considering glance, "and I'd like to run it by you."

She nodded. "Er…okay."

Will quickly related his tentative plan, then outlined the offer. "Doris will have to go for it, of course," he qualified. Since she enjoyed being difficult, it would require some fancy footwork on his part, but Will was confident he could bring her around. "At any rate, I honestly think she'll love your work. What do you say? Would you be interested?"

To Will's supreme annoyance a soft chirp sounded from the vicinity of Rowan's waist before she could respond. She tsked under her breath, then tilted a small beeper-sized gadget away from the front pocket of her shorts to better read the display. Her phone, he realized with an unhappy start.

The 1-900-line, specifically.

She winced regretfully, all business once more. "I hate to be rude, but I can't afford to miss this call." She crossed the room, reached out and opened the door for him.

Will swore silently, annoyed at being thwarted this close to what he knew could be victory, and reluctantly made his way onto the front porch. "But, er...what about my offer?"

A mischievous glint lit her gaze and ultimately infected her smile. "You've got my number. Call me."

CHAPTER FIVE

ALEXA PUSHED a hand through her short curly locks and leaned forward expectantly. "Okay, let me get this straight. The kid's uncle tracked you down, showed up at your house today and, after his failed attempt at chewing your ass, he offered you a job?"

Leave it to Alexa to boil her twenty-minute tirade down to a ten-second synopsis, Rowan thought with a droll smile as she dumped a package of peanuts into her Coke. They'd met at Grady's Pool Hall, their usual haunt. The scent of grease and smoke hung in the air, and the continual hum of conversation was broken only by the clack of pool balls. There was nothing chic about the shabby joint, but Grady made the best burgers in town. Contractors, executives, students and locals typically sat elbow to elbow along the battered bar during the day, then the singles crowd inevitably moved in after five. She and Alexa fell among the latter group.

Rowan finally nodded. Her breath left her in a long whoosh. "Yeah, that about sums it up."

Alexa nodded thoughtfully. Her eyes twinkled with do-tell humor and her lips slid into a what-are-you-hiding? grin, a combination Rowan recognized all too well. Their friendship had been forged on the playground to the tune of ring-round-the-rosy, had survived high-school angst and postgraduation blues.

Alexa had nursed Rowan through the broken engagement

debacle, and Rowan had returned the gesture following
Alexa's nasty divorce. They'd confided every first—first
crush, first heartache, first lover—and shared every significant and not-so-significant event in between. They
were best buds and, Rowan remembered with a fond smile,
they still had the bracelets to prove it.

"That might sum it up—" Alexa leaned back in her seat,
pressed her fingers to her forehead and did her psychic-
moment impression. Her brow folded in exaggerated concentration. "—but something tells me that you've left a
pertinent detail out of your day." She paused. "About this
guy, specifically."

Rowan smothered a laugh. Alexa came from a long
line of clairvoyants, most recently her mother and grand-
mother, and despite the fact that the "gift" seemed to have
bypassed her completely, Alexa still liked to pretend that
she'd been touched as well. Though Rowan suspected that
Alexa was secretly relieved that she didn't possess The
Sight—often more of a burden than a gift—it had nevertheless been hard for her to come to terms with the fact
that she was different from her family.

"Hold on," Alexa said slowly, feigning sudden inspiration. "I'm getting a vision." She nodded, winced, nodded
again. "Yes… Yes…" Her eyes suddenly popped open and
she grinned. "He's a hottie, isn't he?"

Rowan struggled to maintain a neutral expression, but
caved under the unrepentant humor behind Alexa's knowing little stare. Her lips slid into a slow smile and she
slumped under the weight of the confession. *"Oh, God,
yes."*

Alexa's eyes widened, she whooped with laughter
and smacked her hand on the tabletop. "Details," she demanded gleefully. "Now."

Where to start? Rowan wondered as Will's impressive

form leaped obligingly to mind. God, she'd never been so affected by a guy. Had never been so instantly—irrevocably—attracted to one. A soft sigh slipped past her lips. "He's tall, tanned, muscled and gorgeous. Tawny hair—lighter on top, darker around the nape." Her gaze turned inward and she propped her chin in her hand. "He's got those heavy-lidded eyes—bedroom eyes—and they're a very light brown, the shade of warm honey," she said, and decided that the description seemed fitting, particularly since she seemed to have gotten *stuck* in that too-sexy gaze.

Alexa arched a brow. "That close, were you?" she teased.

Rowan blushed. "No. Just that…observant," she improvised.

And she'd been observing closely—almost to the point of obsession—though thankfully, he hadn't seemed to notice. She would have gladly continued that covert, narrow scrutiny, too, if it hadn't been for that ill-fated phone call.

Ultimately, she knew the interruption had been for the best. Rowan rarely made snap decisions—she preferred to mull, to ponder, to consider every angle, weigh advantages versus disadvantages and make informed decisions. She wasn't averse to taking risks—calculated ones—when the opportunity arose, but only when she was sure that risk would be worth the reward. Astonishingly, she knew if Roy hadn't called back, she would have readily agreed to Will's offer without the smallest hesitation. Would he be worth the risk? Most definitely. She knew it without a single doubt.

Which just went show how much Will Foster and his sticky-honey gaze had affected her.

Naturally she'd been annoyed that he'd violated her

privacy, that he'd essentially tracked her down with the sole purpose of delivering a load of brimstone with that sexy mouth of his. No doubt he could do it, too, Rowan thought, remembering the grim expression he'd worn when she'd first caught sight of him. After all, she'd noted that intriguing best-friend-or-worst-enemy element of his too-handsome face right from the get-go. Fortunately, she'd had the pleasure of watching that face dawn with the knowledge of his error, then watching that same countenance scramble for, ironically, a face-saver. Her lips twisted with remembered humor.

Listening to the tapes had been just that, she knew. Will hadn't doubted her. He was a smart guy. He'd known that she wouldn't have offered the proof of her statement if she hadn't had the tapes to back it up.

But after all the trouble he'd undoubtedly gone through to run her to ground—honestly, calling a friend in the P.I. business?—he'd had to follow through, or otherwise risk an item men guarded almost as vigilantly as they did their balls—male pride. And women were accused of being stubborn and vain?

Sheesh.

At any rate, Rowan didn't know precisely why she'd been so intrigued by him. Granted, he was gorgeous and, just like any female with working eyesight, the she-woman in her had responded with prompt and primal efficiency when presented with such a fine specimen.

Meaning, she hadn't been remotely inclined to start cleaning his cave…but she certainly wouldn't mind spreading her fur next to his fire.

The idea sent a dart of heat straight to her womb and her toes involuntarily curled in her shoes. A shiver shook her from the inside out, forcing her to exhale a shaky breath.

At twenty-five, Rowan was no stranger to sexual attraction. Promiscuous? No. She'd been very selective with the few lovers she'd had—given the considerable risks that arose when sharing your body it was just plain stupid not to be—but she had enough experience to know that what she'd felt the few minutes she'd spent in Will Foster's company this afternoon was completely out of her sphere of understanding.

The attraction had been more than intense, more than remarkable. It had been fierce and instantaneous—thrilling. She'd *vibrated* with it, felt it echo off her backbone, tingle through her tummy, and most disconcertingly, gently nudge her heart. A heart that had absolutely no business being nudged or prodded or engaged whatsoever. Not after just meeting him. It was crazy. Rowan let go a stuttering breath.

The connection had been curious, to say the least.

She'd been utterly enchanted by him, from his first irate appearance, to that sheepish "I was pissed," confession, then to that ultimate pathetically awkward apology. Clearly he'd been out of his element, but his character had jumped a notch in her estimation with the follow-through. Her lips twisted. Hell, most guys couldn't admit they'd made a mistake, much less apologize for it. That took integrity, a declining quality among today's men, and one she truly admired.

And if those things weren't enough, he was a landscape architect. Her ridiculous heart had actually skipped a beat when he'd confided that little tidbit. A guy who shared the same enthusiasm as she did for the soil, for the science and wonder of gardening? A rare distinction, that. If she'd pulled through a Build-A-Guy drive-through, she couldn't have custom-ordered a better combo. He was smart, funny, into gardening, with Super-Sized sex appeal. A lethal mix to be sure. Quite frankly—probably stupidly—she was fascinated.

"So when do you start?"

Rowan blinked, jolted back into the conversation. "I'm sorry?"

"When do you start?" Alexa repeated. Her eyes twinkled with knowing humor.

Rowan shifted, feigned indifference. "Who said I was going to take the job?"

"Honey," Alexa chuckled with a shake of her head, "*that* was a foregone conclusion."

Rowan tried to muster mild outrage, but quickly felt her expression turn sheepish. She bit her lip, peeked up at her friend from beneath lowered lashes. "That transparent, am I?" She sighed and took a sip of her Coke. Hell, it had been a foregone conclusion. He fascinated her, made her so hot she threatened to burn right out of her skin. Like she could resist that sort of temptation? Like after months of miserable celibacy she would?

Alexa's brow puckered into a thoughtful frown. "Transparent wasn't the word I had in mind—I was thinking more along the lines of *horny*."

Startled, Rowan almost strangled on a peanut. Her eyes watered as she alternately wheezed, laughed and tried to catch her breath. Geez, nothing like a little truth-therapy from a good friend, Rowan thought, as Alexa silently howled at her expense.

But it would be utterly futile to deny the charge. She was horny. Beyond horny. Succinctly put, something about Will Foster had tripped her trigger. She'd taken one look at him and commenced to simmer. With just a minimal amount of effort on his part, she'd undoubtedly hit a full boil, and just thinking about that kind of singular potential made her loins throb with an achy, hollow sort of heat.

Merely imagining that beautiful mouth of his attached to
hers, or more importantly, attached to her breast, made her
squirm in her seat. Made her fingers itch to slide over that
tanned skin, feel those fantastic muscles bunch and flex beneath her hands. He looked fully capable of *satisfying* her,
Rowan thought, recalling their previous conversation.

She caught her breath, finally nodded magnanimously.
"H-horny works, too," she conceded lightly with a what-
the-hell shrug. "What can I say? He's hot…and he makes
me hot." She grimaced. "That hasn't happened in a
while."

Too long to remember, quite frankly. Months. A year,
maybe. She'd had a little rebound sex with a former lover
after the Mark Mistake, but that had been more about
revenge—a stupid reason, but one that had offered a small
Band-Aid to her injured pride—and less about her needs.
Which was just as well, Rowan remembered now, because
she'd had to finish up post-sex while he'd trotted off to the
bathroom, completely satisfied. She'd been more miserable *after* the sex than before it.

A shrewd gleam glinted in Alexa's bright blue eyes.
"I'm going to make a prediction. I pre—"

Rowan snorted, took another pull from her drink. "Your
third eye is blind, remember?"

"I predict," Alexa continued doggedly, "that he'll call
you."

Duh, Rowan thought. He'd have to, otherwise he
wouldn't know whether or not she planned to come to
work for him. "Well, of course he'll call. I didn't give him
an answer." She grunted. "If he wants that answer, he'll
have to call."

"You're not listening," Alexa chided. "I said, I predict
that he'll *call* you," she repeated meaningfully.

They'd established that, Rowan thought, not following. She quirked a brow.

Alexa heaved an impatient breath, leaned forward and lowered her voice. "For phone sex," she hissed, exasperated. She reclined once more, bobbed her head knowingly. "Mark my words. He'll call. He knows what you do, has seen you in action. He's a guy and he'll call. He won't be able to help himself."

Call her for phone sex? Rowan thought faintly. Surely not. For reasons beyond her immediate understanding, the very idea sent a dart of panic directly into her rapidly beating heart. The mere thought of having phone sex with Will Foster made her mouth parch and her pulse race... and not in a good way.

In fact, she felt distinctly ill.

"What?" Alexa asked, seemingly concerned. "What's wrong?"

Though she knew it sounded utterly ridiculous, Rowan blurted out the awful truth. "I can't have phone sex with *him*," she said, her voice equally incredulous and scandalized. "I *know* him."

It was Alexa's turn to wear the uncomprehending look. "So?"

"So, I— I can't do it," Rowan stammered. This was totally bizarre. She hadn't acted like a blushing virgin when she'd been a blushing virgin, and yet...

"Why the hell not?" Alexa scowled, seemingly bewildered. "I thought you just said he was a hottie, that he made you hot. What's the problem?"

"That's the problem," Rowan explained grimly, struggling to find a reasonable voice for her neurosis. "I *know* him," she repeated. "I can't possibly say all those things to him." She affected her phone-sex voice. "*You make me hot. I wanna get naked and touch myself.* Sheesh. Can you imagine, Alexa? I'd be mortified. Don't you see?"

The clank of cutlery hitting the floor sounded to her left. Rowan turned, and from the stunned, gaping looks of the men seated at the next table, they'd obviously overheard her and wrongfully assumed they'd just witnessed kinky lesbian sex talk.

Rowan groaned as humiliation saturated every pore of her face, painting it red. *Embarrassment,* she thought morosely, *my constant companion.*

Alexa smothered a laugh, and massaged her temples. "Rowan, this doesn't make any sense. You've been pretending for cash with these other yahoos for the past several months, and now you're telling me that you can't do it for real with a guy you're obviously attracted to? Come on," she scoffed.

Rowan winced, conjured a small smile. "Screwed up," she conceded, "but there it is." She paused, vainly searching for the right words to frame her twisted reasoning. "You were right when you'd said I'd been pretending. With other men, it's just a role, Alexa. I can talk some unknown guy through phone sex and not give it a second thought. I'm a catalyst, not a participant. It's not *personal,*" she emphasized with a significant look, "if you get my drift."

Alexa's lips rounded in a silent "oh." "You mean you don't actually have—"

"No. No!" she repeated emphatically. She shuddered. "Ick. How could you— I can't believe you thought I—" She shuddered again, stared in horror at her friend. "With strangers? Eeeew!"

"Well, how was I to know?" Alexa defended with an innocent shrug. "I just assumed…"

"Well, you assumed wrong." She exhaled mightily. "Now do you understand?"

"Indeed I do," Alexa replied as a slow smile dawned on her lips. Unrepentant laughter gleamed in her too-perceptive gaze. "The phone sex queen is a phone sex virgin. But I predict a change in status is imminent." She chuckled behind her beer. "This Will Foster is going to pop your phone sex cherry."

Rowan heaved a long-suffering sigh even as a curious thrill followed immediately by a spasm of dread whipped through her. "You and your predictions," she muttered, unable to muster the enthusiasm for a snarky response.

Alexa inclined her head. "I'm right about this one. You'll see. In fact, I would be surprised if you *waited* on *him* to call *you*." She snorted indelicately. "Hell, when have you ever waited for anything you've wanted? Ha! Try *never*." Alexa considered her once more, looked at her until Rowan was hard-pressed not to squirm. "He's really shaken you up, hasn't he? He's knocked you off your game."

Though she knew Alexa was purposely baiting her, Rowan bristled all the same. The mere idea that she was not in control of every aspect of her person, her world and immediate universe annoyed her no end. "I'm *not* off my game." In truth, now that she thought beyond being embarrassed, she could seriously see herself getting into a lusty conversation with Will Foster...and enjoying it immensely.

"Then you're off your rocker. Ordinarily, you wouldn't hesitate, would you?"

"Who said I was hesitating?" Rowan protested. Hell, she wasn't hesitating. She was merely considering. And she was done. If he didn't call her, then fine. She'd call him. Because she *was not* off her game.

WILL DROPPED the phone back into the cradle, exhaled wearily and massaged the bridge of his nose. Well, that had gone much better than he'd anticipated. *That* being, telling Jim about his son's recent moronic detour down the dial-a-date highway.

"You handled that well." His mother appeared from just outside his office door—her favorite eavesdropping post, the eternal infernal snoop, Will thought tiredly—and, with a weary sigh planted herself in one of the chairs flanking Will's desk. "Going to Jim instead of Lori was a wise decision. A boy needs to hear certain things from his father."

Now that was an interesting comment, particularly coming from her, Will thought. Millie had never considered any topic taboo and had never hesitated to share her opinion or advice regardless of the subject. When those ripening teenage hormones had taken hold of him, it had been Millie, not his late father, who'd given him *The Talk*.

That hadn't been all she'd given him either, Will recalled, still somewhat mortified. She'd also given him his first box of condoms along with the sage advice to "bag it before you plant it because a man shouldn't spread his baby gravy over just any biscuit."

His mother, he thought, fondly exasperated...she was one of a kind. The glue that held his tight-knit family together.

"Lying to him wasn't wise," she continued, "but if buying that cock-and-bull story about science lessons gave Jim peace of mind, then so be it, I suppose." She shook her head. "I don't know why people can't face facts but—"

"It wasn't a cock-and-bull story," Will interrupted before she could really get wound up. His mother could spend hours lecturing on the slippery-slope perils of self-delusion. "It was the truth."

Her eyes widened and she blinked. "Says who? Your 1-900-Lover?" she scoffed.

"She'd recorded the conversations. I listened to them." He pulled a negligent shrug, absently drummed a pen against his desk. "No harm, no foul, and she refunded the charges."

His mother hummed under her breath. "Now that's interesting. A *scrupulous* phone sex operator." She smiled, and that shrewd motherly gleam which had unearthed countless secrets flared to life in her gaze. "I'll just bet that threw you for a loop, Mr. Black-and-White."

Will grunted in response to the nickname. His family had called him that for years. As far as Will was concerned, there were no gray areas, period, and people who saw gray simply weren't strong enough in their convictions. He made a decision and he didn't walk the fence.

But had his mother's keen perception once again ferreted out a hidden truth? Will wondered. Had that been why he'd been so fascinated by Rowan? Because he couldn't find a category for her in his black-and-white, right or wrong world? For instance, the idea of phone sex had been singularly unappealing...until he'd met her. Now he couldn't get her voice out of his head, couldn't stop thinking about her saying those erotic little comments to him in that wonderfully sensual voice of hers.

She didn't fit any mold, Will decided. Didn't fit in any of his preformed categories, that was for sure. He'd have to give it further consideration.

But not right now. Not while under his mother's intuitive radar.

He purposely directed the discussion to business, and after the majority of issues were settled, the conversation turned once again to Dreaded Doris.

"What are you going to do about her?" Millie wanted

to know. "Honestly, Will. This is ridiculous. You can't call it wasted time because she's always paid you. Still…" She frowned. "Something's gotta give."

Will blew out a breath. "She's connected, Mom. If she's not happy, she's going to howl."

A convenient excuse, one his mother undoubtedly saw through, but he hauled the old line out anyway. She knew how he was. Knew that he couldn't stand the idea of having a single unhappy customer. The idea drove him nuts. Naturally Will knew that it was unreasonable for him to expect to be in any form of public service and never have an unsatisfied customer, but he'd managed to do it for the past ten years—*ten years*—and he simply refused to let Doris Anderson ruin it for him. "I'm working on it," he assured her.

"All right," she sighed, then pushed to her feet. "I'm going to call it a day. Shouldn't you go home and get ready for your date?" she asked innocently.

Will smiled at her tenacity. "I don't have a date."

"Which is precisely my point," she needled with a soft harrumph of displeasure. "Keep it up," she told him as she made her way to the door, "and you're going to end up taking the same dial-a-date detour Scott did."

Will chuckled as he watched her leave, but in truth her parting comment triggered Rowan Crosswhite's last edict, one that had plagued him since leaving her house this morning. It had ricocheted around his brain, pinging him at the most inopportune moments.

You've got my number. Call me.

Will speared his fingers through his hair once more and exhaled a long, pent-up breath.

A simple phrase, a simpler request, and yet he found himself completely stymied, a state that was as annoying as it was unfamiliar. Will prided himself on being a decision maker, on being able to swiftly process data, cull the wheat from the chaff, so to speak, and generally make the right call. This mealy-mouthed do-I-or-don't-I? circle he'd found himself in for the past several hours irritated the hell out of him. It was completely out of character.

But just what the hell had she meant, dammit?

He leaned back in his chair and propped his boots on the edge of his desk. Had she wanted him to call her on her regular line...or had that innocuous little instruction held a double meaning? Had it been a subtle suggestion to dial her 900-line? Or was that merely wishful thinking on his part? Hell, who knew?

Too many questions and not enough answers. A quick glance at his wall clock confirmed that he didn't have much time left either. He didn't know what sort of hours Rowan kept—undoubtedly her phone sex business peaked at night, he thought darkly—but in his opinion anything beyond six implied more pleasure than business.

And, against all reason and better judgment, he wanted both.

The question was; which one did he go after first?

Twenty-four hours ago if anybody had told him that he'd be entertaining the idea of calling a 1-900-number for phone sex, Will would have never believed it. Truthfully, he had trouble believing it now. Hell, he hadn't been a participant in the Five Knuckle Olympics since he'd talked Katie Webber into giving him a hand job in junior high. His lips quirked. After that enlightening experience, self-service had lost its tarnished appeal.

But the mere memory of hearing Rowan's sweet throaty voice made his palms itch and a snaky heat writhe in his loins. Made his imagination run reel-to-reel X-rated material starring her in the lead role, and the idea of listening to her tell him that she was hot made him forget that phone sex surely paled in comparison to the genuine article.

Regardless, he had a feeling Rowan Crosswhite could make a man forget the world was round if she were so inclined.

Though logic and intuition had told him her version of events with Scott had been dead on, Will didn't doubt for a moment that she could have easily convinced him even without her "proof."

The minute he'd heard her voice the head without the brain had successfully mutinied, and the one responsible for cognitive control had meekly conceded defeat. He'd tracked her down in order to rock her world and, as a result of that infantile arrogance, he'd been the one to walk away shaken and unsure. An unfamiliar condition he'd discovered he didn't care for in the least.

So what to do? Will wondered for the hundredth time. Ultimately, he knew it would be best to err on the side of caution. If she hadn't meant that she wanted him to call on her 900-line, then he'd look like an opportunistic moron, not to mention heartily embarrassed and, though it was vain, he had too much pride to risk the humiliation. In addition, he still needed her help with Doris Dilemma and he didn't want to risk inadvertently pissing her off and nixing that plan.

On the presumption that Rowan would say yes—and he honestly thought that she would—he'd gone ahead and run the idea past Doris this afternoon. Hell, Will thought with a small smile, anyone who thought phone sex was a pragmatic, practical solution to money woes surely wouldn't balk at helping design a garden. Furthermore, he'd seen Rowan's senses go on point, had watched those gorgeous green eyes brighten with excitement when he'd outlined the offer.

Predictably, Doris had balked, but with a little minimal finessing—which almost made him gag—he'd brought her around. The idea of having a special "team manager" had been more than the hard-to-please old biddy could pass up. Now, provided he could bring Rowan on board, everything should be right with his world very shortly. He liked things being right with his world. Anything out of sync—even something as remarkable as this flash-fire attraction for Rowan Crosswhite—messed with his head. Made him antsy. Which meant he needed to grab the bull by the horns, so to speak, and pull himself together.

So, Will decided as he reluctantly sat up, business had to come first...and if he played his cards right, the pleasure would come later.

Luckily, regardless of what line he dialed, he would still get to talk to her, to listen to that sleepy, sultry bedroom voice. The thought had a consoling effect and left him inordinately—ridiculously—pleased.

Which was pathetic and made him wonder just what the hell had been so wrong with his life that a few mere minutes with this woman would make his entire existence seem that much better. Was he that pathetic? Though it galled him to admit it, that lonely? God knew his mother harped on that enough, Will thought, perturbed at the idea. She was constantly going on and on about finding somebody to settle down with. Sharing his life. He chuckled grimly. His mother was convinced that a woman would make him happy, and his sister was equally convinced that having children would humble him.

They acted like he didn't want either, when in truth there was nothing that he wanted more. But he didn't take the decision lightly, and after his last failed attempt at a meaningful relationship, he was a little gun-shy. Deservedly so, if you asked him.

Will cursed under his breath, bullied the thoughts to the back of his mind where he normally kept them. "Idiot," he muttered. "Just call her." He pulled in a bolstering breath and blamed his shaking fingers and quivering gut on low blood sugar as he reached for the phone. He wasn't nervous, dammit. He had friggin' nerves of steel. It was a simple phone call, an offer of employment, one he'd extended countless times.

But for reasons which escaped him, Will instinctively knew he had more riding on this offer than Doris's displeasure, more than a hundred-percent-satisfaction-guaranteed record.

Precisely *what,* escaped him, but the knowledge was there all the same.

He entered her number—for some idiotic reason, he'd memorized it—and waited for her to pick up. After the fourth ring, he knew she wasn't going to answer. On the fifth ring, her machine picked up. Rather than her voice, a Humphrey Bogart soundalike played over the line.

"Of all the answering machines in the world you had to call mine. Maybe the voice messages between two people don't add up to a hill of beans, but if you'll leave me a message, I'll get back to you. Maybe not today, maybe not tomorrow, but someday. Who knows? Maybe this could be the beginning of a beautiful friendship."

Chuckling, Will left his message. Leave it to Rowan not to have a typical greeting on her answering machine, he thought, once again enchanted. Thus far, he hadn't noticed anything *typical* about her. She definitely put the *U* in unique.

Though initially he'd been annoyed—*not* disappointed because that would be just plain sickening—that she hadn't been home, Will decided it was probably to his advantage…because he'd just officially put the ball back into her court. He kicked back in his chair once more, laced his hands behind his head and a slow smile drifted over his lips.

It would be interesting to see what she'd do with it.

CHAPTER SIX

"SHE SAID CHUNKY MONKEY," Rowan muttered angrily under her breath as she let herself into the house. She slung her purse into the chair by the door, hung her keys on the hook, toed off her shoes, then made her way to the kitchen for a spoon. "I *know* she said Chunky Monkey. The old harpy just wanted my Cherry Garcia."

Note to self, Rowan thought. *The next time I make an ice-cream run, don't make the mistake of showing Ida what I bought for myself.* Better yet, the next time Ida called on her cell phone—man, did she rue the day she'd given *that* number to her landlord, Rowan thought with a grim laugh—she'd simply ignore the call.

She pried the lid off the container, loaded her spoon, then groaned with pleasure as the cool dessert did its magical thing and vastly improved her mood. A Ben & Jerry's antidepressant, she sighed. It did the trick every time.

Honestly, she didn't know why she'd gotten so irritated. Hell, it was only ice cream. It wasn't like Ida had pulled a playground bully trade, for pity's sake. She still had a dessert, one that she happened to be quite fond of. Good grief. What was wrong with her? If this was the worst thing that happened to her today—Ida stealing her Cherry Garcia—then she was in pretty good shape. Yes, she got sick of running Ida's errands—they were usually mortifying—but it was a relatively easy way to make part of the rent. Sheesh. She had to get a grip.

It was Alexa's fault, Rowan decided as she shoveled another spoonful into her mouth. Her eyes narrowed. Alexa, with her little popping-the-phone-sex-cherry prediction. Rowan knew she hadn't picked out that particular flavor because it was her favorite, or because she liked it above all others—she'd picked out Cherry Garcia because she'd been thinking about Will Foster.

Hadn't *stopped* thinking about Will Foster since he'd left her house this morning.

Would he really call her? she wondered. Her gaze inexplicably slid to her answering machine and a bubble of anticipation fizzed in her belly. Or the better question might be, had he called her? The red light, which signaled a message, blinked furiously, and with a sinking heart, Rowan realized he'd probably already called—and, just her luck, she'd missed it. Damn.

Damn.

Damn.

Damn.

Hauling her dessert along with her, she double-timed it to the living room, sank heavily onto her couch, then pulled the machine into her lap and hit the play button. She winced as her initial fear was confirmed.

"Rowan. Hi, it's Will Foster. I was calling about that proposition I'd run by you this morning. If you're interested, you can give me a call back on my cell or at home." He rattled off the numbers. *"I, uh… I look forward to hearing from you. Thanks. Bye."*

Well, hell, Rowan swore, heartily disappointed. No doubt he'd called while she'd been running Ida's ice-cream errand, she thought uncharitably. In all fairness, he could have called while she'd been at Grady's, but right now laying any and all blame at Ida's hideous feet held considerable catty appeal. Her inner bitch was PMS'ing.

Since he'd taken the first step and contacted her, Rowan didn't see any reason—aside from the herd of butterflies which had taken flight in her belly—why she shouldn't just go ahead and call him. She'd told Alexa she would. Had insisted that she wasn't *off her game*. And she wasn't, dammit.

Furthermore, in an hour or so, her 900-line would start a perpetual ring, and she wouldn't have time for something as normal as idle chitchat. Even idle chitchat with a guy who made her hormones sing along to the tacky tune of an eighties porn flick. *Chic-a-wow, chic-a-wow-wow,* Rowan thought with a soft chuckle, instantly imagining them in a similar circumstance.

Once again the idea of an intimate conversation with Will Foster took hold. What naughty things would he say to her? Rowan wondered, her belly clenching at the mere thought. Better yet, how long would it take her to make him set himself off? Her breath stuttered out in a quiet hiss and her very bones seemed to liquefy as an image of him doing just that materialized behind her drooping lids. Sweet Jesus. She wanted this guy.

Truly, desperately, with every fiber of her hopelessly horny being.

So she should do it, Rowan decided abruptly, blinking out of her self-induced lust-trance. She should call him. Was going to call him. Right now. He'd offered her a job—admittedly one that she'd love to do, and frankly, she couldn't afford to turn down the money—so there was absolutely no reason to be nervous or nauseous, or be cursed with any shaky affliction. Because that would imply that she wasn't the mistress of her world, wasn't in control and *that* was unacceptable.

Rowan set her ice cream aside, took a deep calming breath, blew it out, then shook the tremors out of her hands. Okay. She was calling. Right now. She picked up the phone and dialed his home number before she could change her mind.

Shit! She'd called him!

"Hello."

Shit! He'd answered! Rowan squeezed her eyes tightly shut. "Er...Will?" Okay, moron, Rowan told herself. Breathe. Hyperventilating over the phone would not help convey the calm, cool, collected chick she longed to portray.

She was *so* not that chick.

"Rowan?"

"Yeah. I was just returning your call." Very good. She didn't stutter, sounded smooth and offhand, as though she weren't pacing the stain off her hardwood floors. She could do this. *Would* do this.

"Right. I, uh— I'd just wondered if you'd thought any more about my offer." He cleared his throat. "If you're interested, I'd like to bring Doris by your place and let her have a look-see."

"Yeah, I'm interested," Rowan replied with a chuckle. "I'm not as sure as you are that she's going to like my garden—my style isn't for everybody—but you're welcome to bring her by whenever. I'm generally home." So she'd see him again. She did a little happy dance around her coffee table.

"Good. I'll give her a call in the morning, and if she's free, we'll probably come by—" he hesitated, evidently trying to figure out his schedule "—er...sometime before noon. I've got my guys started on the tear-out now. She's got friends coming in soon—Peace Corp buddies," he clarified wryly, "and wants to have everything finished, so we're kind of in a time crunch. Is that going to work okay with your schedule?"

Rowan laughed softly. "Hey, I'm basically unemployed, so I'm flexible."

"Good. You're really helping me out of a bind. I'm, uh— I'm at my wit's end with this one."

Rowan didn't get it. If the woman was that damned difficult, why did he keep going back? Why was this satisfaction-guaranteed thing so important to him? Rather than wonder about it, she decided to ask. "Look, it's none of my business, I know, but if she's such a problem why do you keep dealing with her? Why not let it go?" Rowan settled back down on the couch and took up her ice cream once more. She spooned a bite into her mouth.

A rueful laugh sounded in her ear. "I wish that I could, but I... I just can't."

Rowan grinned. Male pride. Was there anything more powerful?

"And, honestly, I can't complain because she's always paid her bill. She's never tried to stick me. It's just so damned frustrating. She's thrilled, she's ecstatic, she's over the moon—right up until the day we get finished. Then she wants something completely different." He blew out a disgusted breath, punctuating the thought. "You wouldn't believe the work I've put into her damned yard. And all for naught."

Well, that did suck, Rowan thought with a commiserating frown. "So what makes you so sure that she's going to like my garden?" Honestly, if the woman was that hard to please, why *did* he think she'd like her work? she wondered. Why was he so sure?

"Oh, you'll see when you meet her," he readily assured her. "She's a character. Trust me. Your style is right up her alley."

Rowan scowled at the receiver, unable to decide if she should be insulted or flattered. Evidently her lack of response conveyed that message because he quickly moved to fill the yawning silence.

"Damn. That didn't come out precisely right. What I meant is that I think that she'll like your... unconventional approach to landscaping."

Mollified, Rowan felt her lips twitch. "Is that a PC way of telling me that you think my approach to gardening is weird?"

"Nah, not weird." Humor laced his sexy baritone. "Weird has a negative connotation."

Rowan detected the distinct hiss of a bottle being opened, then the muted gulp of a swallow. She found the sound curiously erotic and, to her immeasurable surprise, a flame of heat licked her nipples.

"Unique works," he told her. "Whimsical works better. It's ordered pandemonium, which is completely different to anything I design, by the way, and," he sighed, "is most likely the problem with Doris."

She'd just bet it was different. Though she'd just met him, she could just imagine what he'd design. Lots of symmetrical gardens, regimented lines, plants marching at attention rather than growing at will. Not that there was anything wrong with that, Rowan thought, but it hardly appealed to her.

"Honestly," he continued, "I was impressed. Particularly with your antique roses. Those are a passion of mine as well."

This guy just got better and better, Rowan decided as an unexpected warmth moved through her chest. Well, hell, she thought. He made her warm everywhere else— her chest might as well be infected as well.

She shifted into a more comfortable position and filled

her spoon again. "Thanks. I wish that I could take credit for them, but I got them from my mom." She told him about her globe-trotting parents. Rowan chuckled. "She doesn't know it yet, but she's not getting them back."

"Hey, I know what you mean. I've got a Cornelia that I nursed for my grandfather that he's not getting back either."

A Cornelia, Rowan thought, equally awed and impressed. She stilled as something more than sexual attraction, something cerebral went to work on her. So it wasn't just lip service. He really did have a thing for antique roses. Another sparkler of delight ignited in her chest. "I'm envious. I may have to beg a cutting from you."

A deep, sexy chuckle seduced her ear. "Certainly, but only if you're willing to share."

The distinctive ring of her 900-line sounded, interrupting the easy flow of their conversation, and it belatedly occurred to Rowan that she should have turned it off, or at the very least *down*, before she called him. She mentally swore, then smothered a disappointed sigh as a taut silence suddenly hummed between them, a stark contrast to the lively conversation they'd shared just seconds ago.

"Duty calls, eh?" he said. She detected a gratifying hint of disappointment in his voice as well, and something else. Something not easily read. Irritation, maybe?

"You could say that," Rowan replied. The 900-line shrieked again, an insistent reminder that she really needed to let him go. She took a deep breath and strove for a brisk tone. "So I'll see you tomorrow, then?"

"Yeah. Before noon."

"Great. Well...good night."

He barely hesitated, but she felt it all the same. His

voice, when he finally spoke, was soft and husky and it made a shiver run through her. "Good night, Rowan."

"YOU WERE RIGHT, Will," Doris told him as she gazed in apparent rapture around Rowan's garden. "*I love it.* I *absolutely* love it. Why, I wouldn't be surprised if a flower fairy suddenly flitted through the air. It's...enchanting," she sighed. "Mystical."

He loved being right, Will thought as he struggled to suppress a smug smile. From the knowing little quirk of Rowan's lips, she'd apparently made that deduction herself. Was he that transparent? he wondered, or did she simply have a keen sense of perception where he was concerned? For reasons he couldn't explain, he got the distinct impression the latter was true. And, astonishingly, he found it singularly...arousing. If she carried that same intuition into the bedroom, he'd be—

"This is definitely what I want," Doris continued, thankfully interrupting him before he could take that thought any further and embarrass himself. "And I'd really love some of those whirly-things, and the stained glass ornaments." She shot Rowan an anxious look. "You can make me some, right?" Doris asked. "They're *fabo. Divine.* I absolutely *must* have some."

"I can," Rowan told her with a quick nod. "Or you're welcome to go through my garage—" She gestured to a building snugged against the back of the property. "—and see if there's anything in there that you like." She chuckled softly. "I've got tons of stuff in there."

Doris's pencil thin brows rose in anticipation. "Oh. Would you mind if I..." She left the rest of the sentence unsaid, but leaned expectantly in the direction of the garage.

Rowan shook her head. "No, not at all. Be my guest. The light's on. I've been out there already this morning."

Will resisted the increasing urge to rock back on his heels. The morning was shaping up quite nicely. Doris liked Rowan's work, which meant a) he'd finally heave that albatross from around his neck, and b) he was guaranteed a minimum of two weeks in relatively close quarters with Rowan. Two weeks to explore this bizarre connection, this phenomenal attraction, to listen to that ultrasexy voice.

Talking on the phone had never been one of Will's favorite pastimes. In fact, he typically hated it. It was a way to expedite information, to increase productivity, to relay pertinent details. Even as a teen, Will hadn't been interested in spending hours on the phone like his other counterparts. Hell, he'd had friends who'd kept the lines tied up for hours at a time simply listening to each other *breathe*. It had baffled him then, and baffled him now.

But a funny thing had happened to him last night—he'd *enjoyed* talking to Rowan. It wasn't just the sound of her voice—though God knows that sweet, sultry nonwhisper did it for him—or the fact that he'd needed to talk to her about Doris—he'd simply *liked* talking to her. It had been easy, effortless, and he thought darkly, he could have undoubtedly continued to talk to her until the wee hours of the morning if it hadn't been for her friggin' 900-line.

It was unreasonable, irrational and all those other adjectives which pertained to his asinine reaction, but Will couldn't seem to help himself. When he'd heard that other line ring, his lips had actually peeled away from his teeth, and every muscle in his body had tensed with equal amounts of irritation and dread.

His response had been swift, irrational and—most disturbingly—telling.

Reason told him that he shouldn't care about what she did, or even who she did it with, for that matter. He barely knew her. Had just met her, dammit. What could it possibly be to him? Logically, he knew that he shouldn't give a damn about what she did on her own time. But there was nothing logical about the way he felt. Nothing logical about the instantaneous attraction he'd felt for her, the keen, almost obsessive fascination.

And curiously, even knowing that she merely talked guys through phone sex—he'd seen her yesterday, and knew beyond a shadow of a doubt that she hadn't gotten one iota of sexual gratification from that conversation with Roy. She'd been *weeding,* of all things. Even knowing that, Will still hated the idea of her talking—*that way*—to another guy. It made his brain cramp. Stupid? Ridiculous? Unreasonable? Definitely. But he couldn't help it.

Thankfully this morning when he and Doris had arrived, he'd noticed, among other things—like the way her shorts hugged her curves, the healthy tan on her slim shoulders, and that ever-present twinkle in those gorgeous green eyes—that the phone and accompanying headset were gone.

Will had breathed a silent sigh of relief and had concluded that, after having a chance to think about his offer and the resulting wage, she'd evidently decided to end her career as a phone sex operator. He couldn't know for sure, of course, but it only stood to reason.

She'd been wearing it yesterday.

She wasn't today.

Ergo, she'd quit.

You could drive a truck through the hole in that shaky self-serving deduction, but until he had proof otherwise, he fully planned to delude himself. It was better for his peace of mind.

And the fact that he had to—or was willing to—resort to such tactics absolutely annoyed the hell out of him. It smacked of jealousy—unwarranted, at that—and he knew from personal experience that that hideous emotion could make a man completely lose control. He swallowed a bitter laugh. His unfaithful ex had been a queen manipulator and the number one tool in her secret bag of tricks had been the green-eyed monster.

To his immeasurable regret, he'd let her drag him around by the short hairs for months. Will was embarrassed to admit how many times she'd made a fool of him, and even more embarrassed to admit how long it had taken him to see her for what she really was—a faithless, self-centered bitch.

Never again, he'd decided.

His gaze slid to Rowan. And yet here he was, infatuated to the point of near obsession. This woman had completely monopolized his thoughts since meeting her yesterday. Yet despite the fact that she was a phone sex operator, of all things, and despite the fact that he barely knew her, somehow Will instinctively knew that she had character.

He saw truth in the determined line of her jaw, sincerity in those frank green eyes and just the smallest hint of vulnerability in her dainty chin. Add hot and sexy, smart and funny to the mix and, well…she became particularly irresistible. He studied the delicate slope of her cheek, the lush curve of her bottom lip and felt a bolt of heat incinerate his groin.

He wanted her.

Another disconcerting realization, but he hadn't *truly* wanted anyone in a long time. Wanted sex? Hell, yeah. He was a man. What man didn't eat, breathe and live for the opportunity of getting laid? Just because he'd bowed out of the dating scene didn't mean that he'd abstained. Getting laid, quite frankly, was easy.

Finding a woman that he really *wanted,* however, was a rarity.

Rowan's gaze swung back to him. Her absolute beauty sucker-punched him once more, and that curious electrical current again raced up his spine.

She smiled and released a small breath. "You're right. She's definitely a character."

"I was relatively certain that she'd like your work," Will replied, swallowing the immediate I-told-you-so that had leaped instantly to his lips.

Perceptive humor lit her gaze. She smiled, crossed her arms over her chest, inadvertently forming an impressive view of her cleavage. "Go ahead and say it," she told him. "I know you want to."

"Want to what?" he asked innocently.

"Say, 'I told you so.'" She laughed. "It's practically eating you up, isn't it?"

"Not eating me up, no," Will qualified. His gaze slid to hers. "However, *I told you* she would like it," he improvised, unable to help himself.

Another sexy chuckle bubbled up her throat. "And you were right. Modesty isn't something that comes easy to you, is it?"

Will laughed. "Not really, no," he admitted with a sheepish grin. "What can I say? I enjoy being right."

"Really," Rowan returned drolly. "I'd barely noticed." She gave him another one of those considering looks, the kind that made him feel like she'd just peeked right into his head. "Why do I get the feeling that being wrong isn't something that happens to you often?"

Will grinned, shoved his hands into his pockets. "Because you're insightful?"

Her delighted laugh made his chest inexplicably swell. "Now that's an interesting compliment," she chuckled.

Will poked his tongue into his cheek. "Thanks. I try."

"I'm sure you do." Her laughter petered out into a soft sigh. "So she likes it. What happens next?"

Ah, the good part, Will thought. "I've got a couple of things that I have to take care of today, but I was hoping that we could use this afternoon to cover some preliminary ground. I thought I could swing by and get you later, then we'd head over to Doris's so that you can get a feel for the size and scope of what you're going to be working on." He covered a nervous sigh with a small cough. "Then, we could either come back here, go to my office...or to my house and get started on the initial layout. We'll need to put in at least a couple of hours, if not more, just so I can go ahead and get a materials list." He blew out a breath. "How does that sound to you?"

"Er... How about I swing by and pick you up," she suggested. "Then we'll check out Doris's, and then we can either go to your house or your office, whichever has the best delivery options." She quirked a brow. "I'm assuming we'll be working through dinner?"

Will laughed. "You're right, we will. Actually, the options are about the same, but we'd probably be more comfortable at my house." Will made a mental note to try and get home early enough to straighten up. She wouldn't be able to find so much as a weed or an uneven blade of grass on his lawn, but unfortunately, he'd never carried that attention to detail into his house. He had a cleaning service come in a couple of times a month, but they weren't due until the end of the week. He inwardly winced. Which meant things were particularly messy.

She nodded. "That sounds fine to me. Just give me a call when you're ready."

Will cast a significant glance at her car parked in the drive and smiled. "Are you going to pick me up in that?"

"No, I thought I'd give you a piggyback ride," she deadpanned, causing a startled chuckle to break up in his throat. She laughed at his frozen expression. "Sorry, I didn't mean to be a smart-ass. Yes, I'm picking you up in that."

Oh, but she did mean to be a smart-ass, Will thought, instantly intrigued as he thoughtfully considered her. For reasons which escaped him, he got the distinct impression that the car was a bone of contention. He didn't know why, but he knew it all the same. "Good," he returned smoothly. "Then I'll look forward to the ride. I bet she's a smooth one." He arched a brow. "It's a '62, right?"

She nodded. "Yep."

"I thought so." He hummed thoughtfully, continued to study the vintage vehicle. Honestly, the car was every man's wet dream and, he thought with a covert look at the woman beside him, *her* behind the wheel made it a double pleasure. "A 327 V-eight?"

"That's right."

"Well, it's gorgeous."

"Thanks."

Will's senses went on heightened alert. Her posture hadn't changed, and she sounded friendly enough, but clearly talking about the car hit some sort of nerve and, though he didn't know where the idea came from, he felt like he'd inadvertently stumbled into some sort of test. What? he wondered. Did she expect him to ask to drive? He suppressed a snort. Like he didn't know better.

That Vette was not the sort of vehicle a person *asked* to drive.

It was disrespectful, not to mention presumptuous, rude and tacky. Had that been why she'd insisted on picking him up? Will wondered now. Or did she merely like to be the one behind the wheel, to literally be in the driver's seat?

He didn't know, but he found himself grimly determined to find out. To solve this little mystery as well. Only one of many concerning Rowan Crosswhite, his principled phone sex operator, he thought with a bemused smile.

His gaze slid to her once more—to her mouth, specifically—and a pulse of heat throbbed in his loins. His mouth parched and his scalp literally prickled with awareness. His palms itched and a sluggish sort of heat wound through his limbs. Need landed another direct hit below his navel and another curious emotion, one not easily read, landed an equally daunting hit in his chest.

Luckily, he could start looking for clues tonight.

CHAPTER SEVEN

WILL FOSTER was gorgeous under ordinary circumstances. Will Foster kicked back in her passenger seat—tawny hair blowing in the breeze, slick silver shades over those gorgeous brown eyes, and his long, muscled legs stretched out in front of him—was simply breathtaking.

Since picking him up a little over an hour ago, Rowan had been startlingly aware of him. Every hair on her body had stood on end, a funky quiver had vibrated her belly, and her palms had tingled to the point she'd had to tighten her hands on the wheel to keep from slipping one over his taut thigh.

He hadn't had time to change—in fact, she had the sneaking suspicion that she'd barely beaten him home. She'd caught him shoving an armful of dirty clothes into his kitchen pantry, an act she found stupidly endearing. But he still looked fantastic all the same. Wonderful. Yummy. Delicious.

She'd only been in his house for a moment—the kitchen specifically—but a mere sixty seconds had been enough for her to realize that he didn't concern himself with the finer points of domestication. There were no pictures on the walls, no sentimental bric-a-brac littered about the counter— not so much as a cookie jar—and, horror of horrors, she thought with a small smile, no magnets on his refrigerator.

But despite the glaring lack of decor, the old farmhouse

retained a comforting sense of warmth, a cozy ambiance that made her honey-I'm-home fantasy—the one she normally ignored—zoom into Technicolor focus. She could easily see herself in his kitchen, making his house hers and it had absolutely frightened the hell out of her. In a blink of her mind's eye, she'd instantly redecorated the entire room in cobalt blue, pale yellow, red and green. Blue willow and strawberries, toile fabrics and the like. She'd been so caught up in her mental musings that, embarrassingly, it had taken a significant cough from Will to startle her toward the door.

Those melted chocolate eyes of his had danced with a knowing sort of humor, and the corner of his mouth had tucked into a grin that made her alternately want to shrink out of existence and suckle his bottom lip. Her gaze slid to where he sat in the passenger seat.

After spending the past hour in his company, shrinking out of existence had lost its appeal and the suckling idea had expanded to other areas of his glorious anatomy—the curiously vulnerable patch of bronzed skin behind his ear, for instance. There was something positively adorable— not to mention sexy—about the way his hair curled gently behind his ears.

Yes, to her eternal chagrin and bewilderment, she was looking that closely.

Why? Hell, who knew? Rowan thought, utterly exasperated. But she couldn't seem to help herself. She'd turned into a single throbbing, pulsing nerve of need, and the longer she spent in his company, the more the condition worsened. She wanted him that desperately. More than her next meal. Her next breath.

Even the idea of a virtually unlimited budget and a half acre to landscape in her own unique design hadn't deterred the dogged attraction. If anything, she suspected it had only worsened as a result of it, because now she had more than a serious case of lust going, respect had been thrown into the mix as well.

Landscaping wasn't simply a job to Will Foster, wasn't just a way to earn a living wage—he was truly passionate about it. She'd suspected as much from the beginning, but listening to him talk about sod, fertilizer, trees and flowers while they surveyed Doris's yard had confirmed her earlier opinion. And if that resonating fervor in his voice hadn't clued her in, then one look at his own lawn definitely would have.

Rowan slowed as she neared his house, then guided her car down Will's lengthy gravel drive. The classic two-story house and surrounding property loomed instantly into view, and she found herself just as startled, just as impressed as she had been the first time she'd made this trip.

While he definitely took the minimalist approach to decorating the inside of his house, the outside was another matter altogether. The sloping lawn was graced with mature oak, maple and magnolia trees. Flowering bushes and evergreens hugged the perimeter of the home, and various bedding plants—impatiens, petunias, pinks—lent splashes of contrasting, happy colors to the landscape. Hanging baskets of hot-pink bougainvillea and ivy geraniums lined the porch, and a couple of planters loaded with a variety of flowering plants flanked either side of the front door.

Rowan followed the drive around to the back of the house and found it even more impressive with a second look. A huge antique brick patio butted against the house and surrounded a large kidney-shaped pool with a stacked-stone waterfall. A built-in bar and grill, along with plush patio furniture provided an ample place to simply relax or entertain. Predictably, the entire outdoor room had been accented with lots of greenery and flowers.

In a word, it was gorgeous.

To the left of the pool area, an ivied archway led to a private garden—his antique roses, no doubt—and one she suspected was accessible from the master suite. Though the greenhouse, potting shed and orchard couldn't be seen from the pool area, Rowan had noted them all the same from the road. Every inch of his property had been pruned, clipped, planted and tended with the kind of single-minded tenacity of a passionate perfectionist. She ought to know. It took one to know one, Rowan thought, quelling a grin.

At any rate, recognizing the shared characteristics in him made her chest tingle with a pleased warmth, and her belly clench with another jolt of desire. If he took this kind of care and attention to cultivating a garden, then it simply stood to reason that he'd put that same determined effort into cultivating a lover. The mere idea made her nipples tingle, made her womb quicken. She pulled in a shuddering breath as she shifted the transmission into Park, then let it go with a smile.

"Home, sweet home," Will told her, unwittingly parroting her first thought when she'd walked into his house. "Would you like to have a look around out here before we go inside?"

Most definitely. "Sure, I'd love to."

Time and heat prevented a thorough tour, but her initial impressions were dead-on—he was a perfectionist. She'd also been right about the private garden. His roses were gorgeous, and she made him promise to share several cuttings with her.

Given the perfect state of the yard, Rowan had anticipated a thorough, well-kept greenhouse, but what she hadn't anticipated—an unexpected delight that absolutely thrilled her to her little toes—was his heirloom seed collection. Respect and, curiously, even desire adjusted accordingly.

With the advent of hybrid seeds, many of the open-pollinated varieties were getting harder and harder to find. Hybrids had their advantages, yes. They were disease resistant and consistently produced more uniform fruit and blooms. The trade-off was a lesser scent with the flowers and a muted taste to the fruit, which in Rowan's opinion completely defeated the purpose. Backyard gardeners—like herself, and Will obviously—preferred the nonhybrid varieties. Her gaze slid to Will once more.

Who would have ever thought she'd get this excited over a guy who liked dirt as much as she did? Rowan thought as another flame of warmth tickled her chest and lower extremities.

She fingered a small package of tomato seeds. "Crimson Cushion, Watermelon Beefsteak, Giant Beefsteak and Ponderosa." Impressed, her gaze shot to his. "Wow."

Seemingly uncomfortable, he shoved his hands in his pockets. Soft light filtered through the roof, bathing him in a sepia-looking glow. "It's a hobby of sorts."

It looked like more than a mere hobby to her, Rowan thought, intrigued by his purposely vague description. She picked up a small catalogue. "Some hobby," she said with a small harrumph, for lack of anything better.

Will leaned against a potting table, kicked at a nonexistent rock on the floor. "My father and grandfather were farmers. Farming was too unpredictable for my tastes," he confided with a small smile.

She'd just bet it was, Rowan thought. She'd gleaned enough of his personality to make that deduction in just a few short hours. In fact, Will seemed to enjoy having his way just as much as she enjoyed having hers. The idea that she might have met her match gave her a little thrill, appealed to her more than it should have. "Oh, really?" she asked, tongue in cheek. "I find that hard to believe."

He smiled at her, the grin equally boyish and sexy, endearingly hot. "Yeah, well," he continued. "I still have a healthy respect for it. My grandfather, in particular, was a big proponent of the heirloom varieties." He shrugged lightly, cast a careless glance around the greenhouse. "It's a small way to follow in his footsteps."

Whether it was the offhand way he shared that significant insight—his laudable respect for tradition, or the respect for tradition itself—Rowan didn't know, but her heart inexplicably brightened all the same, and the frightening realization that she could oh-so-easily fall for this guy penetrated her mushy brain and sent a dart of uncomfortable panic right into her overly warm heart.

She'd recognized the Super-Sized attraction. She'd even reluctantly admit to some curiously strong emotions given the short length of time they'd known each other—being with him came easily, made her feel curiously…safe, for a lack of better explanation—but admitting to herself that this could turn into something more than a cavewoman crush was particularly…disturbing.

In fact, though she'd thought she was past the Mark debacle, she suddenly found herself unreasonably spooked.

"Well," Will said, jerking her out of her frown-provoking thoughts. He pushed away from the potting table. "We should probably get started."

"Right," Rowan managed, still unnerved. She pinned what she hoped looked like a natural smile into place and made her way to the door. True to form—getting through a day without embarrassing herself in some way had *never* happened—her sandal caught the lip of the threshold, knocking her off balance and, if it hadn't been for Will's quick reflexes, she would have undoubtedly ended up in a graceless heap face-first, ass-end up on the ground in front of him.

Thankfully, that didn't happen.

Instead, even as her face flamed with a familiar *oh-shit-why-me?* humiliation, another heat spread like a flash-fire over her thighs, up her belly and directly into her breasts. His hands, strong, slightly callused and warm, bracketed her upper arms and her breath left her in a small whoosh as her back came flush up against the hard wall of his muscled chest.

"Whoa," Will chuckled softly into her ear, causing a delicate shiver to dance through her.

Rowan swallowed. Oh, sweet Jesus. His scent, a mesmerizing combination of earth, air and hard work, invaded her nostrils, making her pulse hit an unsteady beat. She made the mistake of shooting an embarrassed glance over her shoulder, and wound up stuck, unable to look away from that warmed honey gaze.

A beat slid into three, and the humor in his eyes swiftly faded, replaced by a heat so intense she barely resisted the urge to melt beneath it.

Every cell in her body sang with joy because she wasn't alone in this unholy attraction—he felt it too. Evidently just as strongly because, thrillingly, a definite bulge nudged the small of her back. His gaze dropped to her lips, an unspoken want she mimicked as well, wordlessly sharing the same desire.

She desperately wanted him to kiss her, could feel that very desire hammering with every beat of her heart, could feel it intensify with every agonizing second that stretched between them.

Then the agony abruptly ended, when he finally swore,

then lowered his head and found her mouth with his. There was nothing tentative about the way he took her mouth, nothing hesitant in the way he firmly molded his lips to hers, nothing shy about the bold sweep of his talented tongue into her mouth.

It was hot and delicious, wickedly tantalizing, and the sheer pleasure coaxed an ecstatic whimper from the back of her throat. She turned in his arms, wrapped one hand around his waist, and anchored the other behind his neck, brazenly pressing herself against him. Out of character? Yes, to some degree. But she didn't care because she wanted him and she would do everything in her power to have him. Because it felt right, as natural as breathing. With any other person, she might have hesitated, but not with him. Not with Will. With Will, she could only feel, and the absolute perfection of this moment left no room for modesty, for doubt, for anything but sensation. The burn of desire charred pride and propriety, left nothing but an urgent sense of need.

With a low growl of pleasure, Will sagged against the door frame, pulling her with him. His hot mouth fed at hers even as his hands charted confidently over her back, then settled warmly over her rump. A hot thrill snaked through her at the intimate contact. Her womb clenched with achy need, her nipples pearled beneath the satiny fabric of her bra, and a moist heat coated her feminine folds and swiftly seeped into her panties.

The bulge she'd felt at her back had grown significantly and was now positioned just below her belly button, a pity since she wanted it lodged firmly between her legs. She shamelessly tippy-toed, trying desperately to put that part of her that ached the most on a firmer level with that part of him she knew would bring release. Her clit pulsed with an itchy insistent heat, and a tingly warmth concentrated in her nipples as his tongue curled repeatedly around hers. Back and forth, a suckle and a sweep.

God, could he kiss, Rowan thought dimly.

She tangled her fingers into those silky curls at the nape of his neck, kneaded his scalp and was rewarded with a masculine growl of pleasure. She smiled against his mouth, empowered by the whip of attraction she wielded over him. He tugged her bottom lip into his mouth, and a wave of gooseflesh leap-frogged up her spine, camped in her neck, forcing a preorgasmic shiver.

Will left off her mouth, blazed a trail of kisses down the side of neck. His hands were suddenly everywhere, molding her more tightly to him, reading her body like Braille, drawing sighs and mewls of pleasure from somewhere deep in her throat.

She slid her hands over his chest, felt the muscles quiver and jump beneath her palms and, before she thought better of it, had tugged his shirt from the waistband of his pants, then sighed when she finally felt his hot skin against her eager fingers. Warm, hot, hard and thrilling…and she wanted more.

Will hummed with pleasure, the sound weaving through her blood, stoking a fever inside her. Not to be outdone, he tugged her shirt down over her shoulder, nipped at her, then tugged it down even more until he bared the top of one breast. He licked a path over the curve of the cup of her bra, then latched his mouth onto her aching peak through the slinky material, unwittingly snatching the breath from her lungs. Rowan arched against him, pushing the needy nipple farther into his hot mouth. Oh, sweet heaven, she thought dimly. She wanted him. Right now.

She *needed.*

With the teeniest bit of effort, she would come right

here in broad daylight, fully clothed, in the doorway of his greenhouse.

The idea drew a whimper, another unspoken plea, one that he readily—*thankfully*—interpreted. He shifted, planted his legs farther apart in order to better align their bodies. She literally shook with the anticipation, her insides vibrated with it. She was so very, very close. She tightened her arms around his neck, shifted closer. Closer...

Ahhhh. There.

Oh, God. Please. Almost—

"Will?" a female voice screamed from out of nowhere, practically on top of them from the sound of it, and abruptly cut through the sensual fog surrounding her fuzzy lust-ridden head.

Startled, Rowan squealed and jumped back. Will jumped, too, as though he'd been hit with a cattle prod, then he swore hotly—repeatedly—and squeezed his eyes tightly shut, seemingly trying to summon patience from a hidden source. "Christ," he muttered.

Rowan wiped the back of her hand over her mouth, darted a guilty look over her shoulder, fully expecting to find the owner of the voice directly behind her. She braced herself for further embarrassment, but curiously, no one was there.

"Will!"

Though she should have been expecting it, Rowan jumped again, squealed. The lips she'd just been kissing tipped into a grin at her reaction. He unclipped his phone—which apparently worked as a two-way radio as well—from his shorts and held it up meaningfully to her. He exhaled a mighty breath. "Yes, Mom?"

Ah. His mother. Rowan bit the inside of her jaw to keep from smiling.

"I tried calling the house, but didn't get you."

His gaze tangled with hers, then he reached out and ran the pad of his thumb over her bottom lip. "That's because I'm not in the house. I'm outside. Was there something in particular you needed?"

"No, nothing particular I guess. I just thought I'd remind you that it's not too late to change your mind about Rebecca Hillendale. I'm sure she'd love to have dinner with you. I could call her back."

Rowan arched a pointed brow and had the pleasure of watching the tips of Will's ears turn red. She kept her expression coolly detached, purposely bored, but inside she writhed with immediate, disproportionate, unfounded jealousy.

She didn't know this Rebecca Hillendale from Adam's house cat, but that didn't keep her from instantly hating the woman, or from forming a less than charitable opinion of her. As far as Rowan was concerned, she was undoubtedly a fat, ugly Class-A bitch and if she knew what was good for her, she'd keep her distance. It was ridiculous. *She* was ridiculous. But she couldn't help herself.

Will massaged the bridge of his nose. "Mom, we've been over this. I'm not having dinner with Rebecca Hillendale. Ever," he added vehemently. "Let it go."

His mother heaved a put-upon sigh. "Oh, all right. But you can't blame me for trying. I don't like the idea of you being lonely."

From the beleaguered look on his handsome face, this wasn't the first time they'd had this conversation. Rowan's intuition went on point. If his mother worried about him being lonely, then that meant he must not date. At least, not regularly. A secret thrill expanded in her chest. But if that was the case, then why? Rowan wondered. Like her, had he been hurt? Or, like so many guys in his generation, was he simply commitment-phobic? Something to ponder later, she decided, filing the information away for future consideration.

"I'm not lonely, Mom," Will insisted. "I'll see you in the morning."

His mother blithely ignored his attempt to end the conversation. "Just because you're not lonely now doesn't mean you won't be in the future—"

Will shot her a long-suffering see-what-I-have-to-deal-with-look and smiled. "I know," he interrupted. "Gotta go, Mom."

"—you know," she continued without the slightest pause. "It's not healthy, a man your age being—"

"Mom."

The pointed edge to his voice finally snagged her attention. "Yes?"

"I'm busy."

Now that was an understatement, Rowan thought with a mental snort, quietly mourning the loss of her almost orgasm.

"Well, you should have just said so," his mother replied primly. "No need to get snippy. I'll see you in the morning."

Will's eyes widened in comical disbelief as she disconnected. "Was I snippy?" he asked. "I don't think I was snippy."

Rowan laughed, shook her head, and crossed her arms over her chest. "Nah, not snippy. Forceful maybe."

Will chuckled darkly. "Trust me. With her, I have to be." A droll smile rolled around his lips. "As you just witnessed, she's not afraid to share her thoughts, opinions or suggestions, particularly when it comes to who I'm dating, or more accurately, *not* dating."

Rowan nodded. "I've got a landlord with the same

annoying proclivities. She's convinced I won't be a whole woman until I've changed my last name." She blew out a breath. "It doesn't take long to get old."

He gave her a commiserating nod, then his gaze sharpened. "So you aren't seeing anyone, then?"

Little late to be asking her that, Rowan thought, considering only minutes ago she'd been practically humping him against the door frame—a hot tingle vibrated her belly at the mere thought—but she found herself immensely flattered all the same. She'd detected a hopeful note in his decadent voice, one that made her toes curl in her shoes.

She shook her head and decided a little plain speaking was in order. "No. If I was, I wouldn't have kissed you. What about you?" she asked pointedly, turning the question around on him. "Are you seeing anyone?"

Her bluntness paid off. She watched a glimmer of respect twinkle in those honey eyes, and something else, something just beyond her understanding. His expression wavered between admiration and uncertainty, and a slow smile edged up his lips. "No, I'm not. If I was, *I* wouldn't have kissed *you.*"

She nodded, inordinately pleased, and barely resisted the ballooning urge to bounce on the balls of her feet. For whatever reason, she got the distinct impression that they'd just cleared some sort of imaginary hurdle, stood on the precipice of something new and exciting, slightly terrifying, potentially wonderful.

New romance, she realized with a delighted start. And she hadn't agonized over making the leap.

In fact, she'd done it already—right into his arms.

CHAPTER EIGHT

WILL SAT ON his front porch steps and watched Rowan's taillights disappear into the darkness. Sheesh, he thought as he passed a hand wearily over his face.

He was pathetic.

Completely pathetic.

There were a half-dozen things that required his immediate attention, and rather than briskly tending to them as he normally would, he'd parked himself on the porch—in the dark, no less—to mope over Rowan's premature departure.

In truth, there was nothing premature about it—they'd been working for hours. It was late. She'd needed to go home. Were he capable of being logical, he'd understand that. Regrettably, the logical part of his brain—the part that ordinarily maintained control—had been short-circuited by single-minded selfishness and a virulent, almost debilitating case of lust.

In fact, Will thought, still unreasonably annoyed, if it had been up to him she wouldn't have left at all. She'd still be seated at his dining room table, poring over designs and catalogues, enthusiastically talking about her plan for Doris's yard in that erotic almost-whisper of hers that made his scalp prickle and his dick strain against his zipper.

She'd be laughing with him, sharing anecdotes and gardening tips. She'd be keeping him company, making this big old house feel a little smaller, a little warmer simply because she was in it. And though he knew it was the most ridiculous thing in the world and it galled him no end because it demonstrated a lamentable lack of control, he found himself curiously reluctant to go back inside, into his own damned house. Why? Because she wasn't there, and he instinctively knew he'd feel the absence more keenly.

How screwed up was that?

Hell, he'd dated. He'd even had the occasional overnight lover, though quite honestly he'd never been completely comfortable sharing his bed *after* sex. Ironically, it felt too intimate, too personal. There was a vulnerability in sleep that required a certain level of trust.

He'd made the mistake of trusting someone once and the outcome had been ruinous.

Naturally, Will knew that it was unfair to paint every woman with the same rotten brush, but his confidence had been badly shaken. He grimaced. Not being able to trust a significant other was disturbing, but not being able to trust your own judgment was considerably worse. He watched a moth flutter around his porch light and absorbed the truth of that statement.

But despite his hang-ups and reservations, Will instinctively knew that he could trust Rowan. He didn't know where the knowledge came from—call it intuition, ESP, whatever—but after less than twenty-four hours in her company, he knew it with a certainty that defied reason and trumped doubt.

From the moment he'd heard her voice—*just her damned voice*—he'd been instantly enchanted. He'd been drawn to her in a way that defied explanation, and every second up until this very minute had reinforced that initial reaction.

Then he'd kissed her and, for all intents and purposes, his world had tilted on its axis, the sky had fallen and time had stood still.

A residual quake shimmied through him at the mere memory, forcing him to expel a shaky breath. Heat stirred in his loins and his fingers involuntarily flexed against his palms.

To be honest, Will had been secretly delighted when she'd tripped—it had given him a reason to touch her—and, though he'd fully intended to kiss her tonight, he hadn't planned on making his move until after their initial work on Doris's design had been finished. Though she had to know that he was attracted to her—she was damned perceptive, after all—he hadn't wanted to seem too transparent, too eager or, God forbid, too needy.

But the moment he'd touched her any preconceived notions of propriety or neediness had fled instantly from his head, burned away by a shock of heat so intense he'd almost staggered from the voltage. The feel of her body pressed against his had been painfully sweet, sinfully erotic…inexplicably *right*. He'd gone from semiaroused to rock-hard in a nanosecond, then she'd turned her head and… Will expelled a long breath.

And he'd been lost.

One look into those gorgeous green eyes—honestly, he'd never seen a shade as compelling as hers—and he'd lost the battle. They were true green, the bright, hopeful color of a new leaf, and that hue coupled with that rueful embarrassment and her wobbly smile had positively sent him over the edge. He'd watched heat chase away her humiliation, then her gaze had dropped to his lips and, lowering his head—finding her mouth—at that moment had seemed as necessary as breathing.

Now, perversely, he felt like he'd suffocate if he couldn't do it again.

Kissing her had been the closest thing to a spiritual experience Will had ever had. Every hair on his body had stood on end, his pulse had tripped, his breathing had gone shallow, and a curious roaring had commenced in his head. She'd tasted like peppermint and fresh peaches, like a sweet rain after a long drought. He swallowed. Like hope, a kept promise, an unexpected gift.

Her lush frame had molded to his effortlessly, as though her body had been specifically tailored and designed to fit his. Will had never believed in "perfect." Like love, it was a word that had been thrown about and overused until the meaning had been diluted, bastardized. Until today, he'd never experienced anything even remotely close to what the true meaning of the word implied...but there was simply no other way to describe the way she'd felt in his arms, the way she'd tasted against his tongue.

That had been flawless.

He wanted her with an intensity that was frightening. Missed her, dammit, of all things, and she'd barely been gone twenty minutes. If he felt this strongly now, just what the hell would happen to him *after* he took her to bed? It was too disturbing to think about, so he firmly closed the door on that line of thinking—as a guy, he was wholeheartedly opposed to thinking/talking about feelings—and instead concentrated on a much more pleasant notion—planting himself between her thighs. Will grinned.

If kissing her turned him inside out, then plunging into her tight, wet heat would undoubtedly rock his world, and God, how he looked forward to the quake.

Tasting her mouth had only been an appetizer, a prelude to the grand event. He couldn't wait to sample her breasts, to feel those tight buds which had raked across his chest this afternoon pebbled against his tongue, flattened against the roof of his mouth. Couldn't wait to slip his fingers between her thighs, then his tongue, and sample the sweet nectar hidden in that secret valley.

A painful ache built in his loins and his breath hissed out between his clenched teeth.

God, he wanted her.

Right now.

Will didn't know where the idea came from, what maggot had taken hold of his brain, but before he could question what he was doing, he strode into the house and dialed her number. Since he'd acted without thinking, he was at a complete loss when she answered the phone.

He squeezed his eyes tightly shut and swore under his breath. "Er...Rowan." Brilliant. Just freakin' brilliant. He sounded like a complete moron. What in God's name had possessed him to call her?

"Will?" she asked uncertainly.

He plopped into his recliner and racked his brain for any plausible reason as to why he'd be calling her when she'd just left his house a few minutes ago. What the hell could be so important that it couldn't wait until tomorrow morning, when he'd see her again?

They had to meet with Doris for design approval— and this time he planned to get something in writing so that she couldn't change her mind again—then, once she signed off, they planned to mock the hardscape into scale so that the next phase could begin.

"I, uh..." *I'm so friggin' pathetic that I just wanted to hear the sound of your voice.* "I forgot to ask," he said, conjuring a brittle laugh. "Who's picking who up in the morning?"

She hesitated, clearly baffled because they'd gone over that right before she'd left. "Er...you're picking me up."

He rested his elbows on his knees, rubbed the bridge of his nose. "Right. That's what I thought."

This was ignorant. He needed to just lay it all on the line.

Will slouched back into his chair, blew out an exasperated breath. "Look, I knew that. That's not the reason I called. To be honest, I have no idea why I called. I just—" He paused, searching the quagmire of his brain for the right words. "I just really enjoyed tonight, more than I've enjoyed anything in a long time, and I— I wasn't ready for it to be over. Can you talk for a while? Do you *want* to talk for a while?" Christ, did he really have to sound so damned desperate?

Several nerve-racking seconds ticked by before she responded, and when she did, her voice held a warm but strangled quality. "Sure, I'd love to. But would you mind if I called you back in a few minutes? I've got a couple of things I need to take care of first."

Will breathed a small sigh of relief. "Sure. Just give me a call back when you're ready. I'll, uh..." He cleared his throat. "I'll be waiting."

ROWAN DISCONNECTED. A slow smile rolled around her lips and the tingly feeling of joy she'd carried home with her tonight multiplied until a giddy burst of laughter bubbled up her throat and she did a little happy *Lord of the Dance* jig around her living room.

Okay, okay, okay. She stopped, pulled in a deep calming breath and tried to act like a rational adult.

The problem was she didn't *feel* like a rational adult. Rational adults didn't skip around their living room simply because a guy had called and said he'd had a good time

with her. Rational adults didn't smile like a donkey with
a mouthful of briers for no particular reason, and rational
adults didn't absently chew on the phone antenna to keep
from squealing with delight.

Rowan knew to an uninformed bystander, she'd look
like a schizophrenic who'd just gone off her meds, but
there was one person who would understand how she
felt right now and that person had left a message on her
machine, and was the sole reason why she'd insisted
on calling Will back instead of continuing to talk to
him—Alexa.

She toed her shoes off, hit speed dial and, while she
waited for Alexa to pick up, she made her way to the back
of the house to change clothes.

"Well?" Alexa demanded when she answered. "How
did it go?"

Rowan shimmied out of her shorts. *"It was fantastic,"*
she said, drawing each word out for maximum impact.

Alexa squealed. "I knew it, I knew it. I had a feeling
about this guy. Tell me everything. Start at the beginning
and don't leave anything out."

Rowan kicked her shorts aside, then rummaged through
a drawer until she found a nightgown. "Hold on a minute."
She tossed the phone onto the bed, shed her shirt and bra,
then quickly tugged the nightie over her head. It settled
coolly over her skin.

Ah. Much better.

She didn't know what sadistic mind had invented the
bra, but she'd be willing to bet the damned torture device
had been a man's idea.

Rowan snagged the phone once more. "Okay. I'm
back."

"What the hell were you doing?"

"Changing clothes."

"So?" she asked meaningfully. "What happened?"

"I've only got a minute—he's called and I've got to call him back—so I'll have to give you the abbreviated version."

An exasperated huff sounded in her ear. "Fine. I'll just ask a couple of questions, then. One...did he kiss you?"

Rowan melted onto the side of her bed. Oh, God had he ever. "Yes, he did."

Alexa whooped into her ear. "Okay," she said with a delighted laugh, "the sound of your voice answered question number two, so I get another one. Did he at any time ask or imply that he'd like to drive the car?"

A flutter of warmth tingled beneath her breast. "No, he did not." He'd complimented the car, her handling of it, specifically, then he'd stretched those gorgeous legs out in front of him, simply sat back and enjoyed the ride.

"Well, there you go," Alexa said matter-of-factly. "We've got a winner."

Rowan silently agreed. Especially if tonight were to be any sort of indicator. Everything about this evening had been absolutely wonderful. From the moment she'd picked him up, to that scorching, belly-clenching good-night kiss, and every second in between, the entire night had been beyond fantastic.

Finding the strength to get into her car, when she knew that he'd wanted her to stay—and more importantly that *she'd* wanted to stay—had been one of the most difficult things Rowan had ever done. Even now, she couldn't say precisely why she knew it would be best to leave, but she'd known it all the same, and since her disastrous engagement, she'd never been one to ignore her instincts.

Physically, she was ready. She barely suppressed a snort. Couldn't be any more ready. Was beyond ready. Mentally, though, for whatever reason, she simply hadn't

arrived. But it was only a matter of time, and a short one
at that. She knew it, could feel it.

I'll be waiting.

A shiver went through her, remembering the heat in
that curiously vulnerable, sweetly poignant murmur.
Three little words, and yet more meaning and promise
lurked in that simple succinct phrase than she could have
imagined.

Shit, she thought with a mental duh. *He was waiting.*

She scrambled from the bed, quickly related this to
Alexa, and promised to call her tomorrow with more
details.

"Wait! Wait!" Alexa shrieked before Rowan could hang
up."

She hesitated, slightly perturbed. "What?"

"Don't forget to turn off your 1-900-line," she advised
sagely.

Oh, hell, Rowan thought. That could have been a disaster. "Right, thanks."

"I mean, you'd hate to have your phone sex line ring
and interrupt your ph-phone sex." Alexa giggled madden-
ingly. "That would be tragically ironic, wouldn't it?"

"You're twisted," Rowan scoffed, even as a wriggle of
something slightly wicked tripped up her spine. Her belly
trembled, but not with fear. With anticipation. "Who said
anything about having phone sex?"

"Nobody has to…but you can kiss your cherry goodbye,
Virgin-Girl, and my money's on tonight."

"We're just going to talk." A token protest, she
knew, but one she felt compelled to make anyway.
Quite frankly, after that wonderful kiss, almost orgasm,
then fantastic dinner where, despite the fact that they'd
gotten their work done, every word had resonated with
sexual innuendo, Rowan was ready for a little sexy

wordplay. To hell with being embarrassed. She was too damned hot.

"Yeah, right. About having sex—"

Rowan rolled her eyes. "Shut up."

"—with each other."

Rowan grinned. Alexa was incorrigible. "I'll call you tomorrow."

As Alexa had so fortuitously pointed out, Rowan booted it to the living room and turned off the ringer on her 1-900-line. She normally tried to keep the same hours—the majority of her clientele were repeat callers—but tonight they'd simply have to do without her. She'd take a B-12 vitamin, and make up the time once she and Will were finished with their…conversation.

Quite honestly, in light of what she'd make from the landscaping job, Rowan had been seriously tempted to disconnect her 900-line—that job alone would float her through until her teaching contract was renewed—but then she'd imagined the big goose egg in her savings account and the balance on her student loan debt, and practicality had won out. She made a moue of disappointment. Given her recent financial straits, she couldn't justify cutting off *any* income. It simply wasn't prudent.

So, while she had the opportunity, she'd decided that she'd be better off to net as much money as she possibly could so that if, God forbid, she ever found herself unemployed again, she wouldn't end up in the lamentable shape she'd been in this time. She'd narrowly missed having to ask her parents for help, and quite honestly, she'd rather be eviscerated with a rusty blade.

Unlike her brother, *she* would not be a source of disappointment.

She would take care of herself.

And if phone sex was what it took, then so be it.

And speaking of phone sex…she needed to call Will back. As for whether or not Alexa's prediction would come true, Rowan couldn't say. Her belly vibrated with anticipation at the mere thought and her feminine muscles clenched, forcing her breath through her lips in a shaky, nervous hiss.

But curiously, what had literally scared the bejesus out of her yesterday didn't seem frightening now and she suspected the antidote had been administered during that inferno kiss this afternoon. *Mama mia,* Rowan thought as remembered heat licked her nipples. Hell, who had time to be nervous? She was too damned horny.

Pop her phone sex cherry, indeed, Rowan thought as she punched in Will's number. Her lips slid into a slow grin.

One could hope.

CHAPTER NINE

WILL BLEW OUT an impatient breath and quietly watched another minute blink past on his VCR display. A screw of unease tightened in his chest. She'd asked for a few minutes. As far as Will was concerned, *a few* implied three to four—five at max.

He'd been waiting for six and every second that had passed in between had felt like a damned eternity, providing him with ample time to second-guess the merits of placing that last call.

Had she changed her mind? he wondered now. Had he frightened her off? I mean, honestly, Will thought, silently cursing himself. She'd just left—had just gotten home—and rather than playing his cards close to his vest, or trying to maintain even the slightest semblance of control—or pride for that matter—he'd pounced on her the second she'd walked through her damned door.

Will's eyes widened. Oh, *hell.* He'd screwed up. A grim chuckle burst from his throat, and a hot poker of stupidity prodded him in the ass, forcing him to leap to his feet. He paced the area in front of his favorite chair, speared his fingers through his hair.

Shit, shit, shit.

He'd screwed up. He shouldn't have called her, he thought faintly. What in God's name had he been thinking? Hell, he hadn't been thinking, Will thought with a miserable groan of disbelief. Hadn't been able to use anything which remotely resembled his so-called gray matter since he'd heard her *voice* yesterday. *I had a good time, and I wasn't ready for it to be over?* Mortification scalded his cheeks, burned the lobes of his ears.

It was the attraction, Will decided with a fatalistic grunt. It had obviously flambéed his brain. There could simply be no other explanation for his over-the-top senseless, moronic, out-of-character behavior.

Clearly, he'd lost his mind.

Lay it all out on the line, indeed, Will thought now, feeling beyond ridiculous.

He'd laid something on the line, all right—his ass. The ass he wished he could kick himself. He swore again and expelled an exasperated breath. Good grief, would he ever learn? Would he ever—

The ring of the phone cut through his self-recriminations. He stopped midstride, and his gaze swung to the phone. Every ounce of worry evaporated as a profound relief saturated every cell in his body. His shoulders slumped and he passed a hand wearily over his face.

Okay. So maybe he hadn't screwed up.

He quickly crossed the room and snagged the phone. "Hello."

"Hey, sorry I took so long," Rowan told him. "I had to return a call—my friend Alexa had left a message—and I wanted to change clothes." She sighed into his ear. "You know, get comfortable."

In other words, she'd shed her bra. His mouth parched at the very idea, making his voice slightly rusty when he spoke. He sank into his recliner. "Yeah, I know what you mean."

She laughed. "So you got comfortable, too?"

Will smiled, glanced at his discarded clothes piled in a

messy heap next to his coffee table. Hell, it was too damn
hot to stay fully clothed. "I guess you could say that."

"Let me guess," she told him, humor lacing that erotic
voice. "Your shirt, shoes and socks are sitting in a pile on
your living room floor."

Will didn't know whether to be alarmed or impressed,
so instead he chuckled. "How'd you know?"

"Because you haven't had time to take them to your
pantry yet."

A startled chuckle burst from his throat. Oh, wow, he
thought. Busted. "You saw that, did you?" Will asked,
somewhat embarrassed. He picked at a loose thread on
his shorts.

"I did," she laughed. "Sorry. I shouldn't have said
anything."

"Nah," he told her. "Don't worry about it. Hey, what
can I say? Keeping up the house isn't one of my strong
suits. I'd rather be outside."

Her laughter tittered out into a soft sigh. "I know what
you mean. Your place is gorgeous, your rose garden in
particular. I'm truly envious."

"Thanks. A lot of work goes into it, but it's worth it.
And yours is nothing to sneeze at," he told her. "You've
done an amazing job." Particularly considering she'd had
no formal training. Honestly, he'd love to add her to his
team permanently. It was something to think about, at any
rate.

Her voice grew warm. "I do love it. There's something
so therapeutic about gardening. I love planning and planting, watching my babies grow and bloom."

"And don't forget weeding," Will reminded her magnanimously. "You're a—" He laughed, he couldn't help
himself. "You're a champion w-weeder." Will didn't have

to see her to know that her face had undoubtedly turned bright pink.

Several beats passed, then, "I'm never going to live that down, am I?"

Still smiling, he sighed and absently scratched his chest. "Probably not. I know I'll certainly never forget it." And he wouldn't. Listening to that sweet throaty voice rise and fall, pant, sigh and moan in orgasmic simulation was indelibly imprinted on his brain, on his eardrums. He'd mentally edited the scenario, had replaced Roy's name with his own, and played it back in his head whenever the urge struck. Which was frequently.

"Well, I wish you would," Rowan said, slightly exasperated. "It wasn't one of my finer moments," she said drolly.

Will quirked a brow. "Really? I was impressed."

She harrumphed. "Well, I can do better."

Will stilled as her unspoken oh-shit hummed between them. He instinctively knew that she'd blurted that out without thinking, and a nice guy—a less horny guy— would undoubtedly let it slide without comment. Unfortunately, the idea that she could do better than what he'd heard yesterday had taken root between his legs and, rather than letting her off the hook, he wanted to make her wriggle for a little while first.

He cleared his throat, lowered his voice. "Do better, huh?"

An audible swallow sounded in his ear, making his smile a smidge wider. "Well...yes, actually."

Too much pride to back down. When push came to shove, this was a chick who'd put her money where her mouth was. An admirable quality, that, Will thought, unreasonably impressed. Besides, he liked the direction this conversation was taking. He reached down and adjusted himself. It lessened the room in his shorts.

"I'd like to hear that," Will told her. "Care to give me a little demonstration?" he asked lightly.

She chuckled, the sound at once sexy and sweet. "Sounds like you're asking for a freebie."

"No, of course not," Will readily replied. He laughed. "That would be tacky. You're the one that said you could do better. I'm merely curious is all."

"Oh, well," she said, humor tingeing that sultry non-whisper. "If that's the case, then that's different."

"I thought so."

"So, what do you want?" she asked. "Just a straight orgasm, or would you like the works? The whole, I-want-to-get-naked-and-touch-myself-because-you-have-the-biggest-rod-I've-ever-seen-and-only-you-can-make-me-sing-the-Hallelujah-chorus spiel?"

Will blinked drunkenly. Just like that, he lost the upper hand. His smile slowly faded and every ounce of blood raced from his extremities and pooled into his loins. His tongue felt huge. "Wha— Whatever you think is best."

"You fed me this evening," she said, an implied shrug in her voice. "I guess I could give you the whole spiel, but it's going to require a little effort on your part." He got the distinct impression that she was laughing at him, that he'd somehow prodded her into this course of action. "Are you up for it?"

He cleared his throat again, considered just how friggin' *up* he was and barely swallowed an ironic grunt. "Sure. Yes. Of course."

"Good. Then let's pretend that you've called me, okay? We're going to take it from the top. Are you ready?"

This time he did laugh. "Oh, yeah."

"Good... *Hello.*"

The difference in the tone of her voice was staggering. Low. Husky. Rife with the promise of a wet dream, and he felt it eddy through him. She was *on,* Will realized. She was ready to play her part.

But he didn't want her just to play her damned part—he wanted her to participate.

If he'd learned one thing this afternoon, he'd learned that she wanted him every bit as much as he'd wanted her. She hadn't merely kissed him—she'd devoured him, had practically tried to crawl up under his skin. She'd been a slave to the attraction just as much as he had.

So why the ruse? Will wondered. What was she afraid of?

He didn't know, but it damn sure wasn't going to be him, and he wasn't going to allow her to turn him into another Roy. His lips tightened.

Not no, but hell, no.

In fact, though now was not the time to ask her, he sincerely hoped there were no more "Roys."

Two could play at this game, Will decided, and while she had the benefit of experience, he had a hard-on that could up-end a Mack truck. In addition to that, he knew her, and he fully intended to press that advantage. He'd noted what had turned her on this afternoon, had committed each and every sibilant sigh and hiss to its coordinating erogenous zone.

So bring it on, Will thought. He was ready to rumble.

ALEXA HAD BEEN RIGHT—she was about to lose her phone sex cherry.

Rowan's heart raced, her mouth parched and a tingly heat concentrated at the apex of her thighs. She didn't know what had possessed her to tell him that she could do better—vanity perhaps, because she knew that she could. She'd been in a hurry that day. But regardless of why she'd said it, the boastful retort had had the desired effect because she and Will Foster were about to scorch the phone lines. She could feel the heat already. Looked forward to the burn.

His voice, when it finally came, was every bit as low and seductive as hers had been. "Hi."

Rowan sank her teeth into her bottom lip. *Oh, yeah,* she thought. *Here we go.*

She made a valiant effort to catch the thread of the conversation. "I'm glad you called," she murmured. "I've been lonely." A standard response, but this time the line rang with a hint of truth that made her swallow.

His soft chuckle seduced her ear. "Lonely, eh? That's a pity. I'll try to do something about that. I haven't caught you at a bad time, have I?"

Rowan shifted against her sheets. "No, I'm just lying here all alone in my big old bed." She purposely lowered her voice, injected that sultry quality that never failed to elicit a response. "What about you? What are you doing?"

"I've been thinking about a girl I met yesterday. Thinking about her a lot, actually."

Her heart rate shifted into overdrive, threatened to beat right up out of her throat. Oh, no. He wasn't following the script. "You have?" Did that thready voice belong to her?

"Yeah, she's pretty damned hot, and she's got this voice that makes me swell out of the top of my shorts. It's soft and husky, sleepy almost. One of those bedroom voices, you know? I've never been so attracted to another person. *Ever.*"

A bud of pleasure bloomed in her chest and, impossibly,

another dart of warmth penetrated her womb. "We've got something in common then, because I've found myself in a similar situation recently. I met a guy yesterday and...*my God*." She slumped against the back of her bed. "He's gorgeous. He's got the most amazing mouth. It's a little full for a guy, but so damned sexy it makes me...wet. Makes me fantasize about kissing him...and having him kiss me...in lots of different places."

She paused, imagined him kissing her right then. Could practically feel his lips melded to hers, the evocative thrust of his tongue into her mouth. Her breath left her in a stuttering whoosh. "In fact, he kissed me today and I came within a gnat's ass of one hell of an orgasm." She winced. "Unfortunately we were interrupted." Rowan felt her lips tip into a grin. "His mother called."

His voice had developed a rasp. "That was unfortunate."

"I'll say," Rowan readily concurred. "We'd been standing against the door frame of his greenhouse—he's a dirt freak like myself, which makes him all the more attractive, I might add—and," she sighed, "if it hadn't been for that fateful call, I'm certain we would have done it right then. I wouldn't have been able to say no, that's for sure. I wanted him. Desperately."

A stuttered breath hissed across the line. "I know what you mean. I want this girl pretty damned badly, too. She's...amazing. I kissed her today, and...*mercy*. Every thought drifted right out of my head and I literally tingled. My palms itched so much that I couldn't keep my hands off of her. I slid them over her ass—did I mention that she's got one helluvan ass?—and... *Wow.* I narrowly avoided embarrassing myself, that's for sure. But I just can't help it. I *want* her and I haven't wanted anyone in a long time." He sighed. "Too damned long."

Rowan absorbed the compliment, smiled as lust and delight commingled in her belly. "So, do you think you and her will get together?"

"Most definitely. It's inevitable." She heard the smile in his voice and just enough confidence to be arousing. "I'm just waiting for the right moment to make my move."

A steady throb built between her legs and her nipples pearled against her nightgown. If she'd ever been more turned on in her life, she couldn't recall it. Need was a living breathing thing inside her, consumed her to the point of complete distraction. "If you—" She moistened her lips. "If you could have her right now, what would you do to her?"

His laugh was rife with anticipation. "First, I'd draw her hair away from her neck—she's got long, gorgeous hair. Very sexy. Makes Lady Godiva look like a troll—then I'd kiss that tender part of her throat where her neck meets her shoulder. I touched her there today, and she melted against me, so I know she'd like it."

Rowan hummed. She knew precisely where he was talking about and the fact that he'd noticed how much she enjoyed it was singularly arousing. Made her wonder what else he'd noticed about what pleased her. Her lids drooped. "Go on."

"I'd like to say that I'd take my time making love to her. That I'd take things slow and easy, savor every second." He sighed softly and she felt that whispery sound simmer in her blood. "But I want her too badly, and the first time, I know I simply wouldn't be able to hold back. I'd devour her. I'd get her naked as swiftly as possible, then I'd lick, suck, kiss and nuzzle every inch of her in short order."

His voice was smooth, yet lightly rough. Like the slide of denim over silk.

"Her breasts are full and ripe, and I felt her nipples

against my chest this afternoon." He hissed. "It nearly killed me. I wanted to feel them in my mouth, wanted to taste them so desperately. I'd have to linger around them for a few moments. Flick them against my tongue. Back and forth, then latch on again. Do you think she'd like that?"

Oh, God, would she ever. What he'd described was right in keeping with her own thoughts. She wanted him to devour her. Wanted him to lick, suck, kiss and nuzzle her. Wanted his hot mouth anchored at her aching, pouty breasts right now. Like he'd done this afternoon through her bra.

Rowan couldn't help herself, needed some small amount of relief. She let her hand drift over one breast, over one distended nipple, winced, then relieved the other one as well. Her blood sizzled. "She'd...like it," Rowan managed to croak brokenly.

"Good." His voice had developed a rasp. "I'd— I'd thought so."

"What would you do next?" When had she become such a glutton for punishment?

A sexy laugh resonated into her ear. "Oh, I'm glad you asked. Next, I'd kiss my way down her belly, then I'd hook her legs over my shoulders and feed at her—fast, remember, because I'm not strong enough to wait—until I made her come and had sipped up every last ounce of her release."

The vision materialized so swiftly behind her lids that she gasped and slid her hand down over her muddled belly. She edged her gown up, dallied beneath her drenched panties. Her back arched away from the bed as pleasure bolted through her.

"Then, once she'd melted for me once, I'd slide right into her wet, tight heat, and pump in and out of her until she did it again." His breathing grew ragged and he seemed to snap under the strain of their sexy wordplay. "Can you feel me there, Rowan?" he whispered. "Tell me you feel me."

"Oh, God yes," she gasped, working her tender flesh beneath her frantic fingers. "Can you feel *me?*" she asked. "I'm clenching around you because every time you retreat, I want to draw you back in. I'm on fire and I— " She gasped as the sharp tug of beginning climax ripened in her sex.

She heard a muttered curse, then a hiss of relief which told her he'd taken himself in hand. The erotic image burned into her brain, made a broken laugh of relief shimmy up her throat.

"Oh, God," she panted. She rolled her head from side to side, barely had the strength to hang on to the phone. Though she knew it was impossible, she could feel him there between her legs, had *felt* every sensual treat he'd described. His hot mouth suckling her breast, that blond head licking a path down her belly, then greedily feasting between her thighs. Then the long hard length of him filling her up, satisfying that itchy, achy heat centered deep into her womb. "I need— I want—"

"Tell me what you want, baby, and I'll give it to you," Will told her.

"Harder," Rowan gasped. "Faster." She upped the tempo, imagined him plunging in and out, in and out, until finally—blessedly—the orgasm crested and broke through her. Her back arched off the bed, her neck bowed and a long, keening howl issued from her throat.

Frantic, masculine hisses rasped into her ear. A gasp, a groan, a guttural growl, then he lost his breath—the telling absence of noise she'd been waiting for—which told her he'd found release as well.

Unable to help herself, Rowan smiled, waited for her labored, wholly satisfied breathing to return to normal. She didn't want to ruin the perfection of this moment with awkwardness, so she conjured a light laugh. "This girl," she gasped, still not completely recovered. "She's going to be one lucky lady."

Thankfully, Will read the tone correctly and played along. He chuckled. "So's your guy. I'll keep my fingers crossed that he lives up to your expectations."

It was Rowan's turn to laugh. *Now he had performance anxiety?* "Oh, I'm not worried about that," she replied confidently. "I'm certain he'll surpass my expectations. I hope your girl does the same."

A beat slid into three. "She already has," he murmured softly. "But I'll let you know how it goes."

"Good." The compliment warmed her, made her heart inexplicably swell with delight. She struggled to find her way out of the foggy realm of release. "Call me again, anytime."

"You can count on it."

"Goodnight, Will."

"G'night, Rowan."

CHAPTER TEN

"I CAN'T BELIEVE you've lived here all your life and you've never had a burger from Grady's," Rowan told him, still apparently scandalized on his behalf. He held the door open for her, followed her inside and then snugged a finger at the small of her back while he waited for his eyes to adjust to the dim interior. The scent of sizzling grease, pool chalk and smoke hung in the air, and the occasional crack of a cue ball finding its mark punctuated the low buzz of conversation.

Rowan led him deeper into the room until she found an empty table toward the back. "Brace yourself," she warned with a teasing smile as she slid into a cracked vinyl chair. "You're about to have the culinary experience of your life."

Will grinned, took the chair opposite her. Apparently this was a week for firsts then. First phone sex. First pool hall burger. Made a guy wonder what could possibly come next.

He'd probably *come* next, Will thought with a smothered snort. Had almost come again this morning when he'd picked her up. Last night had been... Well, there were simply no words for how last night had been, Will decided, because it had been completely out of the realm of his experience. One minute the wordplay had been teasing, the next he'd had his dick in his hand listening to Rowan's *genuine* cries of sexual bliss.

What had once seemed, quite honestly, like a pointless waste of time, or a pathetic option for the undersexed, suddenly held considerable appeal. In fact, though he was hardly an amateur in the bedroom, he could honestly admit that he'd never in his life experienced anything so... erotic.

Hearing those thrillingly graphic words come out of that lush, ripe mouth had literally hot-wired his groin. The air in his lungs had thinned, his mouth had watered, then parched, and he'd had one of the *biggest* hard-ons he'd ever had in his life. His lips quirked in wry amusement. It was enough to give a guy the big head—literally.

Naturally, he couldn't wait to do it again.

And with that in mind, he'd done a little preemptive groundwork this morning when he'd picked her up. Last night, things could have easily turned...awkward, but Rowan had taken care of that by making sure the conversation moved into lighter territory immediately afterward.

In order to avoid the same scenario this morning, the moment she'd opened the door, Will had stepped forward, framed her face and kissed her until he could breathe again—hell, he'd felt like a damned fish out of water since last night—kissed her until he knew beyond a shadow of a doubt that the instantaneous heat had burned up any misgivings or second thoughts she might have entertained.

He meant to continue as he intended to go on, and backtracking simply wasn't an option.

He wanted her. Had to have her. It was more than mere attraction, more than exaggerated sexual chemistry. It was as though she'd unwittingly tapped into a secret power supply. He felt energized, brighter, bigger and better when he was with her. Will let go a shaky breath.

Powerful stuff, that.

And this morning at Doris's had been no exception. Will loved his job, honestly loved what he did. He counted himself among the rare few who actually made a comfortable living doing something that constituted work, but in truth, didn't feel like it. Yes, he ran into the occasional problem—like Doris, he thought uncharitably—but by and large, the majority of his clients were amiable and easy to please, and when he finished a project, he was rarely dissatisfied.

But working side-by-side with Rowan today had been a singularly pleasing treat. He couldn't say that he'd learned any particular character traits—he'd already deduced that she was a hard worker. Her garden alone had told him that. Just like it had told him that she was organized in her own bizarre way, observant and diligent. Still, watching her get in there today and literally get her hands dirty, watching the expedient way her mind worked had jazzed him in a way that defied explanation.

While he had several teams of employees, this was the first time in his professional life that he'd felt like a part of one. It was her, he knew. Something about her just did it for him. She'd unwittingly injected something into his life that he hadn't realized he'd been missing—excitement.

Will leaned back in his chair and took a moment to simply look at her. Her long brown hair had been twisted into a thick braid which curved like a provocative question mark around one generous breast. Those gorgeous green eyes—which seemed startlingly bright against her healthy tan—were framed with thick curling lashes a shade lighter than her hair. Half a dozen freckles dusted her dainty nose and he'd noted a dimple in her left cheek this morning which had previously escaped his notice. He didn't know how he'd missed it since he spent so much time staring at that lush mouth, but it had nonetheless come as quite a shock when the adorable indentation had flashed at him this morning. Will sighed, momentarily lost in the sheer perfection of her face.

There were a million little things that made her beautiful. The sweet curve of her cheek, the smooth arc of her brow, even the delicate skin at her temple. He knew she'd undoubtedly look at herself and find flaws—women typically did, being women—but if she could see herself the way he did... Well, there'd simply be no question.

A slow smile moved across her lips as she suddenly caught him staring. Will blinked, felt his mouth slide into a sheepish grin. "Sorry," he apologized. "I just—" He shrugged, expelled a helpless breath. *Lay it all out on the line,* he thought. It seemed to be working so far. He lowered his voice. "You're beautiful."

Something warm shifted in her twinkling gaze. "Thank you," she murmured. He felt her gaze trace the planes of his face, felt it linger over his lips. "You're not too hard to look at yourself."

A waitress arrived, sparing him an immediate reply. Once she'd moved away, Will found his voice once more. "So how do you think things are going?" he asked. "Are you pleased with the way things are moving along?"

Rowan nodded. "Yeah, I am. You've got a great crew."

Will kicked his chair back, tilting the front legs off the floor. "It makes all the difference in the world, believe me."

"I would imagine so." She leaned back as their drinks arrived. "Doris seems okay with everything so far. What's your take on her?"

"She's happy." He shrugged lightly, grinned. "And like

I told you before, she's connected. I wouldn't be at all surprised if you didn't end up being my competition."

Rowan crossed her arms and rested them on the table. She shot him a wry look. "I seriously doubt that."

"I don't," Will told her, and he meant it. She was seriously talented. "You've got an excellent eye and you know what you're doing. That and a little determination is all it takes."

"Yeah, well, I might consider it once I finish paying for my *first* education," she replied drolly.

"Ah," Will sighed knowingly. "Student loans, the bane of every self-made young professional."

She quirked a brow. "Is that the voice of experience?"

Will bit the inside of his cheek. "Er...no."

She leaned back in her seat and chuckled knowingly. "So which sports scholarship did you land? Wait. No. Let me guess." Her appraising gaze did another thorough inspection and he had the pleasure of watching admiration light a sparkler of desire in those leaf-green orbs. "You've got the lean, athletic look of a baseball player, but given your temper and wit, my money's on football, quarterback. Am I right?"

Will chuckled, impressed. "Yes, you're right."

She laughed and smacked her hand against the tabletop. "I knew it."

"You're good, I'll give you that. I think maybe you're in the wrong profession. Perhaps you should have been a detective."

"Nah." She shook her head. "I don't have the patience."

Will chased a bead of condensation down the side of his drink with his thumb. "What about teaching? Do you like it?"

She barely hesitated, but he felt it all the same. "Er...

yeah, I do. I do," she repeated, and he got the distinct impression that she was trying to convince herself as much as him. Her gaze slid to his, and she winced. "Honestly, I'd much rather be outside doing what we did today, but hindsight's twenty-twenty." She pulled a shrug. "The fact is I've got a degree that I haven't finished paying for yet, and I'm too practical to give it up simply because it isn't as satisfying as I thought it would be."

Well, Will certainly understood that. Still... "Not one of those proponents of the life's-too-short argument?" Will asked lightly.

A self-deprecating smile tugged at the corner of her distracting mouth. "In theory, yes. In practice, no."

Once again the idea of putting her to work for him on a permanent basis crossed his mind. Will instinctively knew she'd be a good choice, a fantastic addition. But if he made the offer now, he was afraid she'd suspect his motives. Better to wait until she'd finished Doris's project, then he could cite her excellent performance. Another thought struck, and though he knew it was none of his business, he simply had to ask. "What about your 900-line?" Will asked lightly. "You probably won't have a lot of time for it anymore, right?"

Rowan shot him a slightly frozen look, then sighed happily as their waitress returned once more, this time with a tray laden with food. She completely ignored his question, which wasn't the least bit encouraging. Will resisted the urge to swear. Why couldn't he leave well enough alone? he wondered. Last night he'd called her after she'd just gotten home, and today he was quizzing her about *her* business, which incidentally had nothing to do with him. Still, he couldn't help it. He didn't want her having phone sex with anyone but him. Selfish? Unrealistic? Yes, but he didn't care. The idea of her talking to another guy the way that she'd talked to him—even pretending—set his teeth on edge and made a red haze swim in front of his eyes.

"Get ready," she warned with a playful smile. "I'm about to change your life."

Will barely swallowed an ironic chuckle. He had a sneaking suspicion she already had. He conjured a laugh all the same, easily caught up in her enthusiasm. "If you say so," he offered skeptically.

Actually, it smelled really good. Quite frankly, he hadn't been the least bit hungry when he'd suggested that they break for lunch—he'd just wanted a reason to be alone with her. Self-serving? Yes. But he didn't care. And evidently she was hungry, so no harm no foul, right?

"Well," Rowan prodded impatiently. "Go ahead."

Will blinked. "Oh, sorry." He glanced at her untouched plate. "What? Are you waiting on me?"

"Yes," she said, heaving a protracted sigh.

"Okay." Will feigned appropriate chagrin, and quickly took up his burger. One bite validated her reverence. His eyes widened in delight as his taste buds experienced what he could only liken to an orgasm. His astonished gaze flew to hers and he made a low growl of appreciation. "It's great," he moaned thickly.

She nodded approvingly and a smug grin drifted over her lips. "I told you so," she said pointedly, a direct dig at his own lamentable tendency to toot his own horn.

Will smiled, wiped the corner of his mouth. "Touché."

For a moment they ate in companionable silence, content to simply enjoy their food.

Then Will made the mistake of looking up.

Rowan's tongue darted out and licked the smear of ketchup from the corner of her mouth.

For all intents and purposes, she might as well have licked his rod.

Without warning that suffocating feeling blindsided him again, and in an instant, he was hard. Not semiaroused, or mildly turned-on—granite-*hard*.

The din around them faded into insignificance, and he wanted her so desperately that he honestly thought his reason might completely snap and he'd make the monumental error of devouring her right now—in public—the way he'd told her he wanted to last night.

She caught him staring once more. The tentative smile she wore faded and he had the pleasure of watching those leaf-green eyes darken into a somnolent mossy shade. Her lids drooped, presumably under the weight of desire, and whether the move was intentional or not, Will couldn't say, but that facile tongue—the very one that had locked his loins in a fiery pit of hell—peeked out once more, glided slowly over that ripe bottom lip. His dick actually strained toward her, as though she were one of Satan's angels, and it her devoted familiar.

She let go a soft shuddering breath, swallowed, then quietly excused herself to the bathroom. Once she was out of earshot, Will squeezed his eyes tightly shut and uttered a sizzling, succinct oath. He rubbed the bridge of his nose with curiously shaky fingers and made a valiant effort to get himself under control while she was gone. Sheesh. He had to get a grip. He simply had to—

His cell chirped and, with an annoyed grunt, he unsnapped it from his waist. He glanced at the Caller ID display, but didn't recognize the number. "Hello."

"You can't look at me like that, Will, especially in public. It…does things to me."

Rowan? Confused, Will blinked, darted a look over his shoulder. His heart rate kicked into overdrive. "I'm... sorry?" Will replied, uncertain as to what she expected him to say.

"You should be," she murmured, her voice a low throaty purr that instantly hissed through his blood. Impossibly, he hardened even more. "When you look at me like that— like you want to eat me up, *devour* me—my joy juice starts flowing and I get an itch that I can't scratch. It's... provoking."

Will grinned, darted a look around the crowded diner, then lowered his voice. "Yeah, well, watching you lick your lips is particularly provoking, too. In fact, you almost wound up with your burger in your lap. I came within a gnat's ass of upending the table."

A stuttered sigh sounded over the line, and when she spoke, her voice was distinctly thready. "Are you telling me that you've got a hard-on? Right now? Right this very minute?" More Rowan, less sex kitten. Utterly impossible to resist. Though he'd never in his life done anything remotely close to what he was about to do—have sex in a public place, a friggin' pool hall, no less—Will quietly stood, then started to make his way toward the bathroom.

"Baby, that's exactly what I'm saying." He chuckled lazily, past caring about control or anything else for that matter. He just wanted her. Had to have her. Right now. "I'm cocked, locked and ready to rock."

A beat slid to three and he listened to the thin, unsteady rasp of her breathing. "I *think* you should come back here."

Will rapped lightly on the door and a startled gasp sounded in his ear. He smiled. "I *think* you should open the door."

A THRILLING TORNADO of anticipation whirled through Rowan's abdomen and her gaze flew to the door. She barely resisted the urge to squeal with delight. It was crazy, what they were about to do. Scandalous, even, and instead of reprimanding herself for being out of control—for being reckless—she simply rode the rush of adrenaline rocketing through her bloodstream, gloried in the efficient way it heightened the need winding through her at warp speed.

This was inevitable, she knew. Had been from the first moment she'd laid eyes on him. Last night had simply been a precursor, a wicked prelude to the grand event. This morning, she'd opened her door and before her mouth had even shaped the word "hello" he'd kissed her so thoroughly that she'd forgotten that she was tired, that she worried about being *weird* around him after the previous night, forgotten everything outside the feel of his lips against hers and the need blistering her veins.

She'd spent the entire day fantasizing about him—about a repeat performance of phone sex, then real sex, and every other sensually depraved scenario she could possibly dream up—had felt his presence, his sheer masculinity, pinging her like sonar all morning long. She'd been a complete wreck, a sexually deprived, single-minded *wreck* and nothing short of feeling him lodged deeply between her legs was going to cure what ailed her.

When she'd looked up a moment ago and caught him staring at her mouth again, saw those honey-brown eyes go heavy-lidded with smoky arousal, she'd absolutely lost it. So she'd calmly excused herself, then hid behind her phone to tell him what he'd done to her, never really intending to let things move to this point. Quite honestly, she simply wanted to torment him the way he'd tormented her.

But then he'd told her about his hard-on—that part of him she craved so very desperately—and uttered that loaded *cocked, locked and ready to rock* phrase, and…she'd snapped. She'd wanted to teach him a lesson, and as it turned out, she was about to get one.

She wanted him now. Not later this afternoon, or even later tonight.

Now.

Rowan opened the door, and Will quickly strode in, seemingly without the smallest regard for the fact that he'd just entered the ladies' restroom. That they were about to do it in a pool hall/burger joint. How sexy was that? she thought, secretly elated. He shut the door, locked it with a purposeful click. Those honey eyes tangled with hers, effectively snatching the breath from her lungs, and the next second Rowan launched herself at him.

With a guttural growl of approval, Will matched her enthusiasm, crushed her to him and she actually whimpered he felt so good. His kiss was hot and frantic, thrilling and impatient, *thank God,* because though she'd undoubtedly relish every single minute of a grand seduction, she simply couldn't wait that long.

With every skilled thrust of his tongue into her mouth, she heard *Now! Now! Now!* An impressive bulge nudged her belly, branded her, and her lips slid into a grateful smile. *Cocked, locked and ready to rock,* indeed Rowan thought dimly as another rush of warmth coated her folds. She clenched her feminine muscles in a vain attempt to stem the flow, but she might as well have been trying to dam the Mississippi with a kitchen sponge—it wasn't gonna happen.

He tore his mouth from hers, then trailed thorough but speedy kisses down the side of her neck, along her jaw. Rowan untangled her fingers from his hair, eagerly jerked his shirt from the waistband of his shorts, then sighed with pleasure when her hands found his bare skin.

Warm, supple and smooth.

Sweet.

A low masculine hum of pleasure hissed out of him, and his belly shuddered gratifyingly beneath her fingers. Getting beneath the shirt wasn't enough—she wanted it off. She tugged the garment over his head, then slung it over the stall door. With a soft wicked chuckle, Will grasp the hem of her tank and swiftly drew it off as well. His hot gaze fastened on her chest and she had the pleasure of watching his eyes darken further. An unsteady breath puffed past his lips as he traced the lacy edge of her bra with slightly shaking fingers.

"It clasps in the front," Rowan told him, just in case he hadn't noticed.

"How fortuitous," he murmured thickly. He slipped his fingers beneath the fastener and gave it a gentle pop. The cups sagged, baring her taut nipples to his hungry gaze. Will let go a thin breath, lifted her from the waist, and gently set her down on the vanity. Then he bent his gorgeous head and fastened his greedy mouth onto her aching peak, expertly palming the other, lest it feel neglected.

Rowan gasped with pleasure and sagged beneath the weight of the exquisite torment. He suckled, kissed, licked and ravished. His tongue blazed a trail from peak to peak, alternately around each globe, then pulled each in turn deep into his hot mouth. A steady throb built between her legs, that itchy sensation intensified deep in her womb and she hooked her legs around his thighs, trying desperately to find some sort of relief. She wanted that weighty pressure, wanted desperately to feel that hard part of him between her legs. At this point she was shameless, wasn't too proud to beg.

She reached out and scored his muscled chest—his nipples—with her nails, leaned forward and nipped his powerful shoulder, then licked the hurt away, savored the salty essence of his skin. His scent invaded her nostrils, drugged her to the point of delirium, and simply shattering into a million little pieces if he didn't finish this soon became a genuine fear.

She squirmed closer to him, let her hand drift over his belly, then boldly stroked his groin. A hot thrill snaked through her at the intimate contact. He was gloriously hard, electrifyingly huge. She slipped the button of his shorts from its closure, then felt his warm breath hiss over her nipple as she lowered his zipper. An instant later, she had him in hand, tenderly working the hot, slippery flesh over his rigid length. She ran the pad of her thumb over his wet tip, then painted his engorged head with the evidence of his desire. Will jerked, shuddered, beneath her ministrations, and a low growl of warning issued from his throat.

She felt his warm fingers against her belly, felt her shorts give way beneath his questing hands. His mouth found hers once more.

A hot probing kiss, the dizzying rasp of his tongue against hers.

She alternately lifted her hips as he tugged her shorts and panties down in agonizingly slow increments. She watched, mesmerized, as Will withdrew a condom from his wallet, then his shorts and briefs sagged to his knees and he efficiently rolled the protection into place.

She blinked drunkenly, astonished at his sheer size, and another thick warm rush of heat seeped into her weeping folds. Her nipples tingled and the air in her lungs virtually evaporated. Her neck suddenly felt too weak to support her head, and anticipation made her belly tremble violently.

Will grasped her hips, scooted her forward, then guided himself to her center. The first nudge of him between her nether lips made Rowan inhale sharply—then he smoothly slid inside her, buried every glorious inch of himself to the hilt—and she exhaled in sublime, wondrous satisfaction. The storm inside her briefly abated, seemingly in awe of the flawless perfection of this moment. It didn't matter that they were hiding in a bathroom, that her panties hung from one ankle, or that, on the other side of the door, roughly fifty unsuspecting people sat calmly eating their lunch.

Nothing mattered but him being inside her—*finally*.

Her world shifted and she clung to him, resisted the curious urge to weep. *Home, sweet home,* she thought. For no particular reason, she tried to tell herself. But she knew better. Knew that she'd never be the same.

Will expelled a harsh breath and he rested his forehead against hers, locked himself inside her. His hands came up and gently framed her face, then with a tender heart-wrenchingly sweet look, he lowered his mouth to hers once more.

One moment of tenderness in a maelstrom of mindlessness was all it took for her silly heart to melt like a pat of butter over a hot bun.

A curiously relieved laugh stuttered out of her mouth. She looped her arms around his neck, threw every ounce of passion she possessed into the kiss and simultaneously clamped her greedy muscles around him. Pleasure barbed through her, and the single wanton act was all it took to make Will forget about being tender. His palms slid down her sides, grazed the margins of her breasts, then wound around until her bottom rested in his hands. He kneaded her rump as he slid in and out of her, a hot thrilling game of seek and retreat that quickly stoked the fire raging through her blood.

A coil of tingly heat tightened in her womb and her breathing came in sharp little puffs as he upped the tempo.

Harder, faster, then harder still.

Will's breathing grew labored as well, and a fine dew of sweat glistened on his shoulders. He pumped in and out of her, a rhythmic, erotic bump and grind that made her nipples quiver and dance as a result of his frantic, manic thrusts.

Rowan couldn't get enough of him. Her hands mapped his body. His shoulders, his belly, the small of his back and, when the first sparker of beginning release detonated in her womb, she anchored them on his ass and writhed wildly against him.

Will growled low in his throat, a masculine sound of pleasure that sang in her veins.

"Will," Rowan gasped brokenly. "I need—I'm almost—"

Will increased his rhythm, pounded into her. One hand left her bottom, came around and massaged her clit. The shock of sensation rent a soundless wail from the back of her throat, and a few clever strokes later she came so hard she honestly feared she might lose consciousness. Her vision blackened around the edges, colors faded into gray, and if he hadn't held her upright, she would have undoubtedly melted into the floor.

Wave after wave of release eddied through her, sucking her under, lifting her up. Heightened sensation bolted through her with every eager spasm of the orgasm.

She heard Will's breath catch in his throat, felt him tense, then a low keening growl sounded next to her ear as three hard thrusts later, he joined her in paradise. A shock of warmth pooled against the back of her womb, sending another tingle of joy through her.

To her unreasonable delight, Will didn't immediately withdraw from her, but rather lingered between her legs. A guy too quick on the dismount was a pet peeve of hers, and she was secretly thrilled that he wasn't going to be guilty of that offense.

He braced one palm on the vanity, then tipped her chin up. His eyes sparkled with latent humor and lingering lust, and just a smidge of something else. Affection, maybe? "That was spectacular," Will murmured warmly, caressing each word with meaningful intent.

Rowan smiled. "I agree."

"Do you have plans for tonight?"

Her smile widened and hesitant joy expanded in her chest. "No," she said slowly.

Will's gaze traced the curves of her face, dropped and lingered on her lips. "Then come be with me. I want to devour you…more slowly…next time."

Mama mia. Rowan barely suppressed a shiver. She nodded, unable to form a coherent reply.

Ever so slowly, he pulled out of her, and she swallowed a wince of regret, already missing his warmth.

A sharp rap on the door interrupted her mini-pity party and her alarmed gaze flew to Will's equally shocked expression. She almost choked on a laugh.

Rowan scrambled from the vanity while Will disappeared behind the stall, presumably to remove the condom. A flush of the commode confirmed her assessment. She snagged a paper towel from the rack on the wall and quickly did a little damage control as well. "Er… someone's in here," she called loudly.

Silence, then, "Rowan, is that you?"

Rowan froze in the process of tugging her panties back up her legs. *Alexa?* She looked up and caught Will's questioning look. "It's my friend," she said quietly. "Yeah," she admitted in slightly carrying tones. She shoved her legs back into her shorts and swiftly pulled them up. "I'll, uh... I'll be out in a minute." Well, this was just great. She'd wanted Alexa to meet Will, but these were hardly ideal circumstances. Her friend, she knew, would roast her mercilessly.

"Get the lead out, would you? You've been in there *forever*. I've got to pee like a Russian racehorse and some old geezer is holed up in the men's room."

Rowan refastened her bra, snagged her shirt then dragged it over her head. She rolled her eyes. "Sorry," she called, exasperated.

"Will!"

Holy shit, Rowan thought, jumping almost out of her skin. Will's mother again. What the hell was with the screaming? she wondered.

Will jerked, startled as well and swore hotly, then patted his shorts down until he found his phone. "I'll call you back, Mom," Will growled, then cut the power to prevent her from saying anything else.

But it was too late. Though she couldn't see Alexa's face, Rowan knew beyond a shadow of a doubt that she'd heard Will's mother—hell, she wouldn't be surprised if everyone in the damned restaurant had heard her.

Sure enough, Alexa's loaded voice sounded through the door. *"Will?"* she asked, her voice rife with happy innuendo. "Rowan, why do I get the feeling that you're not alone?"

Will and Rowan shared a fatalistic look. Oh, well, Rowan thought. It wasn't like she was going to be able to walk out of the bathroom *alone*. She was busted, and truth be told, she'd rather be busted by Alexa than anyone else. She waited for Will to tuck in his shirt, then opened the door to find her friend on the other side. Alexa's twinkling, knowing gaze bounced back and forth between them and she grinned widely.

"It's your third eye," Rowan deadpanned. "I guess it's not blind after all."

"Does that mean my other prediction came true as well?" Alexa asked, her voice a study in mystery.

From the corner of her eye she watched Will's forehead wrinkle with perplexity. Rowan felt her lips twitch, rocked back on her heels. "It certainly did."

Alexa whooped delightedly, shot Will an admiring look. She considered him for a wistful moment, then her mysterious gaze found Rowan's once more. "I just made another prediction," she said softly. "Wanna hear it?"

Not in mixed company, she was sure, Rowan thought, suddenly nervous. Her stomach did a little roll. She had a grim suspicion she knew what her friend *predicted* and she wasn't ready to hear it yet, and most definitely not in front of Will.

Rowan shook her head. "I, uh… I think it'll keep."

Alexa lifted one shoulder in an innocent shrug. "Okay." She glanced at Will, then smiled and leaned forward to whisper in Rowan's ear. "Your shirt's on backward. I doubt anyone will notice that. But you might want to tell Will to close the barn door before you walk back into the dining room. *That,* as I'm sure you know, is *noticeable.*"

Unable to help herself, Rowan chuckled. Alexa disappeared into the bathroom, leaving them alone in the small hall.

"What?" Will asked. "What's so funny?"

Rowan moved in front of him, pressed him up against the wall with her body. A low hum of masculine pleasure vibrated up his throat as her hands went to the front of his shorts. She leaned forward and kissed him, ate his startled wince as she closed his zipper with a quick, telling jerk.

Rowan laughed as his mortification sunk in. He thunked his head back against the wall and swore. "Christ."

"Don't sweat it," she chuckled. "She was impressed."

"And that's supposed to make me feel better?" He passed a hand over his adorably red face.

Rowan sidled closer to him once more, lowered her voice. "Would it help to know that *I* was impressed?"

He stilled, seemingly mollified. "You were?"

"And I'm looking forward to being impressed again," she told him, leaning forward to nip at his bottom lip. Lust kindled again. "What time did you want me to come over?"

He settled his hands on her waist, doodled his thumbs on her sides. "As soon as you can."

"I'll be there," she murmured. Another wicked thrill wound through her.

And she couldn't wait.

CHAPTER ELEVEN

"I DON'T LIKE being hung up on, William," his mother chastised. "It's rude."

"I didn't mean to hang up on you, Mom. I hit a dead spot." Will shut down his computer and tidied his desk, made sure that everything was taken care of before he called it a day. For the first time in years, he was leaving early.

"At Grady's Pool Hall?" she asked incredulously. "It's less than a mile from here."

Will pulled an offhand shrug. "It happens."

She snorted indelicately, pushed off from the door frame. "Indeed it might, but that's not what happened when I called you, and I know it. If you were on a date and didn't want to talk to me, then just say so. Don't tell me you hit a dead spot."

Will glanced up. "Who said anything about being on a date?"

Her eyebrows shot up. "Well, weren't you? The whole crew was abuzz about your *extended* lunch break with the woman you've found to handle Doris's design. A woman I have yet to meet, by the way," she added pointedly, "and to my knowledge, you've never hired a single soul without getting my input first." She drew herself up. "I know that technically I'm just your secretary, Will, but I always thought..." She left the rest unsaid, waiting for the guilt to settle on his shoulders. "Ah, well. An old woman's folly, I suppose."

Oh, shit, Will thought, shifting uncomfortably. He should have anticipated this. He'd avoided the Rowan issue with his mother because, quite frankly, she knew him too well. He knew the instant she saw him with Rowan—or even heard him talk about Rowan, for that matter—the cat would be out of the bed, so to speak, and she'd start planning a guest list for a fall wedding.

Will blew out a breath, rubbed the back of his neck. "Mom, you know that you're not just my secretary. I didn't get your input on this one because there simply wasn't time." He cited Doris's impending guests and shot her a helpless look. "I stumbled into this solution and took advantage of it. End of story. If you want to meet her, come by Doris's."

She was mollified entirely too quickly for Will's comfort and her gaze turned shrewd. "Rumor has it if I wanted to meet her sooner I could come to your house tonight."

Will stifled the urge to grind his teeth. He didn't know which one of those jack-legged bastards had told her that, but come tomorrow morning, someone's ass was his. Still, when faced with an outright question, he found it too difficult to lie. "That's true."

She beamed at him. "So lunch was really a date?" she pressed like a dog with a soup bone.

Will smothered a snort, remembering those wonderful, frantic minutes in the bathroom. In the friggin' bathroom. He'd never lost control like that. Had never been swept up in an attraction so fierce that he couldn't contain himself. But he had with her. His blood heated at the mere thought and an impatient twang strummed across his nerves. "You could call it that, yes."

She sighed, evidently pleased. "Excellent. From what I hear, you and she have a lot in common."

Who the hell was running their mouth? Will wondered, irritated. Wasn't a guy allowed to have any secrets?

"Where did you meet her again?" she queried lightly. Too lightly. "I don't believe I've heard you say."

Speaking of secrets, Will thought, with a mental shudder. That was one he planned to take to his grave. He could just hear himself. *Remember that phone sex operator that Scott called, Mom? Well, she might just be the mother of your future grandchildren.*

Will stilled. Future grandchildren? he thought, suddenly shaken. A queasy feeling swelled in his gut. He'd, uh… He'd sort of made a leap there, hadn't he? One session of spectacular phone sex and a lengthy lunch holed up in the bathroom in a local pool hall having mind-blowing, soul-shattering sex did not a future wife make. Right?

Right.

Was he protesting too much? He didn't think so, and just to prove it he allowed the image of Rowan decked out in a long white gown with a garland of fresh flowers crowning that waist-length mink-colored hair to materialize in his head. The picture made his heart leap and a whirling sensation spin behind his navel. He told himself it was nausea, though he grimly suspected it might be another emotion altogether, one he wasn't anywhere near ready to explore.

Another image surfaced, a snapshot into his fictional future. In this one, she held a chubby-cheeked little girl with brown hair, leafy eyes, dimpled legs and bare feet. His upper lip grew moist.

"Son?"

Will blinked, jerked from the fantasy. "Yeah?"

"Where did you meet her?"

"Er…a mutual friend." He supposed he could call Scott a friend. Splitting hairs, he knew, but he wasn't about to tell her the truth. He'd given Rowan his word that he wouldn't share her secret, and though his mother clearly didn't believe him—and clearly didn't appreciate it—that promise extended to her as well. "Okay," he sighed resolutely. "I'm out of here."

"Out of here? B-b-but it's only f-f-four o'clock," she sputtered, whirling around as he strode past.

"I know," Will replied with exaggerated patience. "I learned how to tell time in first grade." He flashed her a smile. "Bye, Mom. I've got a date." With that parting comment, he headed for his truck.

Before he'd left Doris's this afternoon, he'd asked Rowan to bring her bathing suit and a bottle of her favorite wine, and he'd take care of the rest. Therefore a swift trip to the grocery store was in order, thus his excuse for leaving early. He also intended to get his dirty clothes out of his pantry. The thought drew a smile.

Which brought to mind *her* smile.

Which brought to mind *her* lips.

Which brought to mind *her* kiss.

Which brought to mind sex…with *her.*

Honestly, it was a vicious cycle, Will thought as a vision of her bare breasts and dewy curls leaped obligingly to mind. Tight nipples, the gentle swell of her belly, the perfect curve of her hip, and those tanned thighs wrapped around him, pulling him deeper and deeper into her heat. He let go a shaky breath.

Will had been turned on before, he'd even had great sex. But never in his life had he experienced anything remotely close to the chemistry and heat—the sheer perfection—of being with Rowan Crosswhite. When he'd finally pushed himself between her legs, he'd filled his lungs with more oxygen than they'd ever held—then she'd clenched around him and he'd promptly lost it again.

It had been the strangest sensation. The hair on the back of his neck had prickled, a hum of electricity had raced up his spine, then radiated out over his shoulders, buzzed down his arms and tingled into his fingertips.

The moment had been too rife with some unnamed something to merely let it pass, so he'd drawn her to him and kissed her again...and then he'd been lost. Lost in her sighs and kisses, lost in her heat, lost in a world where the only thing that mattered was being with her—being *inside* her.

He wanted that mindlessness again, Will thought, swallowing as a curious sensation commenced in his chest. Today had merely been an appetizer—tonight he fully intended to devour her. Every freckle, every mole, every white part, every pink part. He smiled in anticipation.

All her parts.

ROWAN FISHED her cell phone out of her purse, then punched in Will's number and waited for him to pick up. Her heart skipped a beat at the sound of his voice. "Hello."

"Hey," she said warmly. "Just wanted to let you know I'm on my way. I'm, uh, running a little late." She shifted into fourth gear, nudged the horses into action, and the purr of the motor had its usual calming effect.

"What happened?"

Rowan rolled her eyes, strummed her fingers on the steering wheel. "*Ida* happened."

His sexy chuckle sounded in her ear. "Let me guess. Another errand?"

"Her new orthopedic shoes came in today. I had to go get them for her."

"Well, look at this way." Though he was trying to be helpful, she could hear the humor in his voice. "At least it wasn't another enema or wart remover."

"In the morning I have to wax her upper lip," she said flatly.

A shocked laugh burst from his throat. "I hesitate to point this out, but she could have asked for a Brazilian, then you would have really been in trouble."

"Too true," Rowan conceded with a laugh, equally relieved and revolted. Though she grumbled, she truly didn't mind running errands for Ida. It gave her something to do to fill up her day, to keep her from thinking about being alone or cast adrift. She turned onto his road, and breathed a curious sigh of relief. Almost there. With him. Where she instinctively knew things would instantly get better.

"Where are you?" Will asked.

"A couple of miles from your house."

"Good," he murmured suggestively, "then we've got time for a quickie. Wanna hear something cool that happened to me today?"

Rowan felt a smile drift around her lips and a secret thrill whipped through her. She'd created a monster. Hell, she was game if he was. She liked shocking him, hearing those wicked words come out of those sexy lips.

In fact, playing the part of the naughty phone sex operator last night had been particularly hard, especially after her *stimulating* conversation with Will, and she grimly suspected it was only going to get harder. But she really needed the money, and it seemed impractical to quit just because she didn't enjoy it. Hell, she'd never enjoyed it. So why should now be any different?

She knew the difference—Will had made the difference.

He'd showed her what she'd been missing, which made it all the more difficult to pretend.

Furthermore, he'd made that leading little comment about her not having time for her 1-900-line anymore, and the only thing which had saved her from an awkward reply had been the timely arrival of their waitress.

Rowan knew that now that she'd gone to work for him, that he fully expected her to give up the 1-900-line. Considering that she'd cited immediate money woes and those woes were now basically nonexistent, it wasn't an illogical deduction. But just because she didn't need the money right now didn't mean that she wouldn't need it in the future. It just wasn't practical. Regrettably, she had more to consider than Will Foster's pride.

Rowan dragged her thoughts back to the conversation at hand. "Sure. What happened to you today?"

"That girl I told you about last night? We had an... interesting lunch date."

Rowan bit the corner of her lip, remembering. Warmth rushed to her core. "Oh? What did you do?"

"We had wild, mindless sex in the ladies' bathroom of a local pool hall." His voice held a strangled quality.

She let go a shuddering breath, felt the tips of her breasts tingle with remembered heat. "Sounds fun. Did you like it?"

A short burst of laughter sounded in her ear. "I more than liked it. I loved it. She rocked my world. She has the most amazing little body. Everything is tight and compact. Her breasts are a mere nod away from my mouth," he murmured, seemingly distracted. "Did I tell you that I tasted them? That the feel of her taut nipple on my tongue made me almost *explode?* That it took every ounce of willpower I owned to take care of her first, to make sure that she came. I didn't want her to think I was a lazy lover," he added.

Rowan swallowed an ironic snort. "I seriously doubt that was ever in question." There was nothing remotely lazy about Will Foster.

"Sliding into her, feeling her greedy body clenching around me was the single most amazing sensation I've ever had. Hell, we were in a bathroom—*a bathroom, dammit!*—with a roomful of people on the other side of the door, and I swear, the building could have tumbled down around me and I—" He sighed. "I wouldn't have blinked. I was too caught up in her. Lost in her."

Rowan let go a soft sigh, felt her goofy heart swell as she listened to him talk about their afternoon. About being with her. "She sounds like a lucky girl."

He chuckled, lightening the curiously tense moment. "I would hope she'd agree."

"I'm sure she would," Rowan said drolly. "Would you like to hear about my day?"

Another sexy laugh, then, "Would I ever."

"Remember that guy I told you about last night?" she murmured softly. "The one who makes me so hot my panties stay drenched when I'm around him?"

"Yes," he replied in a strangled voice. "I r-remember."

"This afternoon, he and I made it in a bathroom as well. *It was fantastic,*" she moaned appreciatively. "One minute I was sitting there calmly eating my lunch. Then I caught him looking at my mouth—looking at me as though I was the last loaf of bread on the shelf before a winter storm—and I... I just snapped. I mean, the nerve of this guy! How could he sit there and look at me like that? Literally light me up—in public, no less—and then not do anything about it? How could he just sit there and expect me to eat my burger, when I wanted to *eat* him, or better yet have him eat *me*." Rowan let go a sigh, pressed her thighs together to stem the flow of heat gathering at her center. "So I did what any pathetically horny girl would do—I excused myself into the bathroom, then I called him, and I called his sexy ass on the carpet."

"That bastard," Will teased unsteadily. "I hope you gave him what he deserved."

"Oh, no. I've just gotten started with this guy. I'm thinking some serious torture sessions are due. I want to blow him until he weeps, then ride him until he his eyes roll back in his head. I want to make him beg," she all but growled. She was so hot she could barely drive, but pulling over would only delay being with him. She couldn't bear it.

Geez, God, she did want to do all these things to him, but she honestly couldn't believe she had the nerve to say them. Would have never believed that she would say those things to a guy and mean them and, even though a part of her insisted on making him lose it as well, Rowan knew that her desire to keep the upper hand only played a small part in why she could let go with him. Why she could say the things she said. For whatever reason, she felt safe with him. Felt the chaos of her world hit a lull and she clung to the hope of that feeling.

Will swallowed audibly. "Make him pay, baby, that's all I can say. Make him pay."

Rowan grinned, swung her car into his drive. She could hear the purr of her car from his end of the line, so she knew he had to have heard her as well.

She pulled around to the back, saw Will standing next to the grill, his barbecue tongs forgotten in his hand. He looked at her and smiled, a grin that was at once hot,

happy and a wee bit stunned. She liked that, Rowan decided. Liked that she'd shocked him.

He was barefoot and shirtless, and from the damp,
slightly curly look of his hair, he'd either spent time in the
shower or the pool, probably both, she decided. He'd slung
a kitchen towel over his shoulder, and looked completely at
home and unguarded. Relaxed. Need and affection broad-
sided her, pushing a wobbly smile into place.

She shifted into Park, killed the engine, then took off
her sunglasses and grinned at him. "I'm here to collect."

He laughed, gestured toward the grill. "Can I have my
last meal first?"

What? Hadn't she made that plain? Didn't she just tell
him he could eat *her?* Rowan barely resisted the urge to
tell him. Honestly, this scandalous behavior was coming
a bit too easily to her for comfort.

She heaved an exaggerated long-suffering sigh, snagged
the wine and climbed out of the car. "I suppose." She
disconnected, then joined him by the grill and sniffed
appreciatively. "Something smells good."

Will flipped the steaks over. "I picked up a couple of
filets on my way home. How do you like yours?"

"Medium rare."

"Ah," he sighed. "A woman after my own heart."

"Is there anything I can do to help?"

"You could pour us a glass of wine." He nodded
toward the table. "Glasses are over there, as well as a
corkscrew."

Rowan grinned, arched a brow. "You're just a regular
Boy Scout, aren't you?"

His honey gaze tangled with hers and a corner of his
sexy mouth tucked into a grin. "Always prepared."

Well, he'd certainly prepared things this evening, Rowan
thought, secretly pleased for all the trouble he'd apparently

gone to on her behalf. He'd set a beautiful table, complete with candlelight, linen napkins and a bouquet of his prized roses. Honestly, she would have been just as happy with a paper plate and a Dixie cup, but this was unexpectedly... nice.

Will transferred the steaks onto a platter and brought them over to the table. "Okay. We're ready."

Rowan dressed her salad. "Thanks," she told him. "This looks wonderful."

"You know, I've been thinking," Will began in that too light tone that usually preceded an awkward conversation. "In light of how fast our relationship has progressed to an intimate level, I uh...really don't know that much about you."

She speared a tomato wedge and dragged it through her dressing, then popped it into her mouth. Rowan chewed thoughtfully, considered him. This was true, she decided. Though she honestly felt like she'd known him forever, other than his name, his profession, his respect for the past, for the soil and every hair, freckle and mole on his body, she really didn't know him at all. She resisted the urge to smile.

Rowan took her time swallowing. "What would you like to know?"

"I guess I could sit here and ask about family, friends, dreams, goals and desires—" Will smiled "—but what I really want to know is this—why aren't you married yet?"

She blinked. "Come again?"

Will exhaled a mighty breath. "You're wonderful," he explained. "You're smart, bright and funny. Sexy as hell," he added with an implied growl. "Why hasn't somebody snatched you up yet? I find it hard to believe no one's asked."

Flattered, Rowan felt the warmth of the compliment down to her little toes. She shot him a droll look. "Someone asked," she admitted.

"And you said no?"

"No," she sighed. "I stupidly said yes."

A puzzled line emerged between his brows and he opened his mouth to ask the obvious question. "But—"

"I called it off."

"Because..." he prodded expectantly when she didn't elaborate.

God, this was so embarrassing. Logic told her that it hadn't been her fault that Mark had cheated, but there was still a small part of her that held on to insecurities, that held on to was-I-woman-enough? worries and all that baggage.

Rowan poked her tongue into her cheek and smiled ruefully. "Because I caught him in bed with another woman. Good enough reason, wouldn't you say?"

Will nodded, winced. "Yeah, I'd say so."

Rowan slouched back in her chair, took a sip of wine and waited for the alcohol to dull her senses. "Do you know what I really regret about all that mess?"

He shook his head, silently encouraging her.

Rowan's gaze slid to her car, felt her eyes narrow into little pissed-off slits. "I let that cheating bastard drive my car. My dad told me when he gave it to me that any guy that would *ask* to drive it wasn't worthy of my attention, to basically kick his ass to the curb."

"Sounds like good advice."

Rowan nodded. "I used that strategy with every guy I dated—I *never* let any guy drive my car—right up until Mark." She chuckled grimly. "He slid right under my radar."

"It can happen," Will told her.

Rowan looked up, her senses going on point. "Since we're sharing, is that the voice of experience?"

He worked a kink out of his shoulders and a dry bark of laughter erupted from his throat. "Oh, hell, yeah."

"What happened?"

His gaze drifted to hers, held it. "Same scenario, but we weren't engaged. She made a complete fool of me."

"I find that hard to believe."

Will laughed without humor. "So do I, now."

Her gaze turned inward. "Why does it always have to be so hard, I wonder? Finding the right person? Other people do it and make it look easy."

He hesitated. "I don't think it's ever easy."

"Okay," she qualified. "Maybe easy's not the right word. But they make it work." She cast him a glance, traced the smooth lines of his face and felt a muddled heat stir in her loins. Her nipples tingled and a bud of need bloomed in her belly. "Is your mother right, Will?" she asked softly. "Are you lonely?"

She was, though she was loath to admit it. For all her independent-woman bravado, there were times when she thought if she spent another minute in her own company she'd scream. Most of the time she was content, but some secret source of information—intuition, maybe?—told her that being content now would never be good enough.

Not after Will Foster.

That sticky-honey gaze found hers and held. "Sometimes," he admitted. Then he leaned forward, bracketed her face with his big, warm hands, forcing a soft sigh from her mouth, and kissed her gently. "But not now," he whispered. "Not while I'm with you."

Her either, Rowan decided dimly.
Not right now.
And definitely not tonight.

CHAPTER TWELVE

NOT WHILE I'M WITH YOU.

Truer words had never been spoken, Will thought as he lowered his mouth to hers, felt her talented fingers slide into his hair. Right up until this very minute he would have denied that he was ever lonely, but the fact was, he'd been lonely all along and had been simply too stubborn or too blind—hell, most likely both—to see it.

Until Rowan, he'd had no frame of reference, no way to put the sentiment in context. The whole suffocating feeling, the fish-out-of-water panic—that had been his body's way of telling him what his mind already knew, which was, he'd be lonely without her.

He needed her.

Thankfully for Will, at the moment one need superseded another, blotted out complicated thoughts of feelings and fears.

He simply wanted to feel.

Wanted to feel her bare skin beneath his palms, her greedy hands stroking his body. Wanted to take her to bed and love her properly.

He tore his mouth away from hers. "Let's go inside," he suggested softly.

She nodded wordlessly. Those gorgeous green eyes had darkened into a shade of mountain fern and glistened with desire so fierce and strong it was simply breathtaking. He laced his fingers through hers, led her silently through the house and into his bedroom.

She looked out his French doors into his rose garden and a knowing smile curled her lush lips, lightened the mood between them.

Will quirked a brow. "What?"

"I was right," she murmured.

"Right about what?"

"Your garden. I thought you'd be able to access it from your bedroom." She sighed wistfully. "It's even prettier from in here."

"You can say that again," Will told her, his voice inexplicably low.

He watched her lips curl into a droll smile and she sidled toward him. "Why do I get the feeling we're talking about two completely different things?"

"Because—and I think I've told you this before—you're very perceptive." He encircled her waist with his arms, smiled down at her, let his gaze purposely caress her lips. "In fact, I think that if you really put your mind to it you could divine what I'm thinking right now."

She laughed. "You mean have a psychic moment?"

He nodded. "Exactly."

Her gaze turned a smidge calculating and something about her wicked smile made him distinctly uneasy. She shrugged lightly. "I'll give it my best shot. I should probably touch something of yours if it's going to work properly." She leaned forward and licked the hollow of his throat, pulling a hiss from between his suddenly clenched teeth.

She smiled up at him, the she-devil, and a startled laugh broke up in his throat.

"Yeah, I think that helped," she told him. "I had a small vision." Her gaze drifted over his chest and she slipped her fingers into the waistband of his trunks. "But I should probably do it again just so that I can make sure I know what I'm talking about. I'd uh…hate to be accused of being a fraud."

She leaned forward and this time her talented tongue darted out and laved his nipple. Will winced and his dick jerked hard against her belly.

Another she-devil grin claimed her lips. "Yes, I think I definitely have a handle on it now."

He strangled on a laugh. He'd give her something to get a handle on, Will thought. He bent his head, found her mouth and then began to slowly propel her toward the bed. He kissed her hard and deep, slow and easy. God, he could kiss her forever, Will thought dimly. He slid his tongue along hers, pulled at it creating a delicious suction between their mouths, which he longed to mimic in their lower extremities.

The backs of her knees hit the edge of the mattress and, with a groan of delight, she sagged onto the bed. Will eagerly followed her down. He'd enjoyed every minute of the first time they'd made love. It had been hot and frantic, mindless and wanton. Fantastic. But he tended to be a little fastidious when it came to making love. He liked to nurture and tease, coax and coddle a bloom of release from a woman. Liked to take his time.

Rowan had blossomed for him this afternoon at the pool hall—*God had she ever*—but he suspected that she was like one of those rare night-blooming flowers and he couldn't wait to see her in all her glory.

He pulled away from her mouth, nuzzled her ear, then licked a slow path down the side of her neck. She shuddered beneath him, a wordless gesture of praise and he smiled against her. "You smell nice," Will murmured. "Like apples and daisies." Her belly shook as his fingers tugged at the hem of her shirt. "I wonder what you smell like here?" he asked, then bent his head and ran the tip of his tongue around the rim of her belly button. Gratifyingly, another shiver shook her.

Will nudged her shirt up farther, treated a couple of ribs to the same treatment. She whimpered, arched her back up off the bed, begging for a kiss of another sort. Will edged up her body, drew the garment over her head, cast it aside with a careless flick of his wrist, then let his gaze drift over her womanly frame. Soft mounds, feminine belly, dainty waist. His mouth parched, then watered. Her womanly scent invaded his nostrils, curled around his senses and suddenly, taking his time, plotting his next move like a road trip didn't seem quite so important.

He popped her bra open once more, then eagerly fastened his mouth upon her breast. Rowan arched again, pushing the tender globe further into his mouth. He hummed with pleasure, ate her up. Her hands were all over him—his back, his shoulders, in his hair. It was as though he'd tripped a secret button, one that sent her wild, and he found it inexplicably—incredibly—arousing. He sucked harder, trailed his fingers over her belly, then took advantage of the extra room beneath her waistband when another startled inhalation deflated her tummy.

She stilled, then squirmed when his fingers brushed her curls. She gasped, then her own fingers made a determined trail to his shorts and she palmed him through the fabric, rubbed determinedly against him. "Oh, Will. I can't— I need— *Could you please hurry up?*"

He laughed. Moved to the other breast. Dragged a finger over her engorged clit. "Are we punching a time clock?"

"No," she growled, rocking suggestively beneath him.

"But I'm burning up. You have to do something. I can't— I can't take it."

Will scooted down between her legs and dragged her shorts and panties over her hips. They joined her shirt and bra on the floor. He glanced at them and an evil little impulse took hold. He pretended to move away from her.

She propped herself up on her elbows. "Where are you going?" she asked incredulously.

"To put those in the dirty clothes hamper. I know how you hate laundry on the floor."

A stuttered laugh fizzed up her throat and her eyes widened in outrage. "Oh, you just wait." Her head sagged against the bed. "I am *so* going to get you."

Will chuckled. "Bring it on, badass," he goaded. "I'm ready whenever you are."

Her head popped back up and a martial glint suddenly sparked in her gaze. He realized at once that he'd made a mistake. He shouldn't have goaded her, shouldn't have teased her. But the power was simply intoxicating. It was the first time in his life he'd ever had this sort of control over a woman and he supposed he'd let it go to his head. It was an appalling abuse of his power, Will decided, and he should be ashamed. He grinned.

Should be...but he wasn't.

"Take those shorts off and we'll see who's the badass," Rowan told him.

He'd made a tactical error, but pride would not let him back down. Besides, he was perversely looking forward to this little game. He stood, shucked his trunks and kicked them aside. Her eyes dropped to his dick, she blinked slowly as though she'd had a little too much to drink, then she licked her lips.

"Come here." She fired the words at him like bullets, short and succinct, and he felt them lodge in his groin.

Will joined her on the bed. She sat up, rolled him onto his back then very determinedly began to lick him in the same thought-shattering, dick-provoking way he'd licked her. His nipples, his ribs, his belly button. Then—and though he'd been expecting it—looking forward to it, even—she still managed to pull a startled hiss from him when she took him in hand.

She worked him up and down, slowly, tenderly, grazed the sides of his stiff shaft. "I've been thinking about this all day," she told him, her voice foggy, sultry, that near-whisper that never failed to set him off. "Thinking about holding you, licking you—" she turned the thought into action, putting the entire length of his throbbing dick into her hot mouth "—having you deep inside of me. Then out of me. Then inside me." She worked him up and down, chasing her hand with her mouth, pulling him deeper and deeper with each steady suck.

Will gritted his teeth against the onslaught, locked his thighs to keep from pumping himself in and out of her mouth. He lay there, listened to her greedy mouth, jerked beneath her talented tongue until he thought for sure he'd explode.

"Enough," Will finally growled, unable to take any-more. Besides, he had something to prove. That he could give as well as he could take. He nudged Rowan onto her back, slid down her belly, parted her curls, then fastened his mouth onto her core.

She gasped, jerked beneath his mouth.

Will lapped at the tiny nub hidden at the crest of her sex, then licked a trail farther down, and pushed his tongue deeply inside her, then flicked it as fast as he could. She bucked beneath him, cried out, but Will refused to stop. He'd told her he wanted to sip up her release and he wasn't moving out from between her legs until he'd lapped up every last drop of it. He continued to flutter his tongue inside her, then worked a finger against her clit, and pressed the pad of his thumb ever so gently against the tight rosebud of her bottom.

It was a risky move, he knew, but one that usually paid off. Rowan momentarily stilled, evidently unsure, but then sensation took over and she went *wild*. She bucked frantically beneath him. Her head thrashed from side to side, arched off the bed. Every muscle in her body went rigid.

"Oh, God," she screamed, her voice a long, guttural wail of release.

He felt her spasm around his tongue, laved up every bit of the sweet release. Unable to stand another minute outside of her body, Will snagged a condom from his bedside drawer, tore into the packet and quickly rolled it into place. She was still recovering when he moved back between her legs.

Pink exertion stained her cheeks. Her breathing was heavy, labored, and she flung an arm over her forehead. "That was— I never—" She smiled at him, seemingly impressed. "There are no words."

Will grinned. "I've got a couple."

"Oh?"

"Open up." And with that he sank into her. Pulled in a satisfying breath as he filled his lungs once more. He looked down and his gaze found hers. Saw wonder, need, happiness and something else, something just beyond his understanding. Sound receded once more and his chest filled with a light, fluttery feeling he'd never experienced before. Something sharp and sweet and akin to awe.

And in a moment of blind comprehending panic he realized what it was—he was falling in love with her. The idea momentarily paralyzed him. In love? he thought wildly. He couldn't be in love? He'd just met her. Barely knew her. How the hell could he be in love?

Rowan rocked suggestively beneath him, smiled up at him. *Dark brown hair fanned over a white pillow, mossy-green eyes, adorable dimple.* She was the picture of perfection. Flushed and lush. His.

He returned her grin, pushed himself more deeply inside her. Ah hell, so what if he'd only known her a few days. Semantics, Will told himself. Screw it. He wanted her. Would always want her.

"YOU CAN STAY, you know," Will told her hours later, after bouts of sex, then rest and then more sex. His voice sounded kind of rusty, unaccustomed to making the offer, and she found herself inexplicably touched.

But something had happened to her tonight, and she knew that if she didn't leave and get some much-needed perspective, she'd lose her tentative grasp on reality as she knew it and she'd be lost. To what, she wasn't quite sure yet. But the knowledge was here all the same.

Curiously, if they'd been at her house, she suspected that she wouldn't have minded spending the night in his arms. Would love to wake up with him.

But being here, in this house, felt too much like a dream she'd wanted for entirely too long—one she typically avoided—and by spending the night, she was afraid she'd set herself up for something that she'd never have. Ridiculous? Probably. But self-preservation had kicked in and rationale was no match for fight-or-flight.

She was spooked.

She was having feelings for Will Foster that simply defied reason when one considered how long they'd known each other. She'd been utterly overjoyed when he'd pulled that little thumb trick, had come until she thought her back would break beneath the strain of release.

But then he'd pushed into her, he'd stilled, the most curiously wondering look had come over his face...and something had happened in her chest. A light winging sensation had flitted from lung to lung, then pushed up her throat, forcing a small disbelieving laugh that had rung too much like an epiphany she didn't dare acknowledge, at least until she was in the relative safety of her own bed.

Will doodled a figure-eight on her upper arm, the motion at once erotic and lulling. "What do you say?"

Rowan winced. "I'd better pass. I look out for Ida, and I really wouldn't feel comfortable being away overnight without letting someone know."

That, too, was the truth. Not to mention she'd have to get in a couple of hours work. Rowan swallowed a dejected sigh. Listening to guys tug on their dongs after she'd just had this amazing, back-clawing sex was *not* what she wanted to do at all, but there it was. Her job. Her extra income. Her dwindling student loan debt and more assurance that she'd never have to sponge off her parents. Sometimes being a rational, practical adult truly sucked.

Will let go a small breath, seemed to accept her excuse for what it was. "Sure. I understand."

"I appreciate the offer, though." She curled closer to him, pressed a lingering kiss on his chest. "I can tell that's not an offer you extend frequently and I'm—" Rowan struggled to find the right word "—flattered."

"Well, you should be," he said, seemingly pacified. She lifted her head and watched him scowl adorably. His hair was mussed and the beginning of a nice hickey had formed beneath his collarbone. "I've never asked anyone to spend the night here before."

Rowan didn't move. "Never?"

He shook his head. "Never."

She waited a beat and when he didn't elaborate, she decided to press him.

"Why not?"

What made her so special? she wanted to know. Wanted him to tell her. He'd pulled the No Fishing sign down off the pond, so he couldn't very well complain if she cast her line out for a compliment or two.

Will hesitated, seemed to be grappling with some momentous decision. Finally, he expelled a breath, then rolled to face her. "Look, Rowan. I'm just going to lay it all out on the line here, okay?" His lips slid into a helpless smile and there was a nervous quality to that sexy baritone she'd never heard before. "It's the only way I know how to be. I say what I mean, I mean what I say. I detest games. I hate being manipulated."

She nodded. Those were excellent qualities, and quite honestly, they sounded reminiscent of many of her own principles.

"The reason that I've never asked anyone to spend the night here is because I've never trusted anyone enough to fall asleep beside them." His matter-of-fact gaze held hers. "I've known you for just a few days, and I felt it with you *instantly*." He reached out, slid a finger down the slope of her cheek. "I don't know what it is about you, but… Well, you just do it for me." His eyes were warm and sticky, drawing her to him. "I think about you all the time. I've been fascinated by you from the first moment I heard your voice." A rueful laugh bubbled up his throat. "I keep a perpetual hard-on. Hell, we had sex in a friggin' *bathroom* today. I've never had in-public sex, or phone sex. Those were firsts, I can assure you. There's a level of intensity, of trust that I can't explain, that I want to explore. If I'm scaring you, then I'm sorry. That's not my intention.

I just— I just want you to know the way I feel, that this is not some wild-wind fling. I want to spend more time with you, see where this goes. I want to follow where it leads, and honestly—" he shrugged lightly, offered another crooked smile "—I've got a good feeling about it. I also want you to stop having phone sex with other guys. I know I don't have a right, that it sounds presumptuous and bossy." He blew out a breath. "But there it is. I can't help it. The very idea makes me want to put my fist through a wall."

Wow, Rowan thought, literally blown away. She was touched, thrilled, ecstatic and flattered all at once. Delight mushroomed in her chest. She was also surprised at his honestly. Though really she had no reason to be. Everything about their relationship had been astonishingly frank. Their racy phone conversations speedily leaped to mind. It only made sense that a certain level of comfort had been achieved early on, otherwise they would have never progressed with such alarming rapidity. And they definitely had.

His smile slipped a fraction. "Come on, Rowan. Don't leave me hangin'. What do you think?"

Rowan cleared her throat, did her best to search for the right words. Finally, she found one that would sum everything he'd said up nicely, and which once again neatly avoided the phone sex issue. She felt her lips form a tentative smile, traced his heartbreakingly handsome face with her gaze. Hope sprouted in her breast. "Ditto."

CHAPTER THIRTEEN

"WELL, DORIS. What do you think so far?"

They were T-minus three days and counting. Rowan had worked tirelessly on Doris's garden, so much so that he'd begun to notice dark smudges beneath her eyes. Of course, he was probably partially to blame for that as well, Will thought with a small grin.

Though she'd still not spent the entire night with him, he'd nevertheless kept her up late over the past week and a half. While he didn't completely buy the Ida-excuse, Will knew better than to press her. Things were going too damned great and he didn't want to do anything to rock the boat. Couldn't risk it.

Instead, he'd *adjusted*—married friends had explained the merit of adjusting—and though he knew it was wrong, he couldn't help but be proud of himself, because, quite frankly, adjustments of any sort seemed contrary to his nature. He made decisions, everyone else fell in line.

Nevertheless, to be more accommodating—because he was such a sweet person and had no ulterior motive hidden in his selfish little heart—he'd left his own bed and spent several nights with her—every night that she'd asked as a matter of fact.

To his eternal mortification, he waited with bated breath every evening to see if she'd invite him to stay. He'd learned that there was no rhyme or reason to her decision and reading her mood was pointless. She was always happy to see him, always eager to share her bed... just not always for the night.

Her mattress wasn't as comfortable as his, but having her sweet bottom snugged against his groin and her delightful breast in his hand while he slept more than made up for it. If Will had ever been happier, he couldn't recall it. His gaze slid to the author of his present joy. She was across the lawn, hanging another one of her whirligig pieces, which Doris had picked out, on a newly planted weeping willow tree.

She'd twisted her long hair into a big, messy bun and had anchored it to the back of her head with a couple of chopsticks. Will frowned. At least, he supposed they were chopsticks, but hell who knew? He didn't keep up with women's hair fashions. All he knew was that he loved her hair. He let go an unsteady breath.

Particularly when she was balancing on his dick, with her neck arched back where it brushed the tops of his thighs.

Or when she leaned forward and kissed him, and it formed a veil around the side of his face.

Or when it slithered coolly over his chest. A hell of an aphrodisiac, her hair, Will thought with a silent sigh.

"Will?" Doris said, her exasperated tone indicating that she'd tried unsuccessfully to garner his attention. She twinkled her fingers in his face. *"Will."*

He blinked. "Er...sorry. Yes, Doris?"

"I said that I'm in love with my garden, and—" her faded blue eyes twinkled with perceptive humor "—if I'm not sadly mistaken, you're in love with someone *in* my garden," she added with a wry smile.

There was that phrase again, Will thought.

In love.

Truth be told, it had strolled in and out of his brain

several times recently, at the most curious moments. Last week, he'd watched her accidentally smear dirt on her face while transplanting a begonia, and a wave of affection had hit him so hard a lump had inexplicably formed in his throat.

Then today, he'd caught her chewing her nail, a thoughtful frown worrying her brow as she tried to figure out exactly where to place Doris's patio set, and the same unnerving sensation had taken hold. Something warm and light had moved into his chest, pushed into his throat, forced him to swallow.

It was the little things, Will realized now. Those small, insignificant little details that somehow added up until he knew he had the perfect person. The perfect partner.

Will shot Doris a look, didn't bother trying to deny it. He shrugged. "What can I say? She's one helluva woman."

Doris readily agreed. "She's fantastic, Will. She suits you. And she's tremendously talented. I think she could bring some much-needed whimsy to your business. Not everybody likes traditional landscaping. Look at me," she offered lightly, as though she hadn't been the bane of his professional existence for three *excruciating* years. "I'm the perfect example."

Will muffled a snort, inclined his head. He shifted, pushed a hand through his hair.

"What does your mother think about her?"

"Mom loves her, thinks she's the greatest thing since sliced bread."

Of course she would, Will thought, because just as he'd predicted his mother had taken one look at them together and deduced the obvious. She'd welcomed Rowan as part of the family without the smallest hesitation, and just yesterday he'd caught her on the phone with a friend who worked at Sylvia Gardens discussing available dates for the Chester-Hollings House, a popular wedding spot in downtown Jackson.

Truth be told, he'd always imagined getting married at the botanical garden. It was gorgeous, a favorite haunt of his. He'd donated countless hours to helping maintain it. Cram-packed with hundreds of naturalized bulbs and perennials, azaleas, camellias and daylilies, the garden changed dramatically from season to season, and in certain grottos, from sunrise to sunset even. Hundreds of songbirds claimed sanctuary there, making it a gorgeous place to hold a wedding.

Rowan strolled over to stand beside him, wiped a hand across her brow, inadvertently streaking dirt across her face. Unable to help himself, he smiled as affection welled within him, then slung an arm over her shoulder, and tugged her closer to him. "You've done a fantastic job," he told her, making sure that she heard the admiration in his tone.

In fact, in appreciation, he'd already planned a special celebration for the conclusion of Doris's project. In addition to wining and dining her, great sex and hopefully more great sex, Will intended to ask her to come to work with him permanently. Doris was right. Rowan had a lot to offer and his company would undoubtedly flourish as a result of her expertise. Foster's Landscape Design needed her, almost as desperately as he did.

"Thanks," Rowan murmured. Her assessing gaze scanned the yard and he had the privilege of watching pride slowly dawn in those gorgeous green eyes, watched her shoulders sag with the accomplishment of a job well done. She'd literally transformed Doris's backyard and it had turned out so much better than either one of them had hoped for. One thing was for certain, his satisfaction-guaranteed record was definitely safe...even if his heart wasn't.

"I was just telling Will here that he should consider—"

"—taking you to lunch," Will finished with a telling glare at Doris. Damn. Couldn't he have a single secret? He nudged her toward his truck. "You are hungry, right?"

Her eyes twinkled. "I could eat. I'm in the mood for something...salty but sweet," she finished, her voice loaded with innuendo.

Will knew exactly what she was talking about and the mere knowledge engulfed his loins in a flash-fire of heat. The image of her lips wrapped around his rod, sucking him until he came hard materialized behind his lids, instantly pushing his dick up behind his zipper.

Will let go a stuttering breath. "I think a trip to the pool hall's in order."

Rowan grinned and her eyes twinkled with equal amounts of heat and humor. "Ah...another psychic deduction."

"I'M NOT SO SURE about this," Rowan said hesitantly as Will fastened a blindfold over her eyes.

"What's there not to be sure of? You trust me, don't you?"

Implicitly, Rowan thought. She truly did. Didn't even have to think about it.

The past couple of weeks with Will had been the most memorable—most pleasurable—of her life. Simply being with him, feeling him unexpectedly sliding his hand into hers, or a tender kiss on her cheek, not to mention those more intimate moments—feeling him inside her, the frantic race for release when nothing existed beyond the exquisite sensation of their joined bodies—had to be the most incredible thing a girl could ever ask for. Did she trust him? Oh, she more than trusted him.

At some point, and she didn't know when precisely, she'd fallen head over heels in love with him.

The idea was singularly terrifying and if she didn't suspect that he felt every bit as strongly for her, she'd have undoubtedly headed for higher ground already. But there was something inexplicably sweet about the way he looked at her, a softer emotion she so desperately wanted to trust, to believe in.

Unfortunately, there was a small part of her that couldn't quite surrender to the feeling, and that part kept her from doing the one thing she knew he wanted her to do—spend the night. The issue would probably come up again this evening, and though she knew Will wouldn't press her, she dreaded it all the same.

She knew that he didn't understand her reluctance, knew that he'd compromised by coming and spending the night with her, but Rowan also knew that one night in this old farmhouse would be all it took for her to be firmly—irrevocably—attached to him and that happily ever after dream that had become brighter and brighter with every moment that she spent with him.

His house had felt curiously like home from the instant she'd walked in the door—hell, she'd started redecorating within sixty seconds of crossing the threshold—and every additional minute spent under his roof, in his yard—with him—made her want it all the more keenly. She had to hang on to some sort of perspective and the only way she knew to maintain that was to go home and climb into her own bed. Crazy? Delusional? Insane? All of the above, but she didn't know what else to do.

She let him make love to her, she relished every second

that they spent together, then she went home and stepped back into reality—a lonely bed and phone sex.

Quite honestly, she could face the lonely bed more easily than she could face her 1-900-line. Keeping that up had gotten increasingly harder. It had always been a quick way to make a buck, had never been anything more than a job, but now that she had some firsthand experience with the genuine article... Well, suffice it to say the very idea of pretending made her ill. And though she'd managed to avoid answering his questions about it, Rowan knew that he assumed that she'd quit. She'd made it a point to hide it from him, which she knew in her heart of hearts was wrong. Anything that she couldn't share didn't belong in their relationship. Which was why she'd called the phone company today and arranged to have the line disconnected at the end of the month. It was paid for until then.

Did she need the money? Yes. She could list a dozen plausible reasons why she could keep it, but only one reason to let it go—*Will*—and that one was enough. If she didn't get called back to school in the fall, then she'd simply find something else. Rowan smiled. Last she heard there was an opening at the Bag-A-Bargain. She'd rather work there for less money than have this funky sense of dishonesty hovering between them.

"Ah, I see that smile," Will told her. "I knew you'd come around. Careful now, watch your step." Will led her down a pair of steps and the sweet scent of roses instantly assailed her senses. So they were in his rose garden. Interesting.

"Tell me again what we're doing," Rowan asked, intrigued.

"We're playing a kinky little game I like to call Name That Smell. It involves a little light bondage and for every scent you correctly name, you get a reward." He drew her to a stop and let go a deep breath. "But first you have to get naked."

Rowan laughed out loud. "Light bondage? I don't remember agreeing to bondage."

"Oh, but you did. This afternoon when we were in the bathroom at Grady's again, I distinctly remember you telling me that I could have anything I wanted if I would just hurry up and fu—"

"Right," Rowan interrupted him, her face flushing with remembered heat and humiliation. She couldn't believe she'd said that, couldn't believe that he'd had her so damned desperate that she'd agreed to give him anything he wanted so long as he'd simply fill her up, put her out of her misery.

Though she couldn't see him, she knew beyond a shadow of a doubt that he was grinning from ear to ear. "You're enjoying this entirely too much, Will."

He laughed. "What?" he asked innocently. "You were the one who said—"

"I know what I said," she interrupted. "I'm here and I'm ready."

"Willing, maybe," Will qualified. She felt him sidle closer to her, felt his fingers tug at the hem of her shirt. "But I don't know about ready. Luckily, I can help you with that."

A laugh stuttered out of her. "Oh, I'll just bet you can."

"Now, onto that naked part I told you about." She felt him move in behind her, draw her shirt up over her head. Her bare back landed again his bare chest, pushing a sizzling sigh from between her lips.

Rowan gasped. "When did you get naked?"

"I've been shedding clothes all the way out here." He

paused. "In fact, I should probably go pick them up and put them in the hamper."

"Don't you dare," Rowan growled with a laugh.

Will chuckled, the wretch. "You're right." His hands slid up over her sides, came around and cupped her breasts through her bra. She sagged against him, let her head fall back on his shoulder. An erotic little thrill moved through her. Curiously, the blindfold heightened her other senses. The feel of his skin, the perfumed scent in the air. He popped the closure, freeing her nipples to the night, to his warm, skilled touch, then thumbed her, pulling another pleased sigh from between her smiling lips. "I've been thinking about this all day," he told her, his voice husky with desire. "Thinking about the moonlight against your naked skin and the scent of roses while I love you."

His hands slid down her belly, unfastened her shorts and ever so slowly, pushed them over her hips. Her wet panties swiftly followed. "God, you're beautiful. I know I've told you before, but I just can't say it enough. I look at you and...and sometimes I can't breathe."

Her heart warmed at the sincere compliment, along with other areas of her body. "I know that feeling," she told him. "It happens to me quite frequently when I look at you as well." And it did. He, too, was beautiful, just in a different way.

Will threaded his fingers through hers, tugged her deeper into his garden room, then helped her lie down on what she could only assume was a mattress...covered with rose petals. A smile inexplicably formed on her lips. A warm wall of hard male flesh moved into place beside her.

"Trite, I know," he whispered, sliding a petal slowly down her belly. "But it's always been a fantasy of mine."

Hers, too, and she didn't care that it was trite. He'd done it for her, which made it incredibly special. "Mine, too," Rowan confessed. She rolled toward him, slid her arm around his waist and licked the hollow of his throat. "I'm…touched."

"Not nearly as much as you're about to be," Will warned with a sexy chuckle. "Which brings me to the light bondage point of our evening." She felt him move, evidently reaching for something, and the next instant, a vine of some sort looped around one of her wrists.

Rowan gasped. "What are you doing?"

"Weren't you listening? I'm tying you up. Your hands are…distracting. I want to touch you. Lick you. Kiss you. And you have to lie back and take it."

Oh, well, in that case… Rowan offered her other wrist up and chuckled. "Am I supposed to argue?"

"A token protest would be nice."

"Will, please," Rowan pleaded, stifling a laugh. "Please don't lick me, kiss me, worship me and make me lie back and take it. It's a torture I can't bear."

He chuckled, attached one wrist to the other. "Smart-ass."

"Hey, you're the one who made the rules. I'm simply going to enjoy them. What are you tying me up with?" A vine of some sort, but she couldn't tell which kind.

"Ivy," Will told her, finishing it up. "You're lying in a bed of rose petals, bound with ivy, and completely at my mercy," he added. His mouth latched onto her breast, effectively pulling the air from her lungs. "What have you got to say about that?"

She laughed again. "Please don't throw me in the brier patch."

She felt a bloom of some sort drift over her belly, do a lazy figure eight around the globes of her breasts and a sigh eddied out of her mouth. She melted into the mattress, fully prepared to take this scene to whatever level he wanted. "Ah," Rowan sighed. "That feels nice."

"I've been thinking about doing this," he confided, his voice a decadent rumble. "Thinking about painting your body with flowers."

A steady throb commenced between her legs. "How about painting my body with kisses?"

"In time," he murmured, dragging the bloom over her thigh, then behind the bend of her knee, over the top of her foot. The delicate flower made the return trek, brushed her curls, then her nether lips, and another sibilant sigh hissed past her lips as sensation bolted through her. Her nipples budded even tighter, tingled. He was priming her, Rowan realized, purposely dragging out the tension, dallying because he knew it drove her wild.

"Will," she murmured, a desperate tone in her voice that she recognized, knew he recognized as well.

"Yes?" She heard the smile in his voice, the triumph.

Rowan could have ranted and raved, could have cursed and begged—that's what she'd done this afternoon, what had put her in this position in the first place. The sheer unadulterated truth had worked before—seemed to be the only way they could communicate—so she opted for honesty.

"I need you." A simple entreaty, the whole truth.

He stilled, she could feel it, could feel the very atmosphere around them change. The night sounds became sharper, the scent keener, and her body literally vibrated with a need so intense, an emotion so true that she felt her eyes water behind the blindfold. She loved their sexy play, loved every instant of every moment they'd been together. But tonight, she wanted something different.

Wanted to strip down barriers and revel in honest love-making. Wanted to lend truth to an act that she knew she couldn't share with another soul.

She felt Will's fingers at her wrists, felt the bonds give way and sag. Then, very gently, he pushed the blindfold away from her eyes. Will's handsome face loomed instantly into view. The pad of his thumb skimmed her bottom lip and those gorgeous honey eyes were rife with emotion, with a quiet intensity and understanding that made her want to weep. "I need you, too."

She looped her hands around his neck and lowered her voice. "Then love me. Just love me."

"I do, Rowan," he murmured softly.

Then he did.

CHAPTER FOURTEEN

WILL DISCONNECTED, clipped his phone back onto his shorts, then hurriedly slid behind the wheel of his truck. It was a little late to be making sure that their reservations were a go, but Will hadn't had time to check in with his mom. Things had been too crazy.

They'd finished up in Doris's yard today—she'd been thrilled, ecstatic, over the moon and this time the sentiment seemed to have stuck. She'd been beyond pleased with the way things had turned out, so much so that she'd added a sizable bonus to her already hefty check.

Will looked forward to giving it to Rowan—she'd earned it, after all—and he planned to hand it over, then offer her a permanent job. He also knew he'd be asking her another significant question in the not-too-distant future as well.

When she'd told him that she needed him the night before last, it was as though she'd inadvertently set the hook and reeled him in. He'd literally felt it—felt the bite, the jerk and the subsequent fall. He might have worried about it, too, had it not been for one thing.

She'd spent the night.

In his rose garden, under a blanket of stars and a hundred-year old quilt, utterly, deliciously naked, snuggled against him as though nothing else mattered in the world, so long as they could breathe the same air. And, though he couldn't be completely certain because the idea that he'd fallen in love—had actually trusted someone enough to make that leap—had just about fried his brain, he grimly suspected that he'd told her that he loved her.

In fact, was almost certain of it, and he imagined that confession was no small part of the reason she'd stayed with him. Whatever the reason, Will could only be grateful. She'd stayed with him every night since and he wanted her to stay every night from here on out. He wanted to be with her all the time, hated every second they were apart, and anticipated the time he knew they'd be together with the sort of reverent, expectant joy that could only be attributed to being madly in love with her. When had it happened? Will couldn't pinpoint an exact time, but if he had to guess, then he imagined he'd been on the slippery slope since the first instant he'd heard that incredible voice of hers.

Which brought to mind another perk—she'd obviously quit answering her 900-line. Will had told himself this for the past two weeks, purposely lied to himself—he'd had to in order to keep from going *insane* every time she left to go home—but given what they'd shared night before last, he knew her well enough to know that she couldn't possibly still be doing it, not when things between them had moved to such an intimate level. She wouldn't betray him that way. Couldn't. She had too much class, and he fully believed that she cared just as much about him as he did about her.

Naturally a small part of Will wanted to question their good thing—a leftover habit from a bad relationship—but he had too much respect for Rowan to let the past ruin what he instinctively knew could be a beautiful future.

She was forever material. That forever kind of love that was constantly lauded in music and film, the ultimate brass ring, and he fully intended to reach for it.

For her.

But one thing at a time, Will told himself. He pulled into Rowan's drive, slowed to a stop, and shifted into Park. A quick glance at the dash told him he was a little early— about thirty minutes to be exact—but he simply hadn't been able to wait to see her, to set tonight in motion.

He'd been waiting for two weeks to ask this question, to essentially put their future on the right track, and waiting another few minutes was simply outside the realm of his control. He felt like an impatient kid with a nickel in his pocket at the penny-candy counter.

He wanted to ask her *now.*

Quite honestly, he'd planned to give her the check and make the offer during dinner, but he seriously didn't see himself being able to wait that long.

Will blew out a breath, exited the truck and made his way to her door. He could probably ask her on the way to the restaurant, then they could celebrate over dinner. Better yet, he could ask her now, and they could start celebrating even earlier. He smiled. The idea held considerable appeal, and gained momentum as he strolled up her steps.

Will lifted his hand to knock, but the sound of her laughter stopped him. A clammy sweat instantly broke out all over his body. He knew that laugh. He'd heard it the first day he'd met her, then had heard it several times since, only in those instances that sexy chuckle had been for him.

Will swallowed and something stark and painful cut through his chest. He didn't know what made him do it, didn't know what propelled him, but rather than knocking on the door, he opened it as quietly as he could and followed that tinkling sultry sound to the back of the house.

"Oh, that's positively wicked. I like the way your mind works." She sighed dramatically, the sound at once sexy and hurtful.

Will stopped in her hallway as she came into view. Rowan stood in front of her bathroom mirror, the be-damned headset in place over her ears. He silently swore, felt that newfound hope he'd just moments ago entertained wither and die like a forget-me-not planted in full sun. His hands fisted at his sides.

She wore a white lacy bra, matching panties and nothing else. Need instantly bombarded him, but he ruthlessly tamped it down. She leaned forward and applied some frosty-looking powder on one of her eyelids. Ordinarily, he would have been content to simply watch her. It was fascinating really, that she went to so much trouble to make herself beautiful, when all she had to do was breathe. But in the next instant he forgot about watching her for pleasure, and watched instead as a too familiar scene—one he'd witnessed two weeks ago—played out in front of his disbelieving eyes.

"Oh, Rick," she sighed. "You can't know how *hot* you're making me. Yes, yes, I know. Oh, I'm wearing a black teddy and spiked heels. No, no panties," she sighed. "I never wear panties. I like to be readily accessible, if you get my drift."

Will told himself that she was playing a part. He plainly saw that. She was getting absolutely nothing out of this exchange. He reminded himself that she needed the money—that she didn't want to sponge off her parents the way her brother had, a tidbit she'd shared recently. He told himself all these things and, though he desperately wanted to laugh like he had the first time he'd seen her do this, Will found himself unable to conjure the necessary humor to complete this scene.

A thousand needles were stabbing into his chest and that near-suffocating sensation took hold, but for a completely different reason this time, he knew. His skin felt like it was going to split and the familiar burn of humiliation and anger tore through like water bursting through a broken dam.

Will smirked as she rounded out her performance once more with another long ecstatic howl of feigned sexual gratification. He was a fool. An utter and complete fool. He didn't wait for her to finish her call this time, but rather lifted his hands and applauded. His hands smacked together, cracking through her small house like the gunfire.

She jumped and squealed and her startled eyes found his. "Will," she breathed.

"Sorry I interrupted," Will told her. "It's a bad habit, but one I'm committed to breaking. I swear it'll never happen again." And it wouldn't. His mind black with hurt and rage, he turned abruptly on his heel and headed for the door.

He heard Rowan call after him, heard her shout his name, but he was too upset to heed her, too caught up in his own stupidity to listen to anything she had to say.

God, he'd been an idiot.

Again.

He heard her screen door bang open as he reached his truck. "Will, *wait!*" she pleaded. "Please let me explain! I'm sorry, I just—" She drew up short. *"Please."*

Will squeezed his eyes tightly shut and his hand hesitated on the car door. God, he wanted to. Wanted to wait and hear her out. He pulled in a harsh breath, waited while pride battled need, battled reason and hope. But reason and hope had won once to a disastrous outcome and this time pride simply wouldn't concede defeat. Though he felt like he was coming apart at the seams, Will jerked the door open, started the truck and shot out of her drive.

Out of her life.

ROWAN WATCHED Will tear out of the drive and felt her heart threaten to explode right out of her chest. Her breath came in sharp, painful gasps and a silent sob formed in the back of her throat.

One look into those devastated brown eyes and she'd felt her own heart break. She'd heard him clap, then she'd turned around and... And that worst enemy mask of his had fallen firmly into place, that damaged smile, so much so that Rowan sincerely doubted she'd ever be able to make him listen to her, make him understand.

Oh, shit.

What had she done? What the hell had she done? Panic crowded her throat, threatened to strangle her. She turned and walked blindly back into her house, pushed a shaky hand through her hair. She muttered a stream of obscenities, paced back and forth in front of her couch, too wired and frightened to sit. She couldn't blame him for being hurt, for being mad. Were the situation reversed, she'd undoubtedly feel the same way.

Oh, God, Rowan silently wailed. Why the hell hadn't she disconnected that damned line? Why had she answered that ignorant call? Because she was an idiot, she thought with a bitter laugh. Because so long as she was paying to have the damned thing, she might as well answer the line. She was too damned practical for her own good, and look at what it had possibly cost her. Will's parting comment ricocheted through her cramping brain.

I swear it'll never happen again.

He couldn't mean what she thought, Rowan thought faintly. He couldn't mean that they were finished. The mere thought terrified her, made her belly tip in a nause-ated roll. Surely not. Surely he'd give her the opportunity to explain. He'd have to, Rowan decided. She'd make him. She knew that his ex had done a number on him, knew that she'd played him for a fool, and though Rowan knew she'd made a terrible mistake, she hadn't done either of those things. Would never purposely try to hurt him. She swal-lowed, felt the burn of impending tears scald the backs of her eyes.

She loved him.

He had to know it. And if he didn't, then she'd enlighten him. The perfect way to do that rose like cream to the top of her churning brain, and she stilled, calmed by the presence of a plan. She knew exactly what to do, Rowan decided. The trouble would be getting him to go along with it.

WILL PULLED a beer from the fridge, then made his way to the living room. Though he wasn't remotely interested in watching television, he turned it on anyway. The noise pushed the quiet away, which helped push his thoughts away. He didn't want to think—thinking de-pressed him.

Truth be told he'd like nothing better than to get blind, roaring drunk, but drowning his troubles in alcohol had never been his thing and he wasn't about to start now. His gaze landed on the phone and he had to force himself to look away. Had to force himself to keep from picking it up and calling her. If he could only hear her voice...

Will swore at the pathetic thought. Her voice was what had gotten him into this mess, his insatiable need to hear her, to be with her. He swallowed. To make love to her. The memory of her greedy body clenching around him, the perfect taste of her pearled nipple on his tongue momentarily took hold of him, making an ache start deep in his chest and infect every cell in his body.

God he wanted her.

Was it really so important to be right? Will wondered now. Was it worth the agony of being alone? Of being without her?

Quite frankly, he suspected that he'd overreacted, that he should have let her explain like she'd asked to do, but having been screwed so royally once before, Will couldn't trust his instincts, couldn't decide if it was truly the case or wishful thinking on his part. And as much as he wanted her, he didn't want to be a fool. Couldn't allow it.

His gaze slid to the phone once more. Which meant that, no matter how much he might want to, he flatly refused to call her. And to his immeasurable disquiet and surprise, she hadn't called him either. Two days had passed without a word, and though he was loath to admit it, it was absolutely killing him. He felt dead on the inside, unable to breathe. Numb and joyless. It was awful.

He'd been humiliated by his ex, that was for sure, but he'd realized something over the past couple of days that he'd never realized before—he hadn't been in love with her. There'd been a sense of relief when they'd split up, one Will instinctively knew he'd never feel about the breakup with Rowan.

The shriek of his phone ringing rose above the din of the TV and Will cursed the instant leap of hope that jumped into his chest. Rowan? he always wondered. Every time the line had rung, his first thought had been her. Hell, who was he trying to kid. *Every* thought was of her.

Irritated with himself, Will refused to answer it, refused to check the Caller ID display. His machine picked up, then her achingly familiar voice—the one he'd desperately been waiting to hear—sounded.

"Will, hi," she said tentatively. "Look, I know I don't deserve it, but I would really like the chance to talk to you. To explain," she said haltingly. "I know it's going to sound strange, and I know I have no right to ask…but I'd really appreciate it if you'd do something for me. Call this number—" To his astonishment, she rattled off her 900-number. "In a few minutes, I'll give you a call back. If you don't answer, then I'll leave you alone." He heard her swallow. "I'll, uh… I'll never bother you again. But things were pretty special between us—at least for me—and I'm hoping that you'll at least give me the benefit of the doubt."

She hung up.

Will sat there for a moment, silently considered what she said. Tried to pretend like the fact that she'd called, or that she'd sounded every bit as miserable as he felt didn't matter.

But it did.

His first impulse was to ease her pain, to let her know that he cared that she ached, that he ached, too, and in that moment he knew that he'd do whatever she asked, he'd believe whatever she told him, because he desperately wanted her back, wanted to be with her, and his pride could go to hell. His need for control could go to hell.

He wanted her. Had to have her.

He blew out a breath, picked up the phone and dialed her 900-line and to his complete bewilderment, he got a recorded message saying that the line had been disconnected, was no longer in service.

His heart began to race and a small seed of hope sprouted once more in the fallow field of his chest. Did this mean— Could she have—

The line rang again, and this time Will didn't hesitate to answer. He cleared his throat of some nebulous obstruction. "Hello."

"Will." The word was drenched in relief.

He rubbed the bridge of his nose, felt that sweet sultry voice seep into him. Felt the backs of his eyes burn. "Yeah?"

"I'm sorry."

Two words. That was all it took for him to literally shake with an emotion so strong it was all he could do not to weep. "No," he sighed. "I'm sorry. I was unreasonable. I—"

"No you weren't," she interrupted. "You were right to be angry, had every right to be mad. I don't blame you. I just—" She expelled a soft breath. "I'd planned on turning it off at the end of the month. I couldn't do it anymore, hated it after being with you." A frustrated growl issued from her throat. "I'm an idiot. I can't offer an excuse that's good enough and the only one I have sounds lame even to me. I was paying for it, so I thought I should answer it. See?" she told him, clearly irritated. "It's stupid. I don't expect you to understand—that's fine—I just wanted you to know that it's off, and I guess what I'm asking is if you can… If you can forgive me? Can we get past this? Because I really want to." She drew up short, let go a soft breath that made his fingers involuntarily curl. "I miss you. I want you to hold me and kiss me and make love to me. I want to fall asleep in your arms. I want to grow things together. A garden, flowers…kids." She stopped again, her voice cracking. "I just want you, what I think we can have."

For a moment Will couldn't speak, couldn't move. He absorbed everything that she said, felt it creep into his chest and take root.

She made a nervous sound, like a sob caught in the

back of her throat. "Well, I guess that's my answer. Sorry to have bothered you. Bye—"

"Rowan, wait!"

"Yeah?" she asked hesitantly.

"Everything you said, about being together and growing things." He swallowed. "Well…ditto."

Another sound, part-laugh, part-cry came through the line, pushing his lips up into a relieved smile. God how he missed her. How he needed her. He couldn't breathe without her. Had to have her.

"I think that you should come over," he told her, desperate to be with her once more.

A knock sounded at his door. "I think that you should open the door."

Will felt another slow smile slide across his lips. He stood and, phone still in hand, calmly made his way to the door and pulled it open. Rowan stood on the other side, an adorable grin on her lush, ripe mouth. His heart inexplicably swelled…as did another equally impatient organ in his lower extremities. He let his gaze trace the woefully familiar shape of her face. "I love you," he murmured softly.

Her eyes misted, searched his. "I love you, too."

Will tossed his phone aside, stepped forward and crushed her to him. She sighed, melted against him.

Then he kissed her…and could breathe again.

EPILOGUE

Two months later...

"COME ON," Will cajoled, steering his new wife determinedly away from well-wishers. "I'm ready to go."

"Me, too," she told him, the heat in that sultry nonwhisper the only proof that he needed that she was every bit as impatient as him to leave. "But we can't be rude."

"Yes you can," Alexa said. "It's the prerogative of newlyweds. No one expects you to hang around after the reception." Her eyes sparkled, and she lifted another glass of champagne in their honor. "I *predict* that no one will mind."

Rowan grinned. "I predict that you're full of sh—"

"Careful," Will interrupted, laughing. "We're in mixed company, remember?"

Will's nephew, Scott, ambled up once more, shot her a curious look. "Are you sure we haven't met? There's something so familiar about you. I feel like I've talked to you before."

Rowan and Will shared a look. Scott had been trying to place her for weeks now and, though Will knew Rowan fervently prayed he never figured it out, Will couldn't help but be tickled by the whole scenario.

"Er...I don't think so," Rowan told him again, her standard answer. Scott scratched his head, shot her another baffled look as though he wanted to argue, then reluctantly walked away.

Rowan sagged against him, her soft breast branding his arm. "Geez, that's nerve-racking. Do you think he'll ever figure it out?" she hissed.

Will smiled down at her. "I don't know. But, like you said, he's pretty bright."

She scowled adorably. "Oh, shut up."

Will pulled a wounded look. "We've been married an hour and you're already bossing me around? Should I be worried?"

Her eyes twinkled with humor and heat. "Definitely."

Will bent his head and kissed her. That lush mouth melded to his effortlessly and within seconds he was so damned hot that self-combustion became a genuine fear. His dick strained against his tux, tenting his cummerbund out in the most undignified fashion.

She chuckled against his mouth. "I want you. Right now. What do you say we find a private little grotto and I'll show you just how much." She lowered her voice. "Repeatedly."

"Get a room!" someone shouted, before Will could reply. His brother, no doubt, Will thought, dragging his lips reluctantly from hers. He rested his forehead against hers and they shared a smile. Happiness saturated every pore of his body.

"I take it you're ready to blow this shindig?" he asked softly. This shindig was costing a fortune, but he didn't care. He'd rented Sylvia Gardens, had spared absolutely no expense. He only intended to get married once and to that end, he'd made sure that everything had been done right, to Rowan's specific instructions.

His heart squeezed painfully in his chest as he looked at her now. Just a few months ago, he'd imagined her like this. Long white gown, a garland of flowers in her hair, and here they were, happier than he ever thought they could possibly be.

"I'm ready when you are," she told him in that too-sultry near-whispering voice. "If you're sure your mother won't be hurt that we leave early."

Will grinned. "She'll get over it," he said drolly. In fact, she'd given him another one of those embarrassing talks yesterday, and had informed him in no uncertain terms that a grandchild was expected posthaste. He was now at liberty to forgo the condoms. Did he have any questions? As if he didn't know how to go about getting his wife pregnant.

Sheesh, Will thought. He thought he could handle *that* without any damned motherly pearls of wisdom. To that end, he made a mental note to leave his phone at home. He didn't want any unsolicited advice on how to conduct his honeymoon.

She sighed softly and those gorgeous green eyes tangled with his. Love, joy, and need shimmered in those mesmerizing orbs, causing his chest to inexplicably tighten.

Will laced his fingers through hers, then whistled loudly to garner everyone's attention. "We're leaving," he said without preamble. "Enjoy the party."

This abrupt announcement was met with laughter and applause. Smiling, they both turned and made their way to Rowan's car. She'd threatened bodily injury to anyone who touched her baby, so there were no cans tied to the bumper, or a Just Married scrawled in shoe polish across the windshield.

She stopped next to the passenger side and calmly waited for him to open the door, as though this were completely normal and nothing out of the ordinary was happening.

Will stilled, then shot her a questioning look. His heart began to pound, to race. "Rowan?"

She smiled, then turned and winked at her dad, who beamed at them and sent her a quiet thumbs-up. Her gaze slid back to Will, then, and she tossed him the keys. "Second sticks a little," she said matter-of-factly, "so you might want to baby her."

Will swallowed, recognizing the gesture for what it was. She trusted him. Fully, completely, without reservation. "Are you sure?" he asked, his throat tight.

She smiled at him and liquid emotion glittered in those gorgeous green eyes. She pulled a light shrug, laughed. "What can I say? I finally found a guy who's vintage-Vette worthy." She swallowed. "I love you, Will."

Will grinned. "Ditto."

* * * * *

SILK CONFESSIONS
Joanne Rock

CHAPTER ONE

TEMPEST BOUCHER had a multimillion dollar corporation to run, a kickboxing class to attend, a board of executives in upheaval and a lecture waiting to be written for a finance seminar she'd promised to give at New York University in a few weeks. But every last bit of it was going to have to wait since *Days of Our Lives* was on in five minutes.

"Eloise!" Juggling her ten-speed bike and the dog leash as she searched for the keys to her building's front door, Tempest whistled to her two-year-old German shepherd. Her spoiled pet seemed utterly unaware of the need to hurry as she gave her best poor-hungry-me look to a corner pretzel vendor in the Chelsea section of Manhattan. Thanks to a new construction site three buildings over, West 18th had suddenly become a prime location for anyone pushing a food cart.

Oblivious to Eloise's irritated owner, the hot-pretzel man tossed the conniving canine a treat. Only then did Eloise deign to obey commands and follow Tempest through the front door. So much for obedience school training.

Tempest grumbled as she repositioned the bike for the trudge up three flights of stairs. She only indulged her soap opera habit on Fridays, for crying out loud. Couldn't Eloise fulfill her inner panhandler on any other day of the week?

Determined to wring some fun—and some sense of normalcy—out of a life overflowing with responsibilities, Tempest had made a New Year's resolution to start living her own life this year. Not every day was her own, of course. After her father's unexpected death eight months ago, the task of overseeing day-to-day operations at Boucher Enterprises had fallen on her shoulders as temporary CEO, taking up most of her time.

But one day a week—Friday—could be hers. For two months now, she had been spending the weekends at the new studio apartment in Chelsea, a run-down and wonderfully normal place where none of her neighbors had noticed the daughter of eccentric corporate scion Ray Boucher in their midst.

And that was just the way Tempest wanted it.

She'd taken so much pride in finding the space on her own and paying for it out of a budget from her meager income as a sculptor. In fact, budgeting a life in Manhattan on a small income took as much financial savvy as running Boucher Enterprises. Possibly more, since the family corporation had a fleet of accountants and financial analysts whenever she needed a business consultation, whereas she had no help with her personal finances. Unless she categorized Eloise's begging on the streets as "help."

Hustling the last few steps to her apartment door, Tempest could already hear the opening bars of music for her soap opera in her mind.

"Like sand through the hourglass…"

Days of Our Lives reminded her to slow down. Enjoy herself. The sand through the hourglass had become her personal transition moment where she left behind Tempest the heiress, who had a schedule so packed she needed— good God—an administrative assistant. This was her time to be Tempest the woman who was passionate about sculpting, soap operas and saving her pennies for a future that wouldn't include running the family company.

But as she moved to put her keys in the lock, she realized the door was already slightly open. Had the superintendent finally decided to fix her broken shower?

Sure that had to be it, Tempest chose to let Eloise go first, just in case. Setting her ten-speed on the landing outside her door, Tempest motioned to the dog. Perhaps feeling compliant after her bonus lunchtime feeding, the shepherd dutifully nudged the door open with her snout.

And revealed Tempest's tiny haven, trashed beyond recognition.

NYPD DETECTIVE WESLEY SHAW didn't normally pay any attention to the calls taken by other officers at his precinct on West 20th, but as he meandered past a throng of desks to start his day, a name slowly repeated by a rookie cop caused a flash of recognition.

"Did you just say Tempest Boucher?" Wes leaned down into Carl Esposito's line of sight, his cop radar blaring an alert.

Ignoring him, Carl continued to copy down information being given to him over the phone.

Wrenching around to peer above the rookie's shoulder, Wes experienced the rush of instinct that always prickled inside whenever he had a good lead—a professional thrill for the chase that he hadn't enjoyed during the two years since his first partner had gone missing. He'd been functioning on autopilot for so damn long, the electric rush was as unexpected as it was welcome.

He'd been coming up empty on a murder case for a week until he'd connected the victim to an online dating service two days ago. And although he hadn't been able to track down anyone at MatingGame.com, he had discovered the business was one of many owned by the successful Manhattan-based conglomerate, Boucher Enterprises.

Seeing Tempest Boucher's name surface in his precinct so soon after his discovery couldn't be coincidence.

"I'll take it." Wes snagged Carl's notes as the officer hung up the phone, determined to follow any lead that gave him the feeling his old partner Steve had called the cop "buzz." Better than your run-of-the-mill Budweiser high, the cop buzz hit your system with the kind of adrenaline surge that solved cases and caught bad guys.

Highly addictive stuff. And Wes had ached for it like a junkie for twenty-four godforsaken months. No way would he let it pass him by now.

"You sure?" Carl reached for his jacket. "I live two blocks from there. I can ask some of the locals if they've seen anything."

Wes was already halfway out the door. "Send a patrol car to meet me. I've been meaning to talk to this woman anyway." He shoved through the double doors into the afternoon gloom when he remembered he needed to inform his new partner.

Yeah, *new.* Vanessa would love that one. She'd been on his back like a bossy sister to pull himself together ever since they'd been paired up eighteen months ago. Jogging back inside, he shouted to Carl. "When Vanessa gets in, do me a favor and tell her where I am."

Ten minutes later, Wes arrived at an address that didn't look anything like the sort of elite building a filthy-rich real estate heiress ought to own. A patrol car already sat out front, attracting some attention from the locals. A few rubberneckers bought hot pretzels from a nearby vendor as if to settle in for any hints of news about what might have happened in the run-down, ten-story building.

Despite New Yorkers' reputation for minding their own business, Wes had yet to see any signs of the phenomenon in nine years on the force.

Making quick work of the stairs, he hit the third floor in no time. A bicycle leaned forgotten in the hall while a woeful-looking black-and-brown German shepherd stood guard at the half-open door to apartment number 35. A skinny old woman clad in a blue-and-yellow floral house-coat watched over the proceedings from number 39, but other than that, the third floor remained quiet.

Pausing to gain the approval of the shepherd, Wes scratched the dog's ears before following a dull hum of voices from inside the airy studio apartment. Light spilled in from floor-to-ceiling windows, illuminating a profound mess of strewn clothing, plants dumped out of their con-tainers and piles of broken statuary. Two uniformed patrol officers were on the scene—one who knelt in the rubble taking fingerprints off some broken glasses and the other who stood near the windows taking notes as he spoke with a petite brunette.

Wes recognized Tempest Boucher from the newspa-pers. She possessed eye-popping curves and seemed to be rocking back and forth on her heels, perhaps an attempt to calm herself since she looked a little shaken. Jittery.

With creamy pale skin and chin-length brown curls, she wore running shoes with a sleekly cut crimson pantsuit that appeared tailor-made for her lush hourglass figure. Something about her extravagant curves and full red lips brought to mind the cartoon image of Betty Boop, except the apartment owner lacked the wide-eyed look of an in-génue. Her tawny gaze was sharp and assessing.

And preoccupied with him as he bent to retrieve a broken piece of statuary.

"Ms. Boucher?" He noted her stare strayed to the

broken piece of clay in his hand. Peering down at the object, Wes discerned a ridge along the top of the foot-long shaft of clay. Only then did he realize the piece he'd recovered was actually a penis.

Reacting on pure male instinct, he dropped the busted piece back on the couch in all due haste. No cop buzz in the world seemed potent enough to make him seek out clues that damn badly.

"Please, call me Tempest." A hint of amusement fled through her honey gaze, although she didn't halt her nervous rocking. She reached for a choker around her neck, a band of silver-gray velvet with a big chunk of smoky quartz crystal dangling just below the delicate hollow at the base of her throat.

"Detective Wesley Shaw." He reached to shake her hand and realized he was eager to touch her. An irritating thought when she might be mixed up in something dangerous. Deadly, even.

Nodding to the note-taking officer, Wes silently took over the questioning. While he sympathized with this woman, if she were truly innocent, he couldn't allow her to bamboozle one of the new guys just because of her famous face and obvious sex appeal. Skinny Paris Hilton had nothing on the more elusive—and deliciously curvy—Tempest Boucher.

"Would you like to sit down?" He gestured to the couch strewn with sketchbook drawings of hands, feet, arms and—damnation—more penises.

While Wes knew he had no business judging her on the contents of her ransacked apartment, the cop in him couldn't help but wonder if the uptown heiress used this downtown address as a love nest. Or something even more sordid.

Her connection to his murder case linked her with some very unsavory characters.

"Sure." She sprang into action, brushing aside the smashed figures and hastily scooping up the anatomical drawings. "Have a seat."

A shiver passed through him as her thumb skimmed the base of a pencil-and-ink penis. A wholly inappropriate reaction. How the hell long had it been since he'd had a woman in his bed if he was getting turned on at work?

He would have made a mental note to call his girlfriend of the month, except that this was one of the many months he didn't happen to have one. In fact, if memory served, he'd only managed to accomplish the girlfriend-of-the-month feat twice in the last year and a half. Hell of a track record.

Since he'd always sucked at relationships—something he sorely regretted telling his new partner—Vanessa liked to hassle him about one month being the longest he could keep a woman in his life. Damned if she hadn't been dead-on accurate. Wes didn't bother to inform her that he'd had a long-term interlude back in the day—before his first partner went undercover and never came back out. His job and his personal life had both pretty much fizzled since then. Even more so after they'd finally found Steve's body in the East River last fall.

Rogue thoughts of the sexy socialite now firmly under control, Wes dropped onto the small pullout sofa a few feet away from her. Too late he realized the open studio apartment contained no bed, meaning she must sleep *here*. Right on this very piece of furniture where he'd parked himself.

Eager to maintain focus on his case, Wes redirected.

"Is that your dog out front?"

"Eloise?" She peered around the apartment as if she'd

only just remembered she had a dog. Inserting two fingers between her lips, she blew a piercing note.

Wes barely heard it since his eyes were glued to her full mouth, her bottom lip still damp from her whistle.

The dog came padding through the rubble of the apartment, its presence seeming to relax Tempest. "Yes, she's mine. I would never bring a shepherd into the city since they really like to run. But I found her in a Dumpster on the way to work one morning and what else could I do? I figured living with me—even if I don't have a few acres for her to romp around—had to be better than the fate she was looking at."

Wes watched her scratch the dog's neck, her shiny red manicure disappearing into the animal's thick ruff. There was no doubt in his mind the mutt had it made.

"She looks pretty well-adjusted." He didn't mention his St. Bernard was twice the size of Eloise and managed to keep entertained in Wes's shoebox of an apartment on Roosevelt Island. "Can you tell me what happened here today?"

"I was coming home from a meeting and I noticed the front door was unlocked." Her fingers buried deeper into the dog's fur. "Eloise went in first because I was a little unnerved by the open door. I had safety measures drilled into my head at an early age, and I can assure you, I've never forgotten to bolt a door in my life."

"Is anything missing?"

"I honestly haven't looked around. I called the police as soon as I saw the mess." Her eyes drifted over the debris. "I'm not sure I'd know where to start looking for missing items."

Wes followed her gaze, his eyes slowing on a haphazard pile of lacy undergarments spilling out of a tall armoire. Black ribbons mingled with pink straps, bright blue satin billowed over yellow see-through netting. He'd have to be a dead man not to notice the distinctly feminine intimate apparel, but he refused to envision Tempest wearing any of the slinky outfits.

Although the thought tempted him. Mightily.

As a compromise, he told himself he would not only work on finding another girlfriend in the very near future, but he would also seek out one who had a taste for lingerie. Of all the times for his libido to make a comeback after staying in hiding for months.

"Consider if you have anything here that someone else really wants. Something with monetary value? Something with significant value to a particular person?" He studied her face for hints of guilt or subterfuge, but only found deep thought. "The level of destruction in the apartment indicates that the perpetrator conducted a thorough search for something specific, or else the person responsible holds a personal grudge."

His thoughts ran to the old lady neighbor he'd seen peering out her apartment door earlier. Had she been monitoring the goings-on in the hallway for reasons beyond general nosiness? Maybe some of Tempest's neighbors didn't appreciate the inevitable media frenzy that followed young, beautiful socialites around New York.

Wes found himself wondering if she brought a lot of men back to this apartment. Was the unassuming address her rendezvous point for booty calls she hid from her ritzy family?

"Obviously my intruder didn't think my sculptures were worth a damn." She clutched the smoky crystal at her neck and Wes spied the rapid beating of her pulse there.

What would it be like to make this woman's heart pound faster?

"You collect statues?" Of naked men?

Perhaps Tempest's snooping neighbor was an old prude who resented anyone with such an obvious interest in male nudity.

"I am the artist." She lifted her chin with vaguely injured pride. "I had been hoping to convince a local gallery to do a showing once I had enough of a collection, but now…"

Certain a wealthy heiress whose face frequently graced the social pages could buy her way into any gallery she chose, Wes wasn't too concerned. He needed answers from Tempest Boucher and he certainly wasn't getting them by being subtle.

Time to be a bit more relentless with his questions.

"Did you keep valuables here? Jewelry? Other artwork besides your own?"

TEMPEST STARED BACK at Detective Heartless Shaw and assured herself he must not have a creative bone in his body. How else could he ask her something so insensitive as whether or not she owned any artwork that was actually *worth* something?

Of all the damn nerve.

"As a matter of fact, my statues were the most valuable items here. I don't keep much at the apartment besides the tools for my sculpting." And a few pictures for inspiration. Could she help it if she liked to mold male bodies? Judging by what her first few pieces had sold for, she wasn't the only woman who appreciated a naked masculine torso around the house.

Detective Shaw might actually make for great male inspiration himself if he didn't have such abrupt crime-scene manners. With his close-cropped dark hair and classic Roman features, he possessed a timeless appeal women would have found irresistible in any era, though his dove-gray eyes and the hint of a dark tattoo curling around one wrist gave him a uniqueness she wouldn't confuse with any other classically handsome male. He wore a vintage suit that had probably cost a fortune in its prime, but the threads had seen better days, settling into softer lines around angular shoulders.

Definitely the sort of shoulders a woman wouldn't mind molding. In clay, of course.

He peered around her apartment as if to test the truth of her assertion that she only came here to work. Curse the man and his unwanted sex appeal. Wasn't she the victim here? Shouldn't he make a passing effort to ask her if she was okay? She'd never been a paranoid woman, but it seemed as if even the toughest of chicks would be shaken by the sight of their personal lives churned through a giant blender and spit out like an aftertaste all over the floor.

"As soon as we've finished collecting evidence, we need to do a thorough walk-through to see if anything's missing. In the meantime, I've got some other questions I'd like to ask you about Boucher Enterprises." His gray eyes slid back to her, fixing her with unsettling directness. And something more? She could almost imagine a hint of male interest there. Then again, she could be dabbling in big-time escapist thinking to drool over Wesley Shaw instead of focusing on the criminal act some scumbag had committed against her.

"You recognized the name?" She had rather hoped he wouldn't want to discuss her connection to the famous family, but no doubt reporters would have jumped on the police report the moment it was filed anyhow.

Her misfortune would be all over the papers and would certainly prompt more irritated phone calls from her mother about the need to move back to the safety of the family's Park Avenue building on a full-time basis.

The media would discover the location of her weekend hideaway and make life in Chelsea impossible. And then there would be the outcry from the Boucher board of directors who never understood her desire to have a life separate and distinct from her commitment to the company.

"There aren't many people in New York who wouldn't. *The Post* ran a feature on you just a couple of weeks ago—"

"I remember." How could she forget the story that implied she had a fixation with younger men? As if her last-minute decision to go to the cinema with the barely-legal performance artist who ran a coffee shop around the corner counted as a date. "Can we move on to your questions, please?"

Adopting her best all-business demeanor, she dismissed the topic, unwilling to think about what kind of man she would have rather been dating than the coffee guy. Tempest might not enjoy her role in Boucher Enterprises as a corporate bigwig, but that didn't mean she couldn't play the part when necessary. After coming home to a trashed apartment, finding her last year's worth of work destroyed and missing *Days* to boot, she wasn't really in the mood to put up with a lot of innuendo. And she definitely didn't want to find herself daydreaming about the detective's shoulders again.

Before he could say anything, however, one of the officers called Wes from the other side of the room.

"Looks like we've got a message from our perpetrator, Shaw." Standing next to the computer armoire, the cop held a pile of clothes that had been draped over the monitor. Now that the mountain of lace and satin had been moved aside to reveal the screen, the neatly typed words in extra large font were visible from clear across the room.

You're in the wrong business, bitch. Rising, Tempest read the message aloud as she stepped closer to the computer, her frustrations with Wesley Shaw forgotten in the sudden onslaught of cold, clammy fear.

The warning written on her computer screen—the cursor still blinking at the end of the last word—had been left by someone who knew her. The break-in was no random act of city crime, but a calculated plan carried out against her specifically.

The thought made her a little woozy. She'd fought so hard for a small slice of independence in a life filled with commitments to her family's business. The unassuming downtown address and her sculpting gave her a taste of normal life where she wasn't under the constant surveillance of security cameras or family bodyguards. But if her weekend apartment haven wasn't safe, did that mean she'd have to return to the Boucher clan compound that was as secure as Fort Knox and just about as homey?

"Tempest?" Detective Shaw stood beside her now, his voice quieter. Softer, even. But the gaze he directed on her remained detached and—could she be reading him right?—suspicious. "I think it's time we talked more specifically about your line of work."

Tempest chewed her lip, trying to figure out what this man was driving at and why she'd roused his suspicions. Unfortunately, he'd roused a different sort of feeling altogether within her. But no matter what she thought of Detective Wesley Shaw, his brusque manners and undeniable sex appeal, she recognized him as her best hope of keeping her studio a safe retreat.

Somehow she would ignore this unwelcome hum of attraction and do whatever it took to help Wes with his case.

CHAPTER TWO

"HOW MUCH TIME do you have, Detective?" Tempest wrapped her arms around herself, clearly shaken by the note on her computer screen. "As the temporary CEO of Boucher Enterprises, I'm involved in overseeing many smaller companies in a wide variety of businesses. I also support my studio with my sculpting, so I consider that a line of work as well."

Wes felt a tug of sympathy for her. He'd had enough years in law enforcement to be pretty astute about sizing up people's stories, and Tempest was either a hell of an actress or genuinely surprised and scared to have found her home ransacked.

Of course, that didn't clear her of wrongdoing. She could still be connected to his murder case, or have some hand in the prostitution ring his informant assured him operated under the guise of the MatingGame.com name. Her genuine fear and surprise might simply stem from dismay that someone was on to her.

Hell, for that matter, maybe his sudden eagerness to clear her name had more to do with the fact that he wouldn't mind getting to know her better. Thoughts of her dressed in some of the skimpy lingerie scattered all over the apartment invaded his brain despite his most valiant attempts to staunch them. Was she wearing an outfit like that under her pantsuit right now?

Shoving aside the thought, he forced himself to focus on the case. On her valid worries.

"Do you have reason to believe any of your assorted businesses could be involved in illegal practices?" This was the revealing question, the one that could give her away if she hid an affiliation to a high-priced call girl ring. She certainly had all the right social connections to provide the city's wealthiest men with escorts.

And damned if he didn't really hate that idea.

The mountains of lingerie strewn all over her apartment took on a more sinister meaning.

"Detective Shaw, I assure you if I had any reason to suspect one of my companies engaged in illegal practices, it would already be shut down." She fixed her tawny stare, eyes as cold and remote as the chunk of smoky quartz at her neck. "If you have any grounds for suspecting one of my businesses is involved in something devious, I urge you to fill me in immediately so I can put the proper balls on the chopping block."

The threat seemed all the more convincing in light of the disembodied clay penis he'd unearthed earlier. He hadn't expected so much fervor from a woman he planned to keep on his suspect list.

Did it make him sadistic that Tempest Boucher and her bloodthirsty promise were turning into the most interesting case he'd had in nearly two years? As the web of intrigue around this mystery tightened, Wes experienced the first hint of enjoyment in his job that he'd had in far too long. "Is that how Boucher Enterprises deals with employees who don't toe the company line?"

"It is while I'm at the helm. My family has been through enough over the past eight months without adding the media frenzy any illegal business practices would cause."

"Do you keep work-related files on your home computer?" His gaze strayed back to the PC where the officer had just finished fingerprinting the keyboard. Wes wanted to get his hands on that computer to see what secrets he could shake loose from the circuitry.

Besides, better to think about laying his hands on the computer than think about using them on the woman in front of him who needed to be off-limits for as long as she was a suspect.

"Nothing related to Boucher Enterprises, but I do the accounting for my sculpting work here." She snorted. "Such as it is. It's not exactly keeping me in high style. And now that all my inventory has been destroyed—"

She broke off, surprising Wes with a hint of vulnerability he hadn't expected. The woman lived her life in a relentless public spotlight, ran a company with a net worth that boggled the imagination, and could afford anything her heart desired. Yet she seemed genuinely distressed about the loss of her homemade statues.

"If it's any consolation, insurance ought to cover their value." Maybe that wasn't what she wanted to hear, but his practical side couldn't help pointing out she wouldn't be hurt financially.

Her curt nod and well-camouflaged sniffle assured him he hadn't consoled her in the least.

"I'm sure you're right. Do you think the person who broke in here was looking for business information of some sort?" She relieved the other officer of his handful of lingerie and the guy got back to work looking around the apartment. Tempest tossed the silky pile of undergarments on the arm of a red floral club chair.

Wes couldn't say how long he stared at the stack of lace and satin, imagining the black silk hugging Tempest's hips, the blue netting cupping generous breasts...

But he knew it took a Herculean effort to pull his thoughts back to reality. Blinking hard, he wrenched his gaze away.

"Possibly." Deciding he was making zero progress by waiting for her to incriminate herself, Wes laid more of his cards on the table, still searching for some telltale reaction. At the very least, by sharing his suspicions he would put her on the defensive if she was guilty. Maybe she'd trip up and give him the lead he needed. "I'm investigating a small company owned by Boucher Enterprises. Mating-Game.com?"

"The Internet dating service?"

"You're familiar with the business?"

"I brought them aboard myself shortly before my father's death." She whistled to her dog and absently petted the animal while she spoke. "They had a talented Web mistress who keeps the site fresh and provides great visibility all over the Web, but they were being inundated by crank dating résumés and starting to flounder under client dissatisfaction. Boucher brought the financial help they needed to screen all their clients by collecting more information. I believe they're turning a very healthy profit now."

"*I* believe they are a front for a prostitution ring." He kept his gaze direct. Detached. That was a crucial part of interrogation unless you had a damn good reason for wanting your suspect to think you were on their side.

Wes didn't know whether he'd struck pay dirt or if he'd merely scared the hell out of her, but she swayed on her feet at the news.

Damn.

"Are you okay?" He reached for her on instinct, pushing aside his need to dig for the truth long enough to steady her.

His hand went automatically to her waist, securing her at the base of her spine. Right away he knew touching her had been a mistake, but what the hell else could he have done? She looked as though she'd seen a damn ghost.

Too bad all he could think of was how tiny her waist felt under her jacket. The tailored cut wasn't nearly tailored enough, the fabric not doing justice to the cinch of her midsection between gently flared hips and incredible cleavage.

Her scent—something rich and warm that made him think of the hot chestnuts sold by street vendors all winter—made him feel damn light-headed too. Good thing he would let her go any second now.

Yup. Any minute.

"I'm fine." Tempest cleared her throat, the soft vibration of her voice reverberating gently against his palm where he still touched her. She stepped away before he remembered he was supposed to be letting go.

Cursing himself and his stupid sex-starved senses, Wes regretted the loss of mental control. He hadn't done anything outwardly inappropriate, but his thoughts were another story. Worst of all, he'd lost track of his instincts since they'd gotten mixed with lust.

Where the hell was the cop buzz when he needed it? It seemed to have been soundly thrashed by a much louder hum of desire.

"I don't know anything about MatingGame being involved in illegal activity, but you caught me off guard since—" She peered over her shoulder toward the other officers in the apartment. "Can we possibly speak in private?"

Surprised at her apparent need to confess, Wes couldn't deny a rush of disappointment. The sexual hunger simmering in his veins had been really rooting for this woman's innocence.

"Sure." He shouted to the cops finishing up their routine search for evidence and quickly cleared the room of everyone but the two of them and Eloise, who curled up in front of the door for a snooze.

Wes hoped Vanessa wouldn't show up on the scene too soon now that Tempest appeared so close to telling him what she knew. His partner had planned to investigate a few other leads on their murder case, but he expected she'd arrive at the precinct soon.

Now he settled in the club chair, a safe distance from the temptation presented by the first woman to send sparks his way in too long.

And didn't it just figure she was going to turn out to be part of a prostitution ring?

Tempest eyed the muscular cop sprawled in a chair two sizes too small for him and prayed she was making the right decision by trusting him. But if he was investigating MatingGame, he might as well know everything she knew.

She sank down into the couch across from him and dug out the old memories that had caused her family so much pain.

"You're probably familiar with the scandal surrounding my father's death last year while he was in Mexico?" It had been the subject of speculation in the papers for weeks, making it nearly impossible to grieve privately.

"Heart attack during sex with a much younger lover, right?" Detective Shaw didn't look scandalized in the least. Somehow, that made it easier to continue.

"Most people assumed it was a heart attack, allowing us to keep quiet the fact that the Mexican officials said he actually died of asphyxiation. You know how some people think cutting off their oxygen supply will increase the power of their release?" She waited for his nod, her cheeks heating at the nature of the discussion. She'd never been a shy woman, but the frank sex talk unnerved her.

Especially in light of her inconvenient attraction to the cop.

"He died during kinky sex?" One eyebrow lifted.

"Yes. And the woman involved might have come under more scrutiny if my mother hadn't assured police my father had been perfecting ways to achieve the ultimate release throughout their marriage. It was one of the core reasons my parents fought." Her mother had been horrified by her husband's increasing obsession with pushing sex to the limit, finally walking out when he'd nearly strangled himself, although they'd never actually divorced. Apparently Ray Boucher demanded as much from his sexual encounters as he had from every other facet of his glittering, over-the-top lifestyle. "And as it happened, the woman my father had been with that last night wasn't really a girlfriend. She was a one-night stand he'd met through MatingGame."

Wes sat straighter in his chair, his long, lean body suddenly charged with alertness. "She never said anything to the press?"

"My mother and I made a trip south of the border to appeal to her sense of common decency and asked her to keep the sordid details to herself since the local officials didn't leak the information to the media." The woman had been nice enough and she'd been as eager as they were to put the ordeal behind her. "We helped her to relocate overseas so she wouldn't be faced with the situation day in and day out over the turbulent months that followed."

"You paid her off?"

"Hardly. She was down on her luck after a divorce

left her broke, which was why my mother and I thought it would be just as well to help her start over again. Last I heard, she'd learned to speak Italian and settled just outside of Florence."

"But you felt guilty enough about the whole situation to confess all this to me," he pointed out with a bluntness Tempest began to recognize as part of his investigative style.

Or maybe it was just his personality. She had found it rather cold at first, but after a lifetime surrounded by people who were often pleasant to her face only for personal gain, she was beginning to find his direct manner more appealing.

Or maybe it was simply all those hard male muscles she found interesting. She hadn't been enticed to get close to a man in a very long time.

"I don't feel guilty about it in the least since no one outside his family needs to know what happened to my father. I was just taken aback when you mentioned MatingGame could be a cover for a prostitution ring." She had thought the scandal of having her father die in bed while having adulterous sex with a woman half his age had been bad. Imagine the repercussions if the adulterous sex turned out to be part of an encounter with a prostitute?

The tabloids would have a field day, her mother would be humiliated and Boucher Enterprises would suffer. And while Tempest and her family were well-insulated from the rises and falls of the business, she couldn't help but think of the people who worked for the company in one capacity or another. *Those* were the people who would suffer the most.

"You're worried about the negative press that will ensue if people learn your father cavorted with a prostitute."

Shaw nodded knowingly, as if that statement summed up the situation.

"It's a lot more complicated than that." Tension built in her forehead, the sure sign of another stress headache coming on. She could have handled all this better if she'd at least had her weekly dose of *Days of Our Lives*. Damn it, melodrama like this belonged on her television screen, not in her living room. "You know how many people depend on our company for their livelihood? Those are the people who get hurt when my family comes under attack.

"My mother will console herself with shopping. My late father's board of directors will unload their stock options and jump on early retirement. But what about the thousands of people we employ around the globe? They don't deserve to lose their jobs because my father suffered a midlife crisis from the time he turned thirty until the day he died."

Levering herself off the couch, Tempest stepped over the piles of rubble from the break-in, slowly making her way toward the kitchen where a bottle of Tylenol waited.

"What about you?" The cool-as-you-please detective merely followed her with his eyes, though his long limbs retained their alert stance, as if ready to pounce at any moment. "What would you do if Boucher Enterprises takes a financial nosedive?"

The question made her head throb all the more. Fishing through a maze of cooking spices and boxes of Milk-Bones in every conceivable flavor, she found the pain reliever and popped two in her mouth. Downing them with a cold glass of water, she took deep breaths and reminded herself nothing catastrophic had happened to the company yet. She could still fix this.

"I'll admit it makes things harder for me. As temporary CEO, I'm eager to unload my job and it will make the position less attractive if the company is struggling."

All the more reason to address the matter of Mating-Game before the problem exploded underneath her. "In fact," she continued, a plan slowly taking shape, "if MatingGame is a front for something sordid, I can have it shut down in a matter of minutes."

Infused with new energy now that she had a strategy, she moved to find the phone, which no longer rested in its usual place on the kitchen counter.

"No." Detective Shaw rose from his seat and was in her face in no time. He moved with a swiftness that surprised her.

"What do you mean, 'no'?" Her breath caught at their sudden proximity, his tall, lanky frame close enough to touch.

Not that she would allow herself the pleasure. She'd been far too aware of him ever since he'd touched her earlier, as if her body had captured that quick impression of his hand on her back and had been seeking to recreate the moment ever since. Ridiculous, maybe. But sort of intriguing considering she hadn't been even remotely interested in any man over the last months of nose-to-the-grindstone work.

What was it about the plainspoken police detective that turned her head and made her—she fidgeted to admit it, even to herself—*horny?* She'd never been the type to get all keyed up over a guy. Why him? Why now?

The timing for her sudden bout of lust surely sucked.

"I don't have the evidence I need to prove MatingGame is a shady business." He had oddly precise articulation for a man who'd probably seen the seamiest underbelly of the city. Glaring down at her from his height, which would have dwarfed her even if she hadn't been wearing her running shoes, Wesley Shaw was warning her in no uncertain terms.

Too bad he was also turning her on—big-time. Her breath hitched in her throat as she envisioned having her way with such a big, powerful man. She'd overcome a lot of personal insecurities in the past year, but she'd never had the chance to test her sexual confidence.

This was *so* the wrong time.

"It would better suit my company to pull the rug out from under them, Detective." Folding her arms across her chest, she glared right back, hoping like hell she wasn't giving out any "do-me" vibe to mirror her sexually charged thoughts. "I don't need any evidence to withdraw my support immediately. I won't allow Boucher Enterprises to be dragged through the mud just so you can make your case."

They stood too close together but Tempest wasn't about to back down now. She hadn't gleaned many of her father's killer instincts when it came to business, but she knew enough about body language to comprehend she didn't dare give this man any ground now.

Of course, there was a whole other dynamic to their body language that didn't have a damn thing to do with prostitution, MatingGame, Boucher Enterprises or even her ransacked apartment.

"I don't care about busting prostitutes." He lowered his voice to a pitch that seemed just right for how close their bodies loomed and all wrong for a detached, intelligent conversation between strangers.

"You don't?" Tempest cringed inwardly to hear her own voice hit a soft note. What was she thinking to engage in guy-girl games with the cop investigating a break-in?

Bad, bad idea.

"No. I'm trying to catch the murderer masquerading as a prostitute."

His words reverberated in her ears, his point resonating until the meaning loomed large and ugly just outside the kitchenette area of her apartment. She blinked hard to gather her bearings, but when she opened her eyes her world still seemed slightly off-kilter and her stress headache now pounded to the forefront of her brain.

Body language be damned, she needed breathing room.

"I think I'd better sit down." Tempest sidled past him, attempting to get her bearings away from the confusing heat that flared between them. She stepped on a piece of statuary, the broken clay crushing into dust on the hardwood floor beneath her sneaker.

"I need your help, Tempest." He was right behind her, following her toward the sofa.

Her apartment seemed to shrink with him in it, his presence big and male and dominating her scrambled thoughts.

"I don't know how I can help you, Detective, and I sure don't understand how having my apartment broken into relates to murder." She paused beside the sofa, unwilling to take a seat if it meant this man would insinuate himself beside her. She couldn't think with him so close.

"You can help me." His gray eyes seemed so confident. So certain. "And you can start by calling me Wes."

"I don't think that's such a good idea." She needed barriers to ward off the train wreck certain to ensue if she ever acted on her newfound lust for one of New York's finest.

She dated artists. Men who weren't afraid to explore their creative side, or at very least, their sensitive side.

Wesley—Wes—didn't look like the type to get in touch with his emotions anytime soon.

"It's an excellent idea because you and I are going to get to know each other a hell of a lot better for the next few days—weeks—however long it takes for me to catch my bad guy." He frowned. "Or bad *girl* in this case."

"That's impossible." No way, no how, would she allow herself to get any closer to this man. She'd already experienced the sizzle of his briefest touch. How could she ward off that kind of sexual firepower for days—possibly weeks—on end? "I've got a multimillion dollar company to run. A CEO to hire. Do you have any idea how much my father's death has compromised his business and all the people who count on Boucher to make their living?"

"No. But I have a fair idea that your earnings will continue to go down once it's made public that the Boucher heiress can't make time in her busy schedule to help police catch a killer."

His words delivered a resounding slap to her conscience, a plea she couldn't very well deny. No matter that her life had been turned upside down, or that her bid for independence from her powerful family would be put on hold until she could recreate her inventory of artworks. She needed to pull her head out of her own problems and remind her body that Wes Shaw was off-limits long enough to help him find his criminal.

She was so caught up in her own thoughts, she didn't realize Wes reached for her until his hands were on her upper arms, the fabric of her crimson jacket practically incinerating beneath that simple touch.

"Please, Tempest." His gray gaze jump-started an erratic and totally juvenile beating of her heart. "Help me."

She was in over her head with this man after knowing

him for less than two hours. But he needed her help and she planned to give it to him, consequences be damned. And not just because she found herself thinking about what it might be like to kiss that blunt mouth of his.

No, Tempest planned to help him because she wouldn't allow her personal space, her private creative haven, to be invaded by street thieves, or prostitutes, or—she took a steeling breath—*murderers*.

Yet, even as she gave him an affirmative nod, she kept hearing a familiar swell of music somewhere in the back of her mind.

Like sand through the hourglass…

In the course of a couple of hours, Tempest's life had definitely become a soap opera.

CHAPTER THREE

OVER THE NEXT HOUR, Wes helped Tempest sort through the wreckage of her apartment. Cleanup wasn't a part of the NYPD response to a break-in, but as a detective and a nine-year veteran on the force, he'd bought himself a little leeway when it came to handling cases.

He used the time to phone his partner, dodging most of Vanessa's questions since he didn't want to discuss the case where Tempest might hear. There would be time enough to catch up with Vanessa tomorrow. For tonight, as long as he had won Tempest's compliance, he planned to find out everything he could about MatingGame and her role in the Internet dating service.

Now, he taped up another box of broken statuary pieces while she swept up some of the dust. She'd changed into a pair of jeans and a simple black blouse at some point, probably while he'd been on the phone. The velvet choker with the smoky crystal remained around her neck, but she'd tied back her curly dark hair with a black and red zebra-print bandana.

He stacked the third box of smashed clay pieces on top of the others and then paused to watch her while she worked. She wasn't at all what he'd expected.

His mental image of a Manhattan socialite pretty much coincided with the stereotype—vain, spoiled, self-involved. Yet here she was, living in a Chelsea studio that had to be far beneath her financial means, with no household help in sight. She swept up her own messes, microwaved her own popcorn and kept stealing glances at a small television that seemed to be tuned nonstop to overblown daytime dramas. Even without the audio, the action on screen snagged most of her attention while she cleaned.

Except for the handful of times he'd caught her sneaking glances at him. Some kind of heat sparked between them and Wes would be stupid to deny it. He didn't plan to act on it—in fact, he would make damn sure to ignore it—but the sexual friction had made for a tense day. He was pretty sure she fought against the chemistry even harder than him.

"Do you mind if I have a look through your computer?" Wes propped his elbow on the stack of boxes and studied her. "Ever since we found the note from the perpetrator, I've been curious to take a look around your files and see if he left a trail." Besides, staring at a computer screen would prevent him from staring at Tempest.

"Sure." Setting the broom aside she washed her hands and pulled two bowls out of a cabinet. "We can have our dinner—such as it is—while we surf. Maybe then you can explain to me what MatingGame has to do with your murder case." She pulled two bottles of water out of the refrigerator. "Is water okay? The secret to my latest diet is not to bring anything in the house that I shouldn't eat."

Wes grabbed the bottles from her and carried them toward the computer, grateful for another topic. "I thought you were going to prove me wrong about jet-setting heiresses."

"I'm not a jet-setting heiress so I'm proving you wrong already." Her voice followed him a few steps behind as the scent of buttered popcorn filled the room.

Eloise lifted her head from her paws as he walked by her, tail thumping the floor.

"You're living on a diet of popcorn and water." He slid into the red, high-backed chair in front of the computer and told himself that finding out more about Tempest was part of his job. The fact that he happened to be enjoying himself was a bonus. "You must know that's exactly what I'd expect from you highbrow types. You probably had a half ounce of cottage cheese on a lettuce leaf for lunch, right?"

"Wrong again." She set down their popcorn on a foldout shelf before pulling over one of the dining room chairs to sit beside him. Before she lowered herself into the chair, she whistled to Eloise and tossed the dog a pink Milk-Bone.

"I bet I'm not far off." Wes concentrated on the scent of popcorn in an effort to shut out the soft fragrance of the woman making herself comfortable next to him.

She sure didn't seem like the prostitution type, even with the high percentage of lacy undergarments still strewn around her apartment like visual sex triggers guaranteed to make him start drooling. And she didn't seem to be hiding anything, either. Other than her lunch menu, of course.

"I skipped lunch actually," she finally admitted, her gaze fixed on the computer screen as he pulled up the "Properties" information box on the unnamed document informing Tempest she was in the wrong business.

"Even worse than a lettuce leaf." He tossed a handful of popcorn in his mouth and jotted down the time the document had been created. 12:53 pm. "You said you got home around two?"

"I got to the building at five minutes before two. My meeting ran late today and then Eloise stopped to beg the hot pretzel vendor for a treat." She glared at Eloise who sniffed the floor for any leftover crumbs.

"It's no wonder your dog has to beg on the street if you feed her like you feed yourself." He cracked open his bottle of water and took a swig before digging into the popcorn bowl again. "But it's a damn good thing you didn't get here any sooner today since you missed your uninvited guest by less than an hour."

Wes didn't want to think about how different his day would have been if he'd been called to Tempest's apartment on an assault case. Or worse.

His popcorn stuck in his throat.

"Tell me why you think MatingGame is involved in prostitution." Tempest tucked her feet underneath her thighs, folding herself up into a more comfortable position on her chair.

Not that he'd let his gaze wander over her delectable body. He was simply making smart cop observations.

Yeah, that was it.

"Anonymous tip." He clicked through a few more screens before opening her browser and surfing to the MatingGame site. "Add that to the fact that our murder victim had a reputation for visiting prostitutes every Saturday night, and then this past Saturday his appointment book had an entry to meet someone he designated simply as a blonde from MatingGame."

She wriggled in her seat beside him, the wooden dining room chair squeaking as she moved.

"Maybe he got tired of paying for sex and decided to use a more tried and true means of getting horizontal." She reached over him to point out a little red box at the bottom of the MatingGame home page. "Click here to move straight to the dating profiles."

"I don't get paid to come up with the most creative

scenarios for a crime. I follow the obvious path first."
Wes took a deep breath to steel himself against the surge
of hunger brought on by the soft shift of her body beside
his. She was close enough that he could hear the whisper
of fabric as she moved. Her shoulder brushed his arm as
she leaned in front of him, and he could have sworn one
wayward curl of her dark hair skimmed his cheek.

Of course, the breath that he hoped would steel his
nerves only filled his nostrils with her warm, nutty
scent—something sultry and feminine and definitely
edible. Whatever it was, he damn well wanted a taste.

He clicked the red box she'd indicated with a vengeance, hoping like hell she wouldn't have any reason to
point to the computer screen again. How could a man keep
his mind on work with such an abundance of soft femininity leaning and bending and stretching beside him?

"Are you comfortable yet?" He turned on her, not
meaning to glare, but didn't she realize how distracting
all that wriggling could be?

"You got the good chair." Frowning, she looped an arm
over the back of the wooden seat. "I can't sit still if I'm
not comfy."

Damnation. He stood, silently rolling the red office
chair toward her until she swapped places with him. He
dragged the wooden chair in front of the computer and
turned it around so he could straddle the seat. They would
both be better off if he didn't get too relaxed in her living
room anyhow.

"So the obvious answer is that his MatingGame date
was a prostitute?" She reached over him again to tap the
blank screen with one manicured finger. "I think the
women's profiles are on the left. Sorry my dial-up connection is slow, but you can go ahead and click here and
it will advance you to the next screen."

This wasn't going to work. Wes was choking on his own lust. The women he'd slept with in the last eighteen months hadn't been people he'd pursued. They'd shown interest in him, he'd succumbed to biology. The encounters had been simple. Neat. Easy.

And completely unlike the heat licking over him because of one curvy, wriggly, delicious-smelling woman. It would be different if he could just take her right now and get it over with. Right there, in her red chair, where she'd damn well be comfortable.

Only she wouldn't stay comfortable for long. If he had his way, she'd be sighing, moaning and writhing all over him until she'd achieved body-rocking sexual bliss.

While they waited for the page to load on the screen, Wes downed the rest of his bottle of water but didn't come close to dousing the heat inspired by Tempest Boucher.

"There we go," she murmured as thumbnail photos of dozens of women appeared on the monitor. "I haven't looked at the site in quite a while, but if I remember correctly, these are the dating profiles for every woman in the system except for the clients who sign up for the Blind Date service. When we took over the company, we helped MatingGame make sure all the e-mail addresses were verified to cut down on bogus profiles. I can't imagine women who were prostituting themselves would give out information where they could be tracked."

"You'd be surprised." Forcing himself to concentrate on his case, Wes enlarged two of the profiles for closer inspection. "The city has slacked off on prosecuting crimes some people argue are victimless. Because of the lack of vigilance, escort services thrive and they can be very aggressive about advertising."

She frowned. "I've never studied the site that thoroughly from anything but a business point of view, but

I know firsthand that valid relationships have formed through the help of MatingGame. One of the company accountants got married last fall to a guy she met through the service."

"Probably most of it is legit. My guess is that there's a protected link, some hidden branch of the business that hires out escorts." He scanned the profiles he'd pulled, not really sure what he was looking for. His professional hunger to solve the mystery seemed to be slowly giving way to a different kind of hunger that wouldn't do either of them any good.

"Preferences—threesomes, foursomes and more." Tempest read aloud one of the entries in the provocative profiles designed to generate plenty of interest for people looking for a date. She sounded vaguely scandalized, but that didn't stop her from reaching for the mouse once again. "Do you think she'll just pick one guy or will she choose four and ask them all to meet her at once?"

"Wait." Wes restrained her wrist, unable to sit still while she stretched her delectable body in front of him for the third time. "I'll get it."

She froze there, body unmoving, her pulse pounding beneath the slight pressure of his thumb. "I just wanted to see what came up when you clicked on the hyperlink for threesomes. I guess I didn't realize people were so... *specific* about what they wanted in a partner."

"But if we start following all the options that catch our attention we'll be here all night." He held her wrist, held her gaze, hoping all the while she'd comprehend his real meaning.

It would have required a supreme act of willpower not to skim his thumb over the silky skin. And after wrestling his growing attraction to Tempest over the last few hours, Wes found he no longer possessed the restraint. He traced a line down the delicate tendons there, absorbing the smooth perfection of her.

Her lips parted, her faded lipstick revealing the natural color of her soft pink mouth beneath. Hypnotized by the perfect shape of the lush Cupid's bow, Wes hovered closer until Tempest pulled away.

"Then I guess we'd better keep our attention more strictly focused." Freeing her wrist, she reached for her water bottle and unscrewed the top. "I'll check out the threesomes later."

Wes wanted to redirect his thoughts but couldn't seem to force himself to turn back to the computer. Lust still surged through him like the Eighth Avenue Express and she just shrugged it aside, as if it was all in a day's work for a pampered, privileged heiress. Did she get off on making men drool and then leaving them wanting?

He didn't know what games this woman was playing, but he damn well wouldn't be leaving her apartment until he found out.

As she STARED BACK into the stormiest gray eyes she'd ever seen, Tempest decided Wes looked angry. No, more like quietly seething.

Well—newsflash—she wasn't exactly thrilled to have him waltz in here and take over her home, her computer and her hormones, either.

"Seems to me you've made concentration impossible." Wes shoved aside their popcorn bowls before taking her water bottle from her hand, carefully screwing on the top, and pushing that away, too. "Has it ever occurred to you all that stretching and reaching over me combined with your infernal fascination with threesomes just might distract a man?"

"I am not fascinated by—" How dare he? Of all the

presumptuous, arrogant things to insinuate. "Are you accusing me of flirting with you?"

"What would you call it?" He didn't raise his voice, instead keeping his tone very, very soft. "I'm not opposed to starting something between us if the appropriate time arises after I close my case. But I'll be damned if I'll let you get away with a lot of suggestive talk and sidling up close only to have you leave me high and dry and completely incapable of getting any work done."

"You think I'm playing the tease?" And didn't that just beat all? "I was nice enough to make you popcorn and I didn't even say a word when you took over my computer keys like you own them, even though I'm more familiar with my computer and this Web site than you are. Can I help it if I'm a little impatient to get through our work for the night so I can clean up the rest of the apartment and get back to my life?"

"But not impatient enough to point out the threesomes link?" He eased back ever so slightly, his self-assured body language somehow conveying a smugness that he'd made his point.

"So sue me for a prurient streak." She had *so* not been flirting with him.

Had she?

Forcing herself to consider the notion, she wondered if her sexual impulses could conspire to act without her explicit permission? What if her artistic persona and businesswoman facade hid yet another facet—a decadent and determined inner seductress? She'd blossomed into a daytime TV heroine in record time today. All she needed was a bout with amnesia.

Maybe she had fallen through the damn sand in the hourglass at 2:00 p.m. today. Instead of transitioning from businesswoman Tempest to artist Tempest this afternoon as usual, she'd walked into a time fugue and ended up in the middle of the drama.

Frustrated with herself, with him and with the undeniable attraction she felt for a man she probably had nothing in common with, she forged ahead. "Look, I'm sorry if it seemed like I was coming on to you. The profiles happened to intrigue me."

"So you're saying your sudden interest in threesomes didn't have a damn thing to do with me?"

"Correct."

He grinned. A slow, sexy, I'm-going-to-have-you grin that incited a sensual shiver down her spine. "Good. Because I'm not the kind of guy who shares."

TEMPEST was still recovering from that grin two hours later as Wes clicked through profile after profile, searching for some clue on his murder case.

She might have been able to forget about their exchange if she hadn't been subjected to reading through all sorts of kinky sexual fetishes and fantasy requirements for every woman in search of a date on the MatingGame site. But honestly, how could she think about motive and intent when every page that scrolled over her screen referenced a new sex act she'd never tried?

She was beginning to feel very deprived and inexperienced, but she had no intention of allowing Wes to read any hint of hunger in her eyes. Restless and on edge, she sprang up from her chair.

"I should take Eloise for a walk." Seizing on the idea like a lifeline, she started picking up their popcorn dishes along with some Thai food take-out containers from the dinner Wes insisted they eat.

"I'll go with you." He unfolded his tall body from the

unforgiving wooden chair that had to be damn uncomfortable by now.

"That's okay. You finish up and I'll be back in a minute." Maybe then she could reclaim her apartment and her wayward sexual thoughts.

"And what if your apartment is being watched?" He took the empty containers from her arms and dumped them in the wastebasket they'd left in the middle of the studio during their clean-up efforts. "If my murder case is linked to your break-in, then you're dealing with a dangerous threat. My guess is the killer came here hoping to erase her profile from the MatingGame database and when she didn't find the Web site files on the computer, she trashed the apartment and left the message to scare you."

If Tempest hadn't been frightened before, she sure as hell was starting to worry now. Almost enough to pack up her stuff and sleep at her family's ostentatious place on Park Avenue, but not quite. "Don't you think this murdering prostitute chick was a little excessive in wrecking the apartment? She broke every statue I ever made."

"Don't forget we're dealing with a criminal mind. Studies show a high percentage of these people are mentally unbalanced in one way or another." He whistled to Eloise, who came bounding over, pink tongue lolling out one side of her mouth. "All the more reason to let me go with you tonight."

"You haven't seen Eloise in action." She couldn't let Wes start thinking he needed to look out for her. She hadn't even managed to free herself from her family business yet, so she definitely couldn't afford to get mixed up with anybody who might start having expectations of her. "She might look sweet and friendly, but she's as kick-ass as any police dog when it comes to watching my back. I couldn't ask for better protection."

"Unless the killer shoots her." Wes pulled Eloise's leash down from a hook by the front door like he'd been living there all his life. "I'm not trying to scare you, Tempest, but you owe it to yourself and your dog to be careful until I catch this person."

She willed herself to nod her head. He was right, and she knew it.

Tempest just hadn't figured out how to reconcile her need for independence with her desire to stay alive. The choice might not have been so difficult except that she wanted to stand on her own two feet and Wes Shaw looked like a man well-versed in sweeping women right off them.

CHAPTER FOUR

WES STUMBLED over his own feet the next morning, bleary-eyed and fuzzyheaded after too little sleep. Blindly he fought his way through the maze of gym equipment that accounted for the sum total of his living room furnishings. Despite his best efforts, he stubbed his toe on a dumbbell and unleashed a string of curses that brought his St. Bernard, Kong, running from the bedroom with a woof.

"All clear," Wes shouted to the dog whose protective instincts would have made Miss Independent Boucher break out in hives.

She'd practically hyperventilated the night before when Wes suggested he spend the night at her place for safety reasons. Suddenly, she'd developed all sorts of plans for beefing up the security around her apartment, insisting she'd be fine without his help. He'd tried to convince her to go back to her family's place where she apparently stayed during the week, but she'd been stubborn on that count, too.

Damned independent woman. Thinking of her there alone had cost him plenty of shut-eye.

He'd stayed up half the night thinking about her, after checking and re-checking every lock in her apartment. Her door had shown no visible signs of tampering, but the only way into the third floor space had been through the front entrance or the door to the fire escape, which had a dead bolt whose lock was collecting dust. Wes had talked to her superintendent along with the old woman who lived a few doors down and had been home during the break-in. Neither of them had heard or seen anything unusual.

After forcing himself to leave her building, he'd gone back to the precinct to go over his case file on the murder and enter an incident report about Tempest's intruder. But late-night brainstorming with Vanessa hadn't helped them figure out the connections between their murder investigation and Tempest or MatingGame.

At least they'd eliminated Tempest as a murder suspect since she had an ironclad alibi for the victim's time of death. A lady photographer caught her date with a local coffee shop owner on film for a tabloid column, and Wes ended up with the distinct displeasure of confirming with the guy that he and Tempest had taken in a movie together that night. Too bad no amount of the man's assurances that they were just friends did a damn thing to improve Wes's mood. Obviously, he shouldn't care who she dated, but it irritated him to picture her with the artsy-fartsy coffee shop guy who managed to weave Kafka references into conversation on two separate occasions.

And as if that wasn't bad enough, Wes now discovered he'd lost his taste for coffee.

Reaching into the refrigerator for a bottle of some bogus energy drink, he chugged a few swigs and started thinking through his day. First and foremost was making a phone call to authorities in Mexico for some more information on Tempest's father. Not that he didn't trust foreign cops—he just didn't trust *any* cop outside his own precinct.

A suspicious nature came with the badge. And Wes had all the more reason to be careful with Tempest since his instincts couldn't be trusted where she was concerned. He planned to check her out ten ways to Sunday so the next time he showed up on her doorstep, he wouldn't have to hold himself back from the attraction that had gnawed at him ever since he'd first walked into her apartment.

Because the next time she leaned and stretched or wriggled those oh-so-fine curves of hers in his direction, he had every intention of showing her how appreciative he could be.

TEMPEST DIDN'T APPRECIATE the stomach-clenching fear her intruder had instilled in her.

She might have given in to her worries and spent the weekend at the Boucher family home if it hadn't been for Eloise. Her dog had slept by her all night, ready to keep away any returning criminals or stray bogeymen who threatened her safe haven. Too bad her faithful canine wasn't as effective at keeping away men who threatened her peace of mind.

This morning, Tempest had been awake since dawn, cleaning and organizing the studio until she'd achieved some semblance of its former order. Now she reviewed the summary of her missed *Days* episode online while she told herself she wasn't listening for Wes's footsteps in the hallway.

She'd read the same line three times about the latest character to come back from the dead—normally a topic she loved—when Eloise ran to the door and barked.

Tempest peered through the peephole in time to spy a familiar figure striding down the hall. Obviously, her dog was even better attuned to the new man in their lives than Tempest. By the time Wes rapped on the door, she was already opening it.

"Did you even check to make sure it was me?" Wes

frowned at her, his vintage suit replaced by faded jeans and a blue T-shirt underneath a long tweed wool coat.

In a word—*yum*. The more fitted clothes were put to good use on a man as ruthlessly toned as Wes Shaw.

"Eloise told me it was you." She opened the door wider, her gaze flicking south as he walked past her into the apartment.

So she noticed he had a great butt, okay? That didn't mean she was going to do anything about it. Slamming the door shut behind him, she braced herself for another round of temptation. She'd already decided today would be all about clearing her name with Wes and helping him find out what was going on with MatingGame.

"She *told* you?" He leaned down to pet her pooch's ears before tossing a folder on the boxes of debris she'd stacked by the front door. "Lucky for you, I own a dog, too, or I might think you were losing your mind."

"You have a dog?" She shouldn't ask him about it, didn't need any reason to like this guy any more than she already did, but curiosity got the better of her.

"Kong. She's been with me since— For about two years."

She sensed more to that story, but it didn't look like he'd be sharing any more of it since he backed closer to her computer.

"Kong's a girl?"

"Trust me, it fits. She's not a girlie girl." He bent over her keyboard and scanned a few lines about her soap opera before moving his hand to the escape key. "You mind if we pick up where we left off last night?"

Her heart slugged in her chest at the images that idea conjured. What if they picked up right at the point when Wes had been sitting beside her, his steely gray gaze drifting down over her mouth? Lingering.

She blinked hard, waiting for her clearheaded thoughts to return. Daydreaming about Wes wouldn't get anything accomplished today and she refused to let a little sexual attraction delay his progress on clearing her business's name.

"That's fine. I placed a call to the MatingGame head Web mistress who still oversees the day-to-day operations of the company. She's out of town until Wednesday, but I left her an urgent message that we needed to discuss the business. I can't imagine MatingGame is involved in anything improper, but if there is trouble in the company, this woman will know exactly where to look for it."

"Good. Were you able to access her files for the site?" Wes slid into the seat in front of the computer and clicked a few buttons to review recently downloaded material.

"Her assistant sent a disk over by courier. It's in the drive now." Tempest watched him go to work on the files, his computer savvy obvious as he opened windows and accessed files.

"Can I get you some coffee?" She could do that much at least, since she would have offered the same to any other visitor.

He grumbled something unintelligible under his breath and then asked for tea.

Three hours and numerous cups of tea later, Wes hadn't found anything unusual in the computer files. He'd forwarded names and addresses to his police station, checking out the women—and even some of the men—who posted profiles on MatingGame. So far not a single person had been linked to prostitution or violent crime. He'd flagged two sex offenders who had snuck through the screening process, however, and reported them to police stations in California and Wisconsin where the profiles originated.

Tempest couldn't help but admire his thorough approach to his work and the noble intentions behind it. She could appreciate the importance of his job, even if it put her on the defensive as owner of the dating company.

Sipping from a small glass of orange juice, she stole past the small desk for the tenth time in the last few hours, curious about his work but not wanting to get too close to him. He'd warned her about sitting beside him last night and she'd taken him at his word. No way would she send him any signals that implied sexual interest.

Even if she felt it.

"If you told me what you were looking for, maybe I could help you find it." She set down her juice to wave her laptop in front of him. "I could work at the table and review files from there."

But Wes scarcely seemed to hear her, his concentration devoted to the text onscreen, which he'd enlarged. "Take a look at this."

She started to lean over his shoulder and then decided she'd be better off just pulling up a chair, since he seemed engrossed in his work anyway. Settling next to him, she retrieved her juice in an effort to keep cool around the sexy detective. "It's the coding for one of the profiles, right?"

Her gaze scanned along the text that suggested the woman who'd written it was especially adept at blow jobs.

Tempest nearly spewed her orange juice.

"Yes. But it's unusual coding since it includes this graphic of an asterisk here and I can't see any explanation on the site for what significance an asterisk has. Do you know?"

Blinking her way past the shock of *blow jobs* written in sixteen-point font, Tempest tried to focus on his question and not wonder if there was actually a technique to good blow jobs. What other key pieces of sex advice had she been missing out on all her adult life?

"I don't know what the asterisk means. Perhaps it only has significance to the site managers?" She congratulated herself on her calm, intelligent words despite her ridiculous thoughts. "Maybe it means the woman in question is a repeat customer or received a good rating from her dates or something."

"But why put it there unless the Web site wants customers to see it?" Wes turned toward her, swiveling in his chair until he faced her head-on.

"Valid point." She half wondered if the asterisk denoted adept blow job givers. "I can put in another call to the MatingGame people and see what they say."

"What if it denotes the prostitutes in the crowd so that visitors who are aware they're available can make sure they choose from the right pool of women?"

"I don't know." Shrugging, she found it hard to believe MatingGame had anything to do with prostitution. Or was it just that she couldn't bear for her business instincts to have been so dead wrong? "Did you check out other women who have the asterisk graphic on their page?"

"I'll put someone on it. I know you don't want one of your companies to be found guilty of trafficking in sex, but one way or another, I have to get to the bottom of it."

"I'm just as eager as you are to figure out what's going on." She didn't need her board of directors questioning her business decisions now.

Reaching down to the floor, she picked up her laptop to show him how helpful she could be in his case.

Except that her arm brushed his leg as she moved.

JUST AN ACCIDENT?

Wes might have written off the barely-there touch as

unintentional, except that coincidences were piling up as fast as he could count them in this investigation. His murder case just happened to be linked to Tempest Boucher, who seemed to be the target of an intruder bent on destruction. And he still wasn't comfortable with the fact that her father had died while out with a MatingGame client, same as the victim in Wes's case.

Maybe the incidents didn't have a damn thing to do with one another and it had all just been chance. But— more likely—the events were genuinely related. He was anxious to speak to the day-to-day operations manager of MatingGame to see if she was selling more than dating advice.

Either way, Wes had reached his personal coincidence quota today. Since Tempest had touched him, he could only believe that she'd meant it.

Shifting beside him, she hefted her small computer onto the desk, her cheeks flushing pink.

"Sorry." She murmured an apology before cracking open the case of her laptop.

"Are you?" He studied her while she flicked through the opening screens as her computer warmed up. One brown curl grazed her temple while the rest remained knotted haphazardly at the back of her head with only a felt tip pen to keep it in place.

She blew the curl away from her eyes impatiently as she huffed out a sigh. "No, actually, I'm not a bit sorry. I can't help you unless I can access the MatingGame site. It's not my fault your he-man sprawl of legs takes up every square foot of space beneath the desk."

He watched her brow furrow in concentration, her lips pursed while she tapped more keys on the laptop. His gaze lingered on her mouth, which appeared deliciously free of lipstick today.

No doubt about it, he wanted her. Her alibi checked out for his case, so he wasn't worried about the ethics of the situation. And although he wanted to find the homicidal hooker who had taken down her victim a week ago, Wes didn't really have any other professional interest in MatingGame. If some facet of the company was involved in prostitution, Wes would stake his reputation that Tempest Boucher didn't know a damn thing about it. Either way, that wasn't his department. Another cop would make that bust, not him.

From where he was sitting, there wasn't a reason in the world not to pursue the only woman to capture his interest in longer than he cared to remember.

"I checked your alibi." He tossed the comment out there, as he navigated his way through a few more profiles of New York–based singles on the MatingGame site.

"Alibi?" Her computer keys stopped tapping.

"For last Saturday night." His gaze wandered over another curly-headed brunette on-screen but the vampish female whose profile touted her S and M expertise left him cold.

What was it about Tempest that set a torch to his libido?

"I almost hate to ask why I'd need an alibi for last Saturday night." She swiveled away from her laptop to face him.

"I wanted to be damn sure you weren't my murderer before things started heating up between us." He downsized the S and M woman and clicked on a—surprise—totally nude chick. There hadn't been many nude photos on the site, but nudity wasn't prohibited by the guidelines either.

"I rescue animals from trash cans, for crying out loud. Why would I ever kill someone?" She huffed out a sigh before turning toward his computer screen and the naked babe whose body was admirable enough, but it wasn't the body he wanted to see. "And on another note, nothing is going to heat up between us."

"Things are already heating up." He reached for the errant lock of hair at Tempest's temple and coiled his finger through the curl. Silky and sexy, the sable strand clung to his skin as if it wanted to linger with him.

Around him.

"You're just getting hot and bothered because you've been reading about every sex fetish under the sun and now you're staring at a disrobed female with perfect breasts." She eased back from him, taking her sweet curves and soft brown waves a few more inches away.

"She's not the one making me hot and bothered." He stared into Tempest's surprised brown eyes, wondering how she could possibly ignore such a blatant come-on. Did she find it that difficult to believe he would be interested? "Tell me, Tempest, do you date much?"

"Is this question of a professional nature?" She tugged on her necklace in what he began to realize was a nervous gesture. Fondling the small pearl at the end of the gold chain, she slid the charm to the right and then to the left, back and forth.

He imagined that mesmerizing touch skimming across his skin instead. Back and forth.

"Yes and no. We were talking about your alibi, but then it made me remember your alibi was a date." He rescued the pearl from her twitching fingers. "It made me wonder if you go out much or if you have a significant other in your life."

She went utterly still as he replaced the necklace just below her collarbone, being careful not to actually touch her. He had the distinct impression that under Tempest's

somewhat shy facade lay a woman of emotions as fiery
as her name implied. If he ever touched her...sparks
would definitely fly.

"I don't have time for significant others." She shrugged,
the movement shifting the pearl along her skin. "I barely
have time to watch my soap opera and feed my dog."

"So the coffee shop guy doesn't hold any special place
in your affections?" Not that he was jealous, damn it.

"I don't date." She said it more firmly, perhaps reading
some of his intent in his eyes. "And I don't think you can
find people who will be remotely compatible with you by
hanging out in your average nightclub or coffee shop. I
always thought a service like MatingGame would be the
better way to go."

"You can't test chemistry online." He couldn't imagine meeting a woman in such a sterile environment. How
would you know what the personal dynamics would be
like unless you met face-to-face? Much better to get
close.

"Chemistry is overrated. What about common interests and shared values? That's the heart of a great relationship."

Wes had heard the same spiel from his partner Vanessa,
but had never given her ideas the time of day. Now that
Tempest seemed to place stock in them, too, he wondered
how a man would go about winning over her mind as
much as her body.

Not that it should matter to Wes. His plans for Tempest
were simple. Straightforward. Soon to be satisfying.

"Maybe you're right." He turned back to the computer,
thinking he'd finish a little business at the same time he
got to know Tempest better. "I thought I'd play around
with the MatingGame application form anyway to get
an idea what they want to know to match people up with

dates. You want to help me? Maybe we can learn a few things about each other."

"We don't need to know much about each other to work together."

Undeterred, Wes started filling in blanks on the application form. "Qualities I value in a woman—loyalty, faithfulness, integrity."

Beside him, Tempest snorted.

"What?"

"What do you mean 'what'? You sound like you're shopping for a dog, not a girlfriend. Everybody wants loyalty in a relationship, Wes. That doesn't say squat about what kind of woman you'd like."

He stared at his application, still liking his answers. "This is the stuff that matters."

"What about creativity and vision? What about finding a woman who follows her dreams and celebrates life? Someone who isn't afraid to thumb her nose at conventional norms so she can immerse herself in her art..." She trailed off, her tawny gaze suddenly a bit horror-stricken.

Wes couldn't help the smile that curled his lips. He leaned in closer to Tempest, ready to find out if she harbored passion and fire beneath her nervous twitches and tendency to wriggle.

"Someone like you?"

CHAPTER FIVE

TEMPEST COULDN'T ANSWER. Couldn't think. Couldn't make herself move away from the six-foot-plus detective inching closer to her with every breath.

If she had reasons for keeping her distance from this man, she certainly couldn't remember them now when her whole body shivered in anticipation of whatever might come next.

His lips brushed hers in a whisper-light caress, just enough to whet her appetite for more. She caught the scent of peppermint tea on his breath and spicy aftershave on his jaw, her senses focusing solely on Wes until the rest of the room around her disappeared. She could only taste this moment, this man.

Sliding her hands up his shoulders, she absorbed the feel of him the way she would test a new batch of clay. Except Wes was already perfectly formed and sharply defined, chiseled by more skilled fingers than her own. She eased her way up his corded neck, molding her hands about his strong jaw until she pulled him closer, deepening the kiss.

He was beautiful. Her hands recognized the physical appeal of his cleanly defined muscles, savoring the supple skin over hard, rippled strength. But the delights for her hands couldn't come close to the feast for her mouth. His kiss teased and invited, daring her to give more of herself to him.

She hoped she knew better, because the languid strokes of his tongue tempted her to fall right into him. Breathe him in. Experience firsthand the most amazing sculpture imaginable.

She skimmed her fingers into his dark hair, winding them around his neck. He growled deep in his throat, encouraging her.

Until he kept on growling.

Arching back, she broke their kiss. Only to discover Eloise doing the growling a scant foot away, her ruff raised in aggressive warning as she snarled softly at Wes.

"No, Eloise," Tempest scolded her, using the stern voice the doggie-school instructor had taught her. "Go lie down."

Eloise cocked her head first to one side and then the other—clearly confused.

"She thinks I was devouring you," Wes supplied, keeping still until the dog trotted off to her open kennel where Tempest kept her blanket and a few toys.

"She's my voice of reason." Tempest knew she should listen to the dog instead of her sex-deprived libido, but Wes didn't make it easy. "And I would think she did you a favor."

"By making sure I didn't get past first base?" His softened tones brought to mind pillow talk and breakfast in bed. "How do you figure?"

She shut out the sound of that seductive voice in an effort to keep her distance. Maintain space. Remember that he suspected a business she'd brought on board at Boucher.

"Kissing me only complicates things for you. For all you know, I'm selling my fellow sisters on the street for a few quick bucks." Growing more indignant by the moment, she straightened in her chair, easing away from him. Where was his sense of honor, for crying out loud?

Wes rolled his eyes. "Whoever is behind this isn't selling anyone on the street. If my informant is right, anything connected to MatingGame would be very high-end."

"Earth to Wes—that's all the more reason you should suspect me. My whole lifestyle is very high-end." She looked around her unassuming little studio with a thirteen-inch TV and a futon couch she'd dressed up with extra pillows. "Okay, so maybe I don't look too sophisticated around here, but you know perfectly well I come from a ridiculously privileged family."

"Who's the cop here anyway? Will you trust me to do my job? I've got great instincts about who to suspect, and frankly, you seem a little too unfamiliar with threesomes to run a call-girl operation." He tipped back in his chair, drumming his hands on his chest. "Besides, when it comes right down to it, I'm not investigating MatingGame, *per se*. I'm only interested in how it relates to my murder case."

"So I should feel fine about you kissing me because you would never have to be the one to bust me?"

"You should feel fine about kissing me because I make you feel damn good."

Was she that transparent? She suppressed the urge to run her finger over her lips that still tingled from his kiss. "Do you always say what you think?"

"Hell no. I've been a detective for nine years, so there have been plenty of times I can't say what I think. Would I have a job that long if I pointed fingers at people and told them they were guilty as hell?" He tugged a curl at her shoulder and watched it spring back into place. "I've got to reserve my professional opinion, but I make snap judgments on a personal level just like everybody else. I know better than to share them."

"Really?" She noticed the ivy tattoo around his wrist and reminded herself to ask him about it. "Does that mean you have personal opinions about me you're not sharing, even though you have no problem telling me how *I* feel?"

His eyebrows shot up. "Lady, what you don't know about men is a lot."

"Didn't I say I don't date much?" Since her father had been too busy wheeling and dealing his way through life, Tempest had learned much of what she knew about men from soap operas. And while she adored her TV heroes, most of the men she met in real life didn't have secret identities, evil twins with ties to underworld gangs or sordid pasts in which they were raised by Gypsies.

"But you've heard the stat that men think about sex something like every ten minutes, right?"

"I thought it was every half hour."

He shrugged, his T-shirt shifting along with his sculpted muscles. "It's a lot. If you take that into account, you can probably guess that men spend an inordinate amount of time thinking about women. Yet I haven't shared any of those thoughts with you."

"Sex thoughts?" The air in the apartment suddenly seemed thick. Heavy. She breathed in the male scent of him and remembered the taste of his mouth.

"Definitely." He turned back to the computer abruptly. "In fact, as long as I'm thinking major sex thoughts, I might as well enter my profile into the computer to see what MatingGame comes up with as a match for me."

"You want to find a date?" Annoyed, she wondered how he could channel sexual energy so easily from one woman to another.

"I want to see if the system pairs me up with a legitimate date or a woman expecting to get paid for her favors." He tapped into the Blind Date section of the site. "But the only section of the company that could really orchestrate something like this would be the Blind Date service."

Intrigued, Tempest watched him fill out the form about what he looked for in a woman. Interestingly, he deleted his ideas about loyalty and faithfulness.

"You want a woman who takes pleasure in her femininity and isn't afraid to show it off." Tempest puzzled over the words, coming up with only a vague image in her mind. "You mean someone who wears short skirts?"

She really hoped he wasn't that tacky. Still, she couldn't staunch the urge to peer down at the long cotton dress she's tossed on this morning because it covered her from head to toe. The fashion equivalent of body armor.

"No. Although short skirts are never a bad thing." A dimple puckered into his cheek even though he didn't crack a smile. "I thought it would be too cheesy to say I'd like a woman with a closetful of lingerie."

Remembering the mounds of silk and lace strewn all over her apartment the day before, Tempest shrank deeper into her chair. "Very cheesy. Women want to be respected for their brains."

Although being drooled over for their bodies wasn't necessarily a bad thing, either. Especially if Wes Shaw happened to be the drooler in question.

Geez, what was she thinking? Thank God she hadn't worn a short skirt. She needed a cynical cop in her life like she needed a few more years in the corporate world. No, thank you.

"But now that I think about it, if I want to test the waters to see if there are women using this service to find paying customers, maybe I'd be better off sounding sex-starved. Cheesy may be the way to go." He continued typing away, finally turning the monitor toward her when he finished so she could see what he had written.

Tempest scanned the parts she'd already read, wondering what he'd thought of her heaps of lingerie scattered around her apartment yesterday. Had he been curious about the fact that there were ten times as many camisoles on the carpet as sweaters?

She happened to really enjoy lingerie.

"Must like dogs?" She couldn't help but focus on the one other characteristic she shared with Wes's cheesy dream woman.

"That's too honest, isn't it?" He tapped his finger along the delete key to get rid of his last line.

"And you honestly want a woman who likes dogs?"

"I've got Kong, remember? She's a St. Bernard, so she tends to scare off all but the most adamant of dog lovers."

There was something reassuring about a guy who had a pet. He could care for something. And chances were he had low blood pressure, right? Pet owners couldn't be too fussy or uptight. "A St. Bernard?"

"I know—you think it's too big for a city apartment, right?"

"Heck, no. I just say that because everybody automatically tells me I shouldn't keep Eloise cooped up in here with me and I'm tired of hearing it."

They compared dog notes, shared frustrations of hair on their favorite clothes and agreed a dog made the Sunday morning trek for the newspaper way more fun.

And somehow, Tempest really wished she'd be on the receiving end of his blind date.

"Are you really going to submit that form?" She wasn't sure if he'd been serious, or if he just wanted to see what kinds of questions the program generated.

"Of course. I need to talk to the woman in charge of MatingGame, but until then, it might help me figure out whether or not the business is legitimate." And before she could say another word about it, he clicked the send button to launch his dating criteria into cyberspace.

Surprise made her stare at the computer even after the form disappeared. "But you won't actually go on the date?"

"Depends." He shut down the screen and swiveled his chair toward her. "Right now I'm only interested in one woman."

Tempest held her breath while she waited to find out who that might be. Like a Friday afternoon cliff-hanger, he left her tense. Anxious. And so much more intrigued than she should be.

But no matter what he said, Tempest knew she couldn't let him stay.

WES TRACED HIS THUMB down her soft cheek, knowing he couldn't let her push him aside like she seemed to shove away everything else in her life. She wasn't close to her family and didn't enjoy being part of her father's business so she lived a secret life in Chelsea when she wasn't a corporate executive.

He liked Tempest. She didn't put on airs. Didn't pretend to be something she wasn't. And after women he'd dated in the past, he found that kind of honesty intriguing.

Hell—to be honest with *himself*—he hadn't found anything about women intriguing during the rough months since they found his first partner's body. So the fact that Tempest Boucher made him sit up and take notice was a major event.

He just didn't want to let her know it or he had the feeling she'd run far and fast.

"I think I've made it obvious I'd like to get to know you better." He'd let his kiss say as much, hadn't he? "But when it comes to my job, I can't afford to overlook any avenue that will achieve my ends. I need to know what's going on at MatingGame and Blind Date seems like the only place on the site that might allow a hooker to ply her trade."

"You think your killer could be working alone? Maybe this woman doesn't go through any kind of service." Tempest remained very still as he touched her cheek.

Wes couldn't afford to encourage the hope in her eyes. "I doubt it. Most women in the business know that's not a safe way to work."

"So you'll test the Blind Date service personally." She raised an eyebrow, clearly disapproving of his methods. Still, she didn't take him to task for it, instead turning her attention to his hand. "Neat tattoo."

He stared down at the green ivy snaking around his wrist. "It was a good save."

"A save?" She wrinkled her nose. "What do you mean?"

"I tattooed an old girlfriend's name on my wrist and came to regret it when she cheated on me with another guy. But I went back to the shop and the artist managed to transform 'Belinda' into a chain of ivy." He'd actually asked for poison ivy at the time, using a twenty-two-year-old's logic that tying yourself to a woman was the equivalent of a bad rash. Luckily, the tattoo lady had ignored him and produced something a little tamer.

Being a horticultural nimrod, Wes didn't even know he'd gotten English ivy instead of the poison variety until a year later.

"Can you imagine?" Tempest shook her head, her brown curls hopping around her shoulders. "How could anyone be so greedy to need two men at once? I never understood the rationale behind cheating. If you want out of a relationship, just tell the other person. Is that so hard?"

"Careful, lady, or I'll start thinking you're harboring a big store of loyalty and faithfulness and all those things you assured me I could only find in a canine."

"I mold penises for a living, remember?" Her teasing tone made it clear she didn't want any part of a serious conversation. "You can't trust a woman who hunts down naked men to model for her."

He knew damn well she was yanking his chain. What could it hurt to yank back?

"Really?" Rising, he reached for the hem of his T-shirt. "I've been looking for an excuse to get naked with you. Why don't you give me your professional opinion?"

He waited for her to say no. Stop. Keep your clothes on. Anything. But as his T-shirt hit the floor and his hands reached for the button on his jeans, he wondered if maybe Tempest Boucher hadn't been bluffing at all.

She watched him in fascinated silence—hell, he hoped it was fascinated and not horrified—her eyes lingering on every inch of exposed skin. And suddenly, blood whooshed through him so fast he was halfway to having a heart attack and an erection that would be evident from two miles away.

Damnation. What kind of stupid-ass idiot started peeling off his clothes around a woman he hardly knew? A woman he really wanted?

Her avid gaze fell to the hard-on that could have been a circus attraction. Eyes going wide, she yanked her attention up to his face, cheeks flushed.

"I don't really hire naked models," she informed him, breathless. Coming to her feet, she tucked strand after strand of brown hair behind her ear.

"It's okay, I don't charge." He found himself stepping closer, incapable of exerting the effort required to keep his distance any longer. The circus erection had only gotten larger when those honey-brown eyes of hers caressed him.

Perhaps the size of his member should have alerted him to the fact that blood was no longer flowing to his brain. But then, his thinking was seriously impaired.

"Speaking strictly from a creative standpoint, I'm impressed." The single pearl she wore around her neck rose and fell with every rapid breath.

"What about from a personal standpoint?" He stopped an inch away from her, breathing in her scent, which he'd begun to recognize as almond.

He wouldn't step any closer without some sort of invitation. A sign.

"Personally speaking?" Now that her hair had been firmly tucked behind her ear, she pulled a strand forward and twisted it around her finger. "I might need more information before I can form an opinion."

"Ask away." He didn't mean to lean forward, but he must have—or she must have—because the soft fabric of her long, cotton dress brushed his chest.

His eyes crossed at the contact, her lush breasts tempting him beyond reason.

Still, she held back. She bit her lip as she seemed to struggle with her thoughts, her face a picture of sensual distress.

When she finally opened her mouth to speak, she murmured a quiet, "What the hell?" before she moved closer. Her hands landed on his waist to skim around his back. "Maybe I just need to feel for myself."

Heat flashed through him like a thunderbolt. His arms banded around her, dragging her into him. Her mouth opened beneath his, soft and warm and so damn inviting. He cupped her head to find the perfect angle, fingers stroking through her thick curls until he found the vulnerable stretch of her neck.

She arched into him, generous curves pressing against him. He wanted his hands everywhere at once, hungry to know the feel of her. Her dress swirled around his calves, clinging to the fabric of his jeans. A blend of soft textures assailed his senses—her hair, her skin, that dress of hers all begged to be touched. Everything about Tempest drew him closer, invited him to linger.

"Wes."

The sound of his name reached his ears, the only discernible word amid breathy sighs and the gentle smack of their lips.

Easing back, he peered down at her in the halo of light emitted by the computer screen, her apartment grown dark in late afternoon thanks to the short winter day.

"Too fast?" He hadn't meant to spin the kiss out, make it so important. But his good intentions had fled when she stared at him with those dark, hungry eyes of hers, and then once he'd kissed her—his body seemed to remember exactly how long it had been since he'd kissed anyone like he meant it.

"No." Shaking her head, her curls bounced restlessly. "Yes. Maybe. I just—"

Prying himself further away, he skimmed his hands up to the safer terrain of her shoulders. "You tasted so good, and it's been a long time for me. Sorry if I rushed you."

"It's not that." Her fingers alighted on his chest briefly, then skittered away again. "I welcomed the kiss and the ah—view."

He resisted a juvenile urge to flex for her. "My pleasure."

"But I don't think you realize what you'd be getting yourself into if we…continue in that vein."

"On the contrary, I think I know exactly what I'd be getting myself into, and after the fireworks of one kiss, I can say with some assurance that anything more than that would rock my whole damn universe." No sense denying the obvious—he wanted her.

"I don't mean that." She reached to flick on a desk lamp, bathing them in dim light. "I know that part would be great, but getting involved with me could be messy."

"I've already learned not to tattoo names on my wrist. What more do I need to know?"

"Every relationship I've ever had has been splashed all over the newspapers. Even taking in a movie with the coffee shop guy turned into a major ordeal, and you found out from him firsthand that it meant less than nothing." Huffing out a sigh, she blew a curl away from her eyes. "I just needed to warn you that hanging out with me will probably only lead to a big headache."

"We could keep things quiet." He traced the golden chain around her neck with his finger. "Private."

"Trust me, I've tried it. I couldn't even keep the results of my college final exams secret. My scores are still available on the Internet if you're interested, by the way."

Finally, Wes's brain began thinking again. Reason returned as he thought about his privacy vanishing the moment he started something with Tempest.

Could he afford to have his life served up for public consumption? Especially when he had a killer to catch?

"So you're willing to back away just because of the potential for a media splash?" Maybe she'd been thinking of him and trying to protect his private life. But what if she didn't want her well-known name linked with average Joe police detective?

He'd be willing to bet he wasn't the kind of man the Boucher family had envisioned for their daughter, even for something short-term. They were megamillionaires with a bona fide fortune to oversee and connections around the globe.

And he was…trying to make the city safer, one crook at a time. Or at least he had been until he'd been forced to face facts that Steve was dead three months ago. He'd been in denial for a long time that his partner had really died, and once his body was found, Wes had been rethinking his job. But whether he decided to remain with the NYPD or move into something with a little less potential for shifting loyalties and career burnout, Wes knew he would never be the kind of man a socialite-turned-corporate-executive needed.

He wasn't sure if he was backing away now for himself or because he sensed she had her own agenda for putting up barriers between them. Either way, he needed to regroup before they made a move that could hurt them both.

"I think it's only fair to forewarn you of the consequences. Think what you want about me or MatingGame, but I'd never purposely mislead anyone."

"Understood. And I appreciate the heads-up." He gathered a few papers he'd printed from the computer, hoping if he got some distance from her, he could make a decision without her almond scent fogging his brain.

Besides, he'd been serious about loyalty and honesty. They were a hell of a lot more important to him than creativity or access to millions of dollars. "I'll keep it in mind next time I get the urge to rip off my clothes around you."

Retrieving his shirt and the coat that he'd tossed over the chair, Wes jammed his arms through the holes and backed toward the door. They were from different worlds, damn it. Walking away from her shouldn't be so tough.

After exchanging quick goodbyes, he was out of her apartment and back on the street.

CHAPTER SIX

COULD THE MAN have sprinted off any faster?

Tempest decided even a hopeless optimist would have to agree that Wes couldn't wait to make tracks out of her apartment. He'd vanished as soon as she mentioned the possibility of media involvement, a surefire libido killer to most men.

Had she chased him away on purpose? Or had he been grateful for the excuse to reclaim a few more boundaries? She didn't know anymore, couldn't tell what had happened with her heart thumping like a pottery wheel overloaded with an uneven lump of clay. Why hadn't she paid better attention to what happened between them?

Whistling to Eloise, she gave the dog free run of the apartment again as she mindlessly clicked through some of the screens on the MatingGame site. If today had been a scene on her soap opera, she would have been damn certain Wes would return the following week to confuse her with more moral-melting kisses.

But this was real life, and she wasn't so sure he'd be back at all.

As regret stole over her, she found herself staring at a new, blank application form for MatingGame's Blind Date service. Who had opened that file? Tapping her finger idly on the mouse, she stared at the questions and found herself mentally penning her answers.

What are your turn-ons? Ignoring the *Playboy* centerfold feel of the short interview section, Tempest started typing the first response that popped into her head. "Men who don't care what I do for a living. Men who are comfortable in their own skin. Men who know what they want and aren't afraid to go after it."

In your face, Wes Shaw.

If he couldn't be the kind of man she needed—and really, what business did she have dating the cop investigating MatingGame?—maybe she should go out and find someone else. Spending time in Wes's arms had made her realize how long it had been since she'd indulged in slow, deep, hot kisses.

So what if she couldn't imagine anyone else's kisses tasting so good, or firing her up half as much as the ones she'd experienced this afternoon? Maybe just this once she'd take her dating fate into her own hands by meeting someone outside her small circle of friends and business associates. Someone completely different from the handful of guys she'd dated in the past.

Through Blind Date, she could remain anonymous, which suited her needs perfectly. Now, any guy who chose her profile wouldn't be dating her for her family connections. Too often in her sparse dating history, men had only been interested in her for one thing and—disappointingly enough—it wasn't even sex.

This way she could find out for herself if the Internet dating business worked legitimately. In her gut, she knew it did, damn it. Still, wouldn't it be nice to have proof firsthand to wave in front of Wes Shaw's handsome face?

Filling out the rest of the form, Tempest submitted her application for her first ever Blind Date before she gave herself time to change her mind. Didn't the old saying preach that what was good for the goose was good for the gander?

With a little luck, maybe she'd find someone else to quench the slow burn Wes had started deep inside her.

DAYDREAMING HER WAY through a board meeting Monday morning, however, Tempest had to admit some things were easier said than done.

Put Wes out of her mind? She must have been engaged in some serious wishful thinking over the weekend if she thought she'd forget about the hottest kisses on the planet. After a day and a half of catching herself remembering Wes's touch, she had to admit that no stray guy she found through a dating service would match up to the red-hot detective investigating her intruder. Entering her profile in the Blind Date system had been a rash act she had no intention of actually following through on.

At this moment, fantasizing about Wes held far more appeal than listening to her board bicker about who to appoint as the next CEO of Boucher Enterprises, so she allowed her imagination to run free. She'd learned that being a good manager involved a fair amount of listening to other people's concerns. Or at least, allowing other people to vent their frustrations even if she wasn't listening quite as closely as she should.

Hands smoothing over the napkin beside her cooling cup of darjeeling, Tempest's gaze dropped to the expanse of shiny mahogany conference table while Kelly Kline, VP of global development, found one excuse after another for why Boucher should look internally for a CEO.

The general consensus among the board was that Kelly wanted the top slot for herself—a feat that wouldn't happen as long as Tempest had any input. Kelly thrived at her job as a public relations guru who spoke three languages and made frequent trips abroad. But she seemed a little too calculating for Tempest's tastes. Kelly had proven to be a corporate shark and a bit of a tyrant in her department, yet extremely effective.

Allowing the woman to have her say, Tempest's thoughts ran to having Wes Shaw at her mercy on the mahogany conference table. She could envision the dark, strong wood as a perfect backdrop for the detective's lean, sculpted muscles.

The private conference room was her stronghold, the one place in the world where she reigned supreme. Because even if Tempest didn't enjoy her stressful job all the time, at least her personal meeting space was familiar terrain and she could be in control here. The sensation was a welcome one after she'd felt so helpless during the weekend with her apartment trashed and her sculptures destroyed. Wes had practically taken over the place with his big, I'm-in-charge presence and his knowledge of catching criminals.

If he set foot in this facet of her world, he would see a very different woman. And next time, Tempest wouldn't give him the upper hand over her again. She might lick every delicious inch of that primo male form of his, but she'd be damn sure to remain in control of the situation.

Remembering his horror at holding the broken clay penis in his hand, Tempest wondered how her artwork measured up to the man. Was he as impressive as her fanciful imaginings? Judging by the eyeful she'd gotten Saturday evening, she'd have to answer with a resounding yes. And if she ever had the man at her disposal on the conference table, she would damn well find out for sure. If he started getting naked with her again, she would make certain he finished the job.

"Tempest?"

Kelly's voice intruded in her fantasies, an unwanted female in the middle of a very hot daydream.

Frowning, Tempest blinked. Remembered she was supposed to be listening sympathetically to Kelly's reasons for why the board shouldn't interview the latest CEO candidate someone had suggested.

"I think we need to come up with a solution before the month is out," Tempest offered, deciding the time had come to put her foot down. The longer she allowed the board to waffle, the longer the company stayed in limbo. And seeing all her artwork destroyed this weekend had made her realize where her real priorities lay. She should be working on her statues and honing her craft instead of operating in survival mode at Boucher. "I'd like to take a private ballot one month from today for who we should interview and I'll pull three candidates from the pool. We're long overdue settling this."

Amid a flurry of protests, Tempest ended the meeting, feeling more sure of herself than she had in a long time. She should have set a deadline and stuck to it months ago. Perhaps her weekend intruder had done her a little bit of a favor in spite of the threat and the rampant wreckage. At least the incident had strengthened her resolve to get her life in order.

The board members filed out while she dumped her cup of tea in the sink at a wet bar. For a minute she thought she'd given herself a shock when a sizzle of electricity shot through her with a definite jolt.

"Knock, knock." The unanticipated masculine voice behind her made her realize that the shock had been of the sexual variety.

Turning, she found Wes framed in the doorway between her office and private conference room. A dark khaki trench coat hugged his shoulders, the stiff fabric dotted with raindrops. The overcoat appealed to her daydreaming mind, making her realize how much she'd like to play cloak and dagger with this man.

Not just any man, curse his hide.

Only Wes.

How had she ever thought she could work up the nerve to accept a blind date with anyone else when Wes seemed to be the only man appealing to her unexpectedly ravenous libido?

"Isn't my assistant out front?" She fumbled with her teacup, spilling a few last drops on her thumb.

"That's a hell of a welcome." He stepped inside the room, taking the long way around the oversize conference table to peer around the meeting space. He took in the long windows looking out over the city, the skyscraper climbing higher than any of the buildings around it so that her window didn't look into another office, the way that so much Manhattan real estate did.

He ran his hand along the conference table as he approached, whistling appreciatively under his breath. "Nice place you have here."

His hand on the mahogany surface called forth images from her bold fantasies. The daydreams taunted her now, sending a rush of desire through her. Funny how she could picture being brash and brazen with Wes so much more easily when he wasn't actually in the room with her.

Coward.

Her conscience railing at her, she washed the tea off her hands and steadied herself. He was just a man, after all.

Just a sexy, appealing man who could kiss her into a near-orgasmic state.

"Thanks." She tugged at the silk scarf around her neck, feeling a bit warm. "I'm just surprised to see you here since Rebecca usually fields all my appointments for me."

"I arrived bearing doughnuts and coffee. Maybe she forgot." He flashed her a disarming smile that would surely fluster the most dedicated of assistants.

Or maybe Rebecca simply thought she'd be doing Tempest a favor by providing her with a mouthwatering diversion to chase away the Monday morning doldrums.

"Can I get you anything?" Tempest opened the door of the minirefrigerator under the wet bar to reveal a wealth of soft drinks and flavored spring water. She might as well be civil, even if he had made it clear the other night that he wouldn't get involved with someone commanding such a prominent public profile. "I've got tea, if you like."

"No, thanks. That's not what I'm here for." Shrugging out of his coat, he folded the garment over one chair and then made himself comfortable in a large swivel seat at the head of the conference table.

Her seat.

"No?" She curbed her annoyance along with her lust, determined not to let either one show. Dropping into a chair midway down the table, she peered into her office and noticed the outer door had been shut, sealing them in complete privacy.

Had that been Rebecca's way of offering Tempest a few moments alone with Wes? Or had the gesture been Wes's attempt to sneak another kiss when he had no intention of giving her anything more substantial?

Neither answer soothed the increased tempo of her heart. She settled for simply casting him a level look and giving him her most businesslike boardroom face. "Then how about you tell me what brings you here."

AN OVERWHELMING DESIRE to get you naked?

Somehow Wes didn't think she'd appreciate the answer after the way he'd lit out of her apartment Saturday night. Thankfully, he had another reason for showing up in her penthouse office this morning.

"I wanted to make sure you were having additional security installed in the Chelsea apartment. Whoever broke into your apartment used some finesse to pick your lock in a way that didn't damage the door at all. You need something more sophisticated to keep out today's crooks." It was a legitimate reason to see her again, right? He'd mentioned security to her over the weekend, but she'd been jittery on Friday and he hadn't trusted that she fully comprehended the importance of the message.

Then by Saturday he'd had more on his mind than safety, a professional error he wouldn't be making again. He'd even taken the liberty of locking her office door behind him on the way in. Not that he really anticipated anyone coming after her on the most elite floor of corporate offices in the building, but it couldn't hurt to be safe.

Private.

Ah, hell, who was he kidding? He'd bolted the door in case she had the urge to take up where they'd left off on Saturday. He might not like the idea of her high-profile career and status as a social figure putting him in the public eye, but he didn't stand a chance at getting her out of his head. By Sunday night he'd realized he just needed to find more creative solutions to their problem of too much publicity because he wanted her too much to concern himself with the inconvenience of his mug in the paper on occasion.

Locking doors behind them seemed like a good place to start today.

"I called a security company this morning. They're going to come by tomorrow to install something." She shifted in her seat just enough to make the leather chair squeak.

And remind Wes of the restless way she'd brushed up against him when they sat at her computer together over the weekend. His body revved at the memory of her scent. Her nearness. He couldn't deny he wanted that again along with a whole lot more.

"They couldn't come out today?" He'd driven by her building twice last night, uneasy with the idea of her alone in apartment 35, guarded only by Eloise. And if he'd entertained a few fantasies involving Ms. Boucher while he was at it, that was his business.

"They already juggled around their schedule just to get out tomorrow." Sitting straighter, she folded her hands together as if to keep herself still. "Is there anything else I can help you with, Detective? I have a busy schedule today."

Her tone verged on frosty, but not nearly chilly enough to cool him off. Memories of their shared kiss had him in a state of perpetual simmer ever since he'd walked out of her apartment.

She looked different today in her executive suite than she had in her Chelsea apartment. She wore a vivid blue suit with a yellow silk scarf tucked into the neckline of her buttoned jacket. Tailored and sophisticated, the suit screamed high-powered exec, but Wes's eyes kept straying to the scarf as he speculated about what she wore beneath the jacket.

A blouse? Some kind of lingerie top like he'd seen strewn all over her apartment? Or nothing at all?

Aside from the sexy mystery of the jacket, her clothes now weren't all that unlike the ones she'd been wearing when they first met. Maybe it was the setting today, or just her attitude that seemed more cool and in-control. But there was a definite difference in her.

"I wanted to see if anything had turned up missing at your place now that you've had more time to look around."

"Nothing." She crossed her ankles beneath her chair, her weekend running shoes replaced by camel-colored leather pumps. "I don't think anything was stolen. All the intruder's effort seems to have been geared toward destruction."

Wes didn't like that one damn bit. "All signs point to the break-in being a threat, probably perpetrated by someone who has a particular beef with you. We didn't find any prints but yours around the apartment, so whoever trashed the place took time to cover their tracks."

Perhaps he'd finally succeeded in scaring her because she nodded with jerky movements, her fingers smoothing the scarf at her neck.

"I won't work at the studio anymore until the security is installed. I usually sleep at the family house during the week anyway."

"Good." He hated upsetting her, but there could be no help for it. "And hopefully we'll have some answers soon on MatingGame. I'm trying to set up a time to meet a date tomorrow night and we'll see if the service works as advertised."

"You're going on the date?" Color returned to her cheeks, her twitchy fingers stilling over her scarf.

"Since your Web mistress never got in touch with me, it's the fastest way to get the answers we need."

"Apparently Bliss Holloway's mother has been in poor health and Bliss is out of touch. I'm sure we'll hear from her soon." Tempest sounded aggravated and looked downright mad.

She couldn't be upset about the date? Maybe she was just annoyed he continued to check into her company, because his brain refused to consider that she could be... jealous?

The idea fanned the slow heat that had been building inside him all weekend long.

"Until then, I guess I'm going on a blind date." He looked back through her office toward her locked door. They were utterly alone, the conference room inaccessible to anyone else. Wicked thoughts came to mind. "Too bad *we* couldn't have enjoyed that kind of anonymity."

She stared back at him blankly for a moment until her honey-colored eyes narrowed. "What do you mean?"

"I mean, wouldn't it have been fun if we could have met under different circumstances?" He eased out of his seat at the head of the table and closed the distance between them, propelled toward her by a deep hunger he didn't fully understand. Halting a few inches away from her, he dropped into a swivel chair right next to her. "What would it have been like between us if I wasn't the cop investigating your company and you weren't a woman I needed to protect?"

Her fingers splayed on the mahogany conference table, her red nails as shiny as the richly polished wood. She stared down at her hand on the table for a long moment before meeting his eyes.

"It might have been very interesting," she admitted, voice soft with sensual promise.

Or was that hopeful thinking on his part?

The air around them turned warm and heavy. The raindrops that had soaked his hair and his coat seemed to evaporate in a slow hiss of steam as their bodies inched closer.

He reached for the length of yellow and blue silk around her neck, gently tugging the scarf from her jacket in one smooth, deliberate motion. She sat perfectly still as he watched the fabric uncoil from her skin.

No blouse beneath.

Just incredible cleavage and creamy smooth skin. Savoring the warm scent of the scarf that had shielded her breasts, Wes rubbed the fabric between his fingers and allowed a darkly erotic idea to take shape in his mind.

A way to accommodate their wish for anonymity.

"Maybe we can still have our own blind date," he whispered the suggestion that had been hovering around his brain, urging him to find a way to be with her. Skimming the silk up her cheek, he twined the material around her eyes. "A few stolen moments with no identities attached if your schedule allows."

When she didn't move so much as a muscle, he allowed himself to secure the cloth behind her head, tying it in a lazy knot.

While he waited for the full import of his suggestion to sink in, he studied the way she looked with the impromptu blindfold wrapped around her eyes. Wild brown curls escaped from beneath the fabric, the bright color of the scarf highlighting the pale perfection of her cheek. But as he watched, a tinge of hectic color brightened the exposed portion of her face. A rosy blush? Or the sensual flush of a woman slowly becoming turned on?

Her lips worked silently for a moment, as if she couldn't quite come to terms with what she wanted to say. The gesture drew his gaze, and sent a rush of heat southward. He thought about what it would be like to personally lick off every last bit of her lipstick before he explored her mouth, the unique taste of her, for hours on end.

"I've got appointments today," she finally managed, although the sighed sentiment didn't sound much like a protest. She wound her finger in one loose end of the scarf that draped carelessly over her shoulder.

"I warned your assistant my business with you might take precedence over everything else." Laying his finger along her lower lip, he stroked the soft fullness of her mouth. "And I locked the door."

The nutty almond fragrance she wore seemed all the more intense as the heat between them cranked up. Tempest nipped his finger before drawing it into her mouth and swirling her tongue around the digit.

His eyes were already crossing when she finally nodded. "Maybe you're on to something with this anonymous thing. But *you're* not wearing a blindfold."

Lowering his damp finger to the valley between her breasts, Wes traced a wet line over her ample curves.

"That's okay. I'm getting off on watching you wear one." The trace of moisture on her full lips was killing him. "And by now I've already forgotten everything we were talking about except how much I want you."

A hum of pleasure escaped her lips before she came up out of her chair and landed in his lap, her knees straddling his thighs.

The heat that had been on slow burn inside him all weekend roared into a full-fledged blaze as her compact curves and creamy legs arrived within reach. Her acquiescence was an unexpected gift. A tempting treasure.

An unbelievable freaking moment he wouldn't ever forget.

And he planned to savor every square inch of her, starting right now.

CHAPTER SEVEN

THERE WAS no stopping her now.

Tempest's bravado seemed to have increased tenfold the moment Wes wrapped the silk scarf around her eyes, relegating her world to a place of touches and tastes. The scent of his rain-dampened skin, the feel of his hands skating over her hips, drove her to the point of no return.

She'd been daydreaming about this an hour ago, and now that he was here, in the flesh, she planned to fulfill her fantasies just this once. Her appointments could damn well wait until another day.

Palms sliding beneath her jacket, Wes smoothed his thumb over her bare waist. She'd always been self-conscious of her curves, even more so after a candid photo of her dancing at a friend's wedding ran in the social pages with a caption implying she must have really enjoyed the bride's cake. But her admittedly ample curves didn't seem like such a bad thing when Wes got hold of them. His fingers sank into her softness, urging her closer to his lap and all the enticing male heat waiting for her there.

"You're sure you're okay with this?" Wes's voice wove through her steamy thoughts, his lips brushing her ear as he spoke. "I don't want to cause a professional flap for you."

She wouldn't allow him to stop. Not now when her mind swam with sensual imaginings, her body more in tune to his touch than it had ever been for any other man's.

"I dedicated twenty hours a day to this company for months on end after my father died." She didn't regret the time since it had given her a chance to finally understand the man who had always been too busy for her when he was alive. She'd come to peace with Ray Boucher in that time. But she wouldn't bury her own needs for the sake of the company forever. "I'm entitled to a few hours of downtime."

If she hadn't been blindfolded, her increased senses might not have picked up the low rumble of approval that went clear through Wes. His body practically hummed with anticipation now, and she couldn't quite believe she possessed so much power over the man.

Consumed with the need to fulfill her daydream visions, she edged backward on the chair, ready to drag him with her toward the conference table. But then his hands found her thighs, his thumbs sliding upward on the inside of her legs until she remembered exactly how much of a barrier stood between her and Wes now that she'd straddled him. Only a tiny triangle of peacock-blue satin shielded her from his wandering touch.

Maybe she could wait to tackle him onto the conference table. Right now, she could only think about what he might do when he discovered the decadent lingerie beneath her conservative suit. Heat licked tiny tongues of flame up her thighs as he nudged the nubby cotton tweed hemline higher and higher.

Cool air breezed between her legs before his fingers touched her. She held herself still, sensing his gaze on her now exposed hips.

"You're gorgeous." His whispered reverence soothed any wounds left by unflattering photos or the occasional broken zipper on her skirts. She delved beneath his suit jacket to touch him through his crisp blue shirt. Fiery warmth radiated from his shoulders, a wealth of heat she couldn't absorb fast enough.

"You just caught me on a good day." She knew she was a far cry from celebrity-perfect, but he made her feel beautiful.

"I've been dying since Friday trying to picture you wearing this kind of stuff." Wes's finger traced the outline of one satin strap holding her delicate G-string in place.

Part of her wanted to whip off the blindfold to see his eyes on her, but somehow it seemed easier to be bold and adventurous this way. With the scarf to keep her in the dark, she could be as brash as any daytime TV diva determined to have her own way.

Licking a kiss along his jaw, Tempest whispered in his ear. "You know I've got lots more where this came from." She gave her hips a little shake to make sure he knew what she was talking about. "If you please me today, maybe you'll be seeing more in the future."

Hooking his finger into the satin strap, Wes tugged gently but didn't pull the panties off. "I'd like that."

"I'd like more of you, Detective." She tugged at his tie, savoring the slide of hot silk between her fingers as she undid the knot. "You seem to be getting all the visuals here."

Nimble, quick fingers went to work on her skirt buttons. "You can't get a visual when you're blindfolded anyway. Why not let me worry about what to see?"

"Only if you let me worry about what to touch." She dropped her hand to his fly, amazed at her audacity. She'd never been this way with a man.

Her palm fluttering over the ridge in his trousers made his fingers move faster on her skirt. And then she lost track of his touch at her waist as all her attention narrowed to the hard heat of him.

She shoved his coat off his shoulders and felt him shrug out of his suit jacket. Clothes peeled off them in every direction, her skirt slipping to her feet, her jacket falling open to expose the peacock-blue satin bra with sheer lace insets.

He sucked in a breath and she almost envied him the ability to see. But she wasn't ready to leave the safety of her blindfold yet, not when it infused her with so much delicious daring. The heat steaming off her skin warmed her perfume and supercharged the light, almond fragrance she wore.

"Like what you see?" She tugged on his belt, while he remained still

"Incredible." His voice hit a hoarse note as she carefully unbuttoned his pants around an erection that would have made any woman's mouth water.

Although it wasn't her mouth going damp right now.

"I've been thinking about you today," she confided, easing his zipper down until his cock sprang free. "Even though I didn't want to."

He rolled the straps of her bra down her shoulders with his palms before lowering his lips to the curve of her neck. "I think I'm insulted."

"Don't be. In these fantasies of mine, you were very good." She shuddered as his lips roamed over the tops of her breasts, the low rumble of normal office conversation on the other side of one wall reminding her what a risk they took, although she knew no one would disturb her while her door remained closed. And no one would be able to hear her and Wes except maybe her office assistant.

But still…the others would know she'd been closeted

with this sexy cop for hours and they would probably wonder.

"Then it wasn't a fantasy." He flicked off her bra and captured a nipple in his mouth. The hot sensation of his tongue swirling over her nearly brought her to her knees. "That must have been a premonition."

He shifted against her and there was a rustling sound before he picked her up and deposited her to sit on the conference table.

Squealing in surprise, she soaked in the feel of the cool mahogany surface beneath her, providing a stark contrast to the hot, lean muscles bending over her. His cock brushed her thigh and she could tell he must have discarded his trousers along the way. He stood in front of her, poised between her thighs.

She wanted him, wanted this, so badly. Part of her longed to tell him she'd like to see him stretched out on the conference table beneath her, but even with the blindfold she couldn't find the words.

Knowing she'd spent long enough in the dark anyhow, Tempest reached for the silk scarf around her eyes and nudged it up and off.

She blinked, her eyes adjusting to the bright fluorescent lighting overhead.

And oh. *Ooh.*

Wes naked was a sight to see. The carved muscle and flat abs appealed to her sculptor's eye, but the weapon he was carrying...yipes. His shaft was pointed her way and looked very ready to strike.

Scooting toward the edge of the table she made her way closer, her greedy flesh hungry for a taste of him. He reached for her panties and snapped the skinny elastic straps, rendering her naked with a flick of his wrist. She leaned back on her arms to support herself, desperate to feel him inside her.

Her finger brushed a paper—no, a foil condom package he must have left on the table. Falling on it gratefully, she ripped it open with her teeth while she silently applauded his foresight. She was so far gone now, she wasn't entirely sure she would have remembered to be careful.

Rolling on the condom, she savored the length and size of him. He gripped her thighs, lifting her off the table until she slid her arms around his neck to hold on. He guided her closer, finding the perfect angle, and gently thrust his way inside.

Stretching around him, her body worked to accommodate his. He eased her back down to the table, settling her there so he could free his hands to touch her.

Eyes falling closed as he spread her with his fingers, Tempest shuddered from the wave of pleasure, a tiny foreshadow of the completion she knew would follow. The skill of his touch amazed her, his finger zeroing in on her clit again and again, even as he moved inside her with long, devastating strokes. She opened her eyes to see his burning into her with enough heat to singe her very soul.

Confusion and pleasure tangled inside her, startling her with how much she wanted this man. He was giving her everything he had, his deft touch taking her swiftly to the highest of sensual peaks, and yet she wanted even more...

Sealing her mouth to his, she kissed away her doubts, her fears, until only the heat remained. Her fingers sank into his skin, clinging, as he played between her thighs. His hips ground against hers, filling her so completely she thought she'd fly right apart.

Waves of pleasure crashed over her, pummeling her

with their intensity. Her thighs locked, squeezing him tight to her until his release claimed him, too. Their shouts mingled, breathless and raw, bodies seizing with aftershocks. Lights danced behind her eyes, a star-studded spectacular just for her. She'd never had an orgasm like that. Not even close.

She almost hated to open her eyes and end this moment in case she never felt that way again. A depressing thought.

Wes's arms coming around her waist saved her from having to make that decision, however. He readjusted her, lifting her off the table where she'd somehow fallen back in a slump, his hands cradling her from the hard mahogany surface.

"Are you okay?" His voice, filled with more tender concern than she'd expected from a man of hard edges, warmed her insides.

She knew that kind of thinking was downright dangerous. As a closet romantic nursing a hunger for soap operas, Tempest knew that real life didn't operate the way she wanted. Therefore, sexy, honorable men like Wes Shaw could never be expected to fork over a bouquet of daisies and start a courtship just because they had wild sex on her conference room table.

Far from it.

The man who had run at the first hint of too much publicity was probably already busy looking for the door. Forcing herself to keep things light between them, she drew in a stabilizing breath.

"Just a little dazed, I think." Smiling with as much composure as she could manage, Tempest pried her eyes open. "That was something else, Detective."

HELL YEAH it was something else. Something out of this world and off his personal record books. Something completely unexpected and mind-blowing. It also happened to be eye-crossing, bone-incinerating and brain-scrambling.

Not that he planned to share any of that with Tempest.

"Damn straight it was." He kissed her, more than happy to allow the heat between them to do his talking for him. "You think anybody heard us?"

"Only Rebecca. And I didn't hire her because she can type fast." She eased up, her naked body brushing his and making him want her all over again. "She's my assistant because we went to school together. I've never had a tryst in my office before, but I trust her to keep all my secrets."

Prying himself away from her before he pushed her back against the table all over again, Wes scouted around for clothes. Did it make him an awful person that he was grateful for the office setting that prohibited intimate post-coital conversations? Not that he wouldn't have appreciated the chance to hold Tempest's body against his a little longer. But the level of their sex connection had thrown him for a major loop.

"Good." He tossed her a skirt while he zipped up. "I meant what I said before about not wanting to cause a stir for you. I didn't expect things to get so…out of hand here."

"Yet you arrived bearing prophylactics." She shrugged into her jacket before retrieving her scarf. "You were well-prepared for a man who didn't expect to get carried away."

Busted.

"Okay. Correction—I *wanted* something to happen, but I didn't think it would happen in the middle of your conference room." He watched her wind the scarf around her neck, carefully tucking the ends into her jacket to cover those incredible breasts of hers. Desire slugged through him as hot as if he hadn't just held her naked in his arms. "Nice view, by the way."

She glanced up, brown eyes wide.

Jerking a thumb toward the wall of windows high above any other building nearby, he dragged his gaze away from her centerfold curves to the panorama of downtown. "You've got great offices here. I can't imagine many buildings in the city rivaling this kind of view."

"You're full of it." She fluffed her dark curls around her face and then pushed a few strands behind one ear. "But thank you."

Her tone seemed different. Remote. Wes watched her, searching for a clue to her mood. She shuffled through some papers on her desk before slamming her appointment book closed.

"I guess I'm done here for the day if you want to walk down with me. I'll have to make up my missed appointments another day."

That was it? They'd just had the best sex of his life and now she wanted to dismiss him like one of her employees? He knew he had no right to be insulted since he'd been wondering how to avoid awkward after-sex conversations himself, but damn, even he wouldn't have tried rolling out the door that fast.

Still, he didn't have any intention of letting her out of his sight just yet.

"I'll walk you down. Better yet, I'll give you a lift back to your family's home." He would make sure she didn't try to stay at her apartment tonight, not until the security system was up and running. "You said Park Avenue, right?"

"Wait a minute." Tempest held out a restraining hand, blocking his exit with a manicured hand to his chest.

"What?"

"I thought you didn't want any part of the public eye." She slid her hand down and away. It surprised Wes how much he mourned the loss of that fleeting touch.

"I'm a cop escorting you home. That's the NYPD doing a damn fine job, and believe me, the good stuff never makes its way into the papers." When rumors had flown about the possibility of his former partner turning bad while undercover, however, the media couldn't shovel up dirt fast enough.

"You know as well as I do that no journalist in the world is going to take that angle." She shut down a coffee machine and flicked off the harsh fluorescent lights. It was only late afternoon, but already the late winter sky outside was hazy and gray. "As soon as they find out who you are and that we come from different walks of social life, they'll either paint a picture of me as a gullible heiress getting taken by a studly fortune hunter, or they'll intimate that I must be slumming it for a little while. I guarantee neither version is going to flatter us."

No kidding. He could feel his nose already out of joint, his shoulders tense. "And you don't like being viewed as gullible or slumming, I take it?"

"Frankly, I don't care. I'm used to it, and I've learned not to buy any newspaper besides the *Wall Street Journal* so I don't have to see things that upset me." She moved from the conference room into her office and straightened a few papers while shutting down her computer. "But I don't want to subject anyone else to that kind of scrutiny without ample warning."

"Consider me warned." He appreciated the heads-up,

but even knowing the downside of dating her, he couldn't seem to talk himself out of it. He wanted her anyway.

On the plus side of things—Tempest didn't seem to care about media flack for her own sake. She wasn't embarrassed to be seen on the arm of your everyday, average cop. Some of the tension in his neck eased. "And if you think I'm studly after a quickie on the conference table, just wait until you see what I can do when I have more time."

"What makes you think you'll ever have another chance, Detective?" She arched a delicate eyebrow and failed to hide a smile.

"I'm on to you now." He tugged at her scarf as she pushed the button for a private elevator that stopped in her office. "You might look like an uptown girl, but you've got downtown, kinky tastes all the way. You can bet I'll find more ways to use that against you."

Her breath hitched just enough to make him want to kiss her again, but the elevator chose that moment to announce its arrival with a short chime. They left the building via her high-speed express car that took them directly to street level.

Her world probably boasted plenty of professional perks he couldn't even wrap his head around, another little reminder of how different they were.

As if her warning about the media hadn't damn well been bad enough. He'd barely had time to wonder how they would face that kind of attention when the elevator doors opened in the lobby and cameras flashed in his face. A crush of reporters moved toward them, although Wes could only make them out in silhouette thanks to the blind spots dancing around his vision. Questions fired at them from all sides while portable floodlights drowned them in a white-hot blaze.

"Do you know who broke into your apartment, Tempest?" A woman's shrill voice shouted from the crowd.

"Who's your friend, Tempest?" Another voice—gruff and male—assailed Wes's ears.

"Is it true police are investigating one of Boucher's companies?"

Still partially blinded, Wes barreled his way into the throng, figuring anyone dumb enough to plant themselves in front of an elevator deserved the trampling. How could she live with this kind of personal invasion all the time?

"No comment." He barked out the same words ten times over as he called on old college football skills to block and dodge his way through the crowd of camera-happy reporters and so-called journalists. Amazing what constituted news these days.

Tucking Tempest under his arm, he protected her the same way he'd protected the ball on numerous carries down the backfield in the days when life hadn't been so complicated. Although he was guessing she wouldn't appreciate the pigskin comparison, the tactic worked beautifully. She was in the end zone—his car, rather—in no time.

He slid into the driver's seat in time to see her pulling down the visors and turning her head to the side, obviously a pro at deflecting media attention. Shoving his unmarked Ford into gear, he drove uptown.

"Short of beating them off with a stick, I'd say we handled that as best as could be expected, wouldn't you?" He relaxed into his seat as they put a few blocks between themselves and Tempest's inquisitors.

"You sound like you enjoyed it." Only then did he detect the subtle sniffle behind her words.

"Are you upset?" He flipped the visors back up to get more light in the car so he could see her better in the twilight of a short winter's day. She looked a little glassy-eyed. Hell, yeah, she was upset. He'd been too busy playing his position to notice. "I just assumed you didn't want to talk to them about the case, so I figured you'd want to get out of there posthaste."

"Of course I did. I'm just sorry you had to deal with it." She cast a dire look across the front seat. "They've obviously discovered my connection to the studio in Chelsea now. You realize they'll know who you are by tomorrow morning's early edition, right?"

"I don't care." At least, not as much as he'd expected he would. Besides, he'd seen firsthand that she could use his help dodging reporters, and somehow that put him more at ease.

"You don't?"

"I've been giving it some consideration, and I realized it doesn't really matter to me since it's not like I go undercover anymore. Having my name linked to one of the most gorgeous women in the city isn't exactly going to hurt my reputation." Although the guys at the precinct would have a field day with Wes's face in the social pages. No doubt there would be a hundred copies of it pasted around his desk by morning—with appropriate comic book detailing and thought-bubble commentary, of course. "You just caught me off guard the other night when you brought up the media spotlight. Sort of blew my mind, I guess. Now, where on Park Avenue?"

She gave him an address that put her overlooking Central Park—a ritzy privilege possessed by very few. Maybe some of his thoughts showed on his face because she hurried to explain.

"It's a little ostentatious, but it was my parents' choice, not mine. My folks stayed there until Mom decided she needed a whole new continent to escape my dad and bought a flat in London. I lived away at school most of the time anyway, and then when my dad died, it was just me knocking around the whole huge place until I found the studio downtown." She stopped abruptly. "Sorry I'm rambling. The house has always intimidated me and no matter how long I wear the family name I think the Boucher brand of extravagance will always embarrass me."

Wes pulled up to the curb in front of a brick facade that screamed "Old New York" and stopped. The understated, elegant building didn't look ostentatious to him, but considering property values in this part of town, Wes knew it had to cost a small fortune. Especially since the family probably owned all ten floors. He knew downtown apartment buildings complete with doormen that were smaller than the Boucher place.

"What matters is that you're safe and this looks like it's got some serious security." He watched her insert access codes into a computer panel next to the front door, then unlock two dead bolts. Much barking ensued on the other side of the door. "You brought Eloise?"

"I dropped her off this morning along with some of my stuff. I usually stay here during the week to take care of family business and then head over to my apartment on the weekends to put it all behind me." She tugged open the heavy door and stepped inside, holding it wide for him. "Do you want to come in?"

Wes could practically smell the money drifting out of the place. From his glimpse of bronze antiques, leather bound books lining the hallway and a grand, sweeping staircase in the foyer behind her, he saw a much different side of Tempest. She could surround herself with soap operas and her statue-making hobby all she wanted, but she'd never be the anonymous downtown artist she tried to project in her Chelsea apartment.

Tempest Boucher had always been the favorite daughter of the social pages, a pampered heiress whose exclusive lifestyle he could view from afar but never truly join.

"No thanks." He'd only be more off his game if he stepped foot inside. "I just wanted to make sure you got home safe. I've got some work to do on the case."

"The murder?" She paused in the door, as if she dreaded entering the huge home as much as he did. Eloise stepped out over the threshold for a greeting, stationing her brown head under his hand just in case he wanted to pet her.

"I'm trying to line up some appointments for tomorrow to check out Blind Date." He scratched Eloise absently while he wondered if he'd be tangling the sheets with Tempest right now if they'd been able to go back to her apartment instead of here.

As she stood framed in the doorway, her luscious curves neatly outlined in her tailored suit, he remembered all the ways he still wanted her, all the things he hadn't tried with that scarf of hers yet. Their time together in her conference room hadn't been nearly enough to sate his appetite for this woman who confused him as much as she tempted him.

He was so caught up in thinking about what might have been, he somehow missed her scowling features. Her tense posture.

Her flat-out glare.

"You're still going on a date through MatingGame?" Her tone could freeze a man at twenty paces.

"It's a *job,* remember?" Damn it, they'd been over this. "I still have to see if the Blind Date service is legit."

"Then by all means, Detective, go make your dates." She reached to pull the door shut between them, giving

him a very literal cold shoulder. She would have slammed
it in his face if he hadn't planted his foot in her way.
   "Wait."

CHAPTER EIGHT

EVEN KNOWING she was being unreasonable, Tempest had no interest in whatever else Wes might have to say. Then again, she didn't want to break his foot. Easing off the door, she glared at him through the narrow opening.

"What?" She bit out the word with every ounce of hauteur she could scavenge because no way would she let him see that his decision to forge ahead with the dates actually stung where she was most vulnerable. Some wishful part of her brain had actually convinced her maybe he'd changed his mind about serial dating after the way they'd connected earlier.

She'd tried to give him his space after the conference table, but apparently he needed *way* more space than her sensibilities would allow. And so what if she was being unfair? She'd grown up chubby and graceless, the bane of her chic mother's existence. Although she'd conquered enough of her insecurities to be effective at her temporary CEO job and a damn good artist, she didn't have the kind of self-confidence required to be with a man whose job demanded he date women with sexually kinky tastes.

Especially not now, when her private haven and her lone claim to independence had been sniffed out by the media. Her apartment would be staked out by snap-happy photographers.

"I can't leave when you're mad at me." He shoved his hands in the pockets of his trench coat. "You know the only reason I'm setting up appointments with these women is to test out MatingGame. I would think you'd be glad to clear your company's name."

"Maybe I'm not upset on my business's behalf." She knew she was being irrational but couldn't seem to shake her frustration—which only made her angrier. She crossed her arms and continued to send out frosty vibes, a feat made difficult by Eloise's damned annoying tail-wagging attempts to shove her aside so she could get at Wes.

Traitorous animal.

"You're offended because…" He genuinely seemed clueless as he searched for the answer, his gray eyes narrowing. Behind him the rain kicked up again, sending pedestrian traffic scurrying for cabs and a nearby subway station. "You're jealous?"

"I am not jealous of a bunch of sex-starved strangers who will try to tear your clothes off the moment they see you." Damn the man. Did she have to spell it out for him? "I'm just not the kind of self-assured woman who can handle being with a guy who undertakes risque assignments after jumping my bones in my conference room a few hours ago. Does that make sense to you?"

He stared at her in calm silence, a frustrating response to angry feelings she didn't know quite where to put.

"You're the detective, Wes. I would think you'd be well-versed in drawing conclusions about people's motivations." She huffed out a sigh as she leaned into the doorjamb and tried to let it go. "I know I'm being way too uptight about the dating thing, I just—"

Don't want any one else to touch you.

Not sure how to complete the thought, she waited. Debated. And spied a photographer adjusting his camera lens no more than twenty yards away.

Crap.

"You'd better come inside." Reaching for Wes's sleeve, she tugged him closer. "There's a snoopy camera guy two doors down."

She had to admire that he didn't immediately swivel his head over to check it out for himself. That was most people's gut reaction and it made for the best full-face shots for press hounds.

"That's just as well." He plowed his way into the house, bolting the door behind him before he peered discreetly through the blinds on a nearby window. Turning to face her, jaw set, his eyes flashed with cool fire. "Because we need to talk, anyway."

"Oh." Thoughts of the invasive photographer fell by the wayside. She felt a bit like she'd baited a beast, egging on Wes until she'd fired him up, and now that she had him, she wasn't quite certain what to do with him. "I thought you had work to do?"

Too bad she couldn't work up the appropriate level of sarcasm since she was beginning to realize that any sensitivity she displayed on the subject only led Wes to believe she cared.

"Lucky for me, I can sign online to set up my work appointments anytime. But I'm not going to be able to get a damn thing done until we get a few things squared away."

His voice reverberated in the cavernous hall foyer, his words softly repeating themselves.

Nodding, she decided sparring with Wes got her nowhere. Better to hear him out and then figure out how to handle the tricky new twists to their relationship once his big, tempting body was out of sight.

And more importantly, out of reach.

"Can we go someplace a little less...echoing?" Gesturing to the twelve-foot ceilings and miles of mahogany wainscoting, he kept his eyes on her. "Your bedroom, maybe?"

"Don't you think that's a little presumptuous?"

"You said this house isn't you. I just want to go to whatever corner of the monolith you have carved out for yourself. If it's not a bedroom, maybe a sitting room?" He shook his head as his gaze scanned the rows of doors visible down the front corridor. "A library? Or do you have your own frigging parlor around here somewhere, Ms. Boucher?"

Sighing, she nodded toward the stairs. "I have the third floor actually. Come on."

She whistled to Eloise, who scampered in the back of the first floor where she liked to reign supreme over an outdoor courtyard. After settling the dog with a few Milk-Bones she'd stashed on the dining room table that morning, Tempest returned to face Wes, along with her fears of what she was getting herself into with him.

He followed her up the steps, a silent shadow near enough to send prickles of awareness through her. Hastening her pace as they reached her floor, she tried not to think about the way she'd given herself so completely into this man's hands today. She'd done such a good job maintaining boundaries with men, up until Wes, and now they were crumbling fast in spite of her good intentions.

She had made a deal with herself long ago that she'd rather be lonely now and hold out for a Grand Passion down the road. No sense having her somewhat tender heart trampled mercilessly until then. And since most men seemed more interested in her connections or her money, keeping her distance hadn't been all that difficult.

But this man had gotten under her skin from the moment he'd walked into her trashed apartment, asking questions, taking names and generally getting in her face. Now that she'd shared a piece of herself with him today, she found herself more attracted than ever, and disappointed with herself that she didn't possess the kind of confidence necessary to be okay with him dating other women all day.

Whatever happened to good, old-fashioned police interviews like they showed on *Law & Order?* Then again, Wes couldn't go that route since the dating service didn't give out any personal information about its clients.

"Here we are," she said finally, leading him into the living area outside her bedroom. Furnished with comfortable wingbacks and inviting ottomans, the room still contained a few of her mother's favorite paintings valued well over the cost of a new car, but at least there was nothing priceless and nothing too precious. Tempest had broken enough irreplaceable objects in her life for her parents to take her at her word when she said she didn't want anything too fussy up here.

"It's better." Wes made the pronouncement without even looking around. Tossing his trench coat aside, he took her hand. "Sit with me."

He tugged her down to a low ottoman covered in faux fur. Tempest had it made for her mother to rest her feet on since she had the beginnings of arthritis in both ankles, but Mom had thought it a little too plebian and chose to be sore rather than risk setting her toes on something unfashionable.

"Just for a minute." She didn't want Wes to think they were going to replay the scene in her conference room today. Not when he had a file folder full of other women he needed to date.

Argh. Did she *have* to keep thinking about that?

He laced his fingers together, hands clasped between sprawled knees as he faced her. "I didn't want to undergo the whole post-sex conversational dance at your office, but I think we made a mistake not talking about what happened today."

"I'm well aware what happened today." She tugged her skirt lower on her thighs, her body already tingling responsively at the man's proximity.

Obviously her body wasn't nearly as offended as her brain.

"I don't want it to be a one-time deal."

That caught her off guard. "But what about the media circus? You've already had a small taste, and it'll be worse tomorrow morning when you see the papers. Especially since they're already staking out my home. I can call some security to keep the worst of the press out of this neighborhood, but it won't be so easy to avoid them at my studio."

She hated the idea of her private sanctuary invaded by camera crews. Reporters seeking sensationalism over the facts.

"I'll tell the world I'm your bodyguard. Cops moonlight with stuff like that all the time." He shrugged it off like it was no big deal when she knew it would be. No man's ego would enjoy the inevitable innuendos that would wind up in the tabloids.

"So you're saying you want something more from this?" She swirled the air between them with her finger, referencing the connection she felt every time Wes got within arm's length.

"I don't know what I want exactly. But I know I'm not ready to let you go." He slid a hand beneath her hair, cupping her neck. His thumb stroked a path down the base of her skull while he ventured closer, devouring her with his gray gaze.

She found it difficult to unglue her tongue from the roof

of her mouth, but she forced herself to speak before she lost herself in his hungry stare. If he could be honest with her, he deserved that much in return. "I know it's not fair to you, but I don't like to think about you dating women who will want you as badly as I do."

She was entitled to a few insecurities as long as she was up front about them, right?

"You just need to remember, I'm searching for a killer, not a sex partner." His voice whispered over her with a bracing reminder, igniting fresh fears in her already pounding heart. She didn't like to think about the risks inherent to his profession. In her world, the big danger was getting flayed by the press. In Wes's world, he put his life in peril on a regular basis.

Admiration stole through her along with the certainty she was being insecure. Overcautious.

Yet she had to admit it soothed her wounded ego that he wanted to see her again. How could she ever overcome her self-doubts if she didn't take a few risks?

Willing away her fears, she reached out to touch him.

"How about right now?" Laying her palm over his chest, she found his pulse beat out the same cagey rhythm as hers. The pounding calmed her at the same time it sent warm ripples of answering heat through her. "What are you searching for now that I've brought you deep into my lair, Detective?"

"I'm looking for the real Tempest Boucher." He smoothed a finger down the delicate column of her neck. "And I'm not leaving until I uncover every clue and explore every last inch."

His touch undid her. Made her forget any reason she might have had for caution.

Her eyes slid closed as she gave herself over to the pure

pleasure of his hands on her skin. After a long draught of no sex in her life, her body ached for more of Wes. Their encounter on the conference table had merely whet her appetite.

He popped the buttons on her jacket, sending them bouncing to the hardwood floor like the first gentle drops of rain before the rush of a full-fledged storm.

Already the warning thunder rumbled through her nerves, rattling her thoughts and vibrating her most sensitive places. She threw her head back, giving him better access to her neck, her breasts…anywhere he wanted.

With Wes, she could almost allow herself to feel beautiful. Confident. Utterly alluring.

"Then I'm turning myself in for a thorough inspection."

HE COULD DO THOROUGH.

For this woman full of surprising contrasts, he thought he could damn near do anything. And *this?* She wanted all the same things he did.

Wes flicked her jacket off her arms, careful to leave the scarf dangling around her neck, skimming her breasts to taste more thoroughly now that they had time. Unhooking the clasp on her bra, he watched her curves spring free from their restraint, the taut peaks evident beneath the sheer barrier of her long scarf.

Sliding the silk fabric down her chest, he twined the material under her breasts until he cradled their weight in the soft fabric. Lifting them as he lowered his mouth to taste her, he rolled each nipple between his lips, sucking hard until she clawed at his shirt. His pants.

Her sensual hunger left him awed. When he first met her, there had seemed something sort of shy and reserved about Tempest, almost as if she wasn't completely comfortable in her pinup girl body. But once her clothes started coming off, she was a different woman, an uninhibited sex goddess ready to feed all her desires with him.

Only him.

Releasing the scarf, he undid a couple of shirt buttons and popped the rest, figuring if she could sacrifice her jacket he could damn well sacrifice his shirt. This was about getting naked, about seeing more of her than he'd seen in her conference room. He wanted to know her better, understand her more.

He couldn't imagine a woman who had so many things going for her harboring such deep-seated insecurities. Maybe he had more than enough ego for both of them, because some part of him kept insisting he could chase away her fears if only he had enough time to lavish every inch of her with his undivided attention.

His pants hit the floor in time with her skirt. She'd lost her panties to his appetite in her office, leaving her fully exposed, a decadent feast for the taking.

While he gawked like a teenager at the spectacular view, Tempest tugged down his shorts, availing herself of his cock. She smoothed her palm down his shaft, her creamy skin a wicked enticement. Circling the head with her thumb, she dropped to her knees in front of him. And then...

His brain short-circuited from the heat blasting through his veins. Her mouth closed over him, gently sucking, flicking her tongue all around the sensitive ridge of the head. She drew him in deeper and deeper, the wet warmth killing him until sweat popped out along his lip.

Two could play that game.

"Who's supposed to be doing the exploring today?"

He drew her up by her elbows, desperate for her taste on his mouth. "Your turn to submit yourself to me."

Licking her lips as she got to her feet, she would have fallen if he hadn't laid her out on the oversize fur ottoman, her thighs dangling off the edge.

Perfect.

He settled himself between her legs, zeroing in on her clit. So much for taking his time. She'd gotten him hot so fast he couldn't think how to control himself or how to hold back. He only knew he needed the taste of her. Now.

Swirling his tongue deep in her slit he made love to her with his mouth the same way he'd make love to her with his cock soon enough. Right after she came for him.

Plucking at the center of her plump sex, he felt the throbbing heat of her pulse hard between her thighs. But still it wasn't enough. With his other hand he roamed her body, over her belly to cup her breast and tweak one tight nipple.

Her cry was his only warning before her body spasmed hard, clenching again and again while her skin suffused with heat. A beautiful sight.

He didn't let her go yet. Not until every last spasm had its way with her. Only then did he kiss her sex one last time and stretch out over top of her, covering her.

Blindly, he sought the condom he'd left near the ottoman where he'd discarded his pants. It rested by their feet now that they'd rolled the piece of furniture into the sofa with their frantic movements. Wes spun them back near the condom so he could protect her, making sure he brought this woman only pleasure.

"Please. Let me." She took the packet from his hands, her movements faster but not necessarily more efficient.

Her hand shook ever so slightly, her body practically humming with sexual energy.

That quiver of hers humbled him, reminding him how damn lucky he was to touch her right now. He watched her as she peeled the condom down his shaft, then lined up his cock with her slick passage. He was more than ready.

His hips thrust gently at first, allowing her to get used to him. She clawed at his back, her short nails a welcome counterpoint to the mind-drugging pleasure of her soft form beneath him, her wet heat clinging all around him.

Driving deeper, he relished the way her hands moved over his chest, then over her own chest. She plucked at her nipple, teasing the tight peak with one finger until she saw him watching. Smiling, she reached up to his mouth to wet two digits and used the dampness to trace a wet circle around one rosy crest.

She made him crazy.

Out of his mind, past obsession-crazy. And with that thought in mind, his gaze glued to the sweet temptation of one nipple, he thrust hard inside her once, twice...

They came together in a rush of harsh cries and ragged moans. Her feet pinned the backs of his thighs down, as if to keep him inside her forever. Her hips arched up against his in the most intimate of matings, her heat pressed tightly to him.

He didn't know what his thorough inspection of Tempest had uncovered about her, but he knew a hell of a lot more about himself for his efforts.

For starters, he now realized he didn't have any idea how he would ever walk away from this woman once the threat that stalked her had been caught.

THE PARK AVENUE mausoleum echoed and creaked after Wes's departure, amplifying Tempest's sense of loss.

Running her palm over the still-warm sheet where he'd laid beside her until a few minutes ago, she breathed in his scent—their scent—until she could almost feel his strong, solid presence beside her again.

Foolish, romantic notion.

She wished she could be the kind of woman who boldly conducted affairs with men, taking the sex and fun, then walking away with heart intact. But she'd been a Sap with a capital S since childhood, surrounding herself in rainbows and unicorns, dotting her very first letter "i" with a heart.

Her fast-living parents had no idea where she came by her love for happy endings. Their own marriage had been a study in dysfunction since her ambitious, east Texas father wed Solange, Tempest's old-money mother, for her family's Louisiana gambling connections. The two of them had plotted and schemed their way into the highest echelons of New York society with their combined drive and Ray's knack for making money, their marriage falling apart once they'd both achieved their material dreams.

They had both looked upon their daughter's tender heart with pity, encouraging her to think big and use her privileges in life to expand the family empire rather than offering leftover meals to homeless people.

So it hardly came as a surprise to Tempest that she was already weaving romantic dreams around Wes Shaw. How could she expect anything less of herself when the man had given her more orgasms in an evening than she'd had in the last three years combined? Of course she was feeling a little bit vulnerable tonight.

And it didn't help to be here, in the empty home of her past where she would never fulfill her childhood dream of seeing her parents happy together, their family whole.

She simply needed to acknowledge her foolish, romantic weaknesses and get over them. Her mother was happy enough being the toast of London society, and her dad had chosen to live his life to the extreme, right up until his last breath. No childish fancies on Tempest's part would change that.

And for his part, Wes would go out with half of the New York–based women using the Blind Date service of MatingGame, so apparently he wasn't nursing any romantic feelings about her in return.

Tempest would get her butt out of bed and the stars out of her eyes before she started pinning any personal hopes on Wes. He'd gone above and beyond professional duty to keep her safe and catch the person responsible for breaking into her apartment. The least she could do for him in return was keep her heart on a leash and pay attention to his ongoing investigation.

Lowering her feet to the floor, she levered herself up and out of bed, dragging the sheet along with her as she sought the laptop in her overnight bag.

Maybe she'd go surf the MatingGame site again just in case she came up with something new, some hint of what really went on at the small company she'd once envisioned as a romantic new way for couples to find each other. Of course, if she'd been completely honest she'd have to admit some perverse part of her also wanted to read the profiles posted on the site and guess which ones had intrigued Wes enough to ask them out.

Switching on a lamp at the scroll-top desk across the room, Tempest flipped the soft bed linens over her shoulder, toga-style. She opened one screen after another on the Web site, hoping to find any clue Wes might have overlooked. Her phone call to the operations manager of the site had gone unanswered since Saturday, but in the woman's defense, she had planned to be away for a few days on personal business.

Then again, what if that business involved leaving town for good? Could she have been aware of misconduct in the company and skipped out before her role was uncovered?

Tempest found it hard to believe that scenario, but given her tendency to see the world through rose-colored glasses, she could hardly trust her own judgment.

That applied double with Wes, damn it.

Punching the keys that took her to her own profile on the Blind Date portion of the site, Tempest reread the words she'd written about herself even though she knew she couldn't go out on a date with a stranger when the only man who interested her at the moment was Wes. To her surprise, there were over one thousand page views on her profile, along with a private message at the top of her screen alerting her that she had mail waiting in her MatingGame account.

Curious, she clicked through the sign-in steps to access the inbox and discovered thirty-two e-mails with subject headers ranging from "Best ride of your life—guaranteed" to "Ever had twelve inches?"

Assured that this was *not* the way a self-described sap would ever meet a man, Tempest nearly clicked the screen closed when an e-mail ID jumped out at her.

KingKong.

It took her a moment to make the connection and recall why it seemed familiar. Wes had named his dog Kong.

Fingers propelled by a rush of curiosity, she clicked on KingKong's subject header that read simply, "Meet Me?" Probably just a coincidence. Then again, Wes said he'd tried to line up a few dates.

Why should her heart speed up at the thought of Wes

choosing her anonymous profile when he'd told her ten times his dates were strictly business?

The letter opened, taking up the width of her screen with white space except for a few simple lines—"I'd like to get to know you better and I'm willing to pick up the tab. Meet you at Mick's Grill on the lower West side tomorrow at 8:00 p.m.?"

The note wasn't signed, but included a link to a profile on the site. A click of the mouse led her to the familiar profile she'd watched Wes create to lure potential prostitutes.

He'd chosen her. Whether he had simply arranged as many dates as possible or he'd spied something interesting in her profile remained to be seen.

Eloise whimpered at her feet and crawled closer to Tempest for an ear scratch.

Sighing, she patted her dog absently. "I know, I know. He's looking for a woman who turns tricks for a living, so why should I be flattered, right?"

Still, she'd be lying if she said the note from King-Kong didn't lift her spirits. Maybe it was because the communication helped prove her theory that MatingGame provided a legitimate service. Or possibly the warm sense of satisfaction inside her stemmed from the fact that she'd found a way to wrangle a second date with the sexiest man she'd ever met.

But Tempest feared her sudden surge of optimism didn't really relate to either of those things. Ridiculous though it might be, she celebrated her small victory tonight because she hadn't included anything remotely sexual in her profile on Blind Date and Wes had said he'd be on the lookout for profiles openly offering explicit sex.

Her profile had none.

Coincidence? Not in her romantic heart, it wasn't.

Detective Wesley Shaw might have been working when he'd chosen to set up dates with the other women on his list, but some deep-seated feminine instinct told her he wanted to meet her for more personal reasons.

And there wasn't a chance she would disappoint her blind date.

CHAPTER NINE

"YOU DISAPPOINT ME, Shaw." Vanessa Torres knotted her long, dark hair into a braid while she squinted down at the morning paper spread out over her desk at the precinct. "You finally made the social pages and you couldn't even trouble yourself to shine your shoes? The trench coat is pretty stylin' though. Maybe there's hope for you yet."

Stationed at the desk beside her, Wes ignored his partner the same way he'd blown off the landslide of jabs from his colleagues, including a life-size blow-up of the newspaper photo some wiseass glued to a piece of cardboard and posted in the break room. The homemade artwork wouldn't have been so bad except that the joker responsible had carefully colored a border of pansies around the photo.

He could take a lot of crap, but any guy who implied he was a pansy had a serious ass-kicking coming to him.

Vanessa chattered on, unruffled by his silence. "So Tempest Boucher is the new Flavor of the Month? It's good to see you getting back in the game, but high-class chicks like this might not appreciate the old Wes Shaw cut-and-run routine four weeks from now."

That got his attention.

Wes spun away from his computer, where he'd been coordinating a dating schedule that would put the world's biggest Casanovas to shame.

"Has it ever occurred to you, Torres, that maybe *I'm*

not the one who does the cutting and running after a month?"

Vanessa leaned back in her chair, her sleek leather jacket rustling with the movement. A five-year member of the force, she still seemed like a rookie. Not that she didn't do her job well. On the contrary, Wes had seen this five-foot-eight, trim woman collar some seriously big guys when push came to shove. But she remained a loner in a job that necessitated strong partnerships, preferring to maintain strict privacy about her personal life and never allowing anyone to get too close to her.

A few guys on the male-dominated force had tried to write her off as an ice princess, but Wes defended her whenever the insults got any worse than that. He didn't know what made Vanessa so aloof with most of the guys, but he understood the need to be left alone better than most. Maybe that's why they made good partners. They might share cases, but they were each content to operate solo for the better part of every day.

"That's an interesting scenario." Vanessa tapped her chin as if deep in thought, but a telltale crease in her cheek—an optimistic dimple in a cynical face—assured Wes she was still messing with him. "You think you possess some sort of time-release scariness that makes women from all walks of life begin to see your true nature after exactly four weeks and decide to give you the old heave-ho?"

"I've had relationships last longer than four weeks." He didn't know why he bothered to hand over that piece of information now, when he had never felt compelled to share as much with her any other time she'd hassled him.

Maybe it was because he couldn't envision getting his fill of Tempest in a few weeks' time. The woman appealed to him on an instinctual level even though their being together made no sense from a logical standpoint.

"You?" Vanessa tipped forward in the ancient wooden office chair, the hardware squawking with the movement. "The king of love 'em and leave 'em? I've been with the NYPD for five years, Romeo, even if I've only been your partner for the past eighteen months. Don't try to tell me you've hooked up with anyone serious in all that time."

"It so happens I haven't, since my stints at long-term predated your arrival." He'd been burning a path through girlfriends in the couple of years before his first partner died—a knee-jerk reaction to two previous relationships where he'd been played. "But what makes you think you knew anything about me from the days before you got assigned to hold my hand and make sure I didn't go off the deep end after Steve went missing?"

He understood that had been a small part of Vanessa's job back then—keep an eye on Wes and make sure he handled the guilt. Wes had blamed himself for not taking a bigger role in Steve's undercover assignment, for not seeing warning signs that he was getting in too fast, too far.

And then once he'd turned up dead, Wes couldn't deceive himself any longer that his friend had slipped into deep cover somewhere to make a big bust or bring down a whole crime syndicate. Wes had never been much for wishful thinking, but coming up with possible scenarios to explain Steve's disappearance had kept him from facing the final truth for over a year.

"Honestly?" Vanessa folded up her newspaper and chucked it in the wastebasket along with Wes's social page debut. "I had the hots for you when I first came on board here."

Wes had never been a man of excess words, and he

couldn't have come up with a response to that one if his life depended on it.

"No need to look so terrified, Clouseau." She whipped him on the arm with a pencil. "I'm long over any feeling of attraction for a guy who sucks at relationships even worse than I do."

Relief smacked him like a tidal wave. Vanessa was nice enough, and he admired her skills as a top-notch cop, but she seemed way too complicated. And although she was Bronx born and bred, something about her still screamed high-maintenance.

Funny that Tempest was about as uptown as a woman could get, yet she didn't strike Wes as high-maintenance at all. Somehow a woman with dog hair on her suits who called microwave popcorn a meal seemed more like his type.

"I've seen that Ginsu crap you do. I could never date a woman who kicks more ass than me." He planned on keeping his head permanently attached to his shoulders, thank you very much.

"It's kendo. Ginsu makes knives." She rolled her eyes. "I guess I just thought—at first glance—that you and I were kind of alike. A couple of loners in the midst of the big cop family where everyone knows everyone else's business. I didn't realize back then you were so much a loner that you were completely relationship challenged."

"Guilty." He could hardly deny the obvious. Thinking he'd reached his quota on personal chat for the day, Wes turned back to his computer to finish logging in his appointments for the afternoon and evening.

"You know, if you decide you want this Tempest woman to stick around longer than four weeks, it couldn't hurt to try trusting her a little." Vanessa pulled a red floral day planner out of a desk drawer and dumped it in her purse.

"No one appreciates it when you expect the worst from them."

"Trust is something earned, not given." He'd learned that the hard way with women. Twice. And even then he'd told himself he could at least trust his partner, a mistake he wouldn't make again with Vanessa even though they got along just fine. But he'd thought Steve was his friend and the guy either sold out to the lure of money or he'd simply gotten way too careless on a job where every breath he took should have been weighed and measured.

Shoving herself to her feet, Vanessa breezed past him, the leather strap of her jacket's belt slapping the back of his chair. "You keep telling yourself that, Wes. I'm sure it will be comforting next month when your uptown girl dumps you." She paused to fill a cup of water from the cooler on her way to the door. "Just don't forget people are very good at living up to your worst expectations. It's a satisfying fact of the cynic's creed."

She lifted her cup of water toward him in a mock toast and then sailed out of the room before Wes realized he hadn't told her squat about his progress on the case.

Damn.

So maybe Vanessa had a valid point about him being a loner. And a tad cynical. That didn't mean he couldn't keep Tempest in his life longer than a month if he wanted.

Although, as he stared unseeing at his computer screen with the list of women he planned to meet starting this afternoon at one o'clock, he had to admit he was already well on his way to pissing her off. She hadn't liked him arranging dates as part of his investigation, but he'd gone ahead and made the arrangements anyway since Tempest hadn't been able to produce the woman at MatingGame who should have the answers to his questions.

The appointments were the only way to find out more

about the women who used the Blind Date service. Forcing thoughts of Tempest from his mind, Wes returned to his private message box at the MatingGame site and found two more responses to his e-mails requesting dates. Guilt nipped him as he realized that one of the notes came from a woman whose profile had caught his eye on a personal level. He'd streamlined his investigation to include only women who posted blatantly sexual profiles on the Web site—except for one that snagged his eye because he'd been thinking about Tempest.

He nearly deleted the post, knowing his dates didn't have a damn thing to do with his personal life, but at the last minute he paused. Thought about it.

Maybe he should meet one woman who hadn't mentioned a lot of kinky sex anyhow, sort of like a standard for comparison in a science experiment. His 8:00 p.m. meeting with the dog owner who described her ideal foreplay as a good conversation would give him a more rounded look at Blind Date's clientele anyway, something Tempest's company deserved.

Confirming the time and place with the last woman on his list via e-mail through Blind Date's private account, Wes had every intention of catching his criminal this week. His time frame for solving the case seemed all the more urgent after Tempest's apartment had been trashed. What if she was next on the killer's list? While he couldn't be sure the break-in had been related to last week's murder, he knew he'd sleep a hell of a lot better once the person responsible had been caught.

Maybe then he'd be able to figure out how to convince Tempest to stick around for more than a few weeks. Because, no matter what Vanessa said about his ability to trust, Tempest was one woman he didn't have any intention of letting go.

TONIGHT SHE WOULD LET GO of all her inhibitions.

Tempest had told herself as much ten times over on the cab ride to Mick's Grill in the lower West side. But while banishing her inhibitions in the bedroom sounded easy enough, she hadn't fully prepared herself for the challenge of being loose and carefree on the streets of New York at night.

And not just loose in a figurative sense. No, Tempest had elected to wear the trench coat Wes left at her place and nothing more for her rendezvous tonight, so her breasts were jiggling around inside the jacket like mounds of unconfined Jell-O.

What had she been thinking?

Her gaze skated up to meet the cabby's eyes in the rearview mirror, hoping he hadn't noticed any unusual breast activity. Luckily he was flipping off the guy in the taxi behind him, completely engaged in his work.

God bless the high level of job commitment in New York cabdrivers.

Swallowing back an attack of nerves, Tempest figured as long as she could pay the man his fare and get out of the car without giving anyone on the street an eyeful of cellulite, she'd be okay. Once she had Wes in her sights again, she would focus only on their night together—the night she planned to shed the last of her hang-ups and concentrate solely on pleasure. After all, she'd progressed beyond the blindfold stage and was now well on her way to making serious strides in the bold and brazen department.

Nervous and a little excited, she tipped the cabby and stepped out of the car with extreme caution. Awareness of her nudity beneath the coat made everything about her surroundings feel sexual. The rumble of a truck vibrated through her as it hurried down the street. The hiss of steam from a subway vent snaked up her thighs to warm her intimately. At the corner, the stoplight turned from yellow to red, bathing a handful of pedestrians in a seductive flush of color.

Amazing how the simple absence of undies filtered all her perceptions through a sex lens.

Tugging on the ends of the coat's belt, she made sure she was still covered before pulling open the door to Mick's Grill. An old Billy Joel tune spilled out onto the street along with scents of spicy teriyaki sauce. The small bar and eatery wasn't jam-packed, but it seemed crowded for a Tuesday night.

Weaving her way past the corporate crowd that liked to invade the quirky establishments on the lower West side in a relentless search for atmosphere, Tempest spied more room in the back where the locals congregated. Squinting through the hazy smoke from the grill, she thought she spied her personal KingKong at the back corner table where he said he'd be. But wasn't that a woman just leaving his booth?

Irritated, she would have stomped straight over to her date's female companion to claim Wesley Shaw for her own, but something about the woman's familiar posture stopped her.

Tall and slim, the redhead possessed a confident stance as she bent to place a flirtatious kiss on Wes's cheek. Her dress was short and sexy, designed to catch a man's eye.

Recognition came when the woman turned on one red-and-white polka-dot heel.

Kelly Kline, Boucher's vice president of global development.

Flustered and not sure what else to do, Tempest darted closer to the bar, ducking under the arm of a short guy in a suit so Kelly wouldn't see her.

"Well, *hello*." The balding Mr. Corporate huffed a beer-stinking breath over her before he nearly fell face-first into her exposed cleavage.

Eyes glued on Kelly's disappearing red dress, Tempest shoved away from the barfly and scrambled closer to Wes, concerned that maybe they'd overlooked something by not examining her work associates sooner. Could Kelly have trashed her apartment in anger? If office gossip held true, the woman probably harbored a fair share of anger with Tempest for not giving her a chance at the CEO slot.

Coincidence that she'd shown up here tonight? Tempest didn't think her driven business associate was capable of murder, but it didn't sit well to see the woman among Wes's suspects when she already had reason to resent Tempest.

Picking up the pace, she reached Wes in a distracted huff, eager to share her suspicions.

"I know that woman." She began without prelude as she latched on to Wes's arm, pointing toward the front of the bar where Boucher's most ambitious employee had vanished.

"What the hell are you doing here?" Wes slid out of the rounded corner booth to stand, rapidly inserting himself between her and the crush of the dinner crowd and assorted happy hour partygoers. "I'm interviewing suspects, damn it."

"I know. I just wanted to—" It was rather complicated actually. She hadn't planned to greet him so abruptly.

What's more, he looked less than pleased and maybe even a little suspicious.

"How did you even know where to find me?" Frowning, he nudged her toward the curved bench seat and settled across from her at the table.

"You asked me to meet you." She hoped he wasn't going to be mad about this. But damn it, she had a right to be here to prove to him Blind Date had set them up legitimately. "I'm the dog owner whose ideal foreplay is good conversation."

"You?" Wes looked confused for about a nanosecond before a small tic started pulsing beneath his left eye. "You entered your profile on Blind Date?"

"I figured if you were trying it out to see how it worked, I could, too." She didn't mention that she'd also toyed with the idea of trying to date her way out of her fixation with him. The tic under his eye warned her this was really *not* the time to bring it up. "Once I saw a note from King-Kong, I remembered about your dog and I knew it was you, so—"

"I'm a trained investigator looking for a killer and I happen to be armed for the job." The tic picked up speed. "You care to tell me what makes *you* qualified to test the system, Nancy Drew?"

Okay, now that pissed her off.

"I own the company, Wes. This might be just another case to you, but Boucher Enterprises is my whole life. I'm not going to sit back and watch it go belly-up because of some deranged prostitute on a killing spree."

A harried-looking waiter arrived before Wes could say anything. The college kid with a crooked bowtie picked up a leftover glass with a red lipstick print on the rim and asked Tempest what she wanted.

"No, thanks, we were just leaving," Wes informed him, tossing a wad of cash on the guy's tray.

"I'll have a vodka tonic with a twist, no ice." Tempest never took her gaze off Wes, refusing to be steamrolled.

As the waiter took off, she leaned forward over the table, needing to clarify one more point. "And furthermore, I don't even think you're right about the whole prostitution angle. The woman you were meeting before me happens to be an employee of my company and trust me, we keep her *far* too busy for her to moonlight as a hooker. She also happens to make plenty of money by using her brain, without having to throw her body into the mix."

"You mean Katrina?" Wes's gaze flicked down to Tempest's breasts, lingering long enough to send a rush of heat through her. By the time he met her eyes again, the tic had faded. "She also happens to have damn kinky tastes."

"Well her name isn't Katrina, it's Kelly Kline and although I can't picture her having any reason to murder a man she met through the MatingGame site, she does have reason to be unhappy with me since I'm the biggest obstacle to her stepping into the CEO shoes at Boucher."

"You think she might have been the person who trashed your apartment?" Wes lifted a skeptical brow as he straightened his skinny silk tie. Between the retro neckwear and a slightly faded pinstripe suit, he looked like a gangster from the forties. All he needed was the fedora.

"I don't know. I just thought it seemed odd that you're here looking for a killer and possibly someone who's upset with me because I'm in the wrong business, and in walks Kelly." She smiled up at the waiter as her vodka tonic arrived. "Thank you."

"I see you brought my coat back." Wes's eyes drifted lazily over her after the waiter left.

Music pulsed through the bar, the light rock changing to old seventies disco tunes. And thanks to a Gloria Gaynor song, Tempest began to feel very bold and brazen as "I Will Survive" blasted over the speakers.

"I did." She smoothed her hands over the lapels and admired the texture of the finely woven garment. "Although I like it so much, I think you're going to have to take it off me yourself if you want to get it back."

His focus narrowed solely to her, his nostrils flaring as

he stared at her across the table. "I'm not willing to part with the coat."

She sipped the vodka, allowing the alcohol to tingle pleasantly through her veins and enhance the buzz of sexual awareness humming through her. "Really? Then why don't we take this in the alley and you can fight me for it?"

Wes reached over the table, suddenly very interested in the coat. He slid a finger under the lapel of the jacket and skimmed it down. Down.

His gray eyes darkened, stormy and foreboding. "Just what the hell do you have on under there?"

SHE COULDN'T be naked.

No. Way. In. Hell. Yet even before her lips curled upward in a wicked grin, Wes knew the truth. The woman didn't have a stitch of clothing on beneath her trench coat. *His* coat, damn it. The same one he'd slung around his shoulders countless times now hugged her nude body, the silky lining caressing her skin the way he wanted to.

"I had the advantage of knowing who I was meeting for my blind date tonight, so I thought I'd dress accordingly." Her voice curled around him like a wisp of smoke from the fat candle flickering on their table.

"How do you know I don't have five other women lined up after you tonight?" He was still frustrated she'd shown up in the middle of his investigative work. What if she'd arrived during an arrest? Or worse, what if she'd gotten caught in a shoot-out with a desperate criminal?

She should have been a hell of a lot more careful. And he shouldn't be contemplating forgetting the lecture she deserved in favor of tearing the coat from her body.

"Do you?" She straightened, her abrupt attention to posture robbing him of the delectable view he'd had down her jacket. "Have five other women lined up to meet you, I mean?"

Peering around the bar she nibbled on her bottom lip and looked unsettled. Worried.

Amazing how that small display of uncertainty could go so far toward evening the balance between them. He hadn't appreciated being caught off guard tonight.

"No." He finished her drink for her, the only sip of alcohol he'd allowed himself in eight hours at a bar. "Somehow I knew to save the best for last."

"So you did choose my profile for personal reasons." She reached under the table to put a hand on his thigh.

Her touch hadn't been the only occasion he'd been groped in his day of nonstop dating, but it was the first time he had enjoyed a feminine hand on his thigh. He pictured those neatly manicured nails clawing hungrily at his skin, her high society facade stripped away so that the real Tempest could have her way with him.

"I thought I should meet with one woman who hadn't blatantly advertised sex in her profile, just in case subversive hookers were more discreet than I thought." He found it difficult to converse with her in a noisy, public place when the only thought in his head right now was how fast he could have that coat off her.

"That's the only reason you picked me?" She slid closer to him in the rounded corner booth, giving herself all the more access to him under the table. Her nails sketched higher on his thigh, lightly grazing his trousers and hovering to one side of his Johnson. "I was your control group?"

"We need to go." He reached beneath the table to imprison her wrist, thinking there was nothing "controlled" about the chemistry between them.

"What about my foreplay?" She wriggled her arm against his grip.

"You'll have all the time in the world to try out your moves as soon as I get you out of the coat." It was all he could think about. Her full breasts even moved differently underneath the fabric. In fact, now that he had realized she was naked, he was certain anyone who looked at her would notice right away.

"Not foreplay for you." She crossed her legs, rubbing one calf seductively against him. "I mean what about our good conversation? The foreplay for *me?*"

Tossing some bills on the table to settle their tab, Wes tugged Tempest out of the booth. "You should have thought of that before you went commando on me."

"Wait a minute—"

Her words were lost in the din of shouted conversations above the blaring disco music.

Wes kept his eye on the door and his arm around Tempest, determined no man in her path would get a bonus feel of anything save her elbow as she moved through the crowd. When he finally reached the door, he plowed through it so hard the metal barricade bounced back on the hinges against the building.

Fresh, rain-scented air blew over him, a welcome relief after the muggy heat of the bar, but it didn't do a damn thing to cool the fire within. Drawing Tempest toward the alleyway between Mick's Grill and the laundromat next door, he figured he'd found the fastest path to a little privacy.

Ducking deeper into the shadows, Wes backed her against the brick wall of the building and reached for the tie of her coat.

"If you need a conversation first, you'd better start talking because we've got about five seconds before you're giving me one hell of a show."

CHAPTER TEN

"I'M AFRAID YOU'VE SEEN it all before, Detective." Tempest shifted on her skinny stilettos, the back of her heel scraping against the rough brick in the darkness. A streetlight shone a few yards away, near the curb, but their alleyway retreat remained shrouded in the comfort of anonymity. "Nothing new to show you tonight."

She loved how dangerous he looked in the shadows, his tall, lean outline tense with restrained hunger.

Loved?

Catching herself romanticizing, she wanted to correct herself but found she'd chosen the best word possible. Still, she could love something *about* the man without falling for him, right?

"On second thought—" growling low in his throat, Wes reached for the knotted belt at her waist, his finger tugging the fabric apart "—you've lost your conversational window, Tempest. Less talk, more nakedness."

A fluttery sensation tickled over her skin as she contemplated baring herself to him here. Now. Glancing sideways toward the street she didn't see anyone nearby. And Wes's big body would shield her from public view anyway.

She couldn't think of anything she wanted more right now than to expose herself to this man's hot gaze. Heat bubbled deep inside her and she welcomed the chance to bury old insecurities and fears forever. She thought she'd been finding herself by buying a downtown studio and defiantly watching soap operas before she threw herself into her artwork every weekend?

Ha! Wes Shaw was artwork in motion.

With him, she lived her hopes and dreams instead of imagining a world she'd never touched before. This moment with Wes was the real deal—the heat, the hunger, the wanting. She needed him so badly she could taste him even before he kissed her.

As the knot on her coat loosened, she pressed herself against the wall, fingers gripping along a mortar seam between bricks. She had to hold on to something before her trembling legs gave way beneath her.

When the belt slipped free completely, the coat hung around her, slightly parted but not enough that he would see anything in the shadows. A thin slice of cool night air drifted through that opening, heightening her anticipation.

"I'm waiting." Hardly daring to breathe in the tension-fogged air between them, Tempest bent one knee slightly and nudged a bare leg through the open slit. Her calf caught a shaft of light filtering into the alley from the streetlamp, her skin pale and luminous in the surrounding darkness.

Wes's hands plunged through the coat all at once, finding her belly and smoothing up, down, palming a breast at the same time he curved a hand around her hip. Releasing her hold on the wall, she twined her arms around his neck, falling into the hard planes of his body. His heat seared her, igniting a forbidden sizzle. Her breasts molded to him, heart beating so hard she could swear it pounded directly on his chest.

The coat cloaked her back and sides, even as it completely exposed her front. The full drape of the garment under her arms made her feel like a bat creature, a naughty, naked vampire on the loose.

For good measure, she shoved aside his jacket and nipped Wes's shoulder through his shirt, sinking her teeth lightly into his hot skin.

His touch grew rougher, more insistent, fingers sliding over the curve of her bottom to lift her against him. The delicious friction against her most tender parts only made her crave more of his wicked touch. Her moan echoed in the narrow alleyway before drowning in the honk of a cab out on the street.

A new fervor swirled low within her until her thighs twitched. She reached for his hand, determined to place his fingers where she needed them most.

His groan made her pause, her ragged breathing loud in her own ears.

"What?"

He stared down at her with enough blaze in his eyes to scorch her before he blinked slowly, deliberately, until some of that fire was banked. Marginally controlled.

"We've got to get out of here." Wes tried to edge away but her arms refused to release him.

"We only just got here." She gave a little shimmy, rolling her hips against his in an unmistakable message. "Besides, I'm the woman who won you fair and square from all the other females swarming around you today. I think I deserve my prize, KingKong."

Stroking her tongue up his jaw, she tugged at his tie, ready for more of him. She had no idea where this week's unexpected sexfest with him was going, but she didn't want it to end yet. He'd touched off some hunger within she hadn't known she possessed and now that the yawning ache had been unleashed, she knew he was the only man capable of fulfilling her.

She'd seen her parents be selfish all their lives, putting their own needs above their marriage. Above her. When would it be her turn to indulge in what she wanted? Just this once—for a few more days, a few more weeks—she planned to live like a hedonist and soak up every sensual touch of Wes Shaw's very capable hands. He would be her private indulgence.

"We can't risk it." His words confused her, but she wouldn't have stopped touching him until he backed away again—farther this time. "Someone might see us and if anyone recognizes you..."

He didn't need to complete the thought since she knew too well how devastating a naked tryst in the alley would be for her family's business. She damned his practicality even as she appreciated the cool head.

So much for her attempts to be selfish.

"You're right." To her horror, her voice broke. Oh God, she couldn't be that upset about delayed completion, could she? Obviously her emotions had gotten all tangled up where Wes was concerned despite her best efforts. Hoping to hide her slip, she reached for the belt on her coat, covering her gaffe with a flurry of sudden activity. "We can go to my house, if you want. The new security system is already in place at the Chelsea apartment."

He was so quiet, so still, she realized how presumptuous—and eager—she sounded. He peered down at her with an inscrutable expression on his face, studying her carefully.

Coat secured around her waist, she blasted forward toward the street, more determined than ever not to romanticize her time with Wes. She had vowed to take control of her own life as one of her New Year's resolutions, and this would be a fine time to prove to herself she didn't need anyone. "Then again you probably have things to do and that's fine, too. I should grab a cab and call it a night."

Wes caught her before she emerged into the light.

"I want to be with you." His words whispered over her ear with unexpected warmth, igniting shivery tingles down her neck until her skin tightened.

Relief, hope, anticipation—too many emotions scrambled inside her, making her aware of how much power she'd given him over her. Bad decision, Tempest. A woman didn't find emotional security and independence by making herself sexually reliant on a way-too-sexy detective.

As long as she kept it short-term, she could handle it. Heaven knew she would have traded her shares in Boucher Enterprises to have her cake and eat it, too, when it came to Wes.

"You do?" She closed her eyes for just a moment, soaking in the musky scent of his aftershave and the sharp cut of his angled jaw against her cheek.

"Trust me, I would have never risked my badge and your public image to cop a feel in an alley if you didn't make me crazy." He squeezed her tighter against him, allowing her to experience exactly how crazy she made him. The proof nudged insistently against her bottom.

"I never thought about the risk to your career." She stiffened in his grasp, uncomfortable with the idea of putting him in danger because of her newfound lust.

"It probably wouldn't have been a big deal, but when a detective is tapped for any kind of misbehavior, the department becomes very unhappy." He threaded his fingers through her hair and tipped her head back, exposing her neck for a kiss. "We shouldn't let the nudity go public again."

Eyes sliding closed at the lash of his tongue on her

throat, Tempest nodded. She could be indulgent. Selfish. Take what Wes had to offer for a little longer before she morphed into the independent superwoman of her New Year's goals.

"Got it. Private shows only. Now what do you say, Detective, your place or mine?"

MINE.

Wes had to continually hold himself back from speaking the word aloud when he was around this woman because he wanted to wrap her up and take her home, shield her from the eyes of the rest of the world so he could keep her for his alone.

A healthy, normal male desire?

Hell, no. He'd never been so possessive with any female in his life. And he had the misfortune of two notably bad relationships to teach him that no person can ever truly belong to another. So this caveman urge he battled around Tempest was stupid. Primitive.

Undeniable.

"Let's go to yours." He forced himself to articulate his choice very clearly, concentrating hard on not giving in to the urge to haul her back to his place. Hers would be safer, less intimate. "I can give the new security system the once-over."

"As long as *I* get more than a once-over." Her white teeth flashed in the shadows as she smiled.

"I can assure you more than once. But keep in mind I'm not one of these mythical soap opera studs who can go nonstop all night and then shower you with rose petals in the morning." Releasing her from his hold, he drew her out of the alley and into the street, relieved to see no reporters, no cameras.

"That's okay. I'm not much for rose petals anyway,

since Eloise is allergic to flowers." She hugged her arms around her waist, her brown curls skimming the collar of her coat. "Why don't you just do what you can for me tonight, and we'll call it even?"

"Your dog has allergies?" Grateful for the reprieve from talking about sex when he wasn't free to act on it, Wes hailed a cab at the street corner.

"She's a very unique animal." Tempest fluffed her hair and slid into the taxi, her long, bare legs giving him a view he wouldn't soon forget.

Seating himself beside her, Wes gave the driver the address of the Chelsea apartment a few blocks away. He'd walked to Mick's Grill from the precinct earlier, leaving the car for Vanessa to use. Now, settling inside the darkened interior, he fought to keep his hands off Tempest.

Because the next time he touched her, he wouldn't stop until he'd gotten his fill. He didn't know how she'd wound herself up in his thoughts so thoroughly that he could barely escape, but maybe once he'd caught whoever trashed her apartment, he'd be able to find his footing alone again.

Not exactly an inspiring thought, but Vanessa had nailed it on the head when she accused him of being too cynical to forge any kind of relationship these days. He didn't possess the kind of trust necessary to play much of a role in Tempest's life.

Hell, he didn't know if he even possessed enough trust to make a good partner for Vanessa. Not that she ever complained. But she damn well deserved someone to watch her back more than Wes had for the past year and a half.

That was going to change. He might not ever be the marrying kind, but he could damn well get his head out of his ass long enough to be a solid partner and an even better cop again. Spending time with Tempest had made him see how antisocial he'd become in the past two years and recognize that he didn't want to tread any further down that path.

As the cab rolled to a stop up the street from Tempest's building, she pulled out her wallet, offending him to his caveman core.

"Your money's no good with me." He paid the driver and helped her from the car while scowling at a handful of photographers who lurked around the doors to her building a few doors up.

"But you bought my drink." She still waved her wallet around like a magic wand to soothe over life's rough spots. She hadn't noticed the looming members of the media—yet. "It's only fair I get the cab. I don't want you to think I'm a moocher."

Grateful the cab hadn't let them out under a streetlight, Wes tucked her under his arm and pulled the collar of her trench coat up high around the lower part of her face.

"Who do you think has to worry more about mooching in this relationship? Me or you?" He plucked the pink leather zipper pouch from her fingers and jammed it back into a staid brown purse. Just like Tempest, her bag looked no-nonsense at a quick glance and hid a softer inside. "Besides, I'm a single cop whose only real bill to pay has been a hefty dog food tab. I think I can afford to keep you in vodka tonics and popcorn for a little while. Now hold on tight because we've got to get past a few camera lenses."

She muttered a couple curse words under her breath, a testament to how nervous the press attention made her. Determined to get her past the reporter vultures who now knew where she spent her free time, Wes ushered her toward her building. They passed a homeless guy sleeping on a hunk of cardboard beneath an awning and a couple dressed in sweats walked their dogs in the unseasonably mild winter weather, carrying a steaming box of take-out pizza between them.

Darting around the press hounds and into the building with only a few flashbulbs blinding him in the process, Wes caught himself envisioning him and Tempest walking together like that. As if they belonged together.

His wrist itched where his tattoo rested, reminding him of the poison ivy effect of women in his life. A knee-jerk reaction after all these years, no doubt. Logically, he knew New York was filled with great women. It was finding the right one that seemed more daunting than tracking a killer.

Tempest wasn't the kind of woman he would have ever pictured himself with, but he had to admit, he'd never been with a woman who would give up roses because her dog had allergies. Maybe there was a chance...

Maybe he'd suddenly morph into a stand-up guy willing to put his neck in the noose for incredible sex and a few good laughs? Seemed bloody unlikely. Hell, he put himself on the line enough at work without dishing up his guts in his personal life, too.

"Is that how long you see us lasting?" Tempest smoothed the collar of the coat back into place once they were safely inside the building. "A little while?"

"You'd get sick of me if I stuck around any longer than that." His gaze scanned the flight of stairs and the rows of mailboxes just inside the front door. Except for an old Beatles tune drifting from one of the apartments downstairs, all was quiet tonight.

"Is that what your girlfriends say when they leave you? They're sick of you?" She started for the stairs but he drew her back, pointing to the elevator which seemed a safer route. Staircases were notorious locations for crime because they were usually more isolated. Did she usually take the stairs by herself?

"No. Usually they say something to the effect of, 'Hey, Wes, meet Jack, the new man in my life.'" He steered her into the ancient elevator car and pressed the button for the third floor. "But I tend to interpret that as being sick of me."

"Hmm." She fiddled with the lapel of her coat, making him recall exactly what she had on underneath.

Nothing.

"What do you mean, *hmm?* Don't go playing psychologist on me today." He pointed a finger in her smiling face. "My partner already took a turn and I think one amateur shrink a day is all I can handle."

"I just wondered if you chased away these women on purpose." Her dark eyes flicked over him with curious intent. "I can't picture anyone being dumb enough to play you for a fool."

The elevator chimed, saving him from having to tackle that one.

"You'd be surprised." He held the elevator door while she stepped out, already thinking how many ways he could distract her as soon as they made it to her door. His gaze zeroed in on the belt of the trench coat and he wondered how fast he could have her naked.

"Oh, my God." She stopped short in the hallway, the tremor in her voice snagging his attention faster than a felony in progress.

Reaching her side in two strides, he caught sight of what had her so upset. The door to her apartment had been spray painted with graffiti, spelling out in fire engine–red letters—*Home of Whores 'R' Us.*

Rage spilled over him, an emotion he'd seldom encountered in ten years of crime scenes far more gruesome than the vandalism on Tempest's door. But this was different. This had happened to *her.*

The Chelsea apartment was her home, the place she'd

bought to give herself the sense of belonging her family never had. And some worthless jackass had mounted a campaign to steal that from her along with the work that was so important to her.

"I'll find whoever did this." Wes slid an arm around Tempest, yanking himself out of his own fierce thoughts long enough to reassure her. He lowered his voice, tucking her close as he scanned the third floor for any hint of movement. "The paint is still wet, so the perp might be close. Do you know anyone well enough in the building to stay with for a few minutes while I look around?"

"No." She shook her head with fast, jerky movements. "No one. And I need to check on Eloise."

Her skin had paled, her whispered words breathless with a hint of panic.

Damn. Investigative work would have to be put on hold.

"Wait here while I make sure the security system is still armed and then we'll check on her together." He tested the lock and found it still engaged before obtaining the day's code from Tempest. She could reprogram later. Right now, he needed to make sure her apartment was safe.

Safe?

He knew damn well she wouldn't rest easy until he caught whoever threatened her. For that matter, he wouldn't rest easy, either.

Like it or not, Tempest was about to get the best alarm system on the market. Since her stalker could very well be a killer, Wes would make sure she received around-the-clock watch from New York's finest.

Him.

TEMPEST WATCHED Wes shake hands with a couple of his cop friends two hours later and knew for a fact she'd never be able to get a good night's sleep in her apartment again. She didn't care that Wes had just sworn up and down her home hadn't been broken into this time, she still felt violated. Watched. Vulnerable.

He'd put in a call to his precinct and wrangled some help lifting prints from her door and an empty can of spray paint found in her hallway, but he wasn't optimistic they'd get anything. Mostly, he'd said it was important to keep a paper trail of the criminal activity so that when he caught the perpetrator, they'd have the right ammunition to prosecute under the harsher stalker laws.

Which was all fine and good, but it didn't give her any assurance she'd be able to sleep here tonight. Or any night for that matter. No matter how many kickboxing classes she attended, she'd never feel strong enough to fight off someone filled with so much hate. Shivering, she tucked her feet between the couch cushions and snuggled closer to Eloise, who she allowed on the furniture only for special occasions.

Like when she was scared spitless.

She'd traded in Wes's trench coat for a pair of sweats and a long sleeved T-shirt that said "Sculptors Do It With Their Hands," a giveaway from an art workshop she'd attended during college. Somehow the "Whores 'R' Us" on her doorway had made her want to cover up, sending her running for comfort clothes even though Wes and his cop friends had covered the offending message with black plastic until she could paint over it.

"Are you okay?" Wes's gray eyes were dark with concern as he headed toward her place on the couch after locking her front door behind his friends.

"I'll be better once you find out who hates me so damn much." She gave Eloise a final squeeze before nudging her off the couch. Time to be a grown-up and figure out what to do next. "I definitely don't want to cross paths with this person face-to-face."

"You need better protection." He dropped down onto the couch beside her.

"I'm not going back to the Park Avenue house." She didn't realize how adamantly she opposed the idea until the protest spilled from her lips. But the home reminded her of all the reasons she'd never fit into her family, and all the ways she wanted to find her own path in the world. As soon as she hired a new CEO for Boucher, she was leaving her parents' superficial lifestyle far behind her so she could challenge herself. She'd been so wrapped up in wealth and privilege her whole life, she'd never had a chance to test her mettle. To see what she was made of.

"That's not what I had in mind." He'd dispensed with his jacket long ago and now sprawled on her sofa in his white shirt, the skinny purple tie loosened around his neck.

"I know the security is good there," she continued, still locked in her own thoughts. "But I'll never feel independent until I— What did you say?"

He picked at the elastic band around her ankle where her gray sweats met her bare skin. "I'm suggesting you bump up security here."

"But I just dumped half my month's salary into a system that—" She was missing something. His intent gray gaze told her as much.

"I'm going to be your new protection." He smoothed his hand up her calf where she'd folded her legs under her, then palmed her knee. "Say hello to your new bodyguard."

She hadn't realized she was already shaking her head until Wes frowned.

"What do you mean, *no?* I'm not giving you an option

on this one." He tugged her leg closer, pressing her shin to his chest. "You need me here."

"I'll figure out something." Letting Wes help her out now would be like opening the door to her heart with both hands and saying, *"Come on in! Do your worst."*

She couldn't allow herself to think about him as her protector or she'd never extricate herself from that safe, comfortable place until Wes left her high and dry and even more of a pampered, over-protected society princess than she'd always been.

"There's nothing to figure out." He sounded damn sure of himself for a man who wasn't in charge of her life. "I need to guarantee your safety, and I can't do that unless I'm with you 24/7."

"My safety is my own responsibility." Maybe she could hide out at a hotel for a few days. Although, if someone was watching her, it wouldn't matter where she went.

"Catching a killer is *mine.* And if that means I have to camp out here until this offender surfaces again, then I'm damn well going to do it."

"I'm never here when your suspect arrives. If you're watching me all the time, you won't even be here when the guilty party shows up because you'll be too busy following me to snooze-fest board meetings and running from camera-happy journalists."

Shrugging, he didn't seem too concerned. "I'll have Vanessa watch the apartment while we're out."

She should be grateful the New York Police Department would go out of its way to offer her around-the-clock watch, but instead, she found herself wondering how many other at-risk women in NYC received this kind of five-star treatment.

Tempest the Over-Privileged Strikes Again.

She could already see the headlines.

Knowing she couldn't argue her way around him, however, she simply nodded, committing herself to his plan until she could come up with a better answer. Yet even as she gave him permission to insinuate himself deeper into her life and her heart, Tempest found herself wondering how she'd ever forge the independence she sought.

CHAPTER ELEVEN

WES COULDN'T REMEMBER the last time he'd caught a lucky break, so his minor victory with Tempest—even if her agreement was grudging at best—definitely tasted sweet.

He skimmed a hand up her sweats-clad thigh, knowing it would probably take more finesse than he possessed to get her naked again tonight. "You won't even know I'm here."

"In a studio apartment?" She lifted a delicately arched brow, her honey eyes glowing with a fire he guessed had more to do with frustration than desire.

Still, a guy could always hope.

"I won't even bring Kong over to join the sleepover." He figured she deserved a few concessions after she'd given in without a marathon protest. "But we'll have to stop by my apartment now and then to make sure she has everything she needs."

"Kong, I could handle. No offense, Wes, and I'm grateful for the extra protection, but I've been trying to snag a little more independence this year and with you here..." She pulled the cuff of her shirtsleeve over one hand and twisted the end like a bread tie as if to cover as much of herself as possible.

As if she could retreat inside her clothes.

Wes wondered if that trick had worked for her in the

past and why she liked to hide from a life most people would have considered a dream come true.

He fished inside her sleeve and tugged her hand free before raising it to his lips. "This doesn't have to be a prison sentence for you. I can go with you to work, or wherever you need to be."

Although, now that he thought about it, the arrangement would make it tough to track suspects when he was committed to be at Tempest's side all day. Then he had a whole host of dates lined up for tomorrow, too. Damned if he knew how to handle winnowing through the next round of possible suspects with Tempest by his side. He'd hardly look like a bachelor with her there.

"I can take off a few days." She brushed a dark curl out of her eyes, a silver bangle glinting at her wrist and making an incongruous touch with her sweats. "I'm sure you've got work of your own and I can devote some time to my sculpting. I'll never have a gallery showing if I don't start replacing the broken pieces."

"You're probably safest in the apartment anyhow now that you've got the security system." Maybe he could have Vanessa stay with Tempest for a few hours tomorrow while he followed through on his dates. "I think that's why your stalker had to be content with spray painting the door this time. I don't think our vandal could penetrate the security."

"I'll call my office and let them know I won't be there in the morning." She picked up the phone from its cradle beside the couch while Wes ran through the new evidence in his head.

When Tempest's apartment had first been trashed, he'd thought the perpetrator might be a pro based on the clean pick of the lock on the front door, even though the rampant destruction within had seemed like a very personal statement. But the spray-painted message tonight confirmed her intruder wasn't a professional criminal. The "Whores 'R' Us" label on her front door had been an emotional act, a crime of anger and passion.

He watched Tempest hang up the phone, wondering where to start with his new line of questioning. She seemed reluctant to venture near her past, but he couldn't avoid it anymore.

"What's your take on the note your detractor left on the door?" On a personal level, he didn't really want to know about past lovers and old boyfriends, but as a cop, he needed to uncover the truth. "Do you have anyone in your life who's said things like that to you before?"

His first instinct on the murder case told him the killer had been a woman since his victim was still naked when they found him, his autopsy confirming he'd been engaged in sexual relations within an hour of the time of death. A woman's negligee had been found at the crime scene, but they'd had no luck tracing the garment to any "blonde from MatingGame" as referenced in the victim's appointment book.

Between that evidence and the fact that the victim had penciled in an appointment with someone from MatingGame on the night of his death, Wes had focused on female suspects, even running a check on the old lady who lived a few doors down from Tempest.

But the message on Tempest's door tonight made him second-guess his conclusions. Why would a hooker leave a message about Whores 'R' Us? Wouldn't a prostitute be more defensive of her profession?

Unless the suspect wanted to draw negative press down on Tempest's head. In which case, the message emblazoned in red all over the front door had been a cagey move.

Shaking her head, Tempest unfolded her legs from underneath her and settled back on the sofa. "Never. I told you, I don't date much because it gets too complicated. The last guy I saw a movie with ended up in the newspapers, and so did you."

He waited, hoping his patience would allow her to think through the people in her life and come up with a more solid lead because right now, he didn't have much.

Shrugging, she splayed open palms skyward as if to suggest she had no idea. "I just assumed the message must relate to MatingGame and your suspicion that it's connected to prostitution."

A likely guess. And yet...

"Not many people know about MatingGame's possible darker side," he reminded her. "It's still one of the most popular singles spots on the Internet."

"So you don't think the average person would trace a connection between me and an escort service." She shifted on the couch so she could turn and face him. "Makes sense. So either Whores 'R' Us is a reference made by someone in the know, or else..."

She stopped short before her gaze narrowed as she looked up at him. "You think the words were intended as a personal slam? On *me*?"

He didn't need a psych degree to know he'd offended her. She bristled and huffed, straightening in her seat.

"In my business, it pays to check out every angle. And I still think our offender might be a woman, but in light of the message left for you tonight, it can't hurt to consider male suspects as well. Some guys will dole out some pretty harsh treatment once they get their asses dumped. That's no reflection on you or any woman who ends up with a psycho bastard on her tail."

"You're right." She slumped back next to him, her

movement stirring the scent of her almond fragrance. "I'm just a little touchy on the dating subject."

"Touchy? Talk to me, Tempest." He stroked a hand over her cheek, his mind turning over possible scenarios for what happened here tonight. "I can't think through this unless you shed a little more light on your past or any men who might have it in for you."

"Honestly, there's almost nothing to share because my parents always gave me a hard time no matter who I dated. Guys in their social circle were written off as complacent trust-fund babies who would never go anywhere on their own. Guys who came from more diverse backgrounds were seen as too uncultured to squire me around to family business commitments. I always found it easier to just avoid romance all together, and I don't think any guy ever got close enough to me to be mad I didn't pay more attention to him."

"Then I'm going to keep looking into female users of the Blind Date service in case a woman has been behind the break-in and the vandalism tonight, but I'm also going to broaden my search because something's not sitting well with me about that theory." His thoughts shifted, trying to put a male suspect into the killer's shoes.

When she seemed lost in thought, he set aside his continual mental review of the crime. They'd been so close to jumping into bed together tonight—until they'd come home to find the painted message on her front door. He told himself a gentleman would hold back, but that didn't stop him from wanting her.

Remembering about Tempest's lack of dating history, he wondered if her mother had eased up on her since her father had died. He sure as hell hoped so, because Tempest deserved to be loved. "You know, maybe for your mom and dad, it was just a classic case of no one being good enough for their daughter. I'll bet there are lots of great parents who think the same thing about their kids."

He eyed her as she twirled her silver bangle on her wrist, thinking he'd rather be stripping off that and a whole lot more. Too bad his attempts to charm her—or even just put her at ease—were falling flat in a hurry.

"That's a nice thought, but I don't think it fits my folks." Rolling the bracelet between her palms, she peered up at him through long, dark lashes. "Did I tell you I already received the call from my mom about you?"

"She saw an imposter on the social pages, I take it?"

"She's been living in London for three years now, but she still subscribes to three New York daily papers. My phone was ringing by noon so she could give me an earful."

"I'll bet it was nothing compared to the crap I took at work." Refusing to concern himself with Tempest's mother's opinion, he thought maybe he'd be better off redirecting. "Aside from a few not-so-subtle hints that any picture in the paper where I wasn't kicking ass made me a pretty boy, I also got serenaded by two guys playing Puccini on harmonica since a social page photo must mean I dig opera."

A giggle snuck free from her somber mood, giving him hope he could still get her to talk. And encouraged him maybe later they could *not* talk for a few hours and communicate on a level where he was a hell of a lot more fluent.

"Sorry about that."

"It's okay. There's a guy on the force who's married to a fashion critic, and he left me a sympathy card since he's been through it all with his high-profile wife." The hand-drawn comic of Wes in a hangman's noose had helped him shake off his frustrations today. Especially since it came from Josh Winger, who along with his partner Duke Rawlins, posted one of the highest arrest rates in the precinct.

When silence met his words, Wes realized the word "wife" still echoed ominously through the room.

And even though there wasn't any chance he'd work things out long-term with Tempest, Wes couldn't help but wonder how a regular guy like Josh had married into glitz and fame while still keeping plenty of street cred on the force.

It had taken Wes a year and a half just to recommit himself to being a cop after Steve's death. And now that he had, he wouldn't allow any uncomfortable conversations to keep him from getting the answers he needed.

Changing the topic abruptly, he called on the blunt approach that always seemed to work when finesse failed.

"So you're sure that no one you've dated could be behind the spray-paint job. What about guys you've turned down? Maybe somebody is upset you said no?"

She thought for a minute before shaking her head—her dark, silky hair an enticement his fingers could scarcely resist. "I've been pretty secluded ever since my dad died, so there haven't been that many people who've gotten close enough to ask me out. My life has been all about work up until January, when I decided to take the studio apartment and make some changes."

From Wes's perspective, it had been about damn time since her parents obviously did a number on her just because she hadn't wanted to follow in their footsteps.

"Then maybe we ought to focus more on your workplace. Tell me about this Katrina— No, wait. You called her Kelly? Tell me more about her."

TEMPEST DIDN'T WANT to think someone she worked with could be so vindictive. Had Kelly really resented Tempest bringing MatingGame on board enough to write something as foul as Whores 'R' Us on her front door?

But still, she appreciated Wes's need to cover all his bases. Besides, the sooner he solved his case, the sooner he'd be out of her life and she would be free to salvage some of her fractured independence. As much as the idea of being alone again stung, she knew it only made sense to talk to him.

"She's been with the company for eight years." Tempest dug out everything she knew about Kelly, including the fact that she'd been relentlessly vying for the CEO spot and that she'd never brought a date to a single corporate function.

Maybe it didn't matter—and Tempest certainly preferred to attend professional parties stag, too—but at this point, she figured she might as well spill everything she could think of about Kelly, Boucher Enterprises and her work there.

Two hours later, she had to admit Wes was a great listener. Or was he just a great cop? Tired and confused, she couldn't be sure if it had been the man or the detective who listened to her, but she knew she wouldn't last an hour more before sleep overtook her.

"You okay?" Wes tucked a finger under her chin and tipped her face up to gaze into her eyes. "You look beat."

"Gee, thanks." She slumped deeper into the couch, heart sore at the way her night had rapidly disintegrated ever since they got back to her place. Thank God Wes had been with her. "I'm just trying to process so much ugliness in the world. I'm depressed after having my apartment ransacked and then vandalized, but you must see so much worse than that every day. Doesn't it bring you down?"

"Not usually. Most of the time it fires me up to fix

things. I catch the bad guys, and all is right with the world again." He switched gears faster than her high-tech ten-speed bicycle, obviously not prepared to dwell on his work. "Sorry for asking you to take the stroll down memory lane tonight, but maybe something you told me will help the pieces fall into place."

"I hope my boring life didn't put you to sleep." Relating all the stories about Boucher made her realize how little she'd ventured outside her safety zone despite her New Year's resolution to be her own person.

She had an apartment and a passion for sculpture and soaps. But how often did she get out in the world to meet new people and see new things? Knowing Wes had made her want to be more adventurous. To take a few chances.

"Nope." He shifted on the couch, slinging his arm along the back of the sofa to dangle one hand just above her shoulder. "But it did make me wonder how you could stand the isolation with no dates and no..."

When his words trailed off, she caught the heat in his gaze, the subtle arch of a questioning brow.

"You mean no sex?" It had been a long time for her before her conference table interlude with Wes. A very long time.

Since she had the feeling Wes was Mr. Sexual Experience, she had no intention of admitting he was only her second sex partner.

"Not sex *per se,* but the pleasure of physical contact. The kisses. The touching." He shook his head all of a sudden. "And it's not a damn bit of my business."

She had the feeling he was just playing the gentleman for her tonight after the ugly message on her front door, but something told her Wes still wanted her the same way she still wanted him. The angry words her stalker had left hadn't erased the hunger she felt for Wes. If anything, she only craved the sensual connection with him all the more.

"Who says I went without touches?" She decided it couldn't hurt to have a little fun with Wes tonight and up the heat with some suggestive conversation.

And maybe she was a smidge offended that he looked at her years of abstinence with what seemed damn close to pity, when that time had helped her to look past sex and desire to see what people really wanted from her.

Of course, that trick hadn't worked with Wes. She still had no idea what he wanted from her since desire had clouded her well-trained eyes from the moment he first strolled into her apartment.

"I got the impression you closed the door on men for a few years." He straightened, his posture no longer lazy and comfortable, but tense and alert.

The new topic of conversation seemed to have his full attention. And didn't that soothe her old insecurities? She couldn't help but enjoy the way Wes took a definite interest in her and her sexual experiences.

"Don't discount the value of solo pleasure." Her heart beat faster at the frank interest in Wes's smoky gray gaze. "I assure you, I can bring myself to orgasm faster than any man on the planet."

Understanding lit his gaze as he followed her line of thinking.

"You realize you've just issued a challenge I can't refuse?" Mischief danced in his dark eyes as he leaned closer.

"That's not a challenge, it's a fact. I'm living this body from the inside, Detective, so it only makes sense that I know exactly what revs it up." What was it about the male psyche that fueled men to tout their sexual prowess at every given opportunity? "It's a physiological advantage no man could fully compete with, although I'll be the first to admit I'd rather have your hands on me than mine."

She scooted closer to him on the couch, putting herself in easy reach. She didn't think she'd recover this level of desire after coming home to find her apartment vandalized. But maybe she needed to be with Wes tonight to feel whole again. Strong. The fears and the worries of a few hours ago faded away as the temperature soared between them.

"You'd prefer I touch you, yet you think you can make yourself hit your personal high note faster than me?" He grinned wickedly, but didn't venture any closer to her.

"It's just biology." And very unimportant considering the way her heart slugged harder against her ribs. She'd had enough time in her life to experience the limited joys of solo sex. As long as Wes was within reach, she planned to make decadent use of that lean, strong body of his. "Besides, the orgasms are much better when there is a friend to share them with."

Refusing to wait for him to touch her any longer, she picked up his hand and tucked it under her shirt. Farther, higher, until he covered her lace-trimmed breast with his palm.

"Really?" Flexing his fingers, he squeezed gently. "What if you did the stroking, but a friend was around to watch? What caliber of orgasms would you achieve then, I wonder?"

Sidling closer, she arched more heavily into his hand, craving the heat of those strong, nimble fingers. She couldn't imagine playing out the scenario he suggested. The vision of him watching while she…

No doubt, it would be hot.

"I already flashed you in the alley." She moaned with pleasure as his other hand snaked up her shirt and molded around her other breast. "Don't you think I've been adventurous enough for one night?"

"Not even close. Whether you admit it or not, I'm guessing you've got a few years of abstinence to make up for. And lucky for you, I'm very glad to oblige." He tugged off her sweatshirt but left her bra on, his gaze lingering in a way that was oh-so-flattering.

"I *do* like it when you watch me," she admitted, wondering if those silver-gray eyes of his could turn any darker. They already glowed with steely intensity as he watched her slip off her sweatpants. She left her white lace panties around her hips since he seemed to like the visual of her lingerie and Tempest planned to give him an eyeful.

"I promise I won't even blink." True to his word, his gaze locked on her undergarments that were semitransparent. "Just tell me where you want me."

Glad he gave her full run of the show, she shouted an order to Eloise to stay put while she stretched out on the couch. She usually slept with the bed pulled out, but with her blood rushing through her veins in a geyser-hot flood, she didn't want to take the time to rearrange the furniture.

She wanted Wes's undivided attention. When he slid deep inside her tonight, she wanted to be able to look in his eyes. And when he found his release, she wanted to see that clench of his muscles, the sheen of sweat over his velvety skin.

Wes made her feel too beautiful, too sexy, to hide behind a silken blindfold.

"You can sit right there." She left him on the edge of

the couch while she flung one leg over his lap, the other resting on the cushions behind him.

Leaning back on a mountain of throw pillows, she peered down the length of her smooth pale skin to his muscular thighs, lean waist and square shoulders. He'd stripped off his shirt and tie at some point, his trousers only partially zipped but still clinging to his hips. His erection strained the fabric even with the fly loosened, his white cotton boxers stretching over the bulge that reached above the waist.

Come to mama.

Breath catching in her throat at the sight of all that delectable manhood on display, she decided she'd never had better inspiration for skimming her fingers over her panties. Simply put, he was the most fascinating man she'd ever met.

Goose bumps broke out over her skin as he followed the progress of her fingers with his gaze. The silk and lace of her lingerie grew damp with heat, the fabric molding intimately to her as she traced a circle around the hard knot of her clit.

Her hips twitched at the thought of him touching her, and with his big male body positioned between her legs, it was easy enough to imagine his hands on her, too. She tugged aside the lace to stroke the slick folds beneath. Little spasms fanned out from her womb, warning her it wouldn't be long until the bigger contractions came, the ones that would wring her body from the inside out.

All because he was here. Watching. Devouring her with his gaze.

Her fingers tracked faster over her flesh grown swollen with want, her fantasies turning more graphic as she imagined him bending over her, taking her in his mouth. Lapping at her most sensitive places.

And then it was no dream.

With a growl of pure animal hunger, he leaned over her, tugging her panties down and off with one hand while he guided her fingers to his mouth with the other. One by one he sucked each digit in turn, tasting her with a thoroughness that left her whole body humming for that most intimate of kisses.

Hot breath fanned over her, stoking the fiery tension inside her. Tighter. Higher.

When he swirled his tongue over her sex she flew apart on contact, her screams thankfully muffled behind Wes's accommodating hand. Lush spasms rolled over and over her, rocking her insides with raw sexual heat until she shuddered from the force of them.

Only then did he pull her up off the couch and into his lap to straddle him, lowering her down onto his shaft. He'd managed to put a condom on, but his pants were still at half-mast, the zipper threatening her most sensitive places until she shoved the trousers down with a trembling hand.

And then she thought no more, surrendering herself completely to the fierce rhythm he set. Her fingers gripped his shoulders as she anchored herself against the next round of waves already dragging her under. Deeper.

Gasping in one last breath, she let her release overtake her as another climax swept through her damp body. Wes didn't bother quieting her cries this time, his own echoing moments behind hers. Their heartbeats hammered so close together the rhythms became indistinguishable, their timing as in synch now as it had been while they made love.

Or had sex.

Or whatever it was they'd just done.

Tempest had no idea. She could barely think. Couldn't

move. Couldn't believe she'd just touched herself for the sensual delight of a man she'd known for all of—how long had it been?—five days.

But, oh God, had it been good.

Body brimming with happy endorphins, she tried not to worry about what it meant that she'd just shared the best sex of her life with a man who'd made it very clear he wasn't a relationship kind of guy. If only she could look at sex like a man, taking her pleasure where she could and to hell with the consequences.

But as Wes guided them down to recline on the couch, his strong arms cradling her close to his heart, Tempest knew she'd crossed some kind of personal line with him tonight. She'd given him too much of herself, shared a little piece of her soul when she'd only meant to follow an intense attraction until it flared out of its own accord.

Too bad she hadn't fully comprehended what it meant to play with fire.

As she drifted off to sleep beside him, wrapped in the musky male scent of him, she told herself she'd figure out some solution in the morning. There had to be a way to reclaim her independence before she fell head over heels for a man who pushed her boundaries as no one else had ever done.

Somehow, she needed to put some space between them again before her old insecurities chased Wes away for good. Until she was strong enough to be a real partner for Wes, she'd keep her distance to make sure neither of them got burned beyond repair.

CHAPTER TWELVE

"OUCH!"

Wes suppressed the string of curses that swelled in his throat the next morning as he nicked his jaw with the plastic straight razor he'd unearthed from a new bag in Tempest's medicine cabinet. Why was it that a microscopic cut from shaving stung ten times more than a gushing flesh wound?

One of those mysteries of life. Kind of as pointless as trying to figure out why walking away from Tempest would hurt exponentially more than the hits to his ego from women who'd taken him deep in the past.

Setting aside the instrument of terror that had left three fresh cuts on his mug, Wes rinsed his face and dried off. Steam from his shower still hung thick in the black-and-white, art deco bathroom as he swiped the towel across the wrought-iron mirror in an effort to clean up after himself.

The shower and shave had done little to clear his head. Sleeping with Tempest again only made him want more, inciting primitive urges to hold her by his side that same way night after night. Maybe part of him had hoped the heat between them would cool after they'd been together a few times, but that was far from the case. If anything, he only wanted her now more than ever.

Flinging a towel over his shoulder, he slid into his clothes, wondering if she'd be awake yet. He'd forced himself to get up and shower instead of succumbing to the far more tempting pleasure of watching her sleep—her red, manicured fingers curled tightly around the sheet and tucked beneath her delicate jaw.

He was getting too close, too involved, the same way his old partner Steve had shortly before his death. Steve had fallen for one of the women involved in a crime ring he'd infiltrated. Wes had followed protocol and refrained from actively contacting his partner when he went silent three weeks into the job, but Steve had checked in with Wes on his own terms during the undercover stint, and his last message detailed his concern for getting his lady friend out safely. Wes still regretted respecting Steve's cover those last few weeks since the woman had ultimately exposed him.

Possibly turned him to crime, if the media coverage was to be believed.

Hanging the towel over the shower door, Wes reminded himself Tempest was nothing like that woman. For that matter, she wasn't anything like any woman he'd ever been with before, his type tending to stray more to fallen angels than uptown girls. What freaked him out was the loss of control when he started to care about somebody, the emotional sucker punch that reminded him it didn't matter how many arrests a guy made or street fights he'd won—when it came to women, men pretty much had no defense.

Except for the one-month rule, of course. Although it wasn't exactly ingenious, at least the time limit made sure he wouldn't be vulnerable to the relationship equivalent of a kick in the gonads.

Until now.

Apparently Tempest was like a fast-acting chemical

agent to his system. A few rounds with her, and he was toast.

Frustrated and out of sorts, he yanked the bathroom door open, startling Eloise to jump up from her mat in the corner with a whine. Tempest lifted a curious brow from her spot in the kitchen where she swirled a tea bag around in a steaming ceramic mug, a morning rain shower beating hard at a window behind her.

"Ghost on your tail?" She shuffled toward a round table tucked in a corner of the studio near the oven range, a pair of ratty pink slippers scuffing along the dark hardwood floor. An untied terrycloth bathrobe flapped open over a T-shirt and a pair of blue plaid boxer shorts.

He refrained from mentioning the spook of morning-after doubts currently haunting her bathroom.

"Just in a hurry to see what New York's reigning society queen looks like in the morning." He wasn't ready to confront the questions between them. Not when he needed to step up his investigation today. Better to keep things light.

Dropping into a seat, she clutched her mug of tea with both hands and smiled. "I'm presiding over an elegant table with perfect aplomb." She crossed her legs and kicked forward a slippered foot with a flourish. "And of course, I'm always a fashion plate. It just goes with the territory."

That's how she does it.

As Wes watched her bend over her tea and sip it with as much ritual and reverence as if it had been a life-saving elixir, he realized she was very good at making him feel comfortable with her wealth and privilege because she downplayed it at every turn. From her self-deprecating comments to her pared-down lifestyle, she gave off a common-person vibe that put him at ease.

But would she always be that way? Or would she tire of her Chelsea apartment and the struggling-artist scene once she'd gotten her fill of sculpting?

Not many people would be able to walk away from a world of luxury for long. Especially if they'd grown up accustomed to life's little extras the way she had.

Maybe he'd figure her out more now that he was staying with her for a few days. Get a better read on a woman who looked all wrong for him on paper, but in reality seemed very right.

"The slippers definitely make a statement." He wandered over to the stovetop and filled the empty mug she'd left waiting on the counter. Even in such a small thing, Tempest remained low pressure with her self-serve attitude.

Dropping the kettle back on a burner, he sifted through her basket of five thousand flavored teas looking for a bag that said plain old "Lipton."

"I don't think we should have sex anymore." Her pronouncement came just as he'd decided he'd try something called cinnamon zinger.

Damned if she hadn't zinged him first.

"Did I miss something here?" His tea bag floated on top of the water since he should have put it in the mug first. Assorted little details filled his cop brain, all the while refusing to process what she'd just said.

"I mean, I hope you'll still consider staying here until you catch the psycho-creep lurking around my apartment, but I don't think it's a good idea for us to keep up the intimacy."

She still clung to her teacup, only now Wes realized it wasn't just her magic elixir, it was a power potion that gave her the nerve to lob verbal bombs at him the morning after they'd shared something pretty damn profound.

"And you came to this conclusion while we were rolling off your couch for the third time last night? Or did you only just make up your mind this morning?" He sucked down his tea in one large gulp, the red-hot liquid frying the inside of his mouth. How in the hell could she be so casual?

"I'm sorry." Bowing her head for a moment, she seemed to study the wood grain in her floor before meeting his eyes again. "I didn't mean to be so abrupt, I just wanted to get the words out before I lost my nerve."

"At least you have the courtesy to admit it takes a hell of a lot of nerve to drop that on a guy at eight in the morning." His brain seemed as scalded as his throat since he couldn't figure out what else to say. What *could* he say to that? "Care to tell me why you're changing your mind? Although, let's be very clear that this doesn't change a damn thing about me staying here. You're not getting rid of me until we catch whoever is stirring up trouble for you."

Nodding, she at least had the good grace to look relieved. Finally, she huffed out a sigh and looked at him dead-on.

"I'm a romantic." She said it with as much drama as if she confessed a cardinal sin.

"Considering my line of work, I'm usually pretty good at connecting the dots, but you're going to have to help me out on this one because I'm not following." He strangled the water out of his tea bag before flinging it in the trash.

And he thought he'd been confused about Tempest while he shaved this morning? He hadn't known the half of it.

Now there weren't just morning-after spooks on his

tail. There was a whole legion of niggling regret demons and one very pissed-off ghost of what might have been.

SHE MIGHT HAVE PLANNED this better.

In the past eight months, she'd learned how to run a board meeting, mastered a travel schedule to oversee her offices abroad and played mediator to countless interdepartmental spats. Surely she could have devised a way to broach this subject with Wes in a way that didn't put him so far on the defensive he was seething at the other end of her kitchen, the steam rising off him faster than their freshly boiled tea.

Too bad she'd been afraid to go to sleep last night, terrified she'd wake up so out of her mind in love with the man in her bed that she would never be free of him. She hadn't even learned how to master her own insecurities. She was jealous that he met with strange women to crack a possible prostitution ring, for crying out loud.

Any guy noble enough to put his neck on the line as a cop didn't deserve that kind of anxiety from his partner. Girlfriend. Whatever she was supposed to be to this man who freely admitted he'd never been able to make a relationship work before.

If only he could give her some time to forge her own path first. To find her own strengths and get a handle on her own dreams. Maybe then she'd be able to commit herself to being the kind of woman Wes deserved. She just needed some more room to breathe. More space to think things through before they plowed ahead at breakneck speed.

"I thought I could brazen out an affair with you, Wes, but I can't. At least, not right now. I'm an old-school, hearts-and-flowers type of girl no matter how tough I try to be in the business world. And I just can't find it in myself to cut off my feelings from sex and simply enjoy what we have." At least, that was part of it.

They didn't need to delve into her lack of confidence now, did they? It was tough enough to deny herself the man she cared about without picking apart her psyche, too.

"Who the hell expects you to cut off your feelings from sex?" He gulped down another slurp of tea that had to singe all the way down. "I sure as hell have feelings about you, and I damn well expect you to have feelings about me after the conference room table, and the Park Avenue encounter, the alleyway…and that's not saying anything about last night."

"You have feelings for me?" Her feminine radar blinked wildly at the thought of this man harboring a hint of deeper emotions for her. All this time, she'd thought she was the only one whose heart was getting involved in their affair. "What kind?"

His brow furrowed as if she'd just asked him to solve quadratic equations. "Hell, I don't know. But you can bet I feel something when I'm with you."

Disappointment fizzled through her, renewing her decision to untangle herself from him before she had more to lose than great sex.

"Well if you ever figure it out, you be sure to let me know. I think we could both use a little time and space to find our footing with whatever is happening between us." She stared at the man she'd clung to half the night, feeding a frenzy of need inside her she hadn't even known existed. It wouldn't be easy to walk away from that, even knowing it was the right thing to do. "More tea?"

Dark clouds rolled through those gray eyes of his, warning her of the storm coming. She braced herself for a tirade in Wes's plainspoken style, but instead of arguing, he suddenly lifted his fingers to his lips and motioned for her to be quiet.

"What?" She peered around her studio, finally noticing Eloise standing on guard at the front door, her ears perking straight up as she stared at the knob expectantly.

Someone was outside her apartment.

Tension crackled as she watched Wes move stealthily across her floor, his steps soundless despite his long strides. For a moment, she hoped maybe it was the paperboy, and then she remembered she didn't subscribe to a paper.

And anyone who wanted to see her should have buzzed in downstairs.

Maybe it could be a neighbor loitering around the hall, looking for a lost key? The superintendent changing a lightbulb? Her brain rushed to supply scenarios even as her gut instinct gave her a bad feeling. She swallowed back a wave of fear, knowing Wes could handle whatever came his way. Still, what if her would-be intruder had a gun? Or worse, what if more than one person lurked outside her door?

She rose, unable to sit still while Wes confronted her problems by himself. She might not be a trained professional, but she had a vested interest in seeing her antagonizer brought low.

Her bravado held right until Wes's gun flashed, the dull gleam of silver sending a chill through her. She paused a few feet behind Eloise while Wes positioned himself by the door and motioned for her to get back.

Too bad her ancient fuzzy slippers were rooted to the floor beneath her. She bent down near Eloise, ready to vault into action if anyone bothered her dog, guns be damned.

Wes reached for the door handle, utterly silent as he listened. Waited. Jerked the door open with a start.

His gun glinted in front of a woman's face.

Kelly Kline's face.

Her hands whipped over her head, raised in surrender, skin going pale on the other side of Wes's gun.

"I'm just here to see Tempest."

Scrambling to her feet, Tempest walked closer to the standoff where Wes drew her co-worker inside, never taking his gun off her.

"It's okay, Wes. She works with me."

He snorted. "All the more reason to suspect her."

Kelly's eyes widened. "You're the guy from last night." She looked from Wes to Tempest, her gaze lingering on her CEO. "Is he here against your will?"

"He's a detective," Tempest inserted, thinking to put her at ease, even though now she was starting to wonder if Kelly's visit today had been a social one.

Could her ambitious VP be vindictive enough to go after Tempest if her path up the career ladder had been thwarted?

Wes pushed Kelly into a chair near the door while Eloise barked intermittently.

"I'll be asking the questions here. Just be kind enough to keep your hands where I can see them, Ms. Kline, and we won't have any problems." Wes tucked his weapon in the back of his trousers and kept his focus on Kelly. "Care to explain how you got into the building without Tempest buzzing you in?"

"A man coming out held the door for me." She crossed long legs in a pencil-slim skirt that rested just above her knees. "Since it was raining, I didn't think twice about coming inside and looking up Tempest on the directory. Now would you please tell me what this is about?"

Perhaps seeing the futility of firing questions at Wes, she directed a haughty stare toward Tempest.

Certain Wes wanted to run the show with their visitor, she said nothing.

"Not until you explain your reason for showing up here unannounced." The scowl on Wes's face suggested he didn't appreciate high-handed attitudes.

Tempest held her breath, wondering if Kelly would turn out to be the intruder who insisted she was in the wrong business. The Whores 'R' Us business.

"When I found out Tempest wouldn't be in the office today, I decided to track her down at home because what I have to say won't wait." Kelly smoothed her hands over her skirt before she looked Tempest in the eye. "I'm handing in my resignation."

"You're quitting?" She hadn't been prepared for that, considering Kelly had done everything but stand on her head to prove how committed she was to Boucher Enterprises. "You had so many plans for development, so many projects in the works overseas."

"Wait a minute." Wes reached out toward Kelly. "I'd like to see the letter please."

"That's between me and Tempest." Her coral-painted lips curled. "And you haven't even explained to me what's going on here. If I'm going to be greeted by a gun in the face, I think I've earned the right to know why."

"The NYPD is helping Ms. Boucher find out who's been harassing her. And you're welcome to leave if you can produce the letter of resignation you say you were submitting today."

"Well I can't do that because I haven't actually drawn it up yet. I wanted to speak to Tempest about what terms I might expect."

As if. The woman was insane if she thought she could dictate terms for quitting.

Wes didn't look overly impressed with her answer either. Nor did he seem any more pleased with the hedging answers she went on to give about her whereabouts the night before, after she'd left Mick's Grill, or her reasons for using MatingGame's services in the first place.

She maintained her dating life was her personal affair, and that she'd gone straight home after meeting Wes. A fact which no one could vouch for since she lived alone and hadn't seen anyone on her way into her apartment.

After another half hour of circular conversation and petulant answers, Wes allowed Kelly to leave with a reminder that she needed to conduct all business with Tempest at the company headquarters and not a private residence.

When the apartment door finally slammed shut behind her co-worker, Tempest didn't even know where to begin. She had more reason than ever to suspect Kelly was up to no good, although Wes said it would be difficult to prove anything until she made her next move.

Did that mean Tempest needed to wait for an escalation in violence against her?

And as if that weren't unsettling enough, she also hadn't even succeeded in getting Wes to agree their affair was over. But with a whole new set of fears and worries churning through her, she didn't know if she could find the emotional fortitude to debate the merits of a relationship built on lust today.

Now, she watched Wes as he stared out the window toward the street, thudding his forehead lightly on the glass. Making sure Kelly really left?

He turned toward her after a long moment, swiping a hand through his dark hair.

"She's lying about why she came over here." He stalked restlessly around the apartment, his body tense as if every muscle was coiled with tension.

Tempest said nothing, sensing he'd entered some kind of thinking zone and hadn't really been talking to her anyhow.

He paced a few more steps and stopped. "And we know she uses MatingGame to meet men. But is she strong enough to—" Pivoting on his heel, he focused on her. "Do you know if she works out?"

Confused, she shook her head. She'd only been on board with the company for eight months, and Kelly had probably been out of the country half that time.

"The murder victim was strangled," Wes continued, picking up his pace again until Eloise barked at him, tail wagging. "And whoever did it would have needed a hell of a lot of muscle."

Tempest bent to quiet her dog while that bit of information rolled over her. Strangulation? Somehow it seemed more brutally cold than a gunshot. She wondered why she hadn't asked Wes about it before.

Her fingers went to her throat, seeking the reassurance of her favorite quartz pendant until she remembered she hadn't worn it today. She was still loafing around the apartment in her bathrobe.

Before she could ask Wes more about how the murder case related to the break-in and vandalism at her apartment, the doorbell rang, raking along nerves already worn raw. This time at least, her visitor had used the buzz-in system connected to the downstairs door.

"That'll be my partner," Wes supplied as he moved toward the intercom speaker and exchanged a few words with a woman on the other end. Turning back to Tempest, he pushed the buzzer to admit the newcomer. "I called her before I took a shower this morning so she could swing by for a couple of hours."

Wes worked with a woman?

A stupid concern when ten thousand other worries bombarded her from all sides, but Tempest couldn't deny the flash of jealousy at the thought.

"You asked your partner to come here?" Why hadn't she at least taken a shower this morning? She probably looked like she'd been cut from one of those real-life cop shows where the women were always wearing mangy bathrobes with their hair shooting out of their heads in twenty different directions.

But logically, she knew that if she wanted Wes to solve his case, it would be a good thing for him to join forces with his partner instead of sacrificing himself to Tempest's insatiable new lust day after day.

"I've got to meet the next batch of women from Blind Date at Mick's this afternoon, but I trust Torres to keep you safe." Withdrawing his gun from the back of his pants, he flipped some little switch under the barrel before dropping it into a holster he'd slung over a chair.

Again with the dates?

She hated the idea of him spending all afternoon getting hit on by women from every borough in the city, but she held her tongue and slowly quelled her old insecurities, reminding herself that just yesterday she'd been looking for a way to get some distance between her and Wes. Today it seemed, she'd have it in spades.

There was a knock at the door behind her, startling her into realizing that Wes would be walking out to hunt for a killer who had strangled his last victim. And it dawned on her in that instant that her jealousy seemed petty and her need for distance seemed incredibly selfish. Right now, only one thing mattered.

She reached out to stop him before he could admit his partner, her hand clenching around his wrist.

"Be careful."

"You, too." Leaning in for a kiss, he covered her mouth with his and clamped his hand around her jaw, holding her steady while he tasted her one more time.

As he released her and Tempest stared up into his eyes, she already regretted that it would be their last.

CHAPTER THIRTEEN

WES WRENCHED OPEN Tempest's door, ready to lose himself in work since his personal life seemed to be disintegrating under his feet. Untangling a murder case seemed easy compared to comprehending the intricacies of the female mind. The taste of Tempest's kiss lingered on his lips as he spied his partner on the other side of the door.

Holding the leash of his 150-pound St. Bernard.

"You brought Kong?" His words were lost in an onslaught of barking and growling as the two dogs spied each other.

Eloise launched in front of Tempest to go head-to-head with the new canine in her territory. Vanessa's body lurched forward with the force of Kong's response, though she clung tenaciously to the leash.

"I thought it would be a nice surprise," Vanessa shouted over the din of woofing. "I didn't know she had a dog."

Tempest's voice cut through the noise. "Eloise, heel."

The terse words seemed to soothe the German shepherd, her barks quieting as she padded behind Tempest, though her fur remained ruffled along the back of her neck.

Vanessa whistled appreciatively while she struggled with Kong. "That's an animal with some pretty manners."

Wes sighed as he took the leash from his partner. "Don't

let her upstage my dog, Torres." Tugging harder, he shouted to Kong until he got her settled down and almost civil. "She's just a little more high-spirited."

Wes quieted Kong as he stroked her head, but there was nothing quiet inside him as he thought about walking out of Tempest's apartment. Sure it might be easier to leave now than to confront the whole host of concerns Tempest revealed this morning, but he'd been choosing that easy route for too long, continually opting for the path of least resistance when it came to relationships.

Something about Tempest made him want to work a little harder this time, to try his hand at untangling the knots and soothing the raw emotions exposed from their night together. And damned if the thought of losing her didn't make him reevaluate things. Rethink what he wanted out of his life.

After making introductions in the foyer, Wes watched the dogs circling each other and inspiration struck. A way to buy himself a little more time.

"Vanessa, how about you take Kong and Eloise down to the street and let them get more comfortable with each other on neutral terrain? They might relax faster that way and you can treat them to a snack." He hoped his partner would take the hint since he really needed a few more minutes with Tempest.

"Are you sure she can handle both of them?" Tempest bit her lip as she looked from the dogs to Vanessa and back. "They're pretty big."

"Vanessa's stronger than me. And she's a ninja." He dug in his wallet for a few bucks and jammed them in his partner's hand before she could protest. He clipped Eloise's leash to her collar and handed it to Vanessa. "She'll be fine."

He pried the door open behind her and steered her into

the hallway as he lowered his voice for her ears alone. "I need five more minutes if I'm ever going to break the one-month barrier like we talked about. Got it?"

Understanding lit her eyes before Tempest followed them out.

"There's a pretzel vendor on the corner," Tempest called over his shoulder. "Eloise is usually more agreeable after a visit with him."

To Wes's relief, Vanessa nodded. Smiled. "No problem." She turned her gaze on him, however, and frowned. "And I'm *not* a ninja. I practice *kendo*, you damn cave dweller."

Steering the dogs toward the stairs, Vanessa walked away, lean muscles flexing as she wrangled the animals and began to lecture them about proper canine street etiquette.

Unwilling to waste his window of time with Tempest, he guided her back inside the apartment, closing the door behind them.

"What was that all about?" She eyed him warily, her bathrobe swinging about her legs as she turned to face him. "What one-month barrier?"

Wes had forgotten women possessed bionic hearing.

"Inside joke." He held out the desk chair for her and waited for her to take a seat before he leaned on the desk. "Vanessa says I can't keep a relationship for more than a few weeks, hence the one-month obstacle. I hoped if she could give us a little more time together, I could figure out what happened to make you do the about-face this morning."

She frowned for a moment before her eyebrows lifted in tandem, her face the picture of surprise. "Because you want to break the one-month barrier with *me?*"

"You find that so difficult to believe?"

"A little." She reached for his hand, smoothing her thumb across the back of his knuckles and then up to the tattoo on his wrist. "You must know even better than me that it's tough to put yourself out there and trust in someone."

"Hell, yeah, I know. I'm a three-time loser in the trust department." He took her hand in his, halting her fingers in their quest. Vanessa told him he shouldn't always expect the worst from people, right? Maybe the time had come to charge into this mess with Tempest and expect—hope for—the best.

She opened her mouth to speak, but he had more to say on that subject. If he was going to put himself out there, he would do it all the way.

"Twice I lost out to women who would probably argue I chased them away by not being committed enough." Maybe they were right. But Wes had always felt like he gave it his best shot. "And a third time I trusted my partner could hold it together while undercover and was blown out of the water when he turned. I still can't fully believe he went rogue, but the reports from an investigation around his murder all point to him being waist-deep in criminal activity. You'd think I'd know better by now, wouldn't you?"

Tempest leaned forward in the desk chair, her hand brushing over his knee. "I'm sorry, Wes. I didn't know—"

"Doesn't matter." He interrupted the sympathetic words he didn't need anymore. He simply wanted another chance with her, and he was determined to secure it before he walked out of her apartment today. "What I'm trying to say is that maybe *I'm* the romantic and you're the cynic if I'm the only one willing to give this a chance."

It was the best he could do, the most forthright he could be. He'd put himself on the line for her this time, showing a side he hadn't shared with anyone for too many years.

He didn't toss aside his pride and call himself a romantic for just anyone, damn it.

Tempest was special.

She blinked hard, as if trying to process what he was saying. Her brown eyes studied him intently.

"I'm not being cynical." She shook her head, denying the obvious. "It's called being practical. I've had my whole life on hold for the last eight months until I figure out who to entrust with my father's business. I'm caught between my dreams and my reality so often, I don't even know who I am half the time. That doesn't seem like a fair way to start a relationship."

"Who cares about fair? I'm not a demanding guy." He'd never asked much of any woman except fidelity for as long as they were together, and he knew without question that Tempest was the kind of woman who would view faithfulness the same way as him. Yet she wanted something else from him. Something he couldn't seem to understand. "You're busy and I appreciate that. So I'll take what you can give and we'll see how it goes."

"But *I* care about being fair," she said softly, seemingly unfazed by his appeal as she tied the belt on her bathrobe, cinching it closed. "And I'm not just worried about what's reasonable for you. When I'm ready to take the gamble with my heart, I want to give myself a real shot of making it work."

He didn't know how to argue his way around that without sounding like an insensitive jerk. His damn tattoo itched again, except he knew it wasn't the tattoo. It was just a stupid head-trip that surfaced with remarkable regularity whenever a woman talked about something like her heart.

"I'm not asking for forever, Tempest." He wasn't asking her to sign her name in blood, for crying out loud. He just wanted to be with her tomorrow. And the next day. And a few more afterward, if she'd let him.

"Believe me, I'm well aware of that." She managed a lopsided smile he'd never seen before, a grin that didn't look entirely happy to his eyes. "I just don't think we should jump into anything when you're not even sure what kind of feelings you have for me."

Hadn't he told her how he felt by asking her to stay with him and work things out? He'd given her more of himself than any other woman, and she was still turning him down. As the sound of dogs barking drifted up to Tempest's third-floor window, Wes realized his opportunity to convince her was over.

And he'd failed.

She wanted to know how he felt? He imagined his condition at this moment in time wasn't all that different from lying facedown on the street after fighting a losing battle. He'd been gutted and left to bleed out while her voice sounded farther and farther away.

The sensation gave him all the more reason to find Tempest's stalker today—to close his case and get on with life. Alone. No matter that he'd put himself on the line, risking heart and pride to a woman too caught up in her own life to make time for him.

There was nothing left for him here.

"WAS IT JUST ME, or did Wes seem a little out of it when he left?" Vanessa Torres had been low-key company for most of the afternoon, staying out of Tempest's way while she showered and then worked on a new sculpture, a male vampire figure with outstretched arms.

Tempest couldn't think of any other way to burn off the mixture of fear, frustration and regret suffocating her ever since Wes seemed to shut her out and had left the apartment without hearing her side of things.

But apparently Vanessa wasn't going to keep quiet on the subject of Wes all day.

"I just assumed he was getting himself into work mode." Tempest didn't want to discuss the trouble between her and Wes with a stranger, especially when she didn't even understand it herself. She only meant to ask him for more time to figure out what she wanted in life, a few more weeks to become the independent woman she knew she could be.

But somehow, Wes seemed to take that as a rejection, even going so far as to tune out half of what she said. Or so it seemed. She couldn't tell what happened any better than Vanessa, but she knew that—in Wes's eyes, at least—she had slighted him by not agreeing to forge ahead with a relationship even though she knew she wasn't ready.

"He's not usually like that at work," Vanessa observed lightly, watching Tempest mold the basic lines of the vampire's bare chest with her hands before she picked up a carving tool. "If anything, he's hyperfocused about the job and today he seemed a million miles away."

The comment echoed in the wide-open studio space, a weighted silence that seemed as much a presence in the room as the two dogs and two women.

She ignored it.

"Have you and Wes been working together for a long time?" Neatly changing the subject, she contemplated the shoulders of her vampire man and wondered what it would be like to be wrapped in those strong arms again.

Again?

Funny how Wes's image was all that came to mind for artistic inspiration today. She'd started work on her male creature to take her mind off Wes, and still found his face staring back at her from the dark, half-formed clay. Her heart ached with a wrenching sense of failure and loss ever since he'd walked out abruptly the moment Vanessa returned with the dogs.

Had she thwarted any chance of a future together by asking him to give her a little time?

"A year and a half." Vanessa stared out one of the windows at the misty rain that seemed to have enveloped the city for nearly a week, her sleek, dark hair falling in a smooth curtain over her profile. Tall and slim, she had the kind of posture Tempest's mother had failed to instill in her despite a considerable amount of effort. This woman possessed a natural poise and elegance that had always eluded Tempest. "He's one of the best detectives assigned to the precinct."

"He said his former partner died on the job." Tempest didn't mean to pry, but figured it couldn't hurt to open the doorway in case Vanessa cared to share anything that would help her understand Wes better.

Not that it mattered now, when she'd already told him she wasn't ready for a relationship. Regret pricked her, even as she knew her decision had been sound. Logical.

Painful.

"Wes *would* say that. He had a hard time believing Steve would do anything illegal." Vanessa traced a raindrop sliding down the glass with her fingernail. "But most people think his partner died after transforming himself into the alter ego he used for a cover. He wasn't as strong a cop as Wes—physically or mentally—and I think he suffered without his role model to keep him in line."

Tempest's fingers slid away from the wet clay, thinking how easily she could lose herself against the force of Wes's personality as well. It would be hard not to lean on someone who seemed so capable.

"Wes deserves a stronger partner." Tempest hoped Vanessa Torres provided that for him. The way Tempest figured, any woman who could single-handedly bring peace between Kong and Eloise possessed a fair amount of strength.

Vanessa peeled her attention away from the misty windowpane to meet Tempest's gaze with clear green eyes. "He sure does. Do you think you've got what it takes?"

Somehow Tempest wasn't surprised that Wes's partner would have a flair for direct speech. She shook her head, determined to be honest with Vanessa—and herself. "Not yet. But I'm working on it."

A ghost of a smile played over Vanessa's lips, but before Tempest could be certain it had been there, it was gone again, her face a smooth mask with wise eyes. "Let me know if there's any way I can help. Wes is a damn good guy—for a cop."

Tempest wondered briefly what Vanessa had against the men on the force, but her most pressing concern now was how to make Wes understand all she wanted was a little more time.

Since he hadn't listened to her, maybe this time she needed to *show* him she was serious. They could have a shot at a future if only he'd give her some more time to pull her life together. To find her own strength.

"Actually, there *is* something you could do to help me." She hoped Vanessa would go for it, but there was a very real chance she might shoot down the idea without even hearing her out since it could be dangerous. "And at the same time, I'll be helping you sew up your investigation all the sooner."

SHE WOULD BE a strong partner, damn it.

Tempest clung to the thought like a personal mantra as

she and Vanessa waited for Bliss Holloway, MatingGame's operations manager, to dispense with social niceties late that afternoon in the woman's midtown home.

Vanessa had quickly agreed they needed to hear from such a key figure in the investigation as soon as possible. Since Wes was in the middle of interviewing potential suspects, that meant Vanessa would talk to Bliss, even if it meant bringing Tempest along for the ride.

After days of silence following the break-in, the MatingGame manager had finally returned Tempest's phone call shortly after lunch. Vanessa and Tempest had set off together—an elegant street cop and a renegade socialite with little in common except for their united effort to help Wes close his files on the MatingGame killer.

The more Tempest thought about him interviewing suspects all afternoon, the more she worried. Maybe it was the way they'd parted that had unsettled her, but she couldn't shake a bad feeling about the day.

Now, she followed Bliss Holloway down a short corridor in a beautifully appointed suite where she said the three of them could talk privately. Bliss, a self-made millionaire before she was thirty, continued to conduct her business from the penthouse floor of an upscale hotel even though Tempest had offered to purchase corporate office space for MatingGame.

Bliss was a woman with unflagging energy and vision, the kind of lit-from-within personality that Tempest admired immediately. Her respect for the woman had only increased the longer they worked together since Bliss actively sought ways to donate portions of MatingGame's profit to private causes that helped a variety of underprivileged people from at-risk teens to low-income single mothers.

Her blond bob swung neatly across the shoulders of her jacket as she turned to look back at Tempest.

"I'll admit, I was worried when I got back from Tokyo this morning and heard your message." Their hostess led them into an open salon in the back of the penthouse after both Vanessa and Tempest had nixed her offer for tea. She gestured to a seating group near the fireplace and took a seat in an elegant wingback covered in dainty yellow flowers. "And now that you've arrived with a police detective in tow, I'm all the more concerned."

Briefly, Vanessa filled her in on the break-in and vandalism at Tempest's apartment, without mentioning the link to the murder they were investigating. And while Tempest had hoped Bliss would be able to offer an explanation that would somehow deflect attention away from the prostitution angle, instead she watched the woman's face turn pale.

"Someone wrote those words on your door?" Bliss turned to Tempest as if for confirmation, her fingers smoothing over a weighty tennis bracelet at her wrist. At Tempest's nod, she took in a deep breath. "What makes you think the vandals referred to MatingGame? Boucher Enterprises must own at least fifty companies worldwide."

Vanessa interrupted before Tempest could answer, no doubt wanting to be in control of an interview where crucial information could be at stake. "The police have additional evidence linking MatingGame to prostitution and perhaps to a more serious crime. Do you have any explanation for this, Ms. Holloway? Do you know of any women—or men, for that matter—using your dating service in an illegal manner?"

Bliss opened her mouth and closed it, as if unsure how to begin. When she tried again, her words were steady and calm. "To my knowledge, no one is using the service illegally, or I would have reported it immediately. But I'm afraid I may have information regarding the origins of the prostitution rumor."

Tempest sucked in a breath, nerves tense. If Mating-Game turned out to be involved in something illegal, it could cost Boucher Enterprises millions in damage control and lost revenues. The hit to their credibility would trickle down through the company to hurt so many people, and yet Tempest couldn't stop herself from thinking she could withstand all of it if only the truth meant Wes wasn't in any danger tonight.

His safety meant more to her than anything.

"As MatingGame has become more commercially successful, I find myself with more opportunities than ever to reach out to people in the city who need a hand." She shifted in her wingback, adjusting her red-and-ivory-colored houndstooth skirt to cover her knees. "Recently, I needed some help around the office and because I work at home, I thought it would be okay to hire some young women away from their careers in the...um...*oldest profession* so they could have a fresh start."

Vanessa leaned forward in her chair, leather jacket squeaking. "You hired hookers?"

"I hired desperate women with small children who really needed a way out of their situations." Bliss straightened in her chair, spinning her words as smoothly as a trained politician.

"Where did you find call girls for hire, Ms. Holloway? I don't imagine you run into your average streetwalker on this block too often."

Bliss offered a tight smile, but her eyes remained cool. "This is New York, Detective. Let's not forget that no matter how lofty your address on Central Park West, you're still hovering on the edge of a playground for crime."

Tempest sensed a subtle tension between the women, but couldn't put her finger on it. Besides, right now, her sole concern was giving Wes whatever help she could to show him she was willing to work with him—for him—as soon as she got her own life straightened away.

She nudged into the conversation, hoping to speed things along. "So you met these women in the park?"

Bliss crossed her ankles beneath her chair. "No. I was simply making a point. I happen to have an old friend in the business who I've never managed to coax over to the other side, and I learned of these two troubled women from her."

While Vanessa continued to quiz the MatingGame manager about the ex-hookers allegedly providing no more than clerical help, Tempest waited impatiently for their conversation to turn back to what seemed most important.

Finally, she interrupted them, too keyed up and worried about Wes to wait. "Do you have any reason to believe either of your office employees might be using Mating-Game as a dating service?"

Bliss shook her head. "It's against the rules for direct company employees, and I post all of the MatingGame profiles so I would see any—" She halted abruptly, her fingers pausing in an idle dance across the tennis bracelet. "Unless they broke office policy and used Blind Date."

Perhaps she had the same bad feeling about the possibility as Tempest did, because Bliss was on her feet and hastening over to her computer before the words had all left her mouth. Vanessa and Tempest followed, their shoes sinking into the room's plush white carpet as Bliss's fingers flew across her keys.

"Should we call Wes?" Tempest whispered behind her hand while Bliss scanned page after page of data on a spreadsheet.

"We'll head over to Mick's Grill right after this and call him on the way." Vanessa never took her eyes off the computer screen.

Bliss paused her scrolling screen to point to an entry in the Web site user log. "This is it. Marianne Oakes's personal e-mail ID." She shook her head, eyes wide with disbelief. "I can't believe she would skirt the regulations and use our service after I gave her a chance to start over here."

"This woman is one of your office staffers?" Vanessa copied down the line entry in a notebook while Bliss pressed a button to print the whole file.

"She's been with me for six months," Bliss confirmed, typing in the user name to search the rest of the log for repeated visits. "A really bright girl with lots of potential, but she fell on hard times last year and got involved in an escort service to pay the bills."

Vanessa tapped the end of her pen on her notebook spiral. "Can you find out how many men she's been in contact with? We have reason to suspect her in a murder committed the Saturday before this past weekend."

Tempest hated the sick feeling in her belly that told her they were finally on the right track.

"It's difficult to trace this since clients can use their private e-mail accounts in addition to the temporary boxes set up through Blind Date." Bliss scanned her screen, shoulders slumping with the defeated look of someone who realizes how severely her trust had been misplaced. "But it looks like she's been in touch with at least three men."

Premonition turned to full-fledged icy dread.

"Is one of them KingKong?" Her voice caught on a hoarse note as she thought about Wes alone with a woman gone off the deep end.

Vanessa looked at her curiously but said nothing while Bliss squinted at the screen.

Tempest knew the answer when the woman paled.

"Yes. Do you think that's the screen name of the murder victim?"

Not yet.

Tempest ignored the fearful part of her that said they might already be too late to help Wes tonight. If ever there'd been a compelling reason to shove aside her fears and scrounge together all her courage, this was it. They had to reach Wes before Marianne Oakes struck again.

Perhaps reading her thoughts, Vanessa pulled Tempest to her feet and warned Bliss that she would be needed for questioning later that evening or the next day. Tempest barely heard the rest of their exchange as she remembered how Wes had been by her side when this person had crossed her path earlier in the week. She vowed this time, she would repay the favor and be there for Wes before anything happened to him.

"KingKong is the ID Wes is using?" Vanessa confirmed the fact with her before pulling out her cell phone as they left the penthouse suite and took the elevator down to street level.

"Yes." She was grateful Vanessa would know how to get in touch with Wes before they drove down to Mick's. The sooner they warned him, the better.

Distracted with worry, Tempest stumbled slightly to keep pace with Wes's supremely athletic partner as they hurried up the street. Squinting through the darkness in a canopied tunnel erected over a construction zone, Tempest listened for Vanessa's call to go through but lost sight of the other woman in the crush of people getting out of work for the day.

By the time she blinked her way back into the overcast haze of daylight along with the rest of the five o'clock pedestrian traffic, Tempest realized Vanessa was nowhere in sight.

Panic skittered over her. Hundreds of people shoved by her in their daily rush from work to home, yet Tempest couldn't remember ever feeling so utterly alone. Peering back into the construction tunnel, she saw no sign of Vanessa. She had vanished completely off a busy sidewalk.

Had something happened to her? Or had she simply jumped in the nearest cab, forgetting all about Wes's girl-friend of the month?

As much as she wanted to figure it out, Tempest was no detective. The person who would know how to help Vanessa was Wes, and right now she needed to reach him before Marianne Oakes got to him first.

Knowing she didn't stand a chance of hailing a cab at rush hour, Tempest stepped onto the first bus she saw, a 7th Avenue local that dropped her on 18th Street, only a few blocks from Mick's. She didn't think anyone had pur-posely followed her onto the bus, but public transportation overflowed with commuters at this time of day and there had been a crowd at the bus stop.

To be safe, she picked up speed as she walked through the lower West side, pedestrian traffic thinning out the farther west she went. After she passed 8th Avenue, the evening had turned completely dark with less street light to brighten the gloom. Just past 9th Avenue, the skies opened in a downpour that sent what few people had been on the streets back indoors.

Leaving Tempest running headlong through the cold, wet night alone.

Finally spying the awning for Mick's Grill, one of the few businesses with a storefront in a predominantly warehouse district, she peered over her shoulder into the dark, relieved to find the street empty for nearly half a block. Her heart had been racing for nothing.

Now she only needed to make sure Wes got the message about Marianne Oakes, and leave it up to him to decide what happened to Vanessa.

She'd wrestled with a guilty conscience ever since she hightailed it out of midtown where Wes's partner had disappeared, but Wes would know what to do. Hurrying past a row of windows outside of Mick's, she had almost reached the shelter of the awning when an iron hand clamped over her mouth.

CHAPTER FOURTEEN

WES TRIED TO BE SUBTLE as he checked his watch for the third time at a booth just inside the front door of Mick's Grill. His sixth date seemed like a nervous, self-conscious woman and he didn't want to give her any more reason to feel ill at ease, but the longer Vanessa went without answering her phone, the more he worried.

He'd tried Tempest's apartment three times and Vanessa's cell phone twice. No answer on either one.

Why did they have to leave Tempest's apartment in the first place? He told himself Vanessa could handle any trouble if they went to the market or ran a couple of errands, but they should have been back by now.

Unease crept down his spine along with restless tension. He peered out the window onto the street, his gaze chasing shadows while darkness cloaked the city. Reminding himself to pay attention to his date so he could finish up their meeting and call it a day, he decided to cancel his last two appointments so he could check on Tempest.

But as he wrenched his attention from the narrow windows, he realized the woman across from him was staring outside with even more apprehension scrawled across her features than churned inside him.

"Everything okay?" The cop in him went on alert. The woman—Mary? Mary Anne?—hadn't said much since she sat down beyond a few cursory replies to questions he'd asked her. He hadn't given her any reason to be so nervous that the trembling of her hands caused the wine in her glass to vibrate with the force of it. "Did you want me to walk you to your car?"

"No!" The very idea seemed to startle her, propelling her out of her seat. She gathered her purse, a well-worn brown leather bag with a frayed handle. "I mean— Sorry we didn't hit it off right away, Wesley. Maybe we shouldn't take this any further."

She extended her hand, catching him off guard by leaving so suddenly. Was it him who made her nervous? Or did she have another reason for an obvious case of jitters?

He held up his hand in the classic surrender pose, hoping to put her at ease long enough to ask her a few more questions. His intuition started buzzing overtime. What if she knew something about his case? She *was* a blonde. Of course, half of his appointments today had been fair-haired as well.

Still, he couldn't afford to check on Vanessa and Tempest now if this was the woman he'd been searching for.

"I understand if you'd like to get going, but do you mind if I ask what's the rush?" He stared meaningfully at the distance between them across the table. "I'm not crowding you, right? And I swear I won't walk you to your car if you don't want me to. But I don't have anywhere else to go if our date doesn't work out tonight, so whether or not we hit if off, I've got nothing but time to talk."

With one more glance over her shoulder she sat back down, perching on the edge of her seat as if ready to take off at a moment's notice. "Maybe for another minute or two."

"Are you meeting someone else?" He couldn't imagine why else she'd need to check the front door so often. Leaning back into his seat, he kept his body posture unnaturally relaxed in an effort to gain her confidence.

As job duties went, Wes would rather take punches from a high-flying druggie right now than force himself to stay so still when tension tightened inside him.

But when she pulled a small inhaler free from her purse and took a long breath of some sort of medicine, he could tell he'd done the right thing in sticking around. He watched some of the tension slide out of her shoulders before she shook her head, her blond dye job shaking loose of the two chopsticks she'd used to hold it in place.

"No. I'm not meeting anyone. But I've got a psycho ex-boyfriend who likes to check up on me, and I really have no business drawing nice guys like you into my life until I figure out how to deal with him." She cast him an apologetic smile, her fingers trembling on the inhaler until she dropped it back into her purse.

A psycho boyfriend?

And with blinding clarity, Wes knew where to look for his murder suspect. He just didn't know how it tied into MatingGame or Tempest.

Lightning flashed outside the bar, the jagged bolt of brightness illuminating the window beside their table for an instant.

"Should I be worried?" He said it with a smile, but deep inside, he was already damn scared. Not for himself, because he could handle whatever came his way.

But, oh God, was he ever scared for Tempest.

"Not for yourself." Her expression changed, her eyes clouding faster than the stormy sky over Manhattan. "But he gets pretty pissed with me whenever I venture out without him. He's a mechanic with a lot of macho bullshit pride. Some guys just don't get the message, you know?"

He was about to ask her more about her ex-boy-friend—a mechanic might very well possess lockpicking skills—when something snagged his peripheral vision. A woman passed by the windowpane beside their table, a brief reflection of a familiar figure outside in the rain.

Tempest?

She was there one minute and then she was gone.

Shooting to his feet, he stepped back from the booth he'd shared with his latest blind date.

"Will you wait up just one minute, Mary?" He wanted to question the woman further, to find out what made her so edgy tonight, but if Tempest was here instead of her apartment, something must be very wrong.

He'd learned a long time ago not to question his instincts, and they were kicking into overdrive tonight. The cop buzz rattled his ears so loudly he felt as though he had a whole hive humming in his head. He didn't know what Mary's crazy ex-boyfriend could want with Tempest, but his gut told him that he'd been looking for a killer in all the wrong places for the last few days.

The murderer wasn't a woman who'd used Mating-Game. It was a furious man who couldn't stand the idea of his girlfriend going out with anyone else. A man who killed anyone who got near his woman.

Darting through the happy-hour crowd that was even thicker tonight than the evening before, Wes wound his way to the exit and wrenched open the door. Rain poured down on the street outside, reflecting the bar lights and streetlights across the slick, shiny surfaces of cement sidewalk, blacktop road and brick buildings.

She was nowhere.

"Tempest." He shouted her name, startling two women sharing a cigarette under Mick's awning.

No reply. No sign of her or Vanessa. No sound but the sheeting rain that drowned out all other noises. He reached automatically for his cell phone and hit redial, hoping like hell he'd been wrong about seeing Tempest. Maybe she'd pick up her phone and he could just write off the vision of her in the bar's window as wishful thinking.

Instead, the phone rang and rang.

Something had gone wrong tonight. Massively, horribly wrong. The realization body-slammed him like one of Vanessa's kung fu moves, scrambling his brain for one valuable instant and forcing him to acknowledge he would be devastated if anything happened to Tempest. He'd been wracked with guilt when Steve went missing, but this... It would level him completely.

Feet already in motion, he sprinted down the sidewalk in the direction he swore he'd seen her. He skidded to a halt in the alleyway where she'd flashed him just last night—her beautiful body full of life and so damn vulnerable.

Cold rain fell harder, pounding him with its wet weight in relentless sheets. Seeing nothing in the alley, he turned on his heel, ready to search the whole damn West side.

His foot crunched something on the pavement.

Bending, he picked up the object. A compact mirror.

Tossing the broken glass in a trash can, he continued back out into the street, slowing his pace enough to do a visual sweep of the sidewalk as he jogged.

And prayed.

She had to be safe, damn it. He wouldn't accept anything less. Couldn't conceive where he would be without her.

And as the rain pelted his brain, it seemed to drive home the message he'd been afraid to face.

He loved Tempest.

The simple truth blared out of him even as he faced a fear unlike anything he'd ever known. He'd been too much of a chickenshit to admit he'd felt something deep and real with her when she'd asked him. And now that he was faced with the prospect of never getting to tell her, the fact that he loved her seemed elementary. Fundamental to who he was and what he wanted in life.

Didn't matter that he'd known her for a handful of days. He'd fallen in love carefully—thoughtfully—in his past and made piss-poor decisions. Maybe it made a weird sort of sense that now—when he'd operated on blind instincts with someone he'd known for less than a week—he was positive he had it right.

But he'd never have the chance to tell her as much unless he found her. Fast.

He called for backup from his precinct, needing all the help he could scavenge when his whole world came down to the safety of one woman.

IT WOULDN'T BE a good night to die.

Tempest couldn't help but think all evidence of her murder would be wiped away in the downpour showering over her nightmare as she struggled against her captor dragging her past 11th Avenue toward the Hudson River. With one clammy palm clamped over her mouth, the man sealed her nose flat to her face, making breathing all but impossible. Screaming was out of the question.

The man who held her was so strong, his grip on her so ironclad, she imagined they looked like a couple running to get out of the rain with half his coat draped over her head. In reality, he had her stuffed inside his jacket to bind her even more tightly to his side, his knife jabbed convincingly against her right hip ever since he'd taken her. Had it been five minutes? Ten? It couldn't be much longer than that since they'd only walked a long block.

A monster of a human being—at least six foot five—

her tormentor had grabbed her outside of Mick's Grill, moments before she would have reached Wes. Safety.

But she refused to think about that now when she needed to figure out how to get away. Back to Wes. He didn't deserve to have another woman forsake him, and she wouldn't let the psycho bastard who held her rob Wes of the chance to know how much she wanted him. How much she already regretted her decision to put off her happiness for the sake of independence.

She'd been doling out a few items from her purse to leave Wes clues à la Hansel and Gretel, but she needed to do more than that if she didn't want to end up as fish food for whatever creatures populated the Hudson River these days.

Scary, scary thought.

Right up there with never again seeing the lines around Wes's eyes crinkle up when he smiled.

She'd wanted her independence, right? What better time to prove to herself that she could be self-reliant? If she could break free of monster man, she would consider herself as kick-ass ready for life as any woman ever had been. And then, by God, if she survived this ordeal, she would embrace Wes Shaw with both hands and allow herself to be happy. Never again would she feel inferior to her poised and gorgeous mother or the dozens of people employed by Boucher Enterprises who seemed smarter and more efficient than her. She was Tempest Boucher, connoisseur of all things romantic, and that would damn well have to be enough.

Remembering a few self-defense moves from her kick-boxing class, she dropped to her knees suddenly, going completely weightless in her captor's grip. He lost his hold on her, his big, meaty paw catching her hair awkwardly as she dashed away.

For about two seconds.

He caught up to her before she could fling herself in the headlight beam of an oncoming car, her desperate attempt to free herself foiled in no time.

"What the hell are you doing?" The man roared at her. It was the only way she could hear him over the unyielding din of the rain. "No one runs away from Luther."

Perhaps he wasn't worried any longer about someone seeing them in this warehouse district of the city because he brandished the knife in front of her as a warning. This part of the West side was deserted, with only a few abandoned buildings and burnt-out shops between them and the river.

She went still against him, frustrated that a total stranger could harbor so much fury toward her. Who was this man and how did he fit with Marianne Oakes? The lunatic's grip tightened around her rain-soaked clothing. Wes's trench coat around her shoulders provided her with little barrier between her and her captor, but it managed to comfort her on a mental level somehow, giving her a little extra strength.

"Why are you doing this?" Tempest shouted back at him without considering the wisdom of engaging in conversation with a crazy man. But maybe he'd get distracted if he started talking. She'd been so close to escape a minute ago. All she needed was a little more of a head start.

"I can't let my Marianne go back to spreading her legs for any guy with a few bucks to spare." He spoke close to her ear, his words angry and cold as he yanked her toward an abandoned gas station. "And I sure as hell can't allow the owner of her whorehouse to go unpunished. I tried to get you today in midtown, but I nailed the wrong damn woman."

Nailed? Dread pooled in her belly as she thought about Vanessa disappearing this afternoon. Had he shot her?

Fear froze Tempest from the inside out as she realized Marianne Oakes wasn't responsible for anyone's murder. It was this man who'd done the killing. A jealous boyfriend who'd come unhinged.

But no matter that she'd finally figured out the mystery, she'd never be able to share it with Wes at this rate. Luther's knife glinted dangerously close to her face again, a tangible reminder that her time was almost up unless she thought of something. Fast.

Too bad the only thing that came to mind was how much she loved Wes Shaw.

With that realization making her more determined than ever to get away, she reached into her purse with her free hand and flicked out the last remaining object. The newspaper photo of her with Wes.

She watched the clipping float down to the pavement for an instant before it succumbed to the deluge, a wet piece of paper plastered to the concrete, no doubt smudged beyond recognition.

WES DIDN'T HAVE a clue where he was going.

He raced through the darkness after disconnecting his distress call to the police dispatcher. They'd send somebody as soon they could.

Probably not soon enough.

Cursing the city's permanently overtaxed department, Wes knew his own efforts would have to be enough this time. He just needed his instincts to kick in. Anytime now, damn it.

Slipping on a piece of paper, he paused long enough to make out the slick magazine-style cover of *Soap Opera Digest,* a trio of glitzy daytime TV stars grinning up at him to mock his total lack of understanding when it came to Tempest.

Or to give him a new direction?

Soap Opera Digest couldn't have been lying in the street for too long since the inside pages weren't soaked yet. Instinct—or the hopeful imaginings of a man in need of a second chance—told him Tempest had dropped it there to give him a lead.

Scanning the street, he searched the rain-slicked darkness for more hints that she'd been here. The deluge hit the pavement so hard it drowned out the rumble of traffic two blocks away, filling his ears with blaring white noise that stifled all other sounds.

Would it drown her out if she cried out? Fear pummeled him at the thought of Tempest alone and vulnerable. Where the hell was Vanessa tonight?

Trying not to assume the worst, he told himself she had to have been nearby. No way would a second partner let him down.

He drew his gun—a Smith & Wesson 9 mm he'd be all too glad to fire tonight—and hastened his step. Even in the darkness, his searching gaze picked out a comb, a gum wrapper that may or may not have been hers and a sopping newspaper clipping of him and Tempest when they'd been photographed together outside her offices.

She'd saved it.

Love for her funneled through him, fueling his steps even when the bread crumb trail of her belongings disappeared outside a deserted gas station near the Hudson. The perfect isolated place to commit a crime.

Jamming the wet assortment of Tempest's belongings in his pants pocket, he raised his gun higher and swallowed back the mixture of fear and fury tangling inside him. Ran like hell for the old Shell station. If the rain impaired his hearing, it would keep Tempest's captor at a disadvantage, too.

Finding the front door locked, he eased around the back to look for a window.

And discovered two figures struggling on the pavement behind the building. A man bent over a woman's prone body.

Tempest's body.

Horror washed through him—a cold, endless wave that sucked out his backbone and left him weak in the knees. But he refused to acknowledge the possibility that anything had happened to her for more than a split second. With a roar of fury, Wes charged the guy as he saw the flash of a blade at Tempest's throat.

Her attacker never saw him coming—he was preoccupied with threatening a woman who rescued stray dogs from trash cans when she wasn't romanticizing the world with her sculptures.

Son of a—

Wes hit him like a freight train, directing all his fury toward her assailant. The guy's head met the blacktop beneath Wes's chest as Wes rolled over him with continued momentum. The knife dropped to the ground, the discordant clank of metal sounding through the downpour.

He forced himself to limit his gun use to a crack across her attacker's temple, coldcocking the bastard into last year. But if he found out the guy had hurt her...

"Wes?" Tempest shouted behind him, her voice soothing a raw wound inside him.

Whipping around, he saw her slowly coming to her knees, her clothes covered in dirt and mud.

"You're okay." He told her instead of asking her, willing it to be so. "Are you okay?"

He couldn't go to her until he'd cuffed the guy who

could only be the jealous boyfriend of the woman he'd been sitting with at Mick's. Still, Wes dragged him to a rusted sign pole and secured his wrists on either side so that he could help Tempest. Pocketing the keys, he finally heard the squeal of police sirens in the distance, the rain slowing enough so that he could hear more than his own heart beating.

"Vanessa disappeared in midtown." Tempest swiped a blotch of mud from her cheek and straightened the skirt she wore beneath Wes's trench coat, which he only just realized he must have left at her place for the second time.

He helped her up off the ground, so damn grateful to have reached her in time. Smoothing his hands over her face, her neck, her shoulders, he reassured himself she wasn't hurt.

And then her words began to sink in.

"What do you mean *disappeared?*" He'd trusted Vanessa to watch over Tempest. She wouldn't neglect her job unless... "Something must have happened to her."

Nodding, she pursed her lips and winced as a result of the cut on her mouth. He hadn't seen it before with a swath of dirt across her chin, but now that the slowing rain washed it away he could see her lower lip was split, the swollen flesh dripping a narrow track of blood.

Regret stung him that she had to be dragged into this at all. Vanessa should have protected her, damn it.

"*He* did something to her." She didn't need to point. She tracked an accusing gaze toward her attacker. "I don't know what, but while he was dragging me down the street he said something about following us after we left Bliss's—"

"Who's Bliss?" Where were those squad cars? He needed

to get Tempest somewhere safe and find Vanessa before this case exploded any further in his face.

He told himself this wasn't a replay of two years ago when his first partner had gone missing. Vanessa was better than that. Stronger than that.

And damn it, he trusted her. Whatever had happened today must have been pretty bad to wipe out his ninja backup who'd never let him down.

Before Tempest could answer, he put in another call to dispatch to provide their exact location, since they'd come a long way from Mick's Grill. Although he had every intention of finding Vanessa, his first priority was getting Tempest—the woman he loved—to safety.

Once he hung up the phone, she related the events that had taken place earlier in the day when she and Vanessa unearthed the source of the call girl rumors. He couldn't help but admire Tempest's determination to wrest answers from the MatingGame operations manager, but his main concern now was finding his partner.

"So Vanessa vanished after you left this woman's house?" Wes waved over the police car that finally found them in the rain outside the forsaken Shell station.

"We went into one of those wooden tunnels they put up around construction sites and—"

"Shaw." A uniformed officer burst from the arriving police car before it came to a stop. "Detective Torres just checked in. She got rolled in midtown and the guy took her phone."

Relief swept through him, making him feel stronger. Taller. And more certain of his judgment than ever. Vanessa hadn't betrayed him.

"She's okay?" He slid an arm around Tempest's waist, surprised how much the feel of her could bolster him. More than anything, he wanted to get her alone. To explore every inch of her firsthand to make sure she hadn't been hurt.

The officer nodded while his partner frisked Luther. "Torres is pissed about letting someone get the drop on her, but other than that she sounded okay." He jerked a thumb toward Tempest's attacker. "Was this the guy who did it?"

Another squad car pulled up and two more officers stepped out. The back door of the car opened more slowly, revealing...

"Vanessa." Wes's grip tightened on Tempest, but he didn't move to help his partner, not even when she wove a bit drunkenly on her feet through the last of the slowing raindrops.

He knew his ninja colleague well enough to know she'd probably drop-kick him if he offered her a hand.

Vanessa held a blood-spattered handkerchief to her temple, her color pale, but her eyes seemed focused and alert.

"I screwed up, Wes." She moved closer slowly, her gaze scanning the gas station parking lot enveloped in thick mist as the rain slowed to a stop. She watched the officers bagging the assailant's knife and reading him his rights. "I let myself get too caught up in the investigation and I took my eyes off her to call you."

Relief poured over him. Sure he was frustrated Vanessa had taken Tempest out of the safety of her apartment, but she was entitled to make mistakes. She'd done her best, and he couldn't reasonably ask for anything more.

Especially since she looked like she'd be carrying around some serious guilt about the incident for a long time. Her normally proud shoulders slumped with the weight of the mistake.

"You did what you could." Wes watched the other officers haul the attacker to his feet. "And bottom line, we've got our killer in custody."

Tempest watched Wes try to cheer Vanessa and admired the way he tried to lessen the woman's sense of responsibility. Still, guilt nipped Tempest as she wondered if she should have done something differently after they'd left Bliss's apartment earlier that day. Should she have spent more time looking for Vanessa?

She moved out of Wes's arm to look at Vanessa's head.

"What happened to you anyhow? You were a few feet in front of me and then you disappeared in the rush hour crunch." She brushed aside the other woman's long dark hair to inspect the cut.

Her own muscles ached from being hauled through the lower West side by a madman. Her feet burned from a hundred little places where her skin had been rubbed raw against the pavement, but none of her injuries seemed significant next to the laceration on Vanessa's temple.

"I heard a noise in the construction tunnel." Vanessa winced as Tempest picked a few strands from the drying blood caked around the wound. "The guy probably just whistled to get my attention. But as I turned into the outlet that connected the tunnel to the subway to wait for Tempest and check out the noise, I got nailed in the head with something."

Tempest watched the mixture of emotions cross Wes's face—anger, worry, the need for vengeance. She didn't know how she'd missed so many feelings within the man before—when he'd asked her to give them another chance—but she could see them now.

And knew she had a lot more to learn about Wesley Shaw.

One of the uniformed officers jogged over to them,

carrying some kind of black handle with a leather strap attached to it. "Guy's name is Luther Murray and he just admitted to winging you with a slingshot." He brandished the weapon that looked like something a caveman would use, along with a Ziploc bag of small silver balls. "The ammo isn't high tech, but I bet it could do some serious damage."

"Great," Vanessa muttered. "Knocked unconscious by a kid's toy. Thanks, Collins."

"You'd better get this stitched up, Vanessa." Tempest told herself she would not be queasy from the sight of someone else's wound. Vanessa had taken the hit because she'd been protecting *her,* after all. The least she could do was offer a little support before she fainted from the sight of all that blood.

And the thought of how much worse the injury could have been.

Vanessa nodded, swiping away a trickle of blood sliding down her cheek. "Will do. But I had to see if Wes needed help first."

Tempest could see the wealth of anguish in the other woman's eyes and she would be willing to gamble it had little to do with the gaping gash just below her hairline. Vanessa simply hated letting Wes down.

"Thanks, Torres." Wes leaned in to clap her on the shoulder before he stepped back to sling an arm around Tempest again. "I found her, and that's all that matters. My last date at Mick's tipped me off when she mentioned a jealous boyfriend who didn't want her dating anyone else, but I couldn't figure out why this woman's ex would trash Tempest's place until she told me about MatingGame hiring former prostitutes."

Tempest watched a dazed Luther ride away in the back of one of the police cars, amazed to find herself still standing strong by Wes's side even after facing abduction. A knife. The threat of missing out on a second chance with Wes.

She didn't know which had scared her the most, but she did know she'd survived to embrace her future with both hands. The time she'd spent keeping herself alive with Luther Murray's knife pressed to her neck had assured her she had deeper reserves of strength than she would have ever guessed.

"Tempest helped me see the connection when she knew your screen name, KingKong." Vanessa gave Wes a soft slug in the arm while the two remaining police officers waited by their squad car, the lights silently flashing through the mist. "She'd make a hell of a partner for someone who deserved her."

Touched that Vanessa seemed to have forgiven her for taking off after she disappeared, Tempest smiled back. She also appreciated the good word of mouth with Wes since she wanted him to see her that way—as a genuine partner and not just a spoiled socialite in need of protection.

Winking with her good eye, Vanessa walked backward toward the squad car. "Besides, I've got an appointment with the E.R. to make sure I don't have a BB pellet lodged in my gray matter."

"That's right. The invincible ninja was taken down by stone age know-how." Wes flashed her a grin as she slid into the car. "You'd better rest up for all the grief you're going to get around the precinct for this one."

Rolling her eyes, Vanessa settled in the back of the police car while one of the officers in the front seat called over to them. "You need a ride, Shaw?"

"Hell, no. I'm taking my own sweet time to get back to the station because I damn well earned myself some slack today. I'll be there as soon as we can scrounge up some dry clothes."

The vehicle pulled away, leaving Tempest and Wes alone in the heavy white mist, which was turning gradually to big, fat snowflakes.

"Are you sure we didn't want that ride?" Tempest blew on her hands to thaw them, her outfit soaked and chilled despite Wes's trench coat around her shoulders.

Wes pulled her closer, tucking her hands inside his jacket. "I wanted you all to myself for five minutes before we head over to the station. You know you're going to have to come with me since I need to take your statement about what happened today?"

Warmth flowed through her at the tender concern in his eyes, the gentle way he touched her. By some miracle, she'd won her second chance with Wes and she didn't have any intention of blowing it.

"Fine by me since I have a lot of statements I want to make to you, Detective."

CHAPTER FIFTEEN

WES GOT HIS SECOND WIND at the precinct two hours later as he typed up his final report for the night.

He'd stuck around long enough to hear Marianne Oakes's tearful apology for using the MatingGame dating service, and the pieces to the puzzle had finally all fallen into place in his mind. Apparently Marianne was too scared of her ex-boyfriend to hit the bars around her home at night or to meet men in the New York dating scene, so she'd hoped Blind Date might help her meet people anonymously in remote locations Luther Murray wouldn't find.

Even Wes's chief of detectives, a hard-boiled cop who'd seen the worst the city had to offer, seemed to sympathize with the former hooker. Especially when her mother showed up at the station with Marianne's three-year-old daughter. Bliss Holloway might have opened a can of worms by hiring an ex-prostitute looking for a way out, but Wes could appreciate the woman's desire to give people a second chance.

Then again, maybe Wes had a particular soft place in his heart tonight for second chances, since his thoughts never strayed far from Tempest and all the ways he wanted to make things work between them. He'd given her the high-pressure pitch earlier that day, thinking he needed to sell her on a relationship before she booted him out of her life for good. But now that he realized he loved her and the feelings he had for her weren't ever going to go away, he didn't see the need to push her into something she wasn't ready for yet.

He'd still be crazy about her tomorrow and next week and next year. She'd get the idea sooner or later, and frankly, he had all the time in the world to wait.

For that matter, maybe he'd get another tattoo. Only this time, he wouldn't put it around his wrist like a ball and chain to keep him tied down. He'd scrawl her name right over his heart where she'd already made a permanent place for herself.

Closing his eyes while he saved his document in progress, he savored the thought of Tempest in his life. His imagination was so strong, so vivid, he swore he could smell her sweet almond fragrance.

"Can we blow this clambake, Detective?" Her voice cut through his thoughts as she leaned over his shoulder to peer at his computer. "I've already given my statement and MatingGame has been cleared of any wrongdoing."

"We?" Anticipation fired through him at the thought of them together for a little longer tonight. He clicked Send on the report before shutting down the computer for the night. "I hope that means you're going to let me drive you home."

Tempest let his words slide over her, grateful for the sound of his voice and the warmth of his presence after those terrifying moments when she'd feared she'd never have another chance to be with him. She pulled his damp suit jacket off the back of his office chair and handed it to him. Although he'd asked their cabdriver to stop off at Tempest's apartment so she could get some dry clothes on the way to the precinct, he hadn't taken time to change.

Always putting her needs first.

"I've been waiting for a chance to talk to you alone."

She stared up into his eyes, remembering that Friday night he'd calmly strolled into the mayhem of her life and helped her restore some order. Her priorities had crystallized since then, her focus narrowing to the things—and people— most important to her. "Besides, Vanessa left Kong at my place. She and Eloise have been alone there for half the day."

"Then I'm definitely driving you home." He shrugged his way into his jacket and retrieved his car keys from a desk drawer. "They've either destroyed your place or they're waking up the neighbors with howls for food. You know how much Kong eats in a day?"

Leaving the building, they found the city streets covered in snow. Tempest took pleasure in holding on to Wes's arm while they slipped and slid their way to his car, but as they drove the handful of blocks to her apartment, she was surprised how quiet he'd become.

For days, there'd been so much to say, so much ground to cover for his case. And now...there wasn't anything left to talk about except for what was happening between them.

Deciding she'd waited long enough to dive into those dark, emotional waters, Tempest was ready to take the plunge when Wes spoke up from the driver's seat.

"Is this Bliss woman going to be in trouble with the company after she went out on a limb to help Marianne?" He pulled into a parking space on the street in front of her building, carefully avoiding a few teenagers lobbing snowball bombs at each other from the safety of parked cars.

"We do need to standardize hiring practices at Boucher, but I like the idea of leveraging company profits to help people in the city who need it most." She'd been thinking a lot about what Bliss had tried to do since the woman's efforts really resonated with her. "Before I step down as CEO, I'd like to change our corporate mission to reflect some charitable efforts. Maybe then I can tell myself that these past few months of company reorganization will have lasting effects that won't fade away just because I'm not in the driver's seat anymore."

"I bet you could do a lot of good with the excess profits." Wes steadied her with his arm as they made their way to the door of her building. "Maybe Kelly Kline won't want to quit once she sees what a forward-thinking company she's working for."

Tempest brushed the snow from her shoulders as they stepped inside and called the elevator. "Something tells me her threat of resignation was just a stunt to make me recognize her value." She suppressed a little shiver of anticipation as Wes entered the elevator with her. The confined space made her all too aware of how much she wanted to resolve the problems between them—and take advantage of the heat that simmered close to the surface. "But she's very good at what she does, so if she doesn't mind supporting the new Boucher mission, I'm glad to have her stay on board."

"The more money she makes, the more money you can spend on worthy causes." Wes remained on his side of the elevator while she stayed on hers, a yawning ache of space between them.

She would fix that, just as soon as they reached the privacy of her apartment. "What better excuse for capitalism at its shameless best?"

"And no need to feel guilty about revenues you're only giving back to the community." Wes stood aside while she disarmed the lock and opened the door to her apartment. "I don't know what your mother will think of the plan, but I really admire you for making the effort."

"Thank you." Her heart warmed to his praise, and she couldn't remember the last time anyone had told her they were proud of anything she'd done. She'd taken pride in her sculptures. And she'd been glad that she held Boucher Enterprises together for eight months without incident, but no one else in her life had ever shared the sentiment.

Still, even though Wes's praise meant a lot to her, Tempest realized she didn't need it to feel strong and secure about herself. She'd waited a lifetime for her mother to dole out a few gentle words, and never again would she pin her self-worth on what anyone else thought about her. Tonight she'd proven to herself that she was made of sterner stuff than she'd ever imagined.

Soft, tired woofs greeted them as Kong and Eloise lifted their heads from the throw rug in the middle of the living room. There was no mess, no signs of massive destruction. Only a shared pillow on the floor where both dogs lowered their big, furry heads before falling back asleep.

"Somebody made herself at home today." Wes bent to give his dog a scratch on the head. "I don't know how I'm going to pry Kong out of here without a fight."

"Then maybe you should make yourself comfortable, too." Tempest figured she owed it to him to spell out what she wanted since she'd been the one with cold feet the last time they talked about any kind of future together.

He stared back at her in the dark apartment lit only by a night-light she liked to leave on for Eloise.

"I'm not sure that would be a good idea." Straightening, he ran his hand along the back of his neck. "I know myself well enough to be pretty certain I can't manage a sleepover without the intimacy. That kind of sensitivity just isn't in my genetic makeup. But that's not to say I couldn't handle it somewhere down the road."

She was still reeling from his polite refusal to spend the night when his last words penetrated her consciousness. "You would give me…more time?"

"Isn't that what you wanted? Some space to straighten out your own life before you think about getting wound up in mine?"

Her heart did a skip-hop in her chest, an off balance beat that reminded her how much she needed to share with him.

Drawing him deeper into the studio apartment, she held one of his hands in hers, thinking she wouldn't let him leave until she'd told him everything important. Everything that mattered.

"I *thought* I needed more time." She'd woken up this morning so scared of the future, so worried that she'd never be able to forge her own way in the world with a strong, take-charge man in her life. "But what I failed to realize is that my life will never be perfect. There will never be a supremely comfortable time to have a relationship because there will always be problems to overcome, a career to worry about or a character flaw to obsess over."

"So you're saying there will never be a good time for us?" His hand squeezed both of hers, smoky gray eyes searching hers in the dim night-light from the range hood a few feet away in her kitchen.

"No, I'm saying I need to stop romanticizing the way people fall in love and just remind myself I'm already there. Whether or not I've gotten my life squared away, the truth is I'm crazy about you *now*, Wesley Shaw. I love you and I don't want to wait for all our stars to be perfectly aligned before I get brave enough to take a chance with—"

She might have stumbled on with words for another half

hour if Wes hadn't slanted his lips over hers and kissed her with all the warmth she felt in her heart.

He slid an arm around her waist, lifting her against him as he pressed her back to the living room wall. He tasted her with a thoroughness that left her weak. Mindless. Hungry for more.

When he broke the kiss, it was only long enough to whisper in her ear.

"I'm in love with you, Tempest."

Ooh.

She wrapped her arms around his neck and held on for dear life as he kissed her again. Staggering with the pleasurable weight of that news, she felt overwhelmed this amazing man could love a neurotic artist trapped in the public eye wearing a business suit.

Easing back, she cupped his jaw with her palm. "Are you sure? Because if you fell in love with the corporate chick on the conference room desk, I have to tell you that wasn't the real me."

"No?" He didn't look terribly concerned. In fact, amusement danced in his eyes as he roamed his hands over her hips and around to her back.

"No. The real me is the soap-opera-watching junk-food junkie." She bit her lip for a moment, wondering how to define herself to this man who had only met her in crisis mode. "I like to ride my bike when I walk my dog and reporters with cameras scare me. I like to create naked sculptures of men and just as soon as I find the right person to head up Boucher Enterprises, I'm leaving behind the corporate world to work on my art full-time."

"Don't worry." He leaned in to nip her ear and soothe the bite with a lazy sweep of his tongue. "I love that woman, too. And maybe if you're a self-employed artist, you won't mind the crazy hours of a cop."

"I promise I can handle the police work. Even if it involves an occasional prostitution bust." A new sense of peace flowed over her, a dose of confidence she hadn't expected from being in love. "Although I may ask you to do some overtime nude modeling for me during your off hours so I can reassure myself how much you want me."

She allowed her hands to roam over his crotch, already feeling very reassured.

"I think I can handle the extra work." He pulled away from her, holding her at arm's length to study her. "But wait a minute. Do you think this new artistic woman wears blindfolds like the corporate chick used to?"

"Oh, I think she can be convinced." She ran her hands over his chest, soaking up the solid strength of him. "I have the feeling she likes playing all sorts of games."

"Sounds like my kind of woman." Wes toyed with the buttons of her blouse, taking his time undoing each one and igniting a wealth of heat deep inside her. "I wonder how she feels about visits to the tattoo parlor."

She arched her back to melt deeper into his touch. "After tonight, I'm guessing she's had enough brushes with sharp objects to last her a lifetime, but maybe if you held her hand…"

"No, she only needs to hold *my* hand since I'm the one going under another needle." He guided her hand to his chest, cradling her fingers against his shirt pocket until she felt the beat of his pulse. "Tempest the romantic deserves a big, red heart. Right here."

Touched more than she could say, Tempest led him toward the bed she wanted to share with him tonight and many more nights to come. Tugging him down to the pullout sofa, she could already see the years of walking their dogs and playing blindfold games rolling out in front of them.

"I think she's going to be very happy right there." She brushed a kiss over his heart, imagining his new tattoo. "Forever."

* * * * *

HARLEQUIN® A *Romance* FOR EVERY MOOD

**If you enjoyed these passionate reads,
then you will love other stories from**

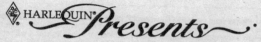

HARLEQUIN® *Presents*

Glamorous international settings...
unforgettable men...passionate romances—
Harlequin Presents promises you the world!

HARLEQUIN® *Blaze*

Fun, flirtatious and steamy books that tell it
like it is, inside and outside the bedroom.

Silhouette **Desire**

Always Powerful, Passionate and Provocative

**Six new titles are available every month
from each of these lines**

Available wherever books are sold

HARLEQUIN® A *Romance* FOR EVERY MOOD™

PASSION

For a spicier, decidedly hotter read—
these are your destinations for romance!

Silhouette Desire®
Passionate and provocative stories
featuring rich, powerful heroes and
scandalous family sagas.

Harlequin® Blaze™
Fun, flirtatious and steamy books
that tell it like it is, inside and outside
the bedroom.

Kimani™ Romance
Sexy and entertaining love stories
with true-to-life African-American
characters who heat up the pages
with romance and passion.

HARLEQUIN® A *Romance* FOR EVERY MOOD™

CLASSICS

Quintessential, modern love stories
that are romance at its finest.

Harlequin Presents®
Glamorous international settings…
unforgettable men…passionate
romances—Harlequin Presents
promises you the world!

Harlequin Presents® Extra
Meet more of your favorite Presents
heroes and travel to glamorous
international locations in our regular
monthly themed collections.

Harlequin® Romance
The anticipation, the thrill of the chase
and the sheer rush of falling in love!

HARLEQUIN® *Blaze*™

*It's said that you have to lose yourself
in order to find who you really are...*

Three intrepid Blaze heroines
are about to test that theory—

in the sexiest way possible!

Watch for
Shiver **by JO LEIGH**
(October 2010)

The Real Deal **by DEBBI RAWLINS**
(November 2010)

Under Wraps **by JOANNE ROCK**
(December 2010)

*Lose Yourself....
What you find might change your life!*

---

red-hot reads